Michael Wood is a freelance journalist and proofreader living in Newcastle. As a journalist he covered many crime stories throughout Sheffield, gaining first-hand knowledge of police procedure. He also reviews books for CrimeSquad, a website dedicated to crime fiction.

x.com/MichaelHWood
facebook.com/MichaelWoodBooks

Also by Michael Wood

DCI Matilda Darke Thriller Series

For Reasons Unknown

Outside Looking In

A Room Full of Killers

The Hangman's Hold

The Murder House

Stolen Children

Time Is Running Out

Survivor's Guilt

The Lost Children

Silent Victim

Below Ground

DCI Matilda Darke Short Stories

The Fallen

Victim of Innocence

Making of a Murderer

Dr Olivia Winter Thriller Series

The Mind of a Murderer

Standalone Thriller

The Seventh Victim

VENGEANCE IS MINE

MICHAEL WOOD

One More Chapter
a division of HarperCollins*Publishers*
1 London Bridge Street
London SE1 9GF
www.harpercollins.co.uk
HarperCollins*Publishers*
Macken House, 39/40 Mayor Street Upper,
Dublin 1, D01 C9W8
This paperback edition 2024
1
First published in ebook by HarperCollins*Publishers* 2024

A catalogue record of this book
is available from the British Library

ISBN: 978-0-00-861856-8

Printed and bound in the UK using 100% Renewable Electricity
by CPI Group (UK) Ltd

To Jamie Cowen
Agent Extraordinaire

Prologue

Sunday, 14 February 1999
Winlaton, Tyne and Wear

Stephanie White had been begging and pleading with her parents for months to buy her a pair of rollerblades for her birthday, and now she finally had them on, she realised she had no idea how to stay upright.

As she rolled carefully down the cul-de-sac where she lived, she could hear from the doorstep the faint sound of her parents stifling giggles. At the bottom of the road, she grabbed hold of a lamp-post, clung to it for dear life, turned back and waved at them with a huge grin on her face to show how pleased she was with the gift. They waved back.

Biting her lip and trying not to show how much pain her ankles were in, she pushed off from the lamp-post and headed for the shops. Her plan was to sit on a bench for half an hour or so before heading back home and saying how brilliant she was at rollerblading and how they were the best present ever.

Stephanie was thirteen years old today. Along with the

rollerblades, her parents had surprised her with a Newcastle United home football shirt which had been signed on the shoulder by her favourite player – Alan Shearer. When she had unwrapped it, she burst into tears and threw herself into her father's arms. The surprises hadn't been over though, and she opened an envelope to find two tickets to the next home game with VIP treatment. This really was the best birthday.

It was a cold and misty February day, but Stephanie had refused to wear a coat as she left the house. She wanted the whole world to see she was wearing a brand-new home football shirt, signed by the living god, Alan Shearer.

There were very few people around, which Stephanie was secretly pleased about, now she realised how terrible she was at skating. The last thing she wanted was to be laughed at, and if her mother found out how unsteady she was, she'd be in for a lecture beginning with the dreaded line 'I told you so.'

She struggled along Church Street, holding onto every lamp-post she passed to keep herself stable. She managed to get across the road without any problems and came to rest at the railings outside the Co-op. She looked at her reflection staring back at her through the window. Her blonde hair, tied back in a ponytail, had come loose, and strands were sticking to her head. Her face was red, and sweat was dripping down her face. She wanted to call on Terry and show him the blades, but not when she looked like this.

Stephanie struggled on down the alley beside the Co-op and almost collided with a man.

'I'm so sorry.'

'That's all right,' he said, holding her up by the elbows. 'Are you okay?'

'Yes. I think so.'

'You were coming down there at quite a speed.'

'I know. Sorry. I can't get used to these rollerblades.'

'Practice makes perfect.'

'That's what my mum always says. She's a teacher.'

'She should know then.' He laughed. 'Are you sure you're all right? You look like you're in a bit of pain.'

'They're pinching my ankles. I think they might be a bit tight.'

'You should take them off. They might have broken the skin. My mum always puts Vaseline in new shoes to help loosen them up.'

'I'll see if Mum's got some. Thanks.'

Stephanie became aware the man was still holding her by the elbows, and she felt uncomfortable. He was very close to her, and she could feel his warm breath on her face as he spoke.

'Is that the new Newcastle home shirt?'

'Yes.' She smiled awkwardly. 'I got it this morning. My dad bought it for me as a birthday present. Alan Shearer signed it,' she said, showing him the signature.

'Wow. That's pretty cool. I'm a massive football fan.'

'Me too. We've got VIP tickets for the next home game too.'

'You're very lucky.'

A car drove past. Stephanie looked up and saw a young girl watching her from the back seat.

'I've got a programme signed by Alan Shearer,' the man said.

'Have you?'

'Yes. And Shay Given too. Would you like it?'

'Don't you want it?' She frowned.

He slowly looked her up and down. 'I think you're a bigger fan than I am. You should have it. Call it a birthday gift from me.'

'That's very kind of you, but Mum and Dad have always told me not to accept anything from strangers.'

'Very wise. Look, see that white van over there?' He pointed to a dirty white van parked in front of the hairdresser's a few car lengths away. 'That's mine. The programme is in there. I can give it to you now, and you can be on your way home.'

Stephanie hesitated.

'It'll probably end up getting torn and ruined and thrown in the bin, which is a shame when you think about it.' He smiled at her. 'It'll only take a couple of minutes. I've also got some cushioned plasters that might help your ankles as well.' He headed off towards the van. He stopped after a few steps and turned back. 'Are you coming?'

Stephanie frowned as she considered what to do. She really shouldn't, but a programme signed by Alan Shearer and Shay Given would be immense. Her father would love it.

'Okay,' she said and followed him.

Part I

THE AFTERMATH

Chapter One

Monday, 7 January 2019

Ryton, Tyne and Wear

'Who the bloody hell is ringing me at this time of night?'

I turned on the bedside light and squinted. It was like having a searchlight shone in my face. I had no idea what time it was. All I knew was that it was still dark, and I should be in dreamland. I couldn't focus on the display of my phone, but it wasn't somebody's name, just a series of random numbers. If this was some knob from a call centre on the other side of the world, I would not be happy.

'Yes?' I answered. I'm not a morning person. Even when it's actual morning and time to get up for work. I like my bed, and I like my sleep.

'Dawn Shepherd?'

Oh God, it *was* someone from a call centre. I could hear the sounds of an open-plan office in the background.

'Yes?'

'Do you know a woman by the name of Rita Shepherd?'

Okay, now they had my attention. Suddenly, I was wide awake.

'Yes, she's my mother. Who is this?'

'My name is Suzanne Hardy. I'm a constable with Northumbria Police.'

'Police? What's happened?' A phone call in the middle of the night is never good news. But when the call is from a police officer, it can only mean one thing. *Oh my God, please don't let Mum be dead. She's the only relative I've got left.*

'A woman was found attempting to break into a shop in the shopping precinct in Blaydon. We arrested her for drunk and disorderly. She gave us the name of Rita Shepherd and your contact details.'

'What? That can't be right. My mother doesn't drink. Are you sure it's my mum?'

'Five foot two inches tall, slim, about seven stone, dark brown shoulder-length hair, a tattoo on the inside of her left arm with a date, the fifth of November 1998.'

'That's my date of birth.'

'In that case, we have your mother in the station. Apparently, the shop she was trying to break into was her own,' said the police officer.

'Hollyhocks?'

'That's the one.'

'Shit.'

'I've spoken to your mother at length and, in between crying, she's told me a rather distressing tale. Do you think you could come and collect her?'

'Erm... yes... of course. I'll be right down.'

This made no sense. My mum doesn't touch alcohol. Why was she trying to break into her own shop when she had a key, and why the hell was she drunk? She won't even have sherry trifle at Christmas.

I kicked off the duvet and immediately felt the chill of the cold winter night. I'm not the neatest person in the world, so I had to scramble around the floor trying to find something decent and warm to wear. I grabbed my keys from the chest of drawers and was just about to leave my bedroom when I caught sight of myself in the mirror. I could not leave the house with dried drool on my chin, a crease in my face and my hair all over the place.

I ran into the bathroom and splashed cold water on my face. That certainly woke me up. I couldn't do anything about the crease running down my cheek – hopefully it would have faded by the time I got to the station – but a beanie hat would hide the Russell Brand tragedy I call my hair.

There wasn't a cloud in the sky when I left the block of flats, just an infinite number of stars. It was bloody freezing, and frost sparkled on every surface under the sodium of the street lamps.

I drive a VW Golf which is almost as old as I am. I slammed the door once I was inside and the sound resounded around the quiet neighbourhood. A light went on across the street. *Oops. Never mind.* The engine started on the sixth attempt. By the time it came to life, more lights had come on in houses along the road. I didn't turn the heater on. My car couldn't cope with driving and warming up the people inside at the same time. It was one or the other. I'd have to remain cold.

As I entered the police station, I realised this was my first time inside one. I'd recently started a new job: I was on the cusp of becoming one of the great paralegals of the twenty-first century… Although, at present, my job was mostly filing, making coffee and asking Sharon if she wanted any post taking to the box on the corner. Still, we all have to start somewhere.

The tired-looking bloke behind the desk took my name, and I sat down on the hard plastic chair, looking around me at all the crime prevention posters. There was a strong smell of disinfectant that was tickling my nostrils. I wanted to sneeze, but the desk sergeant looked like he was about to nod off, and I didn't want to disturb him.

The door to the main part of the station opened, and a short, stick-thin police officer stepped out. She looked younger than me, and her uniform seemed a size too big.

'Miss Shepherd?'

'Yes.'

'I'm PC Hardy. We spoke on the phone. Would you like to come through?'

There I was, five foot seven, twenty-one years old and, despite my mother's many reassurances that I'm big-boned and have childbearing hips, I prefer to speak plainly and call myself fat. Next to me was a teeny-tiny police officer, and we were walking down the corridor looking like a comedy double act. I felt like I was in a farce.

'What happened?' I asked. 'My mum doesn't drink. She doesn't like alcohol. She never has done.'

'Well, I'm afraid she's taken a taste to it now. In a big way.'

'And you say she was trying to break into her own shop?'

'She was kicking the bottom glass panel of the front door. It's going to need replacing, I'm afraid.'

'Are you charging her with anything?'

She stopped walking. I carried on until I couldn't hear her dinky feet catching up alongside me.

'I've had a chat with your mum. She's told me something quite distressing. Have you noticed a change in her behaviour lately?'

I thought for a moment. 'She's been a bit quieter than usual, I suppose.'

'And she hasn't said anything to you about… anything?'

'Like what?'

'Look.' PC Hardy placed a hand on my arm. It wasn't comforting at all. In fact, it was incredibly awkward. The only Hardy I want touching me is Tom, and in that scenario, we wouldn't be fully dressed in a police station. 'There's something your mother has been wrestling with, but I think she's ready to tell you now. I've had a word with my sergeant, and he's perfectly happy to issue your mother with a caution and let her go.'

'Oh my God. She's ill, isn't she? She's dying.' My eyes filled with tears. I felt sick. I could taste last night's disappointing korma.

'It's nothing like that, I assure you. It's just... you should prepare yourself for a bit of a shock.'

The first shock was seeing the state of my mother. Rita Shepherd is the complete opposite of me. She's petite, dainty, wee. She wears size eight clothes and size three shoes. She's always dressed smart, doesn't overdo the make-up and has her hair professionally touched up once every three weeks to hide the grey she's paranoid about. The wreck of a woman waiting for me in the charging suite of the local nick was nothing like the person I've called Mum for the last twenty-one years. The moment she looked up and saw me, the tears started to stream down her face. I took a deep breath. I wanted to cry too but knew I needed to be the strong one here. This wasn't going to be easy.

The drive back to Mum's house in Ryton was fraught with tension. I kept glancing at her as we drove quietly along the deserted roads. Every time we passed a lamp-post, and the bright yellow light entered the car, her face lit up. She was unrecognisable. Who was this woman sitting next to me? She was slumped in her seat, arms rigidly folded, a look of tiredness and embarrassment etched on her face. The car reeked of alcohol. I wanted to talk to her, to ask her what the hell was going on, but now wasn't the right time. I just needed to get her home. Besides, I had no idea where to begin. There were so many questions running around my mind, I didn't know which one to ask first.

Once inside the three-bedroom semi-detached house I'd grown

up in, in the comfort of a warm living room, both of us holding mugs of hot, strong coffee, I couldn't hold my tongue any longer.

'You've got some explaining to do, apparently.' I felt like the mother here. This was a real reversal of roles, and I didn't like it.

Mum nodded.

'What is it? Are you ill?'

'No,' she said, her voice barely above a whisper.

'Money worries?'

'No.'

'What is it then?'

'Dawn, just let me tell you in my own way.'

'Go on then.'

My lips were pursed. I glared at my mum, my role model, my hero. I couldn't begin to fathom what was going on inside her head. We never kept secrets from each other. We prided ourselves on having a very open and honest relationship. I told my mum everything – from the big issues like getting a new job, to the embarrassing ones like the time I was caught having sex in a bus shelter with Mark Foster on the night I passed my driving test. Mum reciprocated. She told me about the time she found a lump in her breast (fortunately, it was only a cyst) and when her business was in trouble (now fully solvent again). There was nothing, as far as I was aware, that my mother could be keeping from me.

'I was hoping I'd never have to tell you,' Mum began. A tear escaped her left eye and ran down her cheek. 'I don't buy newspapers, as you know, but I went into Morrisons, and there it was on the front page of a couple of tabloids. I almost collapsed right there and then. I've been looking online ever since, and it looks like it's definitely happening.'

'Mum… I don't know what you're talking about.'

'It's about your dad,' Mum said, looking up at me for the first time.

'My dad?'

She took a deep breath to compose herself. 'I've been lying to you your whole life. I've always known who your father is. I've always known where he is.'

I could feel my eyes widening. So this was the shock the PC was talking about. When I had been old enough to understand, Mum had sat me down and told me that she hadn't known my dad, that she had just met him at a party, and although it hadn't been planned, she had been over the moon when she discovered she was pregnant. She had known she didn't need a husband or a stepfather to raise me – she was more than capable of bringing me up single-handed, and that's what she had done. I was a credit to her, apparently. Everybody said so. I'm not one to blow my own trumpet, but ten GCSE passes, all As and Bs; three A-levels, two As and a B. And... Screw it, why not brag? A first from Newcastle University.

'Who is he? Where is he?' I asked, the words tripping over each other as I spoke.

My mum cried. The tears fell in a torrent. She couldn't speak. All my life I'd wanted to know who my dad was. It was hurting me seeing Mum so upset, but I needed her to explain.

From under the sofa cushion, she produced a copy of the *Evening Chronicle* and handed it to me.

The newspaper was a week old. The front-page headline was huge: STEPHANIE WHITE'S KILLER TO BE RELEASED. I remembered reading that story in my lunch-hour. Stephanie White was a teenage girl who disappeared on her thirteenth birthday in 1999. Her killer was due to be released early for some reason I couldn't remember; I had only skimmed the story. Why was she showing me this?

'I don't understand,' I said.

'Dominic Griffiths,' Mum said through the tears, 'the man who killed Stephanie White. He's your father.'

My stomach lurched, and I suddenly felt freezing cold. What was she saying to me? I couldn't bring myself to look back at the newspaper I was holding. I couldn't take my eyes off my mum, searching her face for answers. She nodded, confirming what she'd said. Eventually, I looked down at the paper on my lap and at the small photograph of a young Dominic Griffiths staring back at me. He had only been twenty years old when that picture was taken, when he'd butchered little Stephanie. He was tall and had broad shoulders, large brown eyes and dark, floppy hair. I remembered looking at this exact same photo when I read the story last week and thought he looked pretty hot for a murderer. I had no idea I'd been looking at my father.

Oh my God, I actually thought my father was hot. My father, the killer.

I heaved. I dropped the paper and lifted a hand to my mouth, but it didn't get there in time. I vomited all over myself.

Chapter Two

'Are you all right?' Mum asked.

I walked into the kitchen with a spare dressing gown wrapped around me. After being sick all over myself, I'd gone upstairs to the bathroom, peeled off my clothes and jumped straight into the shower. I was in there for ages, just letting the hot needles of water rain down on me, numbing the pain. Actually, I didn't know if I was in pain. I couldn't feel anything. I couldn't make sense of anything I'd just been told.

Less than five hours ago, I was eating a shitty curry and flicking through the channels for something decent to watch. I was living in blissful ignorance. Now, suddenly, I was the daughter of one of the most hated men in Britain.

All through my childhood, I'd asked about my dad. *Where's Daddy? Will Daddy be here for Christmas? Why do Charlotte and Jodie and Teresa have a daddy, and I don't?* When I was old enough, Mum had told me what I always believed to be the truth. She had put on an Oscar-winning performance, and I'd fallen for it. I mean, who would lie about getting knocked up after a one-night stand at a party with a complete stranger?

By the time I'd stepped out of the shower, my skin was red from the heat of the water. I'd felt cleaner, but I didn't feel any better. I'd dried myself and plonked myself down on the toilet lid, still mulling over all the questions running around my mind, wondering which one to ask first. I'd grabbed the dressing gown from the back of the door of my old bedroom and had slowly gone down the stairs. To be honest, I was dreading having to look my mother in the eye.

Mum was standing at the sink, rinsing out the bucket of soapy water she'd used to mop up the sick in the living room. My clothes were whirring around in the washing machine. I hoped they would dry quickly; I wanted to go home.

Mum turned to look at me. Her eyes were wide and full of tears. She seemed to have aged a decade in the past half an hour.

'Are you all right?' she asked a second time, and I didn't answer or move from the doorway.

I shook my head.

'Is there anything I can do? Or say?'

'Everything,' I said, stepping into the kitchen. 'Have you got any wine?'

'No. I don't—'

'I didn't think you did. It turns out you're full of surprises, though,' I said, sitting down at the kitchen table with a heavy thud.

'Would you like me to make you another coffee?'

I nodded. 'Better make it a strong one.'

'I think I'll join you.'

As Mum set about making the coffee, I kept turning to steal glances at her. I had so much respect and admiration for my mum. She'd been a single parent, struggling to run a business and bring up a daughter on her own. It hadn't been easy, but she'd succeeded. When I was young, all I had wanted was to grow up to be like the strong woman she was.

'Do you want something to eat?' Mum asked.

'Sorry?' I'd heard her speak but hadn't heard the words. She repeated the question. 'No. I don't think I could eat anything.' First time for everything.

Mum brought the mugs over to the table, followed by the full biscuit barrel. She sat down at the opposite end of the table and took a sip of the hot drink.

'Wow. That really is strong. Just what I need,' she said, giving me an uncomfortable smile. 'I'm going to have a headache tomorrow.'

I didn't comment. I looked down into my mug as if it had all the answers I was looking for. Usually when I had something to contemplate, I sought solace in a bottle of wine or three. I doubted coffee would have the same desired effect.

'Dawn, talk to me,' Mum pleaded.

It was a while before I looked up. 'I don't know where to start.'

'Tell me how you're feeling.'

'If I knew, I would.'

'Are you mad at me?'

'Yes. I think I am. Why did you lie to me, Mum? All these years. I can understand you not telling me when I was a child asking where my daddy was, but when I was old enough, you could have sat me down and explained.'

'I know,' she said. More tears ran down her cheeks. She grabbed a tissue from the box on the table and wiped them away. 'I've wrestled with this for so long. Every time I decided to tell you, a voice in my head said I shouldn't, that you were better off not knowing the truth. Whenever I started to think you had a right to know, the voice would speak louder and… I don't know.' She blew her nose, wiped her eyes and took a deep breath. 'Ask me anything. It's time to reveal the truth now. Ask me anything you want, and I'll give you an honest answer straight from the heart.'

'Why didn't you tell me before?' I asked firmly.

'When you were a child, I wanted to protect you. There was a lot of ill feeling around here about what Dominic did. There still is. I thought if I told you and you told a friend at school... Kids can be so cruel. I didn't want you being bullied.'

I nodded. 'I can understand that.'

My mum's face softened.

'How did you meet him?' I asked.

'At a party. We didn't go to the same school. It was Lizzie Denham's eighteenth. I met Dominic, and we had a few drinks and a laugh and arranged to meet up that weekend for a date.'

I smiled as I saw the brightness return to my mum's eyes as she remembered a time that was obviously special to her.

I've often wondered why Mum never married or even had a boyfriend. She met the odd bloke, and a couple of them were incredibly odd, but nothing ever went beyond a few dates. She always said she'd been on her own too long and was used to doing her own thing. I can certainly understand that. I may only be twenty-one, but I've been on enough dates to know, more often than not, men can be complete tossers – mentioning no names, Neil Whitaker.

'How long did you go out together for?'

'About a year.'

'What was he like?'

It was a while before Mum answered. It looked like she was struggling to find the right words. 'He was... lovely.' She gave a painful smile.

'Lovely. Is that it?'

'No. He was... sweet and kind and funny, but... he could be a bit overbearing at times.'

'How do you mean?'

'Remember Melanie Pritchard? Had the shop next to me, sold all that crap jewellery?' I nodded. 'Remember her husband? He was always phoning her asking what time she was shutting, what time she'd be home, where she was going, who she was meeting. Well, Dominic was a bit like that. He was… clingy.'

'Maybe he really liked you?'

'Maybe.' She shrugged.

'Did Nan and Grandad meet him?'

'Yes. They got on well with him.'

'So, what happened?'

'We were only eighteen. I was about to go to university. He didn't know what he wanted to do. He wasn't very academic, if I remember correctly. Anyway, people kept telling me not to have a boyfriend when I went to uni, as it wouldn't last and one of us would end up getting hurt. Also, I was planning on going to Sheffield, and I know it's not far, but I didn't want to do the whole long-distance thing. So we decided to end it.'

'How did he take it?'

Mum took a deep breath. 'He cried. A lot. I cried too.'

'He cried?' I was surprised.

'Yes. He told me… he told me he loved me.'

'But you didn't feel the same way?'

'No.'

'Why not?'

'I can't believe I'm telling you this. He was my first boyfriend. I didn't know what love was. I liked him, obviously. But love? No. I didn't love him.'

'Had I already been conceived at that point?'

'No. He asked if we could have one last night together. He picked me up in his van, and we went out for a meal in town. It was a good night.'

'Then what happened?'

'Well, you can imagine the rest.'

'And then you got pregnant. I bet Nan and Grandad went mad.'

'Your nan cried buckets. Grandad went ballistic. It took me ages to build up the courage to tell them, and I'd already started showing by the time I did, but I'd come up with a plan. If they were willing to help me look after you, I'd defer uni for a year, apply to Newcastle and stay at home.'

'And Grandad was okay with that?' I asked. As much as I'd loved Pop-pop and Mee-maw, I knew that Grandad had been tough and old-fashioned. I would have hated to tell him I was pregnant at eighteen.

'Your nan won him over, eventually,' Mum said, with a smile.

'Did you tell Dominic you were pregnant?'

'I did. I thought he had a right to know.'

'What did he say?'

Mum looked away briefly in embarrassment. 'He asked me to marry him.'

'He proposed! I'm guessing you turned him down.' She nodded. 'Why?'

'Like I said, I didn't love him. He didn't have any direction. He had no plan for what he wanted to do with his life. I was eighteen, still living at home and pregnant, yet I knew I wanted to have my own business. I let him down very gently. I told him I wasn't completely shutting him out. I said he could have as much input in raising you as he wanted.'

'So, what happened?'

'His mother happened. The next day, she came over to the house, banging on the door, demanding to be let in. She was a frightening woman.'

'Had you never met her before?'

'No. Dominic always put me off meeting his parents. He said they were very set in their ways.'

'So she came round?'

'She called me every name under the sun. I was a slag, a slut, a bitch, a whore. I'd trapped her son by getting pregnant to force him to marry me. She was furious.'

'Bloody hell. What happened?'

'Your grandfather happened. He read her the riot act and practically threw her out of the house. She left but told us not to have any contact with her or Dominic ever again. I was in tears when she left.'

'Did you ever see Dominic again?'

'Not until about three months after you were born.'

'Did he come to see me?' I asked, with a smile.

'No. I didn't see him in person. I saw him on the news being led to the back of a police car in handcuffs.'

Chapter Three

My stomach rumbled. I was hungry. Mum offered to make me a bacon sandwich or scrambled eggs on toast, but I needed something else, something filling and bad for me. Scrolling through the many takeaway apps on my phone, I ordered a pizza. I asked Mum if she wanted anything, but she just said she'd have a slice of mine. I ordered a fourteen-inch one, just in case she wanted two slices. Screw the diet. The father I didn't know I had had just been revealed to me and, to top it all, he was a bloody murderer. I didn't care anymore if I ballooned up to a size forty. Though I would probably regret saying that when I was next stood in front of my floor-length mirror trying to squeeze into my only work suit.

The large pepperoni stuffed-crust pizza and a large portion of chips arrived within twenty minutes. In that time, the conversation between us was stilted. I went to the toilet and stayed in there longer than usual to marshal my thoughts, while Mum put my clothes into the dryer then went about making up the bed in my old room.

'Why did he do it?' I asked. I'd already devoured a slice of pizza in three bites and was halfway through the second. Mum had placed a handful of chips on a plate and was picking off pieces of pepperoni from a slice of pizza.

'I have no idea,' she replied. It was an honest answer. 'To this day, I still don't know why he killed that little girl.'

'How did you feel when you heard?'

Mum didn't look at me. She busied herself chasing a chip around her plate, scooping up the tomato sauce. 'I felt physically sick. I cried for two days. I just couldn't believe it. It didn't make any sense.'

'What was he like when you were going out with him?'

'I'm not sure.' She sighed. 'I thought he was a sweet boy, but, like I said, he was quite possessive at times. He also…' She stopped and returned to playing with her food.

'What?'

'Once, we were out in his van, and this bloke cut us up. His face just drained of colour. He went mad. I honestly thought he was going to tear after him. I had to tell him to pull over and calm down.'

'He had a violent temper?'

'That was the only time I witnessed anything like that in him. I just put it down to him having a bad day.'

'Something must have happened to him for him to…'

'Evidently, but I wasn't in contact with him. His mother made sure of that.'

I looked at the slice of pizza halfway to my mouth and threw it back down in the box. I'd lost my appetite. I needed a *drink*, not tea or coffee. I needed wine, gin, vodka, turps, anything to numb the raw emotions rising to the surface. Why couldn't Mum have an emergency bottle of Chardonnay in the fridge or a bottle of Stoli in the freezer, for crying out loud? I went over to the sink and filled a glass with cold water. I took a long drink. It didn't have the same effect as alcohol, but it would do. For now.

'What did he do to her?' I asked, leaning against the sink and looking at my mum at the table.

'Dawn, you don't need to know that.'

'Mum, I'm going to be googling him tomorrow anyway to find out everything I can, so you may as well tell me.'

Mum threw her chips on the plate and wiped her hands on a piece of kitchen roll. She had a pained expression on her face like she was struggling to find the right words to use.

'He kidnapped her from around the back of the shops in Winlaton.'

I felt sick again. I looked down and saw the water in the glass wobbling. My hand was shaking.

'Did he… you know… abuse her?'

'No,' Mum answered quickly and firmly. 'There was no evidence of sexual assault.'

'How did he kill her?'

'Dawn…'

'Mum, I need to know.'

'I think she was strangled. I'm not one hundred per cent sure.'

'But… why?'

'Dawn, I've absolutely no idea. All this time I've told myself that something must have snapped, and he just lost his mind. I don't know if it's possible to do that; I'm not a psychologist. I can't answer your questions. I'm sorry.'

'Did you ever visit him in prison?'

'Of course I didn't.'

'Did he ever contact you?'

'No.'

'Didn't he want to see me?'

'I don't know. If he had asked, I wouldn't have allowed it. There was no way I would have taken you into a prison. Dawn, not having a father in your life didn't mean you missed out on anything. Me and your grandparents saw to that. We gave you the best childhood and upbringing we could.' There was real emotion in her voice.

'I know,' I said, struggling to fight back the tears myself.

'I was Mum and Dad to you. You were wanted. You were loved, and I am incredibly proud of you.'

I couldn't hold onto the tears any longer, and I started to cry. Mum jumped up from the table and came over to me. She grabbed me by the shoulders and pulled me into a tight embrace. Being so much smaller than me, she struggled to wrap her arms around me and had to crick her neck back to allow me to rest mine on her shoulder. It was uncomfortable for both of us, but it was what we both needed right then. I suddenly felt a lot safer. I suppose it doesn't matter how old a person gets – they'll always need a hug from their mum occasionally.

'Mum?' I asked, once I'd pulled myself out of her embrace. I grabbed a sheet of kitchen roll and wiped my eyes. 'The girl, Stephanie White, she wasn't Mrs White's daughter, was she?'

Mum nodded.

'Oh my God,' I said, stepping away. The tears began to fall again. 'She taught me English for three years at school.'

'I know.'

'You went to see her on open evenings.'

'I know.'

'Did she know who you were?'

'No. And I didn't tell her either.'

'We knew about her child being killed. We all thought it was tragic. My dad—'

'He wasn't your dad, Dawn,' Mum interrupted. 'He was your father. Any man can be a father, but it takes someone special to be a dad. Look, come and sit down.' She came over to me and led me back to the kitchen table. I sat down, and she pulled out the seat next to me and held my hands. 'I know there's a lot going through your mind right now, and you'll probably be thinking all kinds of things, like if your father was a murderer, maybe you have some of that part of him inside of you, but all of that is rubbish. What made you is the way you were brought up. Me, your nan and your grandad made sure you had the happiest childhood we could give you. You're intelligent, kind, caring, funny, honest and loving. We instilled all of that in you. You are not your father's daughter. I need you to understand that.'

I looked up, but I didn't see my mum. I was looking through her, beyond her. 'I don't know who I am anymore,' I said, crying.

'You are Dawn Mary Shepherd. You're my daughter. You're going to be a successful paralegal and go on to have a family of your own. Whatever happens in your life will be down to you, and you have more confidence and drive than I ever had at your age,' she said, wiping away my tears with her thumbs. 'The past only affects a person if they allow it to. You're not that kind of person. You never have been. Remember when you were eleven and you were bullied by that snotty girl and her mates?'

'Lyla Morris,' I reminded her.

'She tormented you for months. You could have allowed that to get to you, to turn you into a victim and let it ruin your schoolwork, but you didn't. We had a good talk about what you should do, and you went and did it.'

'Not really. I elbowed her in the face.'

Mum tried to hide her smile. 'Well, yes, you went the wrong way about it, but it taught her a lesson and gave you the confidence to stand up to people. You're a lovely, sweet, kind, independent woman. You're not your father.'

I went to bed soon after that. I was exhausted. It was almost three o'clock. I lay in my old bed, shrouded in darkness, but sleep eluded me. Mum was right. Just because my father was a killer didn't mean I would become one too. There was no scientific evidence to suggest a 'killer gene' existed, and I was a mentally stable individual. I'd never expressed any killer tendencies… Well, apart from Lyla Morris. And when Wesley Bishop cheated on me with Rebecca Lucas, I had wanted to rip his tiny head off, but that's only natural, isn't it? I had absolutely nothing to worry about. I was sure of it.

Although, if I could find out exactly what had happened to Dominic, what had turned him into a killer in the first place, maybe that would lay to rest the ghosts currently setting up home in my mind.

I yawned. It seemed like a lifetime ago, but it had been a good day at work. I hadn't been with Schofield and Embleton long, but I'd made a few friends and was settling into my role. I was socialising more, and I'd even been invited to the annual dinner the company had every spring to celebrate its birthday. I had been chuffed when I opened the envelope to see my name on the embossed invitation. I was establishing myself as a valuable member of the team. Then, suddenly, I'd been hit in the face with the bombshell that had torn my world apart. Would I have to tell my manager and colleagues that I was the daughter of an infamous murderer? How would they react? Would they treat me any differently? Would I have to leave the legal profession before I'd even started?

I turned over and pulled the duvet high up over my head. I felt physically and mentally drained. There was a lot for me to deal with in the coming days and I'd need a clear head to do it.

Before I fell asleep, I remembered something Mum had said in the kitchen. She described me as kind, sweet and lovely. As nice as that was, she'd also described Dominic in the exact same way not an hour before. Maybe we *were* similar.

Chapter Four

I woke early. Not that I'd slept much. I kept tossing and turning and decided to get up just after six o'clock. I was cold. At some point during the night, I must have kicked off the duvet and the fitted sheet had come away from the mattress on three corners. Yesterday's clothes were folded on top of the dresser. They'd been washed, dried and smelled clean and fresh. I quickly put them on and went quietly downstairs.

Normally, I can't function without having a coffee and a big bowl of cereal, but I wasn't in the mood to hang around and see Mum. I tiptoed around the ground floor, picking up my coat, handbag and car keys, and as I slipped out of the front door, I breathed a sigh of relief.

Luck was on my side, which made a refreshing change, and the Golf started on the first attempt. I set off without looking back. I wanted to get home, shower, slump in my bed and fall asleep for the rest of the day. Even though it was a workday, and I was due there in less than two hours, I couldn't face it. While waiting at a red light, I dashed off a text to my boss, informing him that I was suffering from excruciating period pains. I had to smile as I hit send. I imagined him blushing as he read the message. He wouldn't question it, as he didn't enjoy talking about anything personal. He would even get embarrassed by us singing 'Happy Birthday' to a colleague.

Once home in my familiar flat, I locked the door behind me and secured the chain. It wasn't a large flat: one bedroom, open-plan kitchen, living room and dining area, and the bathroom was en-suite, so any guests had to trundle through my messy bedroom to use the toilet, but it was all I could afford for now. I lacked storage space and there was only enough room for a two-seater sofa, which isn't easy to relax on when you're of a large build, but to me it was home. It gave me independence; that's what my little flat represented, and I loved it. I was very happy here.

I turned on the shower and allowed the room to fill up with steam and fog the mirrors before I climbed over the edge of the bath and let the hot water cascade over me. It was the longest and most luxurious shower I'd ever had, and I didn't want it to end. When I went into the bedroom, the bedside clock told me I'd been in the bathroom for almost forty minutes. Where had the time gone? What had I been thinking about that had distracted me for so long? I couldn't actually remember, but I had a pretty good idea – my father.

I felt empty and dazed. I wrapped my big pink towelling dressing gown around me, tied it around my waist and slumped, face-down, on the bed. I was asleep within minutes and stayed like that until I woke eight hours later at three o'clock.

I sat up with a feeling of determination running through me, as if my dreams had made me realise what I had to do. I looked at my phone: four missed calls and twelve text messages, all from my mother. She was a worrier. I didn't bother to listen to the voicemails but read a couple of the texts and fired one back saying I was fine and just needed to be on my own for a while.

My stomach rumbled. I hadn't eaten anything since those few

slices of pizza last night. I stumbled off the bed and into the kitchen. Looking through the cupboards, I realised I needed to do a shop, and soon. It would have to be pizza again.

I placed my order on the same app I had ordered from the night before, and while waiting for it to be delivered, I powered up the laptop on the small dining table and opened the Google home page. It was time to find out who my father really was.

Typing 'Dominic Griffiths' into the search engine revealed more than two million hits. The first was a Wikipedia entry for him. I know Wikipedia can't be taken as gospel, as people can edit it whenever they like, but it was as good a place to start as any.

Murder of Stephanie White

Stephanie White (14 February 1986 – 14 February 1999) was a child murder victim in the UK.

Stephanie, from Winlaton, Newcastle, disappeared from nearby shops on the day of her thirteenth birthday. Her disappearance generated a large amount of national and international press coverage. A twenty-year-old man, Dominic Griffiths, was subsequently arrested and charged with her murder.

Search

On Sunday, 14 February 1999, Stephanie's mother, Barbara White, made a call to Northumbria Police when her daughter failed to return home after going out to try out the new rollerblades she had been given as a present that morning. She was unsteady on the rollerblades and was wearing blue jeans and a black-and-white-striped Newcastle United home football shirt, another present she had been given that day by her parents.

The following day, a huge police operation began. Officers went to Stephanie's school to interview teachers and pupils, and television news crews were quick to cover the story. Newcastle United players Alan Shearer and Shay Given gave impassioned pleas for anyone who knew the whereabouts of Stephanie White to get in touch.

By mid-week, Stephanie had not been found, and there had been no sightings of her. British Prime Minister Tony Blair spoke in Parliament, saying the whole country was searching for her.

The following Saturday, Stephanie's photograph was shown on a screen at St James's Park, Newcastle United's home football ground.

Body discovery

At an allotment site in Low Greenside, three miles from where Stephanie disappeared, a spate of break-ins at sheds led police to be called out. Upon checking sheds on the site, traces of blood were found. Samples were taken and identified as belonging to Stephanie White. The allotment was registered to Dominic Griffiths, who had taken over the site when his grandfather, Gordon Griffiths, died eight months before.

Northumbria Police, led by Detective Inspector Ian Braithwaite, went to Dominic's home in Aldwick Road where Dominic still lived with his parents, Anthony and Carole Griffiths. Stephanie's body was found in bin bags in the attic of the semi-detached home.

Trial

The trial of Dominic Griffiths began on Monday, 6 September 1999 before judge the Honourable Mr Justice Hilary. Dominic entered a plea of not guilty to murdering Stephanie but pleaded guilty to cutting up and hiding the body after finding it in his allotment and panicking.

Witnesses called to the court stated that only Dominic had a key to the shed, and nobody, apart from Dominic, had been seen entering or leaving the site since the death of his grandfather.

Samples of Dominic's hair and fingerprints were found on Stephanie's body, though his defence argued they could have been deposited while he was moving the body from the shed to the attic.

On Tuesday, 14 September 1999, the judge concluded his summing up and ordered the jury to retire to consider their verdict. They took twelve hours over two days to find Griffiths guilty of abduction, murder and attempting to pervert the course of justice. On Thursday, 16 September 1999, Griffiths was sentenced to life in prison to serve a minimum of twenty-five years. He appealed twice, only to have them both refused.

Dominic Griffiths has always denied murdering Stephanie White.

The intercom buzzed, and I literally screamed. My pizza had arrived, though I didn't much feel like eating it now. It made me feel sick knowing that my father had murdered a poor, innocent young girl. And worse still, I knew her mother. She had taught me English. She introduced me to the classics. She was my favourite teacher, and all the time I knew her, we had had this horrifying connection.

I didn't even open the pizza box. I tossed it onto the table then returned to the laptop.

I went back to the search page and looked up more information about the case and subsequent trial. I wanted to get a feel for the atmosphere at the time.

NEWCASTLE UTD JOIN HUNT FOR STEPHANIE

Alan Shearer and Shay Given made an impassioned plea for Stephanie White to come home at a press conference yesterday.

Stephanie disappeared last week on her thirteenth birthday and hasn't been seen since. She was last seen leaving her home in Winlaton, wearing blue jeans and the famous black-and-white-striped Newcastle United home football shirt she had been given as a present that morning. She was also wearing rollerblades.

Stephanie, a keen Magpies fan, never misses a home game with her father, Detective Inspector Harry White. Her bedroom walls are adorned with posters of her favourite players.

At the press conference, Alan Shearer looked distressed as he asked for everyone to look for the teenager and help to reunite the family. Goalkeeper Given held up a photograph of Stephanie, which had been taken on the morning she disappeared, wearing the football shirt, and pleaded that if anyone knew anything about her disappearance, or if they knew who had taken her, they were to call the police straightaway.

The Sun has donated £10,000 for anyone with information to come forward in the search for Stephanie.

In a press conference yesterday, Detective Inspector Ian Braithwaite said, 'We are doing everything possible to find Stephanie and bring her home to her family. Police officers are working around the clock and are following up on a number of leads. However, we urge anyone with information to call the police.'

I looked at the photos that accompanied the story. Alan Shearer and Shay Given looked so young twenty years ago. It was strange seeing Shearer with hair. They both had glum expressions as they held up a photo of Stephanie for the cameras. Lower down the story, Detective Inspector Ian Braithwaite was snapped while giving the press conference. He looked drawn and tired, as if he had the weight of the world on his shoulders. That was probably how it felt.

The final photo was of Stephanie in the famous football strip, grinning happily into the camera on her birthday. Little did she know that a few hours later she would be torn from her family and their lives ruined for ever.

I stood up from the table and walked around the room to stretch my legs. It wasn't just the lives of the victim and her family that had been destroyed; it was all those others too. Detective Inspector Ian Braithwaite looked devastated in the photograph, as if it was his own child who had gone missing. How had he reacted when her body was discovered? Would he have considered it a personal failure that he hadn't been able to reunite the girl with her parents? What happened to him afterwards? One man's actions had created a snowball effect and touched many people's lives. I bet even Alan Shearer and Shay Given would often think of poor Stephanie and how it could have been one of their own children.

I wanted to stop reading. I was causing myself unnecessary heartache, but I needed to continue. Within these archived stories there had to be something that would answer the many questions I had racing around my mind. One question, in particular, screamed louder than the rest: why?

STEPHANIE WHITE FOUND DEAD

Teenager Stephanie White has been found dead at a house in Scotswood, Newcastle.

Police were alerted to a house in Aldwick Road and discovered the body of the thirteen-year-old girl in the attic. She had been cut up and stuffed into bin bags. An arrest has been made and other members of the household are helping police with their enquiries.

A post-mortem will take place tomorrow to discover the cause of death.

A statement released by Northumbria Police stated, 'This is the worst possible conclusion to this case. Every single officer is heartbroken that we could not bring Stephanie home to her parents. Our thoughts and prayers are with her family and friends.

'We believe this is an isolated incident. An arrest has been made and we don't believe the public should fear for their safety. The suspect is being questioned by detectives and information from these interviews will be released in due course.

'Northumbria Police would like to thank everyone for their help in searching for Stephanie and ask the media to give Stephanie's family, especially her parents, one of whom is Detective Inspector Harry White, privacy at this incredibly difficult time.'

The house in Aldwick Road has been sealed off, and forensic officers have been spotted entering and leaving the house all day. Uniformed police officers have been conducting house-to-house inquiries with the neighbours as they try to understand the reasoning behind this disturbing crime.

I had no idea Mrs White was married to a detective. What must he have been going through, knowing that his daughter had been kidnapped? I knew he wouldn't have been allowed to investigate, but he must have been climbing the walls, wanting to pound the streets of Newcastle, knocking on every door and not resting until she was found.

My vision blurred as I looked at the photograph of the innocuous house in Aldwick Road through tear-filled eyes. It seemed like a decent neighbourhood where people looked after their properties and gardens. Yet behind one of the painted front doors lurked a murderer. How long had Stephanie's body been in the house? Had Dominic's parents known she was there? Were they covering up for their son? I shuddered.

One question niggling away in my tired brain, which the internet may be able to answer, was: why was Dominic being released after twenty years, when he'd been sentenced to serve a minimum of twenty-five? I found the answer to that straightaway.

DOMINIC GRIFFITHS TOOK 'KILLER' DRUG

Dominic Griffiths, killer of tragic teenager Stephanie White, was taking the now banned drug Fenadine when he murdered the schoolgirl in February 1999.

In a statement released by his solicitor, Clare Delaney, she said, 'Dominic was a disruptive child and was given a mood stabiliser and anti-depressant called Fenadine. This was banned in 2002 following reports in America of users becoming violent and committing criminal acts, including murder and manslaughter, while taking the drug. Makers Maxton-Schwarz have paid out millions of dollars in compensation to people who have had their lives irrevocably changed due to the effects of one of their medications.'

Griffiths, who was sentenced to serve a minimum of twenty-five years in 1999, is now seeking an early release. If successful, he could claim a six-figure compensation payout from the pharmaceutical giant.

'Bloody hell,' I said, as I closed the laptop.

I wondered if that was the reason Dominic had maintained his innocence, because he had been taking a drug that was supposed to help him with his moods, but had ended up tipping him over the edge to commit murder. In his eyes, he wasn't guilty. To the rest of the world, he was.

However, there was no getting away from the fact that he had cut up the body and stuffed it into bin bags before hiding it in his loft. My stomach turned as I pictured the handsome young man from the newspapers standing over a body with a saw. I always thought I was unshockable. A fan of horror movies, I've sat through some disturbing films and haven't shied away from the screen when seeing a helpless victim being cut up with a chainsaw. I've just sat back, eyes wide, and shovelled in more popcorn. I've watched detective dramas on television and read everything Lynda La Plante and Val McDermid have written, but this was real life, and it was incredibly painful.

An even darker thought came into my head. Had Dominic been taking Fenadine while he was seeing my mum? She went out with him for a year – he could have snapped at any time. When she decided to break up with him, he could have killed *her* and cut her up. The tears came then as I wondered just how close my mother had come to being a victim. I wanted to hug her.

So many questions, so many thoughts, all of them making me feel sick. I needed a lie down. No, I needed fresh air. I didn't know what I needed, but maybe wine would help. I pulled a bottle out of the fridge and got a glass down from the shelf. To try to understand what was going on, I would need to speak directly to the people who were involved at the time. Would Mrs White appreciate me turning up on the doorstep? Were Dominic's parents, my grandparents, still alive? I hoped so. If anyone could fill in the background detail, it would be them.

I made a list of all the people I wanted to speak to: Harry and Mrs White. I don't think I'll be able to call her Barbara – she'll always be a teacher to me. Anthony and Carole Griffiths, who are my grandparents. The detective who led the investigation, DI Ian Braithwaite, and Dominic's solicitor, Clare Delaney. How realistic is it that Fenadine turned Dominic into a murderer, and he isn't just a cold-blooded killer? I looked at the list written in my neat handwriting, wondering how many on it would talk to me, how many would tell me to piss off and how many doors I'd have slammed in my face.

I left the list and put the pizza in the microwave to heat up. The best thing I could do for now was to try and forget about it for the rest of the day. If I allowed Dominic to consume me then I'd end up making myself ill, and I needed to be on top of my game here. The microwave pinged. Pizza, a bottle of wine and series two of *Fleabag* on iPlayer. Once Hot Priest appeared, everything else was forgotten.

Chapter Five

I went to work the next day. I had woken up bright and early, showered, put on my attempt at a power suit, did my make-up and hair all nice and headed for work. Mr Schofield asked, very succinctly, if I was feeling okay. I smiled and said I was fine. He blushed and practically ran back to his office, bless him.

Lunchtime couldn't come soon enough. As much as I'm enjoying learning about the legal profession, I'm not doing much work beyond filing and looking over people's shoulders at what they do. I'm aware that I have to learn from the bottom up, and I don't mind paying my dues, but bloody hell, it's dull.

At lunch, I drove to Hollyhocks to see Mum. I hadn't stopped thinking about her since I found out she could have been killed by her boyfriend twenty years ago. I don't think Pop-pop and Mee-maw would have recovered from losing their only child. On the drive over, I wondered if I should tell her what I had been researching. She was already upset enough, and I didn't want to make her feel worse.

'Dawn, I didn't expect to see you,' Mum said, as I entered the shop. It wasn't a large space, but Mum utilised what she had perfectly. Silver buckets of flowers were scattered across floor and shelves. You couldn't help but feel happy when you entered and saw so many vibrant colours and breathed in the heady scents. Mum had a genuine smile on her face when she saw me. It made me smile in return.

It must have been incredibly difficult for her to keep this secret for twenty years. She must have tortured herself, wondering if and when to tell me, hoping it would never come up. When it did, with Dominic's impending release hitting the newspapers, she'd panicked. I suddenly understood everything.

'How are you feeling?' I asked.

'I'm fine, thanks.'

I looked back at the front door with the chipboard covering the bottom panel. 'You'll need to get that replaced soon.'

'I'm waiting for a glazier to come round this afternoon.' She looked embarrassed. 'How are you feeling?'

'I'm fine' was all I could think to say. 'What are you up to?'

'I'm putting a wreath together for a funeral.'

'Oh. That's… nice. Am I okay to make a cup of tea?'

'Of course you are. You don't need to ask.'

'Would you like one?'

'Please.'

I walked past Mum and went into the back room where I flicked on the kettle. Mum followed.

'Dawn, do you want to talk?'

'About what?'

'Climate change. What do you think?' she said, deadpan.

'I don't think so, Mum, not yet. Can I open these Bourbons?'

'Of course. I was thinking, if you have any more questions about Dominic, you can ask them. I don't want him to be something that comes between us.'

I looked up from the packet of biscuits I was struggling to open. Mum had this hopeful look on her face. I bet she wished she could turn back the clock twenty-four hours and do everything differently. Or maybe she'd like to turn it back ten years to when she sat me down and told me I was the result of a shag in someone's back bedroom, and tell me the truth instead. Or maybe she'd like to turn the clock back to 1997 when she first met Dominic, reject his offer of a date and never sleep with him in the first place. However, that would mean I wouldn't be standing here now. Had Mum ever regretted having me, even in her darkest days, when struggling with a crying baby and university work? She probably had.

The kettle boiled, bringing me back from my dark thoughts. A shiver ran down my spine and I shuddered. I made the tea and handed a mug to Mum.

'Are we all right?' she asked.

'Yes.'

'Are you sure?'

'Mum, we're fine.' My goodness, I'm a liar. 'It was a bit of a shock at first. Actually, it was a massive shock to discover my father is a killer, but, well, I can't change it, can I?'

'No. I really am sorry, Dawn. I know I handled everything so badly. At the time I thought I was doing the right thing.'

'I know.'

'Can we have a hug?' she asked.

That's what I needed more than anything. A hug from my mum. Who cared if I was twenty-one years old? I didn't. I wanted my mum to hug me and tell me everything was all right. I smiled, put down my mug and held my arms out. As I'm taller and heavier, it was more like me hugging Mum than the other way round, but it was the sense of comfort and familiarity that was important. When you're being held by a parent, you're indestructible. When the end of the world came, I wanted to be standing right there in my mum's arms. The end of everything wouldn't seem as frightening then.

'What did Nan and Grandad make of all this?' I asked, after the lengthy hug. 'Did they think you should have told me sooner?'

'Your nan did. She was all for being open and honest. Your grandad said—'

'Let sleeping dogs lie,' we both said together, before laughing.

'His favourite saying,' Mum said.

'I miss them.'

'So do I,' Mum said. 'I could have done with having them here over these past few weeks.'

'If Nan had seen the state you were in the other night, she would have killed you.'

'Even at my age, she would have grounded me for a month.'

We both laughed, but it wasn't a genuine display of humour. There was an edge to it, as if we were both holding back. I know I was. Despite the hug, despite saying we were both fine, neither of us were. Our relationship had changed. I felt like I'd grown up by ten years in two days.

'Mum, can I ask you something?' I asked, reaching for another biscuit.

'You know you can.'

I took a lingering sip of my tea as I tried to phrase the question right in my head. 'I was thinking… Stephanie White, the girl who—'

'I know who Stephanie White is,' Mum interrupted.

'Well, with her mum being my old English teacher, do you think I should go and see her?'

Mum's eyes widened. 'What? Go and see Barbara White? And say what? "Remember when you taught me English a few years ago? Well, you'll never guess who my father turned out to be." I'm sure she'd love that,' she said, her tone dripping with venom. 'No, Dawn, I don't think you should visit her. I think you should forget the whole thing and move on with your life.'

'Forget? How can I possibly do that? My dad is a murderer.

Every single person in this city knows his name. He's up there with Myra Hindley, Ian Huntley and Mark Bridger. How can I forget who he is?'

Mum put her mug down and stepped towards me. I really didn't want another hug. 'I'm sorry. Of course you can't forget. I shouldn't have said that. But you didn't know him. He wasn't a part of your life. I was. I still am. Me and your grandparents brought you up. He had no influence on your life at all. I don't want you to think he had anything to do with how you turned out, because he didn't.'

'But he did,' I said quietly. 'Fifty per cent of who I am came from him. His DNA, his genetic make-up is inside me.'

'Oh, sweetheart.' Mum placed her hands on my cheeks. I had to stop myself from recoiling, and I didn't know why. 'You're a kind, sweet, funny person. You're the way you are because of how you were brought up and your own unique personality.'

'You said Dominic was kind, sweet and funny too.'

Mum took a sharp step back. She looked hurt. 'I don't know what to say to you, Dawn.'

'I don't think there's anything else *to* say.' I drained what was left of my cooling tea. 'I'd better be getting back to work.'

'Dawn, you're not going to do anything silly, are you?' Mum called after me, as I left the little staffroom and headed for the door of the shop.

'Like what?'

'I don't know. Something that might jeopardise your career.'

'No.' I smiled coldly. 'I'm just going to go back to my boring job to do my boring work.'

I could see Mum wasn't convinced.

'Do you want to come over for your tea tonight?'

'I can't. We've got staff training after work, and I usually go for a couple of drinks with the girls afterwards.' Bloody hell, where had that lie come from?

'Oh.' She looked dejected. 'Maybe tomorrow night then?'

'Maybe.'

It was only as I headed for my car that I realised I hadn't kissed my mum goodbye. I think that's the first time I'd ever done that.

I think the purpose of going to see Mum was to gauge how she would react to finding out I was researching Dominic to find out more about him and discover how much this Fenadine had played a part in him committing murder. I think I had wanted Mum's approval, but now I knew she wouldn't have given it – the way she kicked off about me potentially visiting Mrs White was testament to that.

As I drove back to work, I started thinking about Mrs White. She was my favourite teacher at school. She never let her grief show, and she must have felt it occasionally during lessons surrounded by young teenagers, all of them reminders of what her own daughter could have become. I remember her always being approachable, kind, and smiling. She never once raised her voice to any kid, even Kevin Sampson, and he was a right little bastard at times.

Mrs White ran an after-school reading club which I joined because I genuinely liked her and thought she might help me with my English. She introduced me to the classics – *Wuthering Heights* is my favourite novel thanks to her. Surely she would welcome a visit from a former pupil.

Chapter Six

I parked at the bottom of the cul-de-sac and turned off the engine. It was only half-past five, but it was dark, and according to the weather app on my phone, it was minus one outside. It felt colder in the car.

It hadn't been difficult to find out where Mrs White and her husband lived, from the many news stories online. A number of photographs of Harry and Barbara entering or leaving their house had been taken at the time Stephanie disappeared. I recognised the street, and I spotted the house as soon as I turned in. It hadn't changed much. I hoped they still lived there. The only way to find out was to get out of the car and knock on the door. I was slightly nervous. Actually, that's a lie – I was shitting bricks. If I was simply paying a visit to my old English teacher to reminisce about our school days together, Mrs White would probably welcome me with open arms, but the dark memories of Stephanie's death were unlikely to be something you'd willingly invite into your home.

'Come on, Dawn, you silly cow.' I often insulted myself. I deserved it for the way I dithered over things. 'You've come this far, just go and knock on the door.' I took a deep breath and shivered. I opened the car door and stepped out into the freezing cold air.

I could hear my heels clacking on the pavement as I headed up the incline. The noise resounded around the empty neighbourhood. It was only early, but there was nobody around. It felt much later than half-past five.

On the doorstep, I hesitated. This really was the point of no return. I badly needed a wee.

I knocked.

It seemed to take an age for the door to open. When it did, I was bathed in a soothing warm glow, and I could feel the heat from indoors.

'Mrs White?' I'm not sure why I asked as I recognised her straightaway. She hadn't changed much. A few more wrinkles, greyer hair, and she may have shrunk slightly, or I'd grown, but she still had a kind face and a sweet smile.

'Yes.'

'I'm not sure if you remember me. I'm Dawn Shepherd. You taught me English at Benfield School. It must have been about six or seven years ago.' My voice was shaking. Was it nerves or the cold? It was hard to tell.

Mrs White glared at me as she seemed to be searching her memory. I wasn't sure if I'd changed much since my school days. I'd put on weight, and my hair was now black rather than brown. Also, she only ever saw me in school uniform – green sweater and a grey skirt – yet I stood on her doorstep wearing black trousers and a black knee-length coat. All I needed was a scythe, and I could stand in for the Grim Reaper on his days off.

'You used to run a reading club after school. I fell in love with *Wuthering Heights* straightaway, and you organised a trip to go and see it when it came to the Royal,' I added, to prompt her memory.

Suddenly, her face lit up.

'Oh, my goodness,' she said, slapping a hand to her chest. 'Dawn Shepherd. Yes, I remember you now. How could I forget? Your essay on *Little Women* had me in tears.'

'Really?'

'Absolutely. Come in, come in.' She beckoned, stepping back from the doorway.

'I'm not interrupting anything, am I? You're not about to sit down to your tea or anything?'

'No. We don't eat until much later.'

She closed the door behind me. There was definitely no backing out now.

'Harry, I have a visitor.' She entered the living room, and I followed. It was warm and homely but slightly dated in its decoration.

On the sofa, staring at the TV, was a man of around seventy. He had thinning grey hair, a lined face and sad-looking eyes. He wore grey trousers and a beige sweater, and looked every inch the elderly man, whereas Mrs White was dressed in a bright coloured top and white trousers. She made the introductions and told me to sit down while she made a pot of tea. On her way to the kitchen, she prodded her husband and made him turn off the game show he was watching.

I took off my coat and sat down. The heat from the radiators was beginning to thaw me out. I looked around the living room, and my eyes immediately fell on a framed photograph of Stephanie on the mantelpiece. She was wearing a hooded sweater and a Father Christmas hat, sat in front of a huge Christmas tree, surrounded by presents. As she looked into the camera, she had an enormous grin on her face. I found myself smiling back. She was a pretty girl with dark blonde hair, a smattering of freckles beneath her eyes that danced across the bridge of her nose. Her eyes sparkled.

There were other photographs of Stephanie dotted around the

room. Some on the walls, others on shelves and bookcases, all showing Stephanie with a smile on her face, enjoying life.

I swallowed hard. I felt sick. Suddenly, it felt wrong to be there. Maybe Mum was right. I heard Grandad in my head telling me to let sleeping dogs lie. My goodness, he was right.

Something moved out of the corner of my eye. I turned and saw Mr White adjusting his position on the sofa. His face was blank. I wondered if he'd noticed me staring at the photos of his daughter.

'So, my wife taught you at Benfield?' he asked. His accent was pure Geordie. He sounded exactly like Pop-pop.

'Yes. She did. My favourite teacher, actually.'

That made him smile. 'She always wanted to be a teacher, right from a young age. She couldn't imagine doing anything else.'

'She was an excellent teacher.'

He leaned forwards and lowered his voice. 'You're not a journalist now, are you?'

'No,' I said, placing my hand on my heart.

'Good. I won't have my wife upset.'

A shiver ran down my spine.

'Here we are then,' Mrs White said, as she breezed into the room carrying a heavy-laden tray.

I hadn't had enough time to react to Mr White's warning. I wanted to leave. The last thing I wanted was to upset either of them.

Mrs White placed the tray on the coffee table. There was a large white teapot decorated with flowers growing up from the base, matching cups and saucers and a matching plate with a mixture of biscuits laid out on it.

She poured the tea and handed the cups round, telling me to help myself to milk and sugar from the matching jug and bowl. She was full of smiles, and I smiled back, but I kept stealing the odd glance at Mr White. Although both of them had welcomed me into their home, there was a hint of sadness about them. Their smiles didn't quite reach their eyes. It was understandable: the murder of their only child would stay with them for the rest of their lives. They wouldn't have got over the loss of Stephanie, but they would have adapted to a life without her. They'd go on holiday. They'd enjoy birthdays and Christmases together. They'd laugh and go for meals out, but at the back of their minds was the knowledge their only child had been brutally murdered, and that would put a dark tinge on any celebration.

'So, what have you been doing with yourself since you left Benfield?' Mrs White asked. She sat back in her armchair opposite me, crossed her legs and blew on her tea before taking a sip.

'I went to Newcastle University. I studied English Literature and Law.'

'You kept up with the English then; that's good.'

'Yes.' I smiled and felt myself relaxing. 'You got me interested in the classics. I was hooked right away.'

'Do you still read them?'

'Not as much as I used to, unfortunately. I started *The Tenant of Wildfell Hall* before Christmas, and I'm not even halfway through yet. Work takes up a lot of my time.'

'What is it you do?' Mr White asked. He too had his legs crossed and held a cup and saucer in his hand, but his expression was sceptical. Always the detective, I assumed.

'I'm a junior paralegal. I work for Schofield and Embleton in town.'

'Oh, I know them,' Mr White said. 'A good firm. Are you enjoying it?'

'So far.'

'That's good. Your mother must be very proud of you.' Mrs White smiled.

'She is.'

'Let me think,' she said, with a frown. 'She had a shop, didn't she? At Blaydon?'

'Yes. A florist. Hollyhocks.'

'That's right. I remember now. Does she still have it?'

'Yes. It's doing very well.'

'Good. I'm glad.'

Mrs White took a sip of her tea and looked at her husband over the top of her cup. I felt as if some kind of question had been asked between the two of them telepathically.

'Forgive me for being so blunt,' Mr White said. 'But why have you come here?'

'Ah.' I could hear my cup rattling in the saucer so decided to place it back on the tray. 'I'm not quite sure how to say this. I don't even know if I should've come here, but… well, you were my favourite teacher, Mrs White—'

'Goodness, call me Barbara,' she interrupted.

I smiled. 'Barbara. Thank you. I felt that if I didn't come and tell you then it would always weigh on me. I don't know if I'm doing the right thing or not.'

'Dawn, slow down. What's happened?'

I closed my eyes for a moment and took a deep breath and tried to draw some energy from somewhere deep inside me to break the bad news.

'I'm not sure if you remember, but my mum brought me up by herself. Well, my grandparents were there a lot, but it was my mum who… Sorry, I'm waffling.' I took another deep breath. 'A few days ago, my mum told me who my father was. She had always told me it was someone she met at a party whom she didn't really know. It turns out that was a lie. She did meet him at a party, but they went out together for about a year. She knew exactly who he was but didn't tell me, as she wanted to protect me from the truth.'

Barbara's face had dropped. The smile had gone, and she looked tense.

'My father… is Dominic Griffiths.'

Barbara visibly baulked at the mention of his name. She let out a noise that sounded like an animal in pain. It was like I'd slapped her in the face. Mr White jumped forwards, grabbed the cup and saucer from her and placed it on the tray. He perched on the edge of the armchair and wrapped his arm around her shoulders.

'I think it's probably best if you go,' he said.

'I'm so sorry.' It sounded insincere, but it was the truth. 'I really didn't mean to upset you like this.'

'Please. Just go.'

I stood up and reached for my coat.

'No. Wait.'

I looked back. Barbara had stood up.

'Don't go. Sit down. Please.'

'Barbara, love, we don't need this.'

'No. We don't. Neither does Dawn. But we're lumbered with it. Now, let's all just sit down.'

Barbara sat first. I followed. It was a while before Mr White took his eyes off me and went back to his place on the sofa.

'I'm guessing you didn't know he had a child,' I said. 'I don't think anyone did. Mum certainly didn't tell anyone. She only told me because… well, recent events have been playing on her mind.'

Barbara's eyes filled with tears. 'It can't have been easy for her,' she said, though her words lacked feeling. She took a breath and continued, 'That man brought so much tragedy into our lives. He stole the most precious thing we had and destroyed our lives.'

'At school… we knew you'd lost a daughter, but I had no idea…' I trailed off.

Barbara turned to the photo of Stephanie on the mantelpiece. I followed her gaze.

'Stephanie was the best daughter we could have wished for.

She had so much life and energy inside her. She wouldn't sit still for a moment, except when she was watching football with her dad.'

I looked across at Mr White. He had tears in his eyes and his bottom lip was wobbling.

'I can't stand the game myself,' Barbara continued. 'Never could. Harry and Stephanie were obsessed though. If they weren't watching it, they were playing it or talking about it. They drove me crazy.' She half-smiled at the memory.

'Have you spoken to him?' Mr White asked.

'I'm sorry?'

'Your father. Have you contacted him?'

'No. No, I haven't.'

'Are you going to?'

'Harry, that's none of our business,' Barbara chastised.

'I really don't know what I'm going to do yet, Mr White.'

He softened at this. 'Call me Harry.'

'Thank you.'

'How do you feel about him being released?' he asked.

'I don't know that either. I'm struggling to come to terms with it all. I'm guessing you've read in the news about that drug he was taking?'

'We've read everything,' he said, reaching across to take his wife's hand in his. 'We knew he'd be released one day. I must admit, we were both shocked when we heard he was coming out early, but I suppose—'

'No.' Barbara snatched her hand back. 'There's no suppose about it, Harry. Whether he was taking a drug that messed with his head or not, at the end of the day, he killed our Stephanie. He murdered a child. He should never see the light of day again.'

'Barbara and I have different views on justice, Dawn.'

'Harry will forever be a policeman,' she said. There was an edge to her voice. 'He believes in law and order, and justice. He doesn't see that the law isn't working, that it's the criminals who are looked after before the victims and their families. Dominic is getting his life back after twenty years. Are we getting Stephanie back? No, we're not. So he shouldn't be released.'

'He's not getting his life back, Barbara. We've been through this countless times. He'll be released on licence. He'll have a probation officer. He'll have to report to the police. He'll have to ask permission to move house, change job, go on holiday—'

'But he'll still be able to do those things, Harry,' Barbara said, jumping up and walking over to the window. 'Stephanie can't go on holiday. She's dead. She's not coming back. He stole her away from us, and he should pay with his own life.' She turned and went into the kitchen.

'I really shouldn't have come here, should I?' I asked.

Harry shrugged. 'You did what you thought was right.'

'Turns out I was wrong.'

'Not at all. We go through stages like this. Something happens that reminds us, takes us back to those dark days, and we have the same argument over and over again. I was a detective for over twenty-five years. I have to believe in the justice system, or it makes everything I worked for a sham. I'm sure you're the same, now you're in the legal profession. Dominic was sentenced in a court of law. He's served his sentence, and he's getting released. That's all there is to it.'

'It's admirable that you think like that,' I said. I meant it too.

'Could you repeat that to my wife?' he said, with a hint of a chuckle.

'Dawn?'

I looked up and saw Barbara standing in the doorway to the kitchen. Her eyes were red from crying.

'I'm sorry for my behaviour. I shouldn't have reacted like that and dragged you into our argument.'

'That's fine. I'm sorry. I probably shouldn't have come here.' I stood up and reached for my coat again.

'No. I'm glad you came. And you deserve to know who your father is. Nobody can help who their family is, can they? Remember your cousin Shaun, Harry?'

'Let's not go down that route, Barbara. The less said about Shaun the better.'

'Precisely my point. There are bad apples in every family.'

I smiled. Once again, Mrs White had a way of making everything seem better. I was suddenly back in English class and worrying because I couldn't understand why Miss Havisham was being such a cow to Pip and Estella.

I started crying. I've no idea where the tears came from or why they were falling, but once they started, I couldn't stop. Barbara came towards me and put her arms around me. I towered over her, so it must have looked strange from Harry's point of view.

'You must be going through hell right now,' she said.

I tried to speak, but my tears were choking me. I sat back down, took a deep breath and composed myself. 'Do you hate me for coming here?'

'Of course I don't. Dawn, I don't want you to worry about us. Don't get bogged down in who your father is and what he did. He is an evil man, but you're not him. Be yourself. Promise me you'll not let it consume you,' she said, looking at me straight in the eye.

My tears had stopped. 'I promise.'

'Good,' she said. 'Now, I'm going to make us another pot of tea, as this one has gone stone cold. When I come back, you can tell me all the fun things you did at university.' She stood up, picked up the tray and headed for the kitchen.

I took a tissue from my pocket and wiped my eyes. No trace of mascara, thank goodness.

'Can I ask you a question, in your capacity as a detective?' I asked quietly, so Barbara couldn't hear us from the kitchen.

'Of course.'

'I've been reading up about Dominic, what he did, and he's always said he was innocent. Is there any way that could possibly be true?'

'No,' he replied firmly. 'No. He's guilty.'

I nodded. 'You didn't work the case though, did you? I'm guessing DI Braithwaite is retired now, but do you think I could talk to him? Do you know where he is?'

'Ian is a very good friend of mine, but you won't be able to speak to him. He had a severe stroke a few years ago. He's living in a nursing home on the other side of Newcastle. He never got over Stephanie's death. He was her godfather, and he had to deal with finding and identifying her body. It ruined him.'

I slowly shook my head. It wasn't only Stephanie my father killed on that day. Barbara and Harry were victims and so was Ian Braithwaite. How many more would I find who had suffered at the hands of Dominic Griffiths?

Chapter Seven

I slept well that night. Reading between the lines of the news stories, it seemed the theory was that Dominic had seen Stephanie and something in his brain had snapped, telling him to kill her. Was that due to the drug he had been taking or was it something that had always lurked in his subconscious that had suddenly risen to the surface?

The next morning, I was scheduled to join one of the senior paralegals at Newcastle Crown Court and observe the more exciting aspects of the job, but when I arrived, I was told the defendant had absconded and an arrest warrant had been issued. The court case was adjourned, and I was back to doing the filing. Typical. I'd worn new shoes for the occasion, too.

At lunchtime, I took myself to Café W in Waterstones next to Fenwick's. I planned on reading a few chapters of *The Tenant of Wildfell Hall*, but I couldn't focus on it. My mind was elsewhere. No prizes for guessing where.

I couldn't get Dominic out of my head. My thoughts kept returning to the picture Mum had painted of him before he had turned killer. What had changed in his life that had caused such a drastic change in temperament? Was it really the drug? I was finding that difficult to believe without more evidence.

I put the neglected book back in my bag and took out my phone. There was another text from Mum which I ignored. Opening Google instead, I typed in Dominic's name and looked up more headlines. I was torturing myself – I knew I was, but until I had all the answers, it was what I had to do.

JUROR COLLAPSES AS DETECTIVE TAKES THE STAND

The murder trial of Dominic Griffiths was halted yesterday when a juror collapsed while a detective recalled how he found the body of his thirteen-year-old goddaughter, Stephanie White, in Griffiths' attic.

DI Ian Braithwaite of Northumbria Police, 43, fought back tears as he told the court of his discovery: 'I knew what the smell in the house was straightaway. I've smelt a rotting corpse several times in my career. When I opened the first bin bag and saw the discoloured limbs, the dried blood, I knew… I knew I'd found her.'

He continued. 'When I opened the third bag, I was looking down at her face. I hardly recognised her as the perfect little girl I'd seen grow up. Her eyes were closed. Her face was bloated and swollen, but I knew it was her. I knew it.'

Trying to control his emotions, DI Braithwaite broke down and took a minute to compose himself before continuing. 'There wasn't much space in the attic. We didn't want to contaminate any forensic evidence, so I had to work with the pathologist to pick out the body parts. She was my goddaughter. I'd helped her learn to ride a bike, I'd played football with her, and suddenly, I'm picking her hands and legs out of bin bags.'

Several jurors were seen wiping away tears, and an elderly

> lady collapsed to the floor. The case was adjourned while she received hospital treatment and will continue tomorrow.

'Oh my God,' I said. I placed the phone on the table and pushed my cooling tuna melt panini to one side.

How long must it have taken Dominic to dismember Stephanie? What was going through his mind as he cut her arms from her body then removed her legs? How could a person physically and mentally bring themselves to cut off someone's head? It defied all reason. But, there had to be one. There was an answer to every question, and no matter what Mum or Barbara said, I needed to know.

FATHER 'SENTENCES' SON

> There were dramatic scenes in court today as the father of Dominic Griffiths screamed at his son from the witness stand.
>
> Working for the defence, Alastair Wimpole QC was questioning Anthony Griffiths, 50, on his son's upbringing, during which the father was having difficulty controlling his emotions. As the questioning continued, Anthony broke down and burst into a vitriolic rant.
>
> 'Why did you do it, Dominic? What had we done wrong? You've ruined so many lives. You make me sick just looking at you, knowing that I brought someone so evil and disturbed into the world. Do you know what you've done to your mother? Do you have any idea what she's going through? You're killing her, Dominic. You're f***ing killing her.'
>
> Mr Justice Hilary halted proceedings while Anthony Griffiths was led away from the courtroom.

So it would seem that even Dominic's parents believed he was capable and guilty of the murder. Hardly surprising. They would have been run out of Newcastle if they'd tried to side with their son against the weight of evidence.

If anyone could tell me everything about what had gone into making Dominic the person he was, it was his parents… my grandparents. Surely, they wouldn't turn me away? I was their flesh and blood, after all, no matter what they thought of their son.

I suddenly remembered what Mum had told me about Carole Griffiths – how she had come to the house screaming and ranting when she discovered Mum was pregnant. She had been a volatile woman back then. Hopefully, age would have mellowed her, but how would dealing with finding out her son was a murderer have affected her personality over the years?

The meeting with Barbara and Harry had gone well, despite a few hiccoughs, but how would it go with my grandparents? How would they react to the granddaughter they had never known turning up on the doorstep demanding to know about her father? There was only one way to find out, but I shuddered at the prospect of facing their rejection. Mum might have liked to say I was confident, but a lot of it was just for show. If it wasn't for the layer of make-up I hid myself behind, I'd have been a gibbering wreck.

I took out the list of people I wanted to talk to about Dominic and ticked off Harry and Barbara. It had been lovely to see Mrs White again after all those years. I hoped I would get another chance to see her, maybe with less crying next time.

I decided to put the list in my phone. I opened the notes app and typed their names in. At the bottom of the list, I hesitated. *What the hell, it's only for my reference, and I don't have to go through with it if I don't want to.* I quickly typed 'meet my dad' before I could change my mind.

Chapter Eight

One of the best feelings in the world is waking up, realising it's Saturday and there's no work. You can turn over, pull the duvet over your head and sleep for another hour or three. And that's exactly what I planned on doing. Unfortunately, my next-door neighbour, Robyn, had other ideas. She'd obviously pulled the previous night, and the sound of her headboard banging against the wall forced me to abandon my lie-in. I had nothing against her having a sex life; I just wished she wouldn't have it so loudly.

Reluctantly, I threw the duvet back and stepped out of bed. Another cold morning. I wrapped my dressing gown around me, slipped my feet into a pair of novelty slippers and kicked the cold radiator as I left the room. I'd complained about the heating to my landlord on a couple of occasions, and it never got me anywhere. He had loaned me a portable fan heater when we had a cold snap in November, but all that did was overheat whatever part of you it was pointing at while the rest of you remained freezing cold. I was like a human Baked Alaska.

Following a huge bowl of cereal and two coffees, I decided the only way to stop my mother constantly texting me was to pay her a visit.

As it was Saturday, I was able to dress how I wanted and didn't have to look all business-like. I still wore black, but I whipped up my hair into a small beehive and added extra make-up to give myself panda eyes. I spent ages on my eyes while listening to Dusty Springfield. I had to laugh when she started singing 'I Just Don't Know What to Do with Myself'. *You and me both, Dusty.*

Leaving the flat, I took one last look at myself in the mirror. I might be a bit on the heavy side but I had style and, if I did say so myself, I looked pretty good.

I parked near Costa and popped in to buy a couple of takeaway lattes and something sugary for a snack for me and Mum. I missed the closeness we had always had, and I wanted it back. I didn't want to hurt Mum by looking into my father's background, but I needed her to meet me halfway and understand it from my point of view.

The door to Hollyhocks opened as I approached. A woman with a smile on her face carrying a large bunch of beautiful flowers held the door open for me. Mum really did have a great job. Everyone left her shop with a smile. Unless they'd been in to pick up a wreath.

'Morning,' I said on entering the shop, trying to sound as jolly as I could.

'Hello, stranger! What a nice surprise,' Mum said, with a huge smile.

'I thought you'd like something to warm you up,' I said, placing the cardboard cup on the counter.

'You're an angel. I was about to flick the kettle on, but this is much better.' She wrapped her hands around the cup. 'I was going to pop around to see you later. I've found something I think you might be interested in.'

She took a sip of her latte, let out a satisfied sigh and placed it carefully on the counter. From underneath, she brought out her handbag and rummaged around inside it. She lifted out a photograph, smiled and handed it over to me.

'I knew I had something somewhere. It took me ages to find it.'

I frowned as I examined the picture. 'Who am I looking at?'

'You mean you can't guess? I didn't think I'd changed that much. Back row, fourth from the right.'

I leaned in closer and squinted. 'Oh my God, is that you?'

It was a group shot of a dozen or so people all huddled together in a kitchen.

'Yes. You can laugh at my hair if you like.' Mum smiled.

'Your hair is fine. I was going to laugh at your clothes.'

'Cheek. I loved that top.'

'When was this taken?'

Mum's smile dropped. 'January 1997.'

'Twenty-two years ago. Before I was…' The penny dropped. 'Is he…?' I asked, looking back at the photograph.

She nodded. 'He's standing to my left. He has his arm around me.'

I held the picture closer to my face and looked deep into the eyes of my dad. I should have recognised him straightaway from all the pictures I'd seen of him on the internet. But he looked completely different here. He was smiling. He was relaxed and happy. He really was a very handsome man.

I felt a tear roll down my face.

'Are you all right?' Mum asked.

I nodded. 'Fine. All my friends have pictures of their parents, either wedding or holiday snaps. I've never had that. It's weird. You really liked him, didn't you?' I asked, looking up at Mum.

She bit her bottom lip and nodded. 'I really did. I mean, you can see how handsome he was. But it wasn't just his looks. He was kind, too. He had his faults, who doesn't? But he always made me feel special when we were together.'

'What kind of faults?'

'He was very insecure. When we went out, he would always be asking me if I was enjoying myself or if I wanted to go somewhere else. He wanted to know if I was happy and if I liked him. I found it sweet at first, but the more it went on the more irritating it became.'

'Irritating?'

'Well, imagine you're in the cinema with someone, and you're trying to watch the film, but you're constantly being asked if you're enjoying it or if your seat is comfortable, if you can see all right, if you're too hot or too cold. It drove me bonkers sometimes.'

'There's nothing wrong with looking out for someone you care about.'

'I know, but it got to the point where I couldn't relax because I'd be waiting for him to check on me.'

'Did you ever talk to him about it?'

'Yes. I said that he didn't need to keep constantly asking me if I was all right or enjoying myself. I wasn't the type of person to keep quiet if I was bored. I'd certainly tell him.'

'What did he say to that?'

She smiled at the memory. 'He apologised. He said he wanted our time together to be wonderful.'

'That's sweet.'

'Yes. It didn't stop, though. And I didn't like how he'd turn up when I was out with my girlfriends either. It was obvious he'd been following me.'

'Mum,' I began, putting the photo down on the counter. 'Did

you ever wonder why he went from being this sweet, insecure guy to being a murderer?'

'Of course I did. At first, I thought the police had got the wrong man. I just couldn't believe him capable of doing something so... horrific. But, well, the evidence doesn't lie, does it? Stephanie's body was found in the loft of his parents' house.'

'He's always denied he killed her. He said he found the body and hid it because he panicked.'

'You've been researching him then?' she said, a heavy frown wrinkling her forehead.

'What else am I supposed to do? You can't just tell me my dad is a killer and expect me to continue life as normal. In every statement and interview he gave to the police he said he didn't do it. His story never changed.'

'Then why cut up the body? Why hide it in his house? How did the body get to the allotment in the first place? He couldn't answer any of those questions to the satisfaction of the police or the jury.'

'Did you hear about a drug he was taking at the time?'

'Yes, I did. Complete bollocks,' she said firmly. It was unusual for my mother to swear, and I was always shocked when she did.

'How can you say that?'

'It's an excuse. He was taking medication that ended up being banned because some people committed crimes while taking it, and he's using it as a way to reduce his sentence. It's a ruse,' she said, crossing her arms firmly.

'Then maybe he's innocent.'

'He isn't, Dawn,' she stated. 'I'm sorry. I know you want your father to be a good man. I want that for you too, but the evidence doesn't lie. You work in the legal profession; you should know that. He killed her. That's all there is to it.'

'Maybe it was one of his parents?'

'No. When all the facts came out, there was no denying it was him. Look, this is why I didn't tell you the truth when you were young. I didn't want you growing up with this hanging over your head. I know it was wrong of me to hide the truth all these years, but you'll understand when you have children of your own – you want to protect them as much as you can.'

I gave her a weak smile. 'I do understand, Mum. I just can't help feeling there's more to this than a bloke suddenly snapping and butchering a poor child like that.'

I could feel Mum's gaze burning into me. She was studying me, reading my thoughts. 'You're going to try and find new evidence, aren't you?' she asked.

'I have to.'

'Why?'

'Because I have more questions than answers.'

'But who are you going to ask? As far as I'm aware there were no witnesses to the murder.'

'I don't know. I just need to know the truth. The Dominic you tell me about and the Dominic I read about online sound like two completely different people. I need to know how he turned from one to the other so quickly.'

'You're going to—' Mum stopped abruptly as the door opened and an elderly couple entered.

The couple wanted to order some flowers for a party they were holding to celebrate their forty-fifth wedding anniversary the following weekend. It was going to be a long discussion. I made my excuses, picked up the only photograph I had of my parents together and left. I looked back through the door and saw my mother looking wistfully after me.

While it wasn't perfect, our damaged relationship was slowly repairing itself, and I was pleased we'd been able to have such a frank and open chat. Now it was out in the open that I was digging into Dominic's background, I felt better knowing that I would no longer have to lie if Mum questioned where I'd been or what I'd been up to.

As I headed back to the car park, my next step was obvious. I needed to locate my grandparents – Anthony and Carole Griffiths. If they didn't know what had turned their only child into a cold-blooded killer, then nobody did.

Chapter Nine

I decided I would have to turn detective to track down my grandparents. First, I tried all the social media sites. There were a couple of people sharing the name Anthony Griffiths living in Newcastle, but I doubted my grandfather was a nineteen-year-old George Ezra lookalike or a forty-year-old plumber with a tattoo of a spider's web on his neck. I couldn't find anyone with the name Carole Griffiths.

From information I had gleaned from the old newspaper coverage of the court case, Anthony and Carole had been around fifty when Dominic was sentenced, which meant they would be around seventy now. As far as I knew, not many seventy-year-olds used Snapchat and Instagram, and I'd been unable to find them on Facebook or Twitter. The only thing I had to go on was the address where Stephanie's body had been discovered on Aldwick Road near Scotswood. I googled 'Aldwick Road' and 'Griffiths' and found an article in the *Newcastle Chronicle* from 2000 which had an interview about the murder with one of the neighbours. I doubted they still lived there, but it was the best place to start.

The latte I'd drunk with Mum had warmed me up, but an hour

of investigating on my phone in the freezing car had made me cold again. As I started the car and headed for Scotswood, I hoped, once I found Dominic's parents, they would be the kind of people who would invite me in for a coffee and a warm by the fire.

Aldwick Road was a long road with a row of semi-detached houses on each side, all uniformly neat and tidy. The front gardens had the equivalent of bed hair from being left unattended during the winter months: grass was uneven, bushes were bare and plants were dead.

I looked at the article I'd been reading on my phone. The main photograph was of the neighbour, Sylvia Hurst, a hard-faced woman with a severe haircut, her arms tightly folded beneath her ample bosom and an expression of disgust on her face, as if she had just been told house prices would plummet now a murderer had been unmasked in the neighbourhood. She was standing on her doorstep with the white door closed behind her.

I looked from the photo to the houses and back again. They all looked so similar. It was difficult to guess which one Sylvia had lived in. I squinted to try and get a better look at the door number, but it was no use. I pinched the screen and zoomed in on the house number above Sylvia's left shoulder, but the close-up was a blur. I thought the first number was a three but couldn't decipher the second digit. It could be a one or a seven. Screw it. It was early, I had nothing else to do. I could knock on every door in the street if I had to. I parked the car and headed for number thirty-seven.

Pausing at the bottom of the short drive, I looked up at the semi-detached house. It looked similar to the one in the newspaper report, same door, same tree in the front garden. I knocked on the door and stood back, glancing around at the neighbourhood. I could imagine myself living on a road like this, maybe with a husband and a couple of kids. There wasn't much room for parking, but… The door opened.

'Hello, I'm looking for Sylvia Hurst,' I said, in my most professional voice.

'Wrong house, love. Across the road. Number forty-six.'

Before I could apologise, the door had closed.

Okay, maybe my detective skills were incredibly amateurish, but at least I'd achieved my goal.

In the nineteen years since Sylvia Hurst had given her interview with the *Chronicle*, time had aged and withered her. Gone was the severe haircut, the bosom had dropped, and her stern expression had softened. She looked the epitome of a sweet old lady. When I told her I was a paralegal investigating Dominic Griffiths, she was only too happy to take the security chain off and invite me in.

The living room was a shock of colour. The carpet was a busy pattern which should have come with a warning to anyone who suffered from photosensitive epilepsy. The feature wall with the fireplace had white wallpaper decorated with huge red poppies. The curtains were a dusky pink, and the sofa was navy blue. It was an assault on the eyes.

I gratefully accepted Sylvia's offer of a cup of tea and made myself as comfortable as I could on the dated sofa. Sylvia returned with two mugs and a chocolate sponge cake. I had made a new year resolution to drop a dress size, and despite a sweet tooth, I was winning the war on snacking between meals. However, if I wanted Sylvia to open up, I would need her onside and that would mean placating the elderly lady when she proffered the cake.

'Just a small slice. I'm trying to lose weight.'

'Get away with you. You're a good healthy size. I blame the television. My granddaughter, she's younger than you, but she watches all those reality programmes. I can't be doing with them. They're full of these stick-thin girls flashing their bits. Men like a real woman, take my word for it. Have a decent slice.'

I didn't need any convincing. I took the largest slice and bit off a huge chunk. It tasted as good as it looked.

'Mrs Hurst—'

'Call me Sylvia.' She smiled.

'Sylvia,' I began. I took a notepad and pen out of my bag to look the part of the legal investigator. 'What can you tell me about the Griffiths family?'

'Where do you want me to start? I could write a book. That Dominic, he was a rotter. From the minute he was born he caused his mother nothing but trouble. Screaming, shouting, wailing day and night he was.'

'They lived next door?'

'Aye, number forty-eight. He was no use, the father. He worked away a lot. You could always tell when he was home, because he'd park his bloody great big lorry outside the house. It used to block all the light from reaching my living room. I'd have to have the light on at three o'clock just so I could see my sewing.'

'How was Dominic a rotter?'

'He terrorised this street single-handed: tipping up dustbins, setting fire to them, pulling up plants, scratching cars, making the neighbour's kids cry, swearing. I don't know how she coped.'

'His mother?'

'Aye, Carole. Bless her. She was a bag of nerves before he even came along. I told my Arthur she wouldn't make a good mother. I was right. She couldn't control him. She was too soft with him. He needed a good hiding, not that you can do that anymore.' She took a sip of her tea and leaned forwards. 'I mean, I had three kids. They weren't angels, and I'm not going to pretend they were. I didn't pummel them, but when they did anything wrong, they got a slap on their legs. They soon learned. That's the problem with kids today – no punishment, no respect.'

I smiled through gritted teeth. My mother had never once

slapped me. There had never been cause, and I'd turned out fine… apart from my addiction to Ben and Jerry's.

'How were Dominic's parents after the murder?' I asked, changing the subject.

'We rarely saw Carole,' Sylvia said, her face dropping. 'She locked herself in that house and hardly ever came out. Some of the neighbours took against them. A few of the kids threw stones at their doors, posted nasty stuff through their letterbox. A few months after the verdict, a big truck pulled up one morning, and they were off. Didn't tell a soul.'

'They just upped and left?'

'Aye. There wasn't even a "for sale" sign up. It was all done privately with the estate agents. I bumped into Carole in town a couple of months later. She'd aged years since I'd last seen her. It was like the life had been drained out of her. She said Anthony had wanted them to have a fresh start, draw a line under everything and start again.'

'Did she tell you where they moved to?' I asked, pen poised.

'Oh yes. We kept in touch, exchanged Christmas cards, that kind of thing. They moved across the river to a bungalow, Langdale Crescent in Winlaton.'

'I know the area.' It wasn't too far from my mum's shop. 'Are you still in contact with the Griffithses?'

'No. I was only really friendly with Carole. I didn't know Anthony that well. He was always a difficult person to talk to. I think he just wanted them to be left alone.'

'So, what happened? Did the two of you just drift apart?'

'Oh… you mean you don't know?'

'Know what?'

'Carole died in 2001.'

'Really? She couldn't have been very old.'

'Fifty-one.'

'How did she die?'

Sylvia leaned forwards once again. 'Killed herself. Police found her hanging from a tree in Axwell Park.'

'Bloody hell. Sorry,' I said.

'Don't be. A shocking way to go. She must have been in such torment, to kill herself like that. Would you like another slice of cake?'

Chapter Ten

I sat behind the wheel of the Golf and thought about what I'd learned from Sylvia Hurst. Dominic had been a problem child, but by the time he met Mum, he was a caring and considerate young man, maybe a touch insecure. Had his issues just been childhood devilment that he'd grown out of? It seemed like it. Then there was Carole Griffiths killing herself two years after her son was sent to prison. Was it because she couldn't cope with having given birth to a murderer? Once again, I found myself with more questions than answers. I took a deep breath and started the engine. It was time for Anthony to meet the granddaughter he never knew he had.

I pulled up outside the row of small bungalows. It was early afternoon, and the brightness of the day was slowly fading. It was going to be another cold night. I rummaged in my cluttered bag for a mirror to check my appearance. My skin looked dry and my face sad, not surprising given what I'd recently discovered. What I'd learned about my father so far was a mass of contradictions. I already had a headache and didn't know if I could face more dark revelations from Dominic's father. But I'd already come this far.

I opened the car door, and it was almost ripped off by a gust of wind. I pulled my coat tightly around me and trotted down the pavement to the door. I rang the bell and waited. The house appeared to be in darkness, as did the ones either side. After a long wait, the door opened, and a small elderly man stood in the dark doorway.

It was difficult to estimate Anthony Griffiths' age. He could be anything from his late sixties onwards. His shoulders were hunched, making him look smaller. What little hair he had left was dark grey and pointing in all directions. His face was a relief map of deep wrinkles, and his eyes were glassy; he gave off the aura of a defeated man.

'Anthony Griffiths?' I asked. I had to squat slightly to make eye contact with him.

'Yes.'

'I'm sorry to intrude on you like this, but… I'm sorry, I'm not sure how to say this.' As soon as I had seen him, I knew I couldn't lie to him. He already looked in pain – this man didn't deserve any more.

'Are you selling something?'

'No, I'm not. I have some news for you. It's about your son.'

His eyes widened. 'I don't want to know.' He started to close the door.

I was losing him. I had a few seconds, maybe, before I would have to shout my news through the letterbox and reveal everything to everyone on Langdale Crescent. 'Mr Griffiths, please, I'm… It's… My name is Dawn Shepherd. I'm Dominic's daughter.'

The wind dropped then blew a fresh gust over me, making me shiver.

'What?'

'I don't know if you remember a young woman by the name of Rita Shepherd. She and Dominic went out together for about a year before… well, before he went to prison. They split up when my mum was moving away to go to university, but then she found out she was pregnant with me. I have a photograph here somewhere.' I opened my bag and began rummaging inside for the picture Mum had given me earlier.

With shaking hands, Anthony took the picture and angled it so the light behind him could give him a clearer view. Judging by his reaction, he recognised his son straightaway.

'The woman he has his arm around, that's my mother.'

'Really?'

'I know. She's pretty and thin, whereas I'm the opposite.'

Anthony looked up, back at the photo, then back at me. 'I think you're a very attractive woman,' he said, with sincerity.

'Thank you.' I felt myself blush.

'You have your mother's eyes.'

'Everyone says that.'

'What do you want from me?' He handed the photograph back.

'I don't want anything. I just want to talk.'

'What about?'

'About your son… my father. I'd like to get to know you, too. You're my grandad, after all.'

Anthony's eyes lit up, and a small smile appeared on his lips. 'I'm your grandad,' he said. He chuckled to himself. 'You'd better come in.'

There was something TARDIS-like about the bungalow. From the outside it had looked like such a tiny building, so I was surprised when I walked along the small hallway and entered the spacious living room. Even with a widescreen TV in the corner, two sofas, a sideboard and a small table and chairs in the opposite corner for having a meal, there was still plenty of walking space. It was tastefully decorated in neutral colours, but there was a hint of sadness in the air. This was not a happy home to live in.

'Can I get you a drink?' Anthony asked from the doorway. He looked uncomfortable, a stranger in his own home.

'I'm fine. Thanks.'

'Would you like to take a seat?' He pointed to the sofa with a shaking hand.

I perched on the edge of the sofa, while Anthony took his place on what appeared to be his regular seat, the one closest to the television and next to a small coffee table where a large mug and a plate with crumbs were placed.

'Is that your wife?' My eyes had been wandering around the room and landed on a framed photograph on the sideboard. It was a large picture showing Anthony and Carole on their wedding day standing in the doorway of a church.

'Yes. That's Carole.'

I picked up the silver frame and looked at my grandmother. She was dressed elegantly in a floor-length, white satin gown. Her hair was flowing down her back along with the sheer veil which was lifted slightly by a breeze. Her skin was smooth, her eyes wide and smiling.

'Friday, the tenth of July, 1970 that was taken,' Anthony said.

'She's beautiful.'

'She certainly was.'

'You look very handsome too. I love the velvet suit.'

'Thank you.'

'You look so happy.'

'We were.'

I replaced the frame and returned to the sofa.

'When did you find out Dominic is your father?' Anthony asked, breaking the silence.

'Last week.'

'Oh. It must have come as a shock.'

'You could say that. Mum always said I was the result of a one-night stand and that she couldn't remember who the boy was. I never questioned it.'

'What made her tell you the truth?'

'It was the news of Dominic being released from prison. It had a bit of a strange effect on her.'

'I see. I don't think I can be much use to you. I don't know Dominic that well.'

'He's your son.'

Anthony appeared to buckle at the mention of his relationship to the killer. 'I don't need reminding.'

'I'm sorry.'

A silence fell between us, and Anthony's expression plunged into a deep sadness.

'I made a stupid mistake,' he said, wiping away a tear that had formed in the corner of his eye.

'In what way?'

'I thought moving away would solve everything. I thought we'd be able to start afresh, a new life, put Dominic and everything behind us. It didn't work. It backfired.'

'How do you mean?'

'Carole needed to talk about Dominic. I refused. I banned his name from this house. All she wanted to do was talk, and I wouldn't let her. She kept everything bottled up until she couldn't stand it any longer. Then she…' His voice broke, and he bowed his head.

'I heard about what happened.'

'Who from?'

'An old neighbour of yours. Sylvia Hurst.'

'Bloody hell, is she still going? She must be about a hundred by now,' he said, with a chuckle. 'Is she still on Aldwick Road?'

'Yes.'

'I think they probably built those houses around her – she's been there that long. Lovely woman, well, Carole liked her, but bloody nosy.'

'I really am sorry... about your wife. Could I ask you some questions about my father?'

'What do you want to know?'

'What was your relationship with him like? I've read that you worked away a lot – that must have been a strain.'

Anthony's eyes darted from me to the floor and back again. 'I was a long-distance lorry driver. I was away a lot. I phoned Carole every night, asked her how she was, but it wasn't the same as being there. Depending on what routes I was working, sometimes I was only home at weekends.'

I didn't say anything, but I had noticed how Anthony said he called home every night to ask how his wife was, not his son.

'There was an atmosphere in the house,' he continued, his gaze fixed straight ahead. 'Dominic was a sullen child, and Carole, well, those tablets she was taking turned her into a zombie. I knew the problem wasn't with her.'

'Did you spend much time alone with Dominic?'

'No,' he answered firmly, after a short silence. 'I... there was nothing there between us.'

'What do you mean?'

He looked at me with watery eyes. 'Tell me, do you and your mother have a good relationship?'

'Yes.' I smiled. 'We're very close.'

'Do you do things together?'

'Yes. We go for meals, the cinema. Sometimes it doesn't feel like we're mother and daughter.'

He gave a weak smile. 'That's nice. We didn't have that, me and Dominic. He was a difficult boy to like.'

I hope I didn't let my facial expression show my revulsion. Had Anthony really said he hadn't liked his own son?

'Sylvia said he was a problem child, always in trouble. Yet at the time my mum was going out with him, she paints him as being a very caring and affectionate man. How can someone go from one extreme to the other?'

Anthony adjusted himself on the sofa. 'Not long after he was sent to prison, that drug he was taking was taken off the market.'

'Drug?' I felt bad for playing dumb and deceiving him, but I wanted to hear everything in his own words.

'Yes. I can't remember what it was called. Carole went to the doctor's many times, because she wasn't coping with Dominic, and they gave her tablets for her nerves. It was only when this new GP arrived at the surgery and said he wanted to see Dominic that we realised it was Dominic who should have been on medication, not Carole. So, she was weaned off her tablets, and he was given some kind of new wonder-drug.'

'What for?'

'To stabilise his moods. He was an angry child. He didn't mix well with others. He wanted to be friends with other children but didn't know how to, and they all thought he was weird. I suppose nowadays he'd be labelled as autistic or as having that ADHD or whatever it's called.'

'So, this drug he was taking was taken off the market? Why?'

'I can't remember the full details. There was something about a woman in America who killed her husband while taking it, I think. You'd need to speak to Dominic's solicitor about it. She knows all the information. I've got her card here somewhere. Would you like it?'

'Please.'

Anthony struggled out of the comfortable armchair and went over to the sideboard. Walking, even a few steps, seemed to cause him pain.

'Why would Dominic need a solicitor?' I asked. That sounded false – I doubted I'd be nominated for a BAFTA anytime soon.

He found the card and handed it to me. Clare Delaney's name was written in gold lettering on an embossed card. Very classy.

'I didn't agree with it. I told her all this, too. Nobody will thank her.'

'Thank her for what?'

'She was working on the theory that it wasn't Dominic who killed Stephanie White, that it was this drug that made him do it. She was putting together a case to sue the makers of the drug and have the murder conviction quashed.'

'I did read a couple of articles online where Dominic said he didn't do it. He said it a number of times. Do you think that's possible?'

'No,' he answered, without hesitation. 'He's guilty. I know it.'

'Did he tell you so when you visited him in prison?'

'I never visited him. Carole did. I didn't. I couldn't. I couldn't believe what he'd done. He disgusted me.'

I felt bad for bringing up buried trauma and emotions. I could see the agony etched on Anthony's face, the sorrow in his glassy eyes.

'Dominic's solicitor.' I looked at the card. 'This Clare Delaney. Does she believe in Dominic's innocence?'

'I've no idea what she believes. If you go to see her, look very closely at her eyes. She doesn't have pupils – she has pound signs,' he said, with a chuckle.

I smiled. 'Should I not have come here this evening? I can tell I've upset you.'

'Don't be silly. I'm pleased you've come. You're a lovely young woman and obviously a credit to your mother.'

'That's kind of you to say, thank you.'

'Let me give you a piece of advice,' he began, leaning forwards in his chair. 'Forget all about who your father is. Don't let him into your life. I don't care what he says, and I don't care what that solicitor says. He killed Stephanie White. I can feel it in here,' he said, tapping his heart with gnarled fingers. 'He cut her up, hid her in our attic, and he killed his mother, too. You don't want someone like that in your life.'

I suddenly felt very cold. It couldn't have been easy for a man to call his own son a killer. I felt such sympathy for him. I wanted to give him a hug, but having only just met him, it didn't feel appropriate.

I looked back at the business card. A solicitor wouldn't get involved in a case like this, if he was guilty, would she?

Chapter Eleven

Every Sunday, I went to Mum's for lunch. I'd tried making my own Yorkshire puddings, but they just wouldn't rise. I still have no idea what I'm doing wrong. Hollyhocks was closed on Sundays, and I didn't work weekends, so we'd get together, and Mum would roast a chicken. It was a relaxed occasion and the conversation would flow freely. We'd always end up having a giggle.

That week I wasn't looking forward to going. The subject of Dominic's impending release was bound to come up, and I knew we would both be treading on eggshells, neither of us wanting to speak up first in case we hurt the other.

'I went to see Anthony Griffiths yesterday,' I said, within ten minutes of entering the house. I'd have got indigestion if I'd eaten with that knotted feeling inside me.

We'd already spoken about the weather: how cold it was and how my car was struggling in the minus temperatures. I had said how the cooking chicken smelled delicious and asked if Mum needed help peeling the vegetables. Our body language had been stiff and the lingering looks fraught with tension. In the end, I had got fed up with biting my tongue and decided I would just have to deal with any fallout.

'Who?' Mum asked, looking genuinely puzzled.

'Anthony. Dominic's father.'

'Oh. I didn't expect him to still be alive, for some reason.'

'He's in his early seventies. Maybe. He could be older. I'm not sure.'

'What about the mother?' Mum asked, her tone severe.

'She died not long after Dominic was sent to prison. She killed herself.'

'Did she?' Mum looked genuinely shocked.

'Yes. Hanged herself from a tree in Axwell Park.'

'Good grief. I didn't know her, but she seemed a very volatile person, especially the way she was when she came around to the house that time. The look in her eyes was frightening. How… how is Anthony?' she asked tentatively.

'I'm not sure. I got the impression he's lonely. He misses his wife.'

'How did he take it – you turning up on his doorstep out of the blue?'

'He was fine. He smiled and looked happy, briefly, when I said he was my grandfather. There was a glint in his eye. He's not too keen on Dominic being released from prison.'

'I'm not surprised,' Mum said, as she prepared the gravy.

I took the cutlery from the drawer and headed over to the table. 'Would you like to see him?' I asked, my back to Mum.

'What?'

I could feel Mum's gaze burning through my clothes.

'Anthony. Would you like to see him?'

'Why would I want to see him?'

'Because he's lonely,' I said, turning around. 'He's sad. I thought it might be nice for him to realise he has family.'

'But he doesn't. He has his son. That's it.'

'And me. I'm his granddaughter.'

'Oh my God,' Mum said, pinching the bridge of her nose. 'I knew it was a mistake telling you. That's why I put it off for so long. That's why I had to get pissed to try and block everything out. Dawn, they're not your family. You've survived this long without Anthony and Dominic in your life. You don't need them.'

'But Anthony needs me.'

'No, he doesn't. Sweetheart, I don't want you getting involved with them.'

'Why not?'

'Because it's not going to be any good for you,' she said, almost snapping. 'There's a lot of hatred towards Dominic in Newcastle. You weren't old enough to understand, but I saw it all.' She sat down with a slump at the table. 'He denied killing her, but nobody believed that. His defence was weak. He could have admitted it, got himself a lighter sentence, avoided the pain of putting Stephanie's parents, and his own, through a lengthy trial, but he didn't. They had to sit through all the evidence and hear what he did to that poor girl. He was found guilty, and he should stay locked away for the rest of his life.'

'Do you honestly believe that?'

'Yes, I do.'

'You don't believe in rehabilitation and people atoning for their crimes?'

Mum took a deep breath. 'People like Dominic Griffiths don't atone for what they've done. You can't rehabilitate a psychopath,' she said slowly.

'Then what's the point of prisons?' I asked, sitting down opposite her. 'Why do we put people in prisons, if there's no chance of them coming out a changed person?'

'They're locked away to protect the public.'

'But if they're going to be locked away forever, why not just bring back the death penalty? Why not string them up in Eldon Square for all to see?'

'Now you're being ridiculous. Sorry, but I just don't believe someone who doesn't admit to their crimes can be properly rehabilitated. He's never owned up to it; he's never apologised.'

I started to cry. I wasn't usually so emotional, but lately, it didn't take much to set me off.

'I'm sorry to be so harsh,' Mum said. 'I don't mean to hurt you, but you need to understand what a person like Dominic Griffiths is like.'

'You're right. I do,' I said, after taking a deep breath.

'What does that mean?'

'I'm going to visit him in prison.'

'What?'

'I need to talk to him. I need to hear everything in his words.'

'Dawn, that is probably the worst decision you've ever made. You'll regret it.'

'I'm sorry, Mum, but I have to do this. I want to know if he's sorry for what he's done.'

'And if he isn't?'

'Then I'll know what kind of person he is.'

'You know that already. Look at the crime. Look at what he did.'

'I've looked,' I said, more tears falling. 'I know exactly what he did. But I have to believe a person can regret their actions and be sorry for them. If I don't believe that, then how can I be a paralegal? How can I represent people in court?'

'Shit!' Mum jumped up when she saw smoke coming from the oven.

I watched as she brought out the roasting tin and slammed it on the counter.

'Well, dinner's bloody ruined,' Mum said. She stood on the

pedal to the bin and threw the whole lot into it, including the roasting tin.

'I'm sorry,' I said feebly.

'I think you should go,' she said, turning away and standing at the sink.

'Mum?'

'I'm sorry your father turned out to be a murderer, but there's nothing I can do about that. I told you because I couldn't keep it to myself any longer. I didn't want you hating me if he turned up on your doorstep wanting to meet his daughter. I honestly thought I knew you better than this.' I could tell she was struggling to hold onto her emotions. 'You're making the wrong decision by wanting to meet him, allowing him into your life, and I know you'll regret it. I don't know what else I can say to make you change your mind.'

'But there's a strong possibility he didn't do it.'

'Dawn, I'm sorry, but we're in serious danger of falling out. I really think you should go.'

I looked at the back of her with wide eyes. I loved her with all my heart. Mum was hurting, that much was evident. But it takes two people to make a child, and what kind of a narrow-minded, bigoted person would I be if I took what the media said at face value? I needed to hear the truth from the only person who could give it to me.

I stood up slowly from the table and left the room, not once taking my eyes off my mother who was now audibly crying. I picked up my bag and coat from the hallway and left the house, closing the door firmly behind me.

I felt bad for upsetting her, but the truth was never easy to live with.

Chapter Twelve

I sat in front of the mirror in my bedroom doing my make-up. I was on the bed, and the mirror was on top of the chest of drawers, propped up against the wall. I chose a dark red lipstick, a thick layer of black eyeliner and a new kind of mascara that was supposed to make my lashes longer and thicker, but I hadn't noticed any difference so far. During working hours, I had my thick, dyed hair tied back professionally into a ponytail rather than the beehive I wore at weekends and for nights out. My style was old-fashioned; I loved the look of the Sixties and often joked to Mum I had been born forty years too late.

My mobile rang. I'd been playing a Dusty Springfield album on it, but the music abruptly stopped when the call came through. I looked at the display and saw Mum was ringing. I rolled my eyes. I didn't need another lecture. Not right now. I already had enough to contend with that morning, and my nerves were playing havoc with my stomach. I had made up my mind and didn't want it changing for me. The ringing stopped, and Dusty went back to singing about the son of a preacher man. I loved that song. I knew it by heart. I had sung it once at a karaoke night in the local pub. By the time I finished there was only Robyn left. If she hadn't been with me on the night out, I think she'd have left too. Singing wasn't my thing, evidently.

I left my flat, locked the door and trotted down the stairs. In the hallway, Robyn was at the post boxes collecting her mail. Robyn Shelley was in her early thirties and worked shifts in a call centre while designing her own clothes in her spare time. Often when I came home and passed her flat, I could hear a sewing machine whirring away.

'Morning, Dawn. Off to a funeral?'

'That joke is getting very old, Robyn.'

'Why do you always wear black? It makes you look ill.'

'It's a slimming colour.'

'You've got such a hang-up about your weight. I wish you wouldn't. You're gorgeous. You should flaunt yourself more. I wish I had boobs like you've got.'

'You wouldn't say that if you'd ever run for a bus with them.' I smiled. 'You working today?'

'Not until later. Listen,' she said, pulling me to one side of the hallway and lowering her voice. 'Did you see the new bloke move in yesterday?'

'No.'

I had heard the sound of someone walking up and down the stairs but had been too busy searching the internet and worrying about the fractured relationship with my mother to care.

'Oh my God, Dawn, you should see him. He's absolutely gorgeous. He looks just like Chris Hemsworth. Or is it Chris Pratt? Actually, I think it might be Chris Evans. Anyway, one of the hot Chrises. I held the door open for him while he was bringing in a couple of boxes, and the way he smiled at me, I'm sure my ovaries did a little dance,' she said, with an excited grin on her face.

'There's a mental image I'm not going to be able to unsee,' I said.

'I'm going to pop round later, see if he's all right for coffee and sugar.'

'I'd get your roots done first, if I were you.'

'Bloody hell, they're not showing through again already, are they?' she asked, going over to the window in the door to see her reflection. 'That's the last time I go there. I knew she wasn't putting enough colour on.'

'Well, as much as I'd love to watch you make a tit of yourself with the new hunk, I've got to get to work.'

'I'll try and get a photo of him and send it to you,' she said, with a smile.

'You're a tart, Robyn, do you know that?'

'You say it like it's a bad thing.' She stuck her tongue out.

I left the building with a smile on my face. For a brief moment, I'd forgotten the huge tasks ahead of me that day. The chat with Robyn had been exactly what I needed to settle my nerves.

It was another cold morning. The sky was cloudless, and the sun was slowly rising. There was a thick layer of frost on the windscreen, and while the engine of the Golf ticked over, I set to work on the windows with a defunct credit card.

Once in the car, while waiting for the rest of the frost to melt, I made a call. Listening to the call pick up, I took a deep breath and cleared my throat.

I had wanted to sound professional and strong, as if I knew what I was talking about, but I ended up chastising myself for stuttering and sounding wet. However, my call had had the required effect, and an appointment was made for later that morning. I just hoped my boss would accept my request for some compassionate leave.

I arrived at work, but I didn't take my coat off. I smiled at my colleagues and headed straight for Mr Schofield's grand office. The second I sat down opposite him, I did something I hadn't expected: I cried. Despite believing myself to be a confident and independent woman, I was still scared of authority and upsetting people. I hoped to plead my case with Mr Schofield and tell him I'd just discovered who my father was and would like some time to get my head sorted. I'd even take unpaid leave. However, the unexpected tears worked in my favour. Mr Schofield, uncomfortable in the company of a weeping woman, called his secretary to come in while he disappeared to another room. Less than an hour later, I left the building. I was to take the rest of the week off, longer if I needed it, and I would still be paid. I made a mental note to buy Mr Schofield a bottle of whisky on my return. He likes a tipple.

By the time it came to eleven o'clock, I had composed myself. It was time to see Clare Delaney.

Clare Delaney worked for Ripley, Blumenthal and Partners. Their head office was on Collingwood Street, not far from where I worked at Schofield and Embleton. The street had imposing Victorian buildings on either side, and the clacking from my heels echoed as I walked as confidently as I could manage. I could see the offices up ahead. The gold lettering above the oak door looked regal and the plaque beside a downstairs window was shiny and new, not tainted by the harsh north-eastern weather. This was a company with money, and they wanted their clients to know it.

I pushed open the heavy door and stepped inside. I was hit with a smell of newness coming from the deep blue carpet which padded my footsteps. The ceilings were high with low-hanging chandeliers, and the walls were painted a brilliant white to accentuate the original artwork adorning them.

'Can I help you?'

I recognised the haughty voice I'd spoken to on the phone earlier that morning and turned to face a receptionist sitting behind a very grand desk. She was young, slim and pert. Her face looked pinched, and her lips were thin. She eyed me with an arched eyebrow and made a point of showing she was judging my dress and size.

'I have an appointment with Clare Delaney. My name is Dawn Shepherd.'

The raised eyebrow went further up the receptionist's forehead. She was obviously wondering how an overweight goth could possibly afford the services of one of the junior partners.

The stick-thin receptionist led the way down a long corridor where even more original artwork hung on the walls. I supposed these solicitors' clients must have six-figure salaries and more than two cars in the garage, which made me wonder how Dominic could afford the fees. She knocked lightly on a solid polished door and pushed it open, stepping back to allow me to enter and closing it with a loud bang once I was inside.

Clare Delaney stood up from behind the oversized desk that seemed bigger than my entire flat. 'Ms Shepherd, I'm Clare Delaney, pleased to meet you. Have a seat.'

She held out her hand which I didn't notice at first because I was so distracted by the grandeur of the room. When we eventually did shake hands, I wasn't totally shocked by the powerful grip. I sat nervously on the leather chair and tried to look like I belonged in a room like this. It wasn't working. To quote Victoria Wood, I felt like a sausage roll in a bag of Twiglets.

'Angelina tells me you have information regarding Dominic Griffiths,' Clare began.

'Angelina?'

'My receptionist.'

'Oh.' It made sense she had a name as pretentious as Angelina. I wondered if it was a real name or one she'd made up to sound like she came from a privileged background.

Clare Delaney was a tall and broad woman. She wore her dark red hair like a huge mane cascading down around her shoulders. Her make-up was severe, as was her power suit and killer heels.

Her accent, although loud and authoritative, was obviously fake. She seemed to be trying to hide her Geordie roots.

'That's right.' I licked my lips and swallowed hard a couple of times. Nerves were getting the better of me. I'd really need to work hard on my confidence, if I was going to survive in this industry. 'I recently discovered that Dominic Griffiths is my father.'

Clare's eyes seemed to light up. 'Really?' she asked, leaning forwards on the desk, interlocking her fingers. 'Tell me more.'

The fact she was genuinely intrigued, or maybe just loved a bit of gossip, made me smile, and I relaxed. I leaned back in the firm leather chair and told the story of my mum having a year-long relationship with Dominic and falling pregnant on their last night together.

'That's quite a story. So, why have you come to see me?'

'I want to know who my father is. I'm getting very conflicting images of him. The press paints him as the embodiment of evil, yet my mum tells me he was a considerate, caring and romantic young man. The two pictures don't match.'

'Very true. They don't. I first met your father… let's see, when was it?' she mused. 'It was probably about five or six years ago. Have you heard of a drug called Fenadine?'

'No.' I didn't mind lying to a solicitor. Besides, she should be used to it.

'No. You're too young to know about it. Fenadine was an anti-depressant drug used in the Eighties and Nineties. It was removed from the market in 2002. Dominic was taking this drug at the time Stephanie White was killed. At first, Fenadine was seen as a wonder-drug. It was used on children in America who had difficulty concentrating and modifying their behaviour. These days we'd say they had ADHD. It was successful too. Clinical trials continued, and the drug was used to treat adults with depression and anxiety. Unfortunately, there was a snowball effect.'

'What does that mean?'

'Well, one person who is going through a brief depressive episode goes to the doctor and is given a low dose of Fenadine for a couple of weeks. The patient recovers, no longer needs the medication, and the doctor presumes it is the medication that was successful in the patient's recovery. Another patient may have required longer on Fenadine before they noticed any difference, or maybe a higher dosage. But it was successful for this patient in just a short time, and suddenly Fenadine is the go-to drug whenever a patient presents with symptoms of depression.'

'But every patient is different. You can't measure depression, can you?' I asked.

Clare smiled, impressed with my ability to keep up with the narrative. 'No, you can't. Like you said, everyone is different. Every brain is different, and each brain reacts differently to every type of drug. Not to mention other immeasurable factors going on in people's lives.'

'So, Dominic was taking this Fenadine, and he had a reaction to it?'

Clare opened her laptop, and with long, slender fingers, nails painted bright red, she hammered on the keyboard. 'Dominic started on a low dose, just ten milligrams per day. After two weeks, there was no change, so the GP increased the dose to twenty milligrams. There was a marked improvement, so he remained on that dose for three months. By then, his body had become used to the drug, and an increase in the medication was needed. By the time he met Stephanie White, he was taking one hundred and fifty milligrams of Fenadine every day.'

'Bloody hell!'

'Exactly.'

'You said Dominic was depressive and suffered from mood changes, what did that involve?'

'Are you sure you want to hear all this? It might be upsetting.'

'No more upsetting than finding out the father you never knew you had is a murderer.'

Clare shrugged and continued. 'Dominic was very withdrawn. He wouldn't mix with children of his own age, and he would either be very disruptive in class, or he would spend the whole day sitting in the corner of the room not talking, not interacting with anyone. I suppose, if tested, Dominic would have been classed as autistic, or a variation of autism. He seems to have been ignored and fed medication as if doping him up was the answer. At first, Fenadine helped to balance his behaviour. As the dose was increased, instances of his erratic behaviour became more severe.'

'Severe? How?'

'At the age of eight, Dominic slapped a girl in the head, so hard she permanently lost the hearing in her right ear,' Clare said, almost nonchalantly.

'My God.' I gasped.

'When he was ten, he picked up a mug from a teacher's desk and threw it at the head of a fellow pupil. That child ended up losing his right eye.'

I closed my eyes and put my hand over my mouth. This was shocking. 'But Dominic wasn't taking Fenadine then.'

'No. These are the reasons for him taking Fenadine.'

'How do you know all of this?'

'I've done my research,' she said with a smile. Or was it a grin? It could have been a smirk. Either way, it reminded me of Jack Nicholson's 'Here's Johnny!' line in *The Shining*. Even my goosebumps had goosebumps.

'Who told you?'

'Client confidentiality,' she said. Now, it was a sneer.

'So, when he was on the drug, he was much calmer?'

'Considerably.'

'So it worked then?'

'Until he murdered Stephanie White.'

'But how do you know that was the drug and not just Dominic?'

'The last recorded piece of evidence of Dominic's violent behaviour was at the age of fifteen, five years before he killed Stephanie. Towards the end of 1998, Dominic suffered a setback. He'd finished school with very few qualifications. He went to college to retake some GCSEs and hoped to get on an engineering course. He failed. He applied for twenty-six jobs in a three-month period and was turned down for every one of them. He sank into another depressive episode, and his mother sent him back to the GP for a medication review. All they did was increase the dose from eighty milligrams per day to one hundred and fifty.'

'That's quite a leap.'

'Which turned him into a killer. He was no longer thinking for himself. His mind, his senses, were dulled by the medication. He wasn't in control. Go and speak to his father, your grandfather, he knows a great deal more about his son than he ever let on to me.'

'How do you know that?'

A smile appeared on her lips. 'I meet a great deal of people in my line of work. I can spot a liar from across a crowded room. I've met Anthony Griffiths on many occasions and spoken to him at length about his son's behaviour, before and during taking Fenadine. He knows things he won't share with me. With you being a family member, he may open up more.'

I was frowning. Surely if Anthony knew more, he would have told me when I visited him. Unless he thought he was protecting me.

'Why is Dominic seeing you?'

'How do you mean?'

'I mean, what is it you're doing for him? How did he come into contact with you?'

'It was me who contacted Dominic. I was researching Fenadine, trying to track down people who had taken the drug and committed acts out of character. In 1995, I represented a woman who assaulted her ex-husband. She was found guilty and given a suspended sentence. However, she felt that, as she was taking Fenadine at the time of the assault, she was not responsible for her behaviour. Following the court case, she came off the medication and had no more outbursts of violent behaviour. Unfortunately, having a conviction had a negative impact on her getting employment. It's taken years, but I successfully sued Maxton-Schwarz, the makers of Fenadine, on my client's behalf. I've since found eighteen similar cases of people taking Fenadine who committed unlawful acts, and I've had their convictions quashed and received settlements from Maxton-Schwarz totalling more than ten million pounds. In America, settlements have totalled almost fifty million dollars.'

'Bloody hell,' I said. 'So, Dominic could receive a payout?'

'Dominic was sentenced to life in prison to serve a minimum of twenty-five years. Although he is still in prison, he will be getting released in the near future. Based on Dominic's good behaviour over the past twenty years in prison and the fact he was under the influence of a prescription drug, now banned, at the time of the murder, I have put together a case that the parole board and the Home Office have accepted. I am hopeful that once this gets to court, I should be able to secure a seven-figure compensation claim from Maxton-Schwarz for your father.'

'Seven figures? You mean one million pounds?'

'At least.' She shrugged, as if she dealt with seven-figure sums every day. 'It's a small price to pay for twenty years of your life.'

'Oh my God.'

'Quite,' Clare said, with a smirk on her painted lips.

'Dominic has always denied killing Stephanie. Has he ever said anything to you about it?'

'No,' she replied quickly and firmly.

'Why not?'

'That has nothing to do with me,' she said, looking away.

'But you're his solicitor.'

'I'm representing him in suing Maxton-Schwarz. Whether he killed Stephanie or not is of no consequence to me.'

I was shocked. How could she possibly say that with such coldness?

'Let's say, for argument's sake, that he is guilty,' I began. 'Doesn't it worry you that you're helping a convicted killer be released from prison before his time, possibly get his conviction quashed and receive a life-changing amount of money?'

Clare smiled and leaned back in her seat. 'Dawn, if he's guilty, we are still presented with the question of whether or not he killed her because the balance of his mind was disturbed due to the drug he was taking. Would he have killed her if he wasn't taking Fenadine? Who knows?' She shrugged. 'It's the fact that he was convicted of a crime, and he was taking a drug which has been proven to alter people's state of mind, that makes his sentence unsound.'

'But he could have still killed Stephanie, even if he wasn't taking Fenadine.'

Clare squeezed her lips tightly closed. She had no intention of replying to that.

'This is a lot to take in,' I said.

'Let me tell you something,' Clare said, leaning forwards on her desk once again. 'In January 1992, Joshua Clarke was made redundant from a car manufacturer in Austin, Texas. He applied for other jobs, but his age went against him – he was in his mid-fifties. He spent his days at home and his wife was the sole wage-earner. She started working more hours to cover the shortfall in income and was eventually promoted at the hospital where she worked in administration. Her wages increased considerably, and although they were still earning less, with a few cutbacks, they were solvent once again.

'Joshua Clarke, however, couldn't get a job. He received rejection after rejection, and it got to the point where he rarely left the house. He became depressed. His wife took him to the doctor, and he was prescribed Fenadine. At first, there was no change, so his dosage was increased. He eventually began to feel better and started to leave the house more. Unfortunately, he became paranoid and suspected that his wife was having an affair with someone at work. She had started wearing nicer clothes, make-up and perfume than she had before. She said being in management meant she needed to look the part, but he was convinced she was cheating on him. One night, she was late home from work. There had been a power cut at the hospital and the automatic doors had failed, trapping the staff inside. When she arrived home at eleven o'clock that night, she found her husband waiting in the living room with a loaded shotgun in his hands. He shot her twice in the chest. She was dead before she hit the floor.'

'Oh my God.'

'He was sentenced to life in prison. Seven years later, he was released with a cheque for two million dollars in his back pocket, signed by Maxton-Schwarz.'

'So, even though he killed his wife, he was released from prison?'

'He hadn't been in his right frame of mind, because he was taking Fenadine,' Clare stated clearly.

'But he killed his wife.'

'Yes, he did. And it's tragic,' she said, without emotion in her voice. 'But he wouldn't have done that had he not been taking Fenadine.'

'But he might have done.'

'We can spend eternity arguing what someone may or may not do, depending on what was or was not happening at any particular time. All we have to go on is facts, and in the case of Joshua Clarke and your father, they both committed murder when they were taking Fenadine.'

I felt conflicted. Suddenly, I understood what Mum had been talking about. Even if Dominic hadn't meant to kill Stephanie, he still did, and by releasing him early, it was a slap in the face to Stephanie's memory and her parents who deserved justice.

'Dawn, have you spoken to your father?'

The question snapped me out of my thoughts, and I looked up. 'No.'

'I think you should,' she said, with a glint in her eye. 'I think it could be beneficial for both of you. You obviously have a great many questions, and I can't answer all of them. He, however, can. And I believe he will, if you're the one asking them. I think you should write to him.'

'Maybe. I'll give it some thought.'

'The thing is—' Clare said. She stood up from her chair and walked slowly around her desk, perching herself on the edge, crossing her legs. She was inches away from me and loomed over me like a lion in the jungle glaring down at its trapped prey. 'Although there is no statute of limitation against bringing a case against Maxton-Schwarz, there is a moral angle we need to consider.'

'In what way?'

'Like you said, your father said he didn't kill Stephanie, but he did plead guilty to hiding the body. It's a grey area and one that we could do with adding a dash of colour to, so that when Dominic is released, and the story hits the press, we can draw a line under the case and the public won't be in uproar.'

'But you said the conviction would be quashed. He wouldn't be a murderer then.'

'I was getting a little ahead of myself there,' she said, with another twinkle in her eye. 'The case would go under review. If the panel was to prove Dominic killed Stephanie, the conviction would still stand. Our argument is that he wasn't in the right frame of mind, couldn't be held responsible, but he'd still be a killer in the eyes of the law.'

'So, you think if he confessed and atoned, or was able to prove his innocence, it would help?'

'Exactly.' She grinned. 'I tell you what I'm going to do. I'll contact your father on your behalf. Don't worry, I'm incredibly discreet. I'll set the ball rolling, and we can arrange a meeting.' She smiled, leaned forwards and gave my shoulder a patronising rub like I was a child who'd gone to the toilet on my own for the first time.

Clare jumped down from her desk and went back around to her side. She licked her lips and rubbed her hands like the money-hungry vulture she was. She sat down, picked up her expensive-looking fountain pen and began frantically scribbling notes.

She looked up and stopped as if she'd forgotten I was there. 'Was there anything else?'

'Oh. No. I don't think so.'

'Leave your contact details with Angelina, and I'll be in touch.' She put her head down and continued writing.

I stood up and tentatively walked to the door, guessing the meeting was over. As I left the room and stood in the empty corridor, I couldn't quite understand what had just happened. All I knew was that I had passed the point of no return.

Chapter Thirteen

'Anthony, it's Dawn. Dawn Shepherd. Could I come and see you?'

'Of course. You don't need to ask.'

I could have gone to my mother's shop and poured my heart out, wept on her shoulder and asked for guidance, but that's not what I wanted. I wanted someone who knew Dominic to help me with my dilemma. I walked out of the solicitor's as I ended the call and looked back at the imposing building of Ripley, Blumenthal and Partners. I physically shuddered.

I decided not to turn up at my grandad's house empty-handed so popped into a supermarket on the way and bought a pack of muffins. The subject we'd be chatting about might be heavy and disturbing, but in my opinion, everything is better with cake.

As I pulled up outside his house, the front door opened. He'd been waiting for me. Something about that made me smile, and I felt warm inside.

'You look smart,' he said, as I trotted down the path.

'I'm in my work clothes.'

'Quite the businesswoman. Come in. I've got the kettle on.'

'Lovely. I've brought some muffins.'

'You certainly know the way to my heart.' He smiled.

While Anthony set about making tea, I filled him in on my conversation with Clare Delaney.

'I did tell you she was a formidable woman,' he said.

'She oozes confidence. She's quite scary.'

'I suppose you have to be if you're going to be arguing in court.'

'Did she tell you she could get Dominic a seven-figure settlement?'

'She did.'

'What do you think about it?'

'Blood money,' he spat. 'Maybe it *was* this Fenadine he was taking that altered his mind, but at the end of the day, he killed a little girl, and he shouldn't be compensated for taking her life and destroying the lives of her family.' While he spoke, Anthony had both hands pressed firmly on the countertop in the kitchen. He wasn't old, but what life had thrown at him had taken its toll, and he was fragile. His body was stooped, and his movements were slow. He didn't look well.

'Don't you want your son released?'

'Not like this. Will you carry the tray through to the living room for me?'

I picked up the tray with ease, and Anthony led the way. I set it down on the coffee table and poured us both a cup from the teapot.

'You look pensive,' he said.

'I really don't know what to do for the best,' I said, sitting back on the comfortable sofa, wrapping my hands around the mug. 'Clare said I should visit him in prison and ask him the questions she can't answer.'

'Don't listen to a word she says,' he said firmly. 'All she's interested in is money. She doesn't care about reuniting a father with his long-lost daughter. She doesn't give a damn if we all live happily ever after. The second that massive cheque is cleared and in the firm's account, she'll move on to the next case and forget all about you.'

'You're right.'

'I know I am. What you need to ask yourself is, will your life be any richer for having Dominic in it? Do you want your father to be part of your future?'

'If you'd asked me that a week ago, I would have said a definite yes.'

'And now?'

I thought for a long moment. 'He killed someone.' There was a catch in my throat. 'Whether he meant to or not, he killed a child.'

'There's your answer.'

'But what if he's spent the last twenty years in prison regretting it?'

'Could you forgive him then?'

'Maybe. I-I'm not sure. Could you?'

'No,' he answered firmly.

'Why not?'

He adjusted himself in his seat. He was obviously wrestling with something he didn't want to bring up. 'I know Dominic. You only know about what you've read in the news. I know what wasn't reported – I lived it. Carole kept some diaries. I'll dig them out for you. However, I think you should speak to a man called Joby Turnbull.'

'Who's he?'

'He was a friend of Dominic's. He knew him before and during the Fenadine years. Speak to someone who doesn't have an interest in whether Dominic is released or not. You might find him useful.'

'How do I find him?'

'You're a child of the internet age – you tell me,' he said, with a smile.

Chapter Fourteen

I always hated pulling up at red lights, as I worried my poor wee car would stall and everyone would stare at me. The engine was ticking over noisily, and I tried not to think about it conking out. My eyes drifted. I was next to a row of shops, and I saw a poster for the *Evening Chronicle* in a newsagent's window. The headline screamed DOMINIC GRIFFITHS TO BE FREED NEXT MONTH. Clare Delaney hadn't mentioned that. Had she known? She must have done, surely. Why hadn't she told me? My God, what a bitch. I could have prepared Anthony for it, even warned Barbara and Harry. They'd see the paper, watch the local news and have it hit them in the face. They all deserved better than this.

I drove home at speed. Well, what passed for speed in my Golf. I was fuming. I parked in my usual spot at the back of the building, tore up the stairs and into my flat, my sanctuary, and slammed the door behind me. I had a lot to do. I also needed a drink. While I booted up the laptop, I went to the fridge for a bottle of wine.

The stories I'd read on the internet about my father were

understandably focused on the crime. However, nobody seemed interested in his not-guilty plea. Even now, twenty years later, he was still saying he didn't kill her. Did the police in the original investigation just assume he was lying? Shouldn't they have investigated his claim and tried to find someone else who could possibly have murdered her? It was hard to tell if all the evidence led to Dominic or if the police just hadn't bothered to gather any evidence beyond Dominic.

I grabbed a pen from the empty coffee jar I used as a pen holder and scribbled a note on a pad. I needed to speak to someone who had worked on the original investigation. Yes, on the face of it, Dominic was guilty – blood was found in his allotment shed, and the body was in his attic – but a thorough investigation should have taken place. Someone would be able to answer my questions. I'd no idea how I could question police involved in the case, especially as DI Braithwaite was in a nursing home. I could hardly just walk into a police station and ask to go through their archives.

I refilled my glass. I didn't even remember drinking the first one. I sat down at the table and logged on to Google. Now to find this Joby Turnbull. Unfortunately, all I knew about him was that he was roughly the same age as Dominic. He could be anywhere in the world. He might even have changed his name. Fortunately, Joby wasn't a common name. He shouldn't be too difficult to find.

I tried the usual social media sites: Facebook, Twitter and Instagram. There were several Jobys but no Joby Turnbulls. Eventually, I struck lucky with LinkedIn and found one living in Newcastle who was a social worker. Fingers crossed he was the one. I sent him a vague message saying I was a paralegal working with Dominic Griffiths' legal team, and if he was the Joby Turnbull who knew Dominic as a child, please could he get in touch. It wasn't a complete lie, and I didn't give him all the gossipy details in case he turned out to be someone entirely different.

There was a knock on the front door, and I jumped. I hardly ever received visitors. I closed the laptop, went over to the door and, closing one eye, looked through the spy-hole. It was Robyn. I wasn't in the mood for her cheeriness right now, and the last thing I wanted was to hear if she'd slept with the hunky new neighbour. I opened the door and put on my best fake smile.

'Hello. I can't stop,' she said, as she barged her way in. 'First of all, guess who's got a date with the incredibly sexy new neighbour on Friday night?'

'I'd say you but that seems too obvious,' I said, closing the door.

'It bloody is me. I saw him heading out, so I thought I'd properly introduce myself. I told him when bin day was, and if he wanted to take advantage of the milkman—'

'Like you've done many times,' I interrupted.

'It was twice, actually. Anyway, we got chatting, and we had a laugh and he asked me out,' she said coyly, like an excited schoolgirl.

'Well done. That's the fastest you've ever bagged a bloke. Wine?' I asked, heading back to the fridge for another bottle. There must have been a leak in my glass.

'Better not. I need to lose half a stone by Friday.'

'There's nothing on you.' I looked her up and down in her tight skinny jeans and skimpy bra top.

'I'll give you all the details on Saturday lunchtime. I'm bound to stay at his for breakfast.' She sat down on my sofa and picked up the copy of the local paper from the coffee table. 'Have you read this?'

'I've glanced at it,' I said, as I handed her a glass of wine.

'I can't believe it's been twenty years since he was put away. God, I remember it like it was yesterday.'

'You remember Dominic Griffiths going to prison?'

'Yes. Wait. Didn't I tell you?'

'Tell me what?'

'I knew the girl he killed – Stephanie White. I was actually on the local news. I went to place a bunch of flowers outside the school, you know, like you do, and the BBC were there filming it. My one claim to fame.' She smiled. 'Actually, that's not true. I'm pretty sure I was sat two tables away from Will Young in Patisserie Valerie in St Pancras station last year.'

'How did you know Stephanie White?'

'Well, we weren't best friends or anything, but we were in the same class at school.'

The penny suddenly dropped. Stephanie would have been thirty-three now, and Robyn had kept mentioning her thirty-third birthday being on a Friday night this year and how we should definitely have a pub crawl around Newcastle.

'I saw her on the day she went missing actually,' Robyn said, sipping her wine and playing with her hair with her free hand.

'Really? Did you say anything?'

'Yes. They held a big assembly at school the next day. The police turned up and everything. I remember it being quite a frightening time. After Stephanie went missing, my mum picked me up and dropped me off for ages.' She half-laughed at a sudden memory. 'My dad, right, he said that—'

'What did you say to the police?' I interrupted, sitting down next to her. I didn't want to seem too eager, but this was brand-new information. Well, it was to me anyway.

'I told them what I saw. Stephanie was at the back of the shops in Winlaton. Do you know them? There's an alley between the Co-op and… What's the one next door? Is it a Premier? Anyway, Stephanie was leaning against the wall. She was wearing rollerblades and a Newcastle United top. I only recognised her because of the top. It stood out.'

'Where were you?'

Robyn rolled her eyes and tucked her hair behind her ears. 'We always had to go and visit my gammy on Sundays. She wasn't really my grandmother – my father was adopted. She was horrible. Face like a slapped arse. And she was tight with her Christmas presents. Do you know what she gave me when I was ten? A bloody apron. Anyway, we were driving past the shops when I saw her.'

'Was she with anyone?'

'Yes. She was talking to a bloke.'

My heart almost stopped beating. This was almost too perfect. An eyewitness to Stephanie's disappearance right on my doorstep. I could feel the blood thundering through my ears.

'What did he look like?'

'I only saw him from behind,' Robyn said.

I deflated. 'You must have been able to tell something about his appearance.'

'Well, yes. I mean, he was taller than Stephanie. Thin, but not skinny. He was wearing a tracksuit. Dark blue, I think. Or it could have been black. He was wearing white trainers.'

'Did you say all this to the police?' I asked excitedly.

'Oh yes. At school the next day – I told you the police came round – anyway, they had a designated room where you could go in and chat to some of the detectives. I went to speak to this woman in uniform. I told her what I saw, and she went off to get this plain-clothed detective, and I had to repeat my story. Then, I had to go to the police station with my dad and tell them the story again, so they could turn it into a proper statement. You always think police work is exciting, but when you're involved in it, you realise how boring it really is. I must have told my story to about ten different people.'

'So, what happened after that?'

'Nothing.'

'Nothing?'

'No. Well, not nothing. I remember Mum and Dad talking about me having to go to court to be a witness. Mum was dead against it. She kept saying I was too young, and I'd find it too distressing. I had no idea what was going to happen, but I remember feeling scared about it.'

'Did you go to court?'

'No.'

'Why not? As far as I know, there were no other witnesses.'

'One night, we were sat having our tea when this big knock comes on the door. Dad answered it, and this bloke came in ranting and raving, demanding to know who I saw with Stephanie. I burst into tears. My mum burst into tears. My dad's shouting for our Luke to call the police. It was frightening. I thought he was going to hit me.'

'Who was it?' I asked.

'Stephanie's father.'

'What? He came round and shouted at you?'

'Looking back, it's obvious he was upset about his daughter being murdered, but he was in a real rage. My dad grabbed him to drag him out of the house, and Stephanie's dad punched him. That just made me and Mum worse. We were screaming bloody murder.'

'What happened?'

'He seemed to come to his senses after he'd hit my dad. He knew he'd gone too far. Luke had called the detective who'd taken my statement – he'd given us his card – and he turned up about ten minutes later, full of apologies. He calmed everything down and took Stephanie's dad away.'

'Bloody hell.'

'I know. My claim to fame, eh?' she said, pointing at the newspaper with a silly grin on her face. 'I wonder if ITV will do a drama about it. They're pretty hot at the moment – true crime dramas. I wonder who'd play me.'

'So why didn't you have to go to court?'

'Well, I didn't find out this until a long time later, but my dad told this detective that he could have Stephanie's dad charged with assault, but he wouldn't if they'd let me off having to give evidence in court.'

'So, let me get this straight.' I needed to get this organised in my head. 'Stephanie's dad comes to your house and causes hell, and this other detective removes your statement from the case, in return for your dad not pressing charges against Mr White?'

'That's right.'

'Who was this other detective?'

'Him,' she said, pointing at the photo in the newspaper. Leading Dominic into court was, according to the caption underneath, Detective Inspector Ian Braithwaite.

'I wonder if Barbara knows about this,' I said, almost to myself.

'Who's Barbara?'

'Barbara White. Stephanie's mother.'

Robyn shrugged. 'What do you know about it? Are you working with the firm who's getting him out?'

'No. I'm…' I decided not to tell her. 'Listen, Robyn, would you come with me to meet Barbara White and tell her what you've told me?'

'Why?' She frowned.

'To find out if she knows already, but if she doesn't, she definitely should.'

'I don't know.' She squirmed.

'Please, Robyn. It could be important.'

'If you think so, then I guess I could. I'd rather not though. Is there something you're not telling me?' she asked, a look of suspicion on her face.

'No.'

'Are you sure?'

'Positive.'

I don't think I convinced her.

'Hmm. Well, anyway, I'd better be going. I've got some trousers to take up.' She stood up to leave.

'Robyn, this man you saw with Stephanie on the day she disappeared, was it Dominic Griffiths? I mean, was he the same height and build?'

She paused for a moment in contemplation. 'Looking at that photo of him on the front of the paper and the picture I have in my head of the bloke talking to Stephanie, I'd say it was the same person. I'll see you later.'

Robyn left the flat, closing the door firmly behind her.

I looked back to the newspaper. So, an eyewitness saw a man matching Dominic's description at the scene. My theory that the wrong man had been convicted seemed to be going up in flames.

The only defence left for Dominic seemed to be that the balance of his mind was disturbed from taking a high dose of a now banned drug. However, that left me with a moral dilemma. Should someone be released from prison, for a crime they committed, just on a technicality?

I knew my answer. I just didn't want to admit it.

Chapter Fifteen

It didn't take long to hear back from Joby Turnbull. There was a message waiting for me the next morning when I checked LinkedIn. He was indeed the person who knew Dominic Griffiths as a child, and although his message was brief, he said he had information that would give me an insight into Dominic's personality as a young man. However, he warned, 'What I tell you may not be what you want to hear.'

That was enough to pique my interest. I fired off a reply, including my mobile number, and asked him to call to arrange a meeting.

I had a strong sense of foreboding. Every time I uncovered something new, I ended up with more contradictions to add to the pile, and still no closer to discovering if my father was a killer or not. Robyn had seen a man talking to Stephanie on the day she disappeared, and she thought he had looked like Dominic. That was a massive tick in the guilty column. If Joby gave me further evidence that pointed towards my father being a killer, I wasn't sure how I was going to react.

I showered and spent time styling my hair and putting on thick eyeliner. It felt strange not going into work, but I was grateful for the time off. I needed to gather my thoughts and feelings towards my father and find a way to understand who he really was.

By the time I returned to the living room, my mobile showed I had a voicemail from Joby Turnbull. He was free at lunchtime if I was able to meet. I gave him a quick call back, and we arranged to meet in a coffee shop close to where he worked, just outside the centre of Newcastle. He had a soft Geordie accent which I really liked the sound of. When I ended the call, I found I was smiling. He'd put me at ease with his smooth tone and confident attitude.

I wanted time to work on some questions to ask him and knew I'd be distracted in the flat, so I decided to head into town and find a quiet café. As I was leaving, I looked at myself in the mirror. Maybe dressing all in black was a bit too severe. Did it put people on their guard when talking to me? I needed Joby to open up, and if he was intimidated by a plump goth sitting opposite him, he might be reticent. I threw off my coat and stormed back into the bedroom.

Half an hour later, I was ready. The black sweater had been replaced by a white shirt, open at the neck. My hair was no longer whipped up into a small beehive but tied loosely in a ponytail which softened my features. I'd made the eye make-up more subtle, and the harsh red lipstick had been toned down with a lighter shade. I changed the black choker around my neck for a delicate cameo Mum had given me for my eighteenth birthday. As I studied my reflection once again, I had to admit that I liked this new, softer image.

Joby was a social worker at Children's Social Care at Barras Bridge. The civic centre was a massive concrete eyesore of a building just outside the centre of Newcastle. I arrived at Nero's early and sat near the entrance with a latte. I felt slightly conspicuous in my new softer style. I was rarely given a second glance in my usual clothes, which was how I liked it. However, I'd already had a couple of blokes look over and smile. One wasn't bad looking, the other was old enough to be, well, I'll not say my dad. I was on my second latte by the time a tall, slim man approached me.

'Are you Dawn Shepherd?'

I looked up from my notebook where I'd been writing down more questions to ask. 'Joby Turnbull?'

'Yes.' He smiled.

'Pleased to meet you,' I said, proffering my hand for him to shake, which he did.

Joby towered over me, standing at about six foot four inches tall. He was slim with fluffy blond hair and bright blue eyes. His suit was designer, as were his shoes, and his fingernails showed signs of a regular manicure. He asked if I wanted a drink, but it was a while before I answered, thanks to me being bewitched by his gorgeous eyes. I told him to sit down while I bought him a coffee. It was good of him to give up his lunch-hour for me, and it was the least I could do.

'I wasn't expecting anyone to get in touch with me about Dominic Griffiths. Your message came quite out of the blue. He's not someone I like to think about, if I'm honest,' he said. There was no hint of nerves; he sat tall in the high-backed chair and, although his tone was serious, he had a twinkle in his smiling eyes.

'I'm afraid I wasn't totally honest in my message.' I leaned forwards and lowered my voice. 'I am a paralegal, but I have nothing to do with the case surrounding Dominic being released.' I took a deep breath. 'I'm his daughter.'

'His daughter?' he asked, clearly taken aback, the smile dropping from his face. 'I didn't realise he had one.'

'No. I've come as quite a surprise to many people.' I attempted a casual chuckle, but it sounded forced.

I could sense the revelation that I was Dominic's daughter had unnerved him, so I quickly explained how I had only just found out, and I was on a mission to discover everything I could about the father I never knew.

'Wow. And you only found out all this a week ago?' he asked, picking up his latte and taking his first sip. 'That must have been a shock and a half.'

'You could say that. Do you mind talking to me?'

'No. You're his daughter. You have every right to know all about him.'

'Thank you. You mentioned in your message that I might not like what you have to say.'

'Ah. Yes,' he said, looking down. He took a deep breath. 'Are you absolutely sure you want to know?'

Suddenly, I was no longer sure. If he was going to tell me something that would convince me of Dominic's guilt, then I would be forced to come to terms with it. Draw a line under everything and tell Clare Delaney I wanted nothing to do with him being released.

I bit my lip and thought. It wasn't too late to stand up and leave the coffee shop. I didn't have to know everything. But if I didn't, I would have 'what if' running around my mind for evermore.

'Yes. I need to know,' I said quietly.

'Right. Okay then. I met Dominic in the spring of 1997. I was fifteen, and he was seventeen. Both our grandads had allotments, and they tried to get us interested, but what teenager is interested in growing onions? We spent most of our time in his grandad's shed reading magazines. We got on well to begin with.'

'Did he tell you anything about his home life?'

'He told me about everything. When you're in a shed together for several hours each day with no television, you have to fill the time somehow. I knew his dad worked away a lot.' He frowned as he remembered. 'And his mother was a bit… I don't know. I can't remember his exact words, but they didn't get on.'

'What made you think that?'

'He said she cried a lot. She'd be sat watching television in the evenings, and she'd just burst into tears for no reason. She'd fly off the handle over the littlest thing, like if he left a dirty cup in the living room or something. That's why he spent time with his grandad. His mother couldn't cope with him at home all day during the summer holidays. He didn't call her Mum either. He called her Mother. I remember thinking at the time that it was a bit weird. I still call mine Mum, even at my age.'

I smiled. 'So do I.' I settled back into my seat.

'Dominic was quite sad. I'd look up from whatever magazine I was reading, and he'd have this look on his face like he wasn't really there. His body was, but his mind was a million miles away.'

'Did you ever ask him about it?'

'I'd ask him what was wrong, and he'd just say, "Nothing."'

'Did he like staying with his grandad?'

'Yes. His grandad allowed him a can of beer in the evenings and let him stay up late. There were no rules with his grandad.'

'Whereas there were with his mum?'

'There were too many with his mum, by the sound of it.'

'What about his dad? Did he mention him at all?'

'No. Never. I thought he'd left them or died, so I didn't bring it up. It was only when my grandad mentioned him that I knew he worked away a lot.'

'Did Dominic ever mention taking medication?'

'Fenadine? Yes.'

'You know about Fenadine?'

'Only what I've read about in the news. I didn't know what it was called at the time I knew him. He did say he'd been given tablets to take. He said he suffered with low moods. I could certainly understand that, given how volatile his mother was.'

'Did he mind taking the tablets?'

'He didn't say,' Joby said, and took another sip of his latte.

I leaned forward and picked up my mug. I took a long sip while I marshalled my thoughts. 'When you heard about Dominic being charged with murdering Stephanie White, what did you think? Were you surprised?'

It was a while before Joby answered. I wondered if he was trying to find a way of putting it without upsetting me. 'I'm afraid not,' he eventually said.

'Something happened between you, didn't it?'

Joby nodded.

'This is the something I might not want to hear, isn't it?'

He nodded again. 'It's not too late for you to say you don't want to know.'

'No. I'm fine. Go on.'

Joby drained what was left of his latte. I asked if he wanted a second cup, but he refused. He leaned forward in his seat and interlocked his fingers. He lowered his voice. The twinkle in his eyes had faded, and he suddenly looked very sad.

'It was a really hot, sunny day. My grandad said we shouldn't be cooped up in a shed all day. He slipped me twenty pounds and told us to go and get some dinner or something. So, we went into town. We went to Burger King and then down by the Tyne. It was a good day. The thing was, I'd been wrestling with something for a long time, and I needed to get it off my chest. I thought me and Dominic were close enough that I could tell him, and he'd be supportive, give me some advice. So, we were in the park, and I told him that I thought I was gay.'

'Oh.' Typical. I looked at his hands and noticed a wedding ring.

Joby followed my gaze. 'Craig and I have been married for eight years next Thursday.'

'Congratulations.'

'Thank you,' he said, the sparkle returning to his eyes momentarily.

'How did Dominic take your news?'

'He was very understanding. It actually gave me a bit of a confidence boost, you know, like I could come out to my mum and dad.'

'So, what happened?' I asked when Joby stopped talking.

His face seemed to drop as the sadness swept over him. I couldn't stop looking at him. I was captivated by his story.

'He called me that night and asked if I wanted to meet up at the allotments.'

I frowned. 'Had he ever asked to meet at night before?'

'No.'

'Did he say why he wanted to meet?'

'He said he was bored. His grandad always went to bed early, and he had nothing to do.'

'What did you think?'

'To be honest, I thought he was going to tell me he was gay too.'

'Did you suspect he was?'

'No, but when you're fifteen and you realise you're gay, it's nice to think there's someone, a friend, who is the same as you.'

'So, you met at the allotments?' I prompted.

'Yes. It was dark. I can't remember what time it was. Dominic was there, waiting for me. He'd brought a few cans of lager he'd taken from his grandad, but I think he'd had a few already. He was slurring his words. He said he wanted to talk about what I'd told him earlier.'

'What did he say?'

'He was full of questions about when I had realised I might be different and what being gay involved.'

'Did you think he was asking because he suspected he was gay himself?'

'I did, yes. So, I asked him. That's when he... you know, snapped.'

'Oh God. What happened?'

'Are you sure you want me to go on? You've gone very pale.'

I didn't speak. I couldn't. My mouth had gone dry. I nodded.

'I think I said it in a joking kind of way. He asked me if I thought it would hurt, you know, sex with a man. I asked why he was so interested; did he want to try it out for himself? Something like that, anyway. I was laughing, and that seemed to set something off in him. His face just changed in a split second. He hit me across the head with his open hand, and I fell backwards onto a bench. I was dazed and confused and shocked. I had no idea where it had come from. It didn't seem real. I didn't even see him raise his hand, that's how quickly it happened.' Joby stopped and took a breath; he couldn't meet my gaze. 'The next thing I remember, he was pulling my trousers down. He held my arms behind my back and pushed my head down on the bench, and he... well, you can guess what he did.'

'He had sex with you?' My voice was loud with shock. Several customers in Nero's turned around to look at us. I lowered my voice. 'Sorry.'

'He tried to. He couldn't get it up. I managed to break free from his grip. I pushed him off and threw something at him, I'm not sure what. Then I pulled up my trousers and ran as fast as I could. I don't know if he followed me. When I got home, I was going to pretend nothing had happened, but as soon as I saw my mum I started crying. I had to tell her. I told her everything.'

'Did you report it to the police?'

'No. My mum wanted me to. My dad was all for going around to Dominic's to kill him. I was looking for comfort from them, and it ended up being me who had to calm *them* down.' He smiled. 'I knew that if we went to the police, I'd have to go through the whole story over and over again, and then go to court, and it would be in the papers, and everyone would know. I didn't want that. What fifteen-year-old would?'

Joby was staring at the floor, and my heart broke for him. Such a traumatic attack, and at the hands of one of his friends too. So now attempted rape could be added to my father's rap sheet. Had he graduated from rapist to murderer?

'Did you ever see Dominic again after that?'

'No.'

'And the next time you heard about him was…?'

Joby nodded. 'It took a while for it to sink in. I remember reading all the stories about it in as many newspapers as I could, just in case one of them had got it wrong, and it was someone else. For some reason, though, I wasn't surprised. It was like I had been waiting to read about him doing something like that. I've struggled with it for many years. I wondered if there was something I could have done to stop him. I was broken for a long time.'

Joby looked back at the ground. He took a deep breath. He lifted up the sleeve on his left arm and showed me the scars from a suicide attempt on his wrist. His voice was shaking. 'I blamed myself for not reporting him to the police when he attacked me. My mum found me unconscious on the bathroom floor and called for an ambulance. While I was recovering in hospital, I thought about what would have happened if I had reported Dominic to the police. It would have been my word against his. There was no actual rape, so there were no forensics. It was then I realised reporting him wouldn't have got a conviction; it wouldn't have changed anything. Only then did I start to forgive myself and heal.'

A wave of sadness swept over me. I wanted to cry. 'I'm so sorry. I didn't mean to drag all this up…'

He reached across the table and placed his warm hands on top of mine. 'No. It's okay. I'm a social worker – I ask difficult questions all the time. It's just strange being on the receiving end of them.'

'Is that why you went into social work – to help others?'

Joby nodded. 'I want children to know they have someone to talk to if they need it. If they don't think they can talk to their parents or any family members, they can come to me. In a way, I'm a survivor. I tell them that. I survived, and they can too. I can be their voice.'

'You do a good job.'

'Thank you.' He looked at his watch.

'Sorry, I'm keeping you. Let me ask one last thing, what did you think when you heard Dominic was being released?'

'I don't know. I wasn't surprised. I always knew he'd get out one day. I just didn't think it would come around so quickly.'

'What are your feelings towards him?'

'I don't have any.'

'Do you hate him?'

'Hating him would take too much energy. I let it go a long time ago.'

'I can understand that.' I smiled weakly. 'I'm struggling with how I should be feeling towards him. I really appreciate you agreeing to see me, Joby. It can't have been easy.'

'You're welcome.' He stood up. 'Have you been to see him yet?'

'No. I'm still in two minds whether to or not. Do you mind me asking your opinion, if you think I should see him?'

'That really is a question only you can answer. If I were in your shoes…' He paused while he thought. 'I have no idea. I'm sorry. He's served his time in prison. I like to think that in the past twenty years he's repented and is genuinely sorry for what he's done.'

'Even though he still claims his innocence?'

'Maybe he really believes he is innocent, especially if he's been reading all the reports about that drug.'

'What do you think about the drug?'

'I don't know enough about it to form an opinion. However…' He sat back down again on the edge of the chair. 'Every brain reacts differently to that kind of medication. One person sues the company who made it, then others jump on the bandwagon, looking for a way to excuse their own behaviour. Unfortunately, we're living in a time where people look to blame others for their actions and don't take responsibility for what they do. Fenadine could have made Dominic react violently towards Stephanie. Or maybe he's spent twenty years looking for a way out and finally found one.' He stood back up again. 'I really hope you find the answers you're looking for.' He held his hand out for me to shake.

'Thank you so much.'

'You're welcome.' He gave me a smile then turned away, buttoning up his coat as he left the coffee shop.

I watched as Joby Turnbull headed back to work with his head held high. I smiled at this remarkable man. He had been through a horrific ordeal at a very difficult age. He had attempted suicide but had managed to come through his nightmare and out the other side a better person. He was doing good work. He was settled in a loving relationship, and he seemed happy with life. He was the perfect example of someone facing adversity and pulling himself back from the brink to achieve greatness.

I was no closer to discovering the truth, but I had been given another snapshot of my dad's behaviour while he was taking Fenadine.

I pulled my phone out of my bag and saw I had two missed calls from Mum. I felt tears prick my eyes. I really needed her right now. More than ever, I wanted my mum to put her arms around me and tell me everything would be all right.

The problem was, I didn't think it would be.

Chapter Sixteen

I wasn't quite sure what to do with the information I'd received from Joby Turnbull. Could everything Dominic had done be due to a drug, or did it just lie in his own dark personality? I needed some fresh air. I suddenly felt claustrophobic in the coffee shop, surrounded by chattering lunchtime drinkers and squawking machines.

It was another bloody cold day in Newcastle, but the sky was a brilliant blue, and the low sun was shining. I buttoned my coat up and walked aimlessly, hands thrust deep into my pockets. One problem I had was that only one person had had anything good to say about my father, and that was my mother. His own father wanted nothing to do with him. His mother had killed herself over what he'd done, and he had no friends, it would seem. Even an ex-neighbour had called him a bad egg. So who knew the real Dominic Griffiths? Did he suffer from multiple personalities? Was he a cold-blooded killer using the Fenadine scandal as a way to get out of prison early? Was he innocent, panicked when he found the body in the allotment shed and hid it, like he'd always claimed? If so, he'd suffered a massive miscarriage of justice.

I stopped walking and let out a huge sigh. I was really struggling, and I felt completely alone. This was too much for me to do on my own.

A possible answer lay across the road. I looked up at St Andrew's Catholic Church. I'm not a religious person, and I've never even been in a church. I went into a mosque for a school project once, but that was the closest connection I'd had with religion. One issue I was wrestling with was whether I could actually forgive Dominic when he was released, especially as all the signs were indicating that he did actually kill Stephanie. And who knew more about forgiveness than the Catholic Church? In for a penny…

The church was a beautiful building from the outside. I walked through the iron gates and saw a gorgeous wooden door ahead. There was a plaque on the wall in honour of the church's founder, Father James Worswick, whom the street the church stood on was named after. The background noise of traffic and twenty-first-century life faded away. I felt calmer just being within the grounds.

The inside was bright and airy with pure white walls and tall, beautiful, ornate stained-glass windows above the altar. The pews were empty. I walked slowly down the aisle, my footsteps resounding around the space. I looked about me, marvelling at the beauty of the place. It was so clean and welcoming and peaceful.

'Can I help you?'

I almost jumped out of my skin. I hadn't thought there was anyone there. I almost screamed out 'Jesus' but managed to bite my tongue at the last moment.

I hadn't seen the priest come into the main part of the church. He'd obviously been alerted by my footsteps.

'Sorry, I didn't mean to startle you,' he said, in a soft, smooth accent that I couldn't quite place.

I was slightly disappointed. In my head, I had pictured

Andrew Scott from *Fleabag* walking out. Unfortunately, this was no Hot Priest. He was tall and gangly. He had a warm smile, but his crooked teeth were off-putting. He wore Hot Priest's costume, but it didn't seem to fit him as well. Never mind. I wasn't there for an illicit tryst.

'Sorry, I was wondering if I could have a word.' I sounded like I was shouting. My voice echoed around the space.

'Of course.' He held out a hand to offer me a seat at a pew.

I unbuttoned my coat and tentatively sat down. It wasn't very comfortable, and I could have done with a cushion for my back.

'I haven't seen you here before, have I?'

I smiled. I wondered if he knew every single one of his parishioners. 'No. I'm afraid this is my first time in a church,' I said, pulling an apologetic face.

'The first of many, I hope.'

'Maybe.'

'So, how can I help you?'

'I'm really struggling with something at the moment, and I don't know what to do. I've never known who my father is. Last week, my mum finally told me the truth. The problem is, he's in prison for committing a murder. He's always denied doing it, but the evidence against him is... well, all signs point to him being guilty. He's due to be released next month, and I'm not sure what to do about it or how to feel.'

'Wow, that's quite a story,' he said, with a smile. He wouldn't be bad looking if he straightened his teeth, maybe had a decent haircut and put on a few pounds. He thought for a moment. 'You don't have to tell me, but I'm guessing you're talking about Dominic Griffiths.'

I laughed. 'Everybody seems to know about him but me.'

'You're his daughter?'

'I am.'

'And you want to know how to forgive him?'

'I don't even know if I want to do that. Sorry, I'm feeling very conflicted right now.'

'That's perfectly understandable. Murder is wrong. We all know that. The law is very clear on that. Even the Bible is clear on that.' He smiled again. 'You said Dominic has always maintained his innocence – is he still sticking to that story?'

'I believe so. I haven't seen him yet. I'm not sure if I want to.'

He nodded as he thought. 'Luke 17, verses three to four, says: "If your brother sins, rebuke him, and if he repents, forgive him, and if he sins against you seven times in the day, and turns to you seven times, saying 'I repent', you must forgive him."'

'But he hasn't repented,' I said. 'If he was sorry for what he'd done, I might be able to forgive him.'

'Could you? Truthfully?' he asked, looking deep into my eyes.

I thought for a moment. 'I'm not sure, actually. My mum can't forgive him. Stephanie's parents can't forgive him. His own father can't forgive him. Why should I?'

'They can't forgive him because he hasn't admitted his crime. Pleading guilty, owning up to our actions, is the first step to repenting. Because he hasn't, everyone connected has been suffering in a limbo state, waiting either for him to finally admit his guilt or for the real killer to come forward.'

'Some cases never get solved, though. What if the real killer is out there, and we never know it and wrongly believe Dominic is the killer?'

'You will be forgiven in God's eyes, as you're taking the only evidence you've been given,' he said, with a smile.

'But Dominic has said he's innocent, and we've ignored him.'

'Numbers 35:30 says: "If anyone kills a person, the murderer shall be put to death on the evidence of witnesses. But no person shall be put to death on the testimony of one witness." You, yourself, will be forgiven for not believing in him.'

'You really know your Bible, don't you?' I said, with a chuckle.

'It's my job to know it.' He smiled. 'I understand you want a father whom you can love and develop a relationship with, but it's not easy to love someone who has committed a mortal sin, especially if he doesn't repent.'

'So, there is nothing against me turning my back on him?'

'Nobody will judge you for doing so.'

'I'll judge me.' I could feel myself tearing up.

'You're being too hard on yourself.'

'Can I ask you a non-religious question?'

'You're going to ask me what I would do if I were you, aren't you?'

'Wow, you really are good.' He might not be Hot Priest, but he was very personable. I liked him.

'Well, personally, I'd go and see him. I would ask him if he killed Stephanie. Listen to what he had to say and base my decision on that. If you can forgive his past sins, accept him into your life. But you can also choose to walk away, get on with your life, and know you did the right thing in pursuing the truth.'

I thought for a moment about what he had said. He was right. The only way I could get peace from all this and relieve myself of the headache was by going to the source.

'Thank you,' I said.

'Have I helped?'

'You really have.'

'Good.'

'Do I pay you or something?'

He threw his head back and laughed. 'No. You're more than welcome to make a donation. We run many events and charities from here. It's not obligatory, though.'

'I'd like to make a donation. You've been very helpful.'

'The box is on your way out. I'm always here if you want to speak to me again. And you'd be more than welcome to come to our services.'

'I'm not sure about that.'

'Think about it. The Church isn't the scary place people think it is.'

'I will. And thank you again.' I stood up and held my hand out to shake, which he did.

As I walked away, I rooted around in my bag for my purse. I rarely use cash. Everywhere I go I pay with card or my mobile, so it was a relief when I found a screwed-up tenner behind a bunch of receipts and smoothed it out before pushing it into the slot at the top of the box. I hadn't even realised I'd had the note, so I wouldn't miss it.

I turned around. The priest had gone. I looked up and saw Jesus on the cross looming over the whole church. I don't know why, but I curtsied before leaving. It felt like the proper thing to do.

Chapter Seventeen

On my way home, I pulled into the supermarket to pick up a few items. My mind wasn't focused, and I walked up and down the aisles in a daze as I grabbed the odd tin and packet to throw in my trolley. I was thinking about what Joby had told me. I wondered how Dominic would have felt the morning after the attempted rape. I could understand Joby's parents not wanting their child to have anything more to do with him, but if his actions had been caused by the medication he was taking, then it wasn't completely his fault. I imagined, in the cold light of day, that Dominic would have been full of remorse. Or was that just wishful thinking on my part?

I paid for the items at the self-service till and headed back to the car park. Once in the car and heading for the exit, I saw a familiar-looking shape ahead struggling to carry a couple of heavy carrier bags. I waited until I had driven past before looking back over my shoulder.

'Anthony!' I called out, as I pulled over.

His face was red and his breathing laboured as he trundled along. He looked to be in pain. He smiled when he saw me.

'Would you like a lift?'

A look of relief spread across his face. 'That would be wonderful.'

I jumped out of the car and took the bags off him. I expected them to be heavy, but they didn't seem to be as heavy as Anthony had been making out.

'I do this every time,' he began, as I placed them in the boot. 'I write a list of the things I need, but I see items on offer and think I may as well buy them while I'm here. I forget I've got to get the bloody things home.'

'I'm the same. If it's on offer and it's covered in chocolate, I'm throwing it into my trolley.'

Anthony climbed into the front passenger seat and pulled the door closed. He shuddered and held his hands in front of the heater to warm them up.

'Sorry, the heater doesn't work too well,' I said. 'I'm saving for a new car, but there's always something else to buy.'

I drove out of the car park and made my way slowly up Blaydon Bank. It was a twenty-miles-per-hour speed limit, but my car struggled on the steep incline. I put the Golf into second gear and floored the accelerator. It managed to pick up speed, and I hoped I wouldn't have to stop or slow down as I'd struggle to get the speed back up again. I turned to Anthony and gave him a painful smile. He was staring at me.

'Everything all right?'

'Yes. I was just looking. You've got a look of my Carole about you.'

'Have I?'

'Yes. In profile. It's strange. I was aware a girl Dominic had been seeing had got pregnant, but I must have put it to the back of my mind or something, because until you turned up on my doorstep, I never thought about it.'

'You've been through a great deal over the years,' I said, as I turned onto Langdale Road.

'Oh God!' Anthony said.

'What's the matter?'

'I recognise that car.'

'Which one?'

'The dark red Range Rover. It's Dominic's solicitor.'

'Clare Delaney?'

'That's her. The viper. What could she possibly want?'

I pulled up behind Clare's car. It was showroom-bright and clean, and it screamed of wealth. It had the personalised number-plate 'BO55 BCH', and when Clare opened the door on the driver's side, a step came out from underneath, so she didn't have to jump down to the ground.

Clare was wearing a black trouser suit and a knee-length leather coat with a fur trim around the collar which I guessed was probably real fur. Against the brightness of the sun, she was wearing large-framed sunglasses. As soon as she saw us, she beamed a toothy grin.

'Two birds with one stone. I was going to call you later, Dawn. Mr Griffiths, how are you?'

'I'm fine, thank you. What do you want?' he asked. There was tension in his voice.

'I've come to update you on your son's case.'

'Ms Delaney, we've spoken about this on many occasions – I'm really not interested. Dawn, could you bring my shopping in?' he asked, as he pulled a key out of his pocket and hobbled to the front door.

'Of course.' Then I turned to Clare. 'What did you want to see me about?'

'I have a letter for you from your father.'

'What?' My head was in the car as I was in the process of

scooping up Anthony's shopping. I stopped and looked daggers at Clare.

'I gave him a call, told him all about you. He was very interested,' she said, with a devious smile.

'You had no right to do that. I said I'd let you know if I wanted to contact him.'

'The health and wellbeing of my client are my number-one priority. He's feeling a tad low and worrying about his impending release. He's frightened about what kind of a world he's going to be living in. I thought it would be beneficial to his mental state to know there was someone for him on the outside.'

'I don't believe a single word you just said.' I slammed the car door closed, and the alarm went off. 'Shit.' I fumbled in my pocket for the keys and pressed a button hard on the fob to silence it.

'Expensive things, cars, aren't they?' Clare said. 'I'm sure your father would help you out once he receives his settlement.'

I wanted to slap that grin off her face, but judging by the amount of make-up she was wearing, she probably wouldn't even feel it.

'I pay my own way in this world, thank you. Now, if you'll excuse me,' I said, pushing past her and heading for Anthony's front door.

'I have the letter right here if you want it.'

I turned back from the doorway. Clare stood holding up an envelope like it was a golden ticket.

I placed the bags of shopping on the ground and walked over to Clare with my head high. I snatched the letter and returned to the house.

'There's a visiting order in there for you, if you'd like to pay him a visit. He's currently in HMP Holme House, not far from here to prepare him for release. Did I tell you his release date? It's the thirteenth of February. Not long to go.'

I closed the door firmly behind me, as I went into Anthony's house. Clare Delaney really was a viper.

'Are you all right?' I asked Anthony. He was in the kitchen, leaning on the work surface, his face tense and angry.

'No. I can't stand that woman. Do you know, when she first made contact with Dominic, he wasn't interested in this compensation claim from that drugs company? She came here asking me to try to convince him. She wrote, phoned, knocked on the door, day and night.'

'You should have called the police.'

'She's not stupid. She wasn't hassling. She stayed on the right side of intimidation. She must have worn Dominic down herself, because she soon stopping calling. When I read in the papers about him suing and possibly getting early release, I was fuming. I'd never been so mad.'

'Did you hear what she just said about Dominic's release date?'

'Yes.'

'I guess he'll go to one of those halfway houses first to get him used to life in the outside world.'

'I know. I've done plenty of research. He's never stopped writing to me.'

'Really?'

'He wrote to his mother all the time.' He filled the kettle, flicked it on and set about getting the cups and teapot ready. 'I told him to stop. She'd visit him in Wakefield Prison and come back in a terrible state: crying, headaches, feeling sick. It wasn't doing her any good seeing him in there. I put a stop to it. I told her no more visits, no more letters. We should draw a line under it. Move on.'

'But she couldn't?'

'No. That's why she... she couldn't cope. It was what he'd done to that poor girl that made her kill herself. She used to visit her grave, lay flowers, leave notes and cards for her parents saying how sorry she was for bringing such a monster into the world.'

'Did they ever get in touch with her?'

'No. When Carole died, I wrote to Dominic, the first and only time I'd done so. I told him what she'd done, what he'd made her do. I told him not to contact me ever again. As far as I was concerned, I had no son,' he said, slamming teaspoons and mugs onto a tray.

'Did he write back?'

'Constantly. I recognised his writing on the envelopes. They went straight into the shredder. I didn't even open them. I've never been free of him.' He looked up at me with tears in his eyes.

'You don't want him to be released, do you?'

'No,' he answered quickly. 'I know he's always maintained his innocence, but at the end of the day, his actions led to the death of an innocent young girl. I'm sorry,' he said, leaving the kitchen and heading for the bathroom.

I began to put his shopping away. I looked in cupboards and drawers to try and find where things went and saw the shelves were mostly empty. I noticed he was taking a lot of medication. His fridge only contained a tub of butter, a bottle of milk and a packet of cheese, and the freezer was empty except for a box of Cornettos. I felt incredibly sad for him.

By the time Anthony came back into the kitchen, I'd put everything away.

'Do you want me to go?'

It was a while before he answered. 'No. It's nice having you here. She gave you a letter, didn't she, that viper?'

'Yes. From Dominic.'

'Are you going to read it?'

I nodded. 'Look, I'd better be going.'

'You don't have to.'

'I have frozen food in my car. I don't want it thawing out.'

'Oh, of course,' he said. 'Here, before you go.' He headed for the living room and returned with a shoe box. 'Those diaries of Carole's I told you about.'

'Are you sure you don't mind me reading them?'

'No. She started writing them after we got married. She said she wanted to document our married life and pass it on to our children and grandchildren.'

'That's a good idea.' I smiled.

'So, you see, it's only right you should have them.'

'Thank you. I'll take good care of them.'

'I know you will. Will you come back to visit me again?'

'Of course.'

His smile was genuine. 'I'd like that. The only person I seem to speak to these days is whoever's presenting the weather after the news. They never get it right. I tell them so, too.' He chuckled.

Chapter Eighteen

Dear Dawn,

I was surprised when I received a visit from Clare Delaney, and she told me you had been to see her. It made me smile for the first time in years. I've often thought of you. I did think of writing to your mum, many times, over the past twenty years, but I didn't think she'd want to hear from me. I guessed she knew where I'd be, and if she wanted me to be involved in your life then she'd contact me.

I'm getting out in a few weeks. Clare has probably told you all about that. I was planning to look you up. I don't know if you're interested in meeting me for a coffee or a chat to get to know each other, but it would be nice for me to have something to look forward to when I come out. I don't know anyone.

Clare told me you've been in touch with my father. How is he? I hope he's well and looking after himself. I write to him regularly, but he never replies. That's understandable, I suppose. I've caused him a great deal of pain over the years.

Your mum kept my identity from you for a long time, I hear. That couldn't have been easy for her, but I'm pleased she finally told you about me. I'm guessing you weren't pleased to hear the father you've longed for is serving a prison sentence for murder. I'm not a murderer, Dawn, I promise. I'm not any of the things the newspapers have said I am. I'm no good at letter writing, but I would like to explain everything to you. I've included a visiting order with this letter, so you can come and see me. As I've said, I'd really like to get to know you, but if you don't want to, or if, after we've talked, you want nothing more to do with me, I'll completely understand, and I'll leave you to live your life.

Love,

Dad

It was a while before I could bring myself to read the letter. I arrived home, put all my shopping away and left the envelope on the table. I seemed to be able to see it from wherever I was in the flat. It was taunting me, always on the edge of my peripheral vision, begging, pleading with me to open it.

I gave Mrs White a call. I asked if she'd like to meet for a coffee, and she told me she was free tomorrow. I didn't mention anything about bringing Robyn along and her having seen Stephanie on the day she went missing. When I ended the call, I wondered whether I should have prepared her. It didn't seem fair to ambush her. Eventually, with nothing left to distract myself, I opened the letter from Dominic.

I was surprised by how neat and tidy his handwriting was. I suppose he looked to me as a silver lining on his dark horizon, a prospect of happiness on the outside. All I could think about was the pain Anthony was in. How would he feel if I met my father – his son – and began to forge some kind of relationship? The same question could be asked of my mum, too. We often went out for meals or trips to the cinema together, but what if I couldn't make it on a particular evening because I was going to the pictures with my dad instead? How would Mum feel about that, after all these years of being my sole parent?

On the other hand, I had every right to get to know my dad, and people should understand and be supportive of that.

'Oh, I don't bloody know,' I said out loud, falling back on the sofa in frustration.

The visiting order was on the coffee table in front of me. I'd got this far into investigating my father – I couldn't stop now.

I'd always wanted to meet my father. Even when I was a child and had no idea of his identity, I'd pictured him in my head. He had been tall with dark hair and smiling eyes. He was clean-shaven, strong and always looked happy. He'd hold my hand firmly as we went to the park, and he always bought me an ice-cream. I was far too old for all that now – although I never turned down the offer of ice-cream – but I'd be denying my younger self if I didn't meet him now I had the chance. And meeting him might finally answer all the questions that were burning inside me. It might bring me the peace I so desperately needed.

Chapter Nineteen

I spent most of the night in bed with a tub of Ben and Jerry's while reading Carole's diaries. It wasn't long before I was so engrossed that I forgot about the ice-cream, which wasn't like me at all. They gave me a snapshot of what life was like for Carole and Anthony in those early years of marriage. Some of the entries had Polaroid photos stuck beneath them. I looked at them closely, smiling at the fashions of the Seventies and the hairstyles and the Griffithses' gaudy choice of decoration. It was amazing to see Anthony looking young, cheeks full of colour and standing upright. And he was right, there *was* a resemblance between me and Carole. They looked genuinely happy in those early years.

Smiling at the photos, exhaustion from the past few days finally caught up with me, and I fell asleep while reading – I hadn't even got to Dominic's birth yet.

The next morning, when I eventually woke, the cardboard tub of ice-cream was a soggy mess of melted chocolate, and there was a suspicious-looking brown stain on the carpet which would take some explaining and probably a great deal of effort to get out. I immediately got back to reading the diaries. In the first few years of wedded bliss, Carole had written about how happy she was to be married, how much she loved her husband and how excited she was to move into their first home together. Soon, the subject of motherhood came up, and she was looking forward to giving her husband a child. She actually used that phrase, as if having a baby was a gift to present to the man of the house. There were several false alarms and a couple of miscarriages, and by the end of the Seventies, Carole was beginning to suspect she'd never have a child. From the language she used, this was unacceptable. She *had* to become a mother. The mental anguish she felt was evident in the way the writing on the pages became more untidy and deeper-etched, as Carole vented her anger on the pages. She began to despise herself, and I felt tears of sympathy begin to run down my face as I read about how my grandmother hated waking up each morning as a failure of a woman, incapable of performing the most basic function of her gender – to have a child.

Over breakfast, I read more of the diary entries:

Wednesday, 10 March 1976

Another fucking miscarriage. That's four now. Why don't the doctors just scoop out my insides and have done with it? What is wrong with me? If I hear the sentence 'it's just one of those things, Mrs Griffiths' one more time I'm going to kill someone. Why is my alien body rejecting life?

Thursday, 11 March 1976

I finally told Anthony about the miscarriage today. He looked upset. No, that's the wrong word. He looked mortified. He hates me. I know he does. His hair is going grey at the temples. We're getting old. It's going to be too late soon.

Friday, 12 March 1976

I've told Anthony to leave me. He needs to be with a real woman who can give him a child, two children, a whole rugby team of children. He said I was being silly, and he was with me because he loves me. How can he possibly love me? I'm a freak!

Saturday, 13 March 1976

I don't think I'm going to write in this diary anymore. There's no reason for it. It was my intention to chart my married life: talk about the pitfalls, the highs and lows, my feelings and emotions as Anthony and I had children and grew old together. It was supposed to be something I could pass on to my kids and grandchildren, but as there aren't going to be any because of my poisonous womb, then there is nobody to hand this to. So, I may as well stop. This is to be my last entry. I have nothing left to say.

Wednesday, 8 September 1976

I'm three months pregnant. THREE WHOLE MONTHS pregnant. This is the longest I've gone. It's been a long, hot summer, and Anthony and I have had a few holidays – only weekends away, but they've been happy and relaxing, and we've enjoyed ourselves. I think it's this change that's helped me fall pregnant. I've not been worrying. I've just relaxed and gone with the flow, and it's worked. I'm bloody pregnant. I'm so happy. Anthony is thrilled. There's joy and excitement in our house again.

Thursday, 9 September 1976

It's funny watching Anthony fuss over me. I could get used to it. He's making sure I'm comfortable and not doing anything too strenuous. He's even arranged for a cleaner to come in twice a week to help around the house. He says he wants me to do nothing for the next six months. I can see the love and happiness in his eyes. He's going to make a great father. I hope I'll be a good mother. I've read so many books. I'm sure all first-time mums worry. I'll be fine. I know I will. Fingers crossed.

Wednesday, 15 September 1976

Life is incredibly, incredibly cruel.

A knock on the front door made me jump. My cereal had gone soggy in the bowl while I'd become engrossed, once again, in Carole's diaries. Maybe I should use them as a way to lose weight: read them at mealtimes so I'd forget to eat.

I opened the door to see Robyn on the doorstep, dressed up smart and conservatively but wearing far too much fragrance. I coughed.

'You either got lucky last night or you've forgotten all about it,' she said, taking in my bed hair, dressing gown and novelty penguin slippers.

'What?'

'I don't believe this. You badger me into meeting Barbara White and then forget all about it.'

'I haven't forgotten. We're not meeting her until half eleven.'

'It's eleven o'clock now.'

'What?' I leaned back and looked at the clock on the wall in the kitchen. 'Fuck!'

Robyn looked at her watch. 'I'd say you've got about ten minutes to get ready before we can leave without being late.'

'Fuck. Fuck. Fuck,' I said as I ran to the bedroom.

'What are these?' Robyn asked, when I came back into the main part of the flat.

I'd had the quickest shower I'd ever had and taken great care not to get my hair wet. I pulled on a pair of black jeans and a cream sweater I'd forgotten I had, deciding once again that it was probably better to tone down the severity of my usual dress code. I'd applied the basic amount of make-up and sprayed myself liberally with an expensive fragrance Mum bought me for Christmas. I smelled nice, looked decent, but felt scruffy. It would have to do. I grabbed my bag, rushed into the kitchen and saw Robyn poring over one of Carole's diaries.

'You shouldn't be reading those. They're private,' I said, snatching it from her hand.

'Who wrote them?'

'It doesn't matter.'

'It's Dominic's mother, isn't it?'

'What makes you say that?'

Robyn took the diary back and opened it. '"Thursday, the second of June 1988",' she read. '"James Flint came around earlier and told me to stop bad-mouthing him to the neighbours. He told me the real reason why he hadn't invited Dominic to his youngest's birthday party, despite inviting all the other kids in the street. It turns out all the other children are frightened of Dominic. He hasn't done anything wrong. He's just quiet, that's all. I've tried to get him to play with the other kids, interact, but he's not interested. He just sits there, staring at them. I tried to defend Dominic to James, but I don't think I did a good enough job. I don't even know what words I used. The thing is, I perfectly understand. Dominic scares me, too, sometimes, with his silence and his staring."'

Robyn stopped reading and looked up at me.

'I haven't got that far yet,' I said.

'Why have you got all these diaries? What's going on?'

'Look, Robyn, we're going to be late. I'll explain everything on the way.'

By the time I found a parking space in Eldon Square, Robyn knew everything.

'Oh my God, you should *so* sell your story,' was the first thing she said.

'What? I don't bloody think so.'

'Why not? You could make a fortune out of this. The newspapers would make you a good offer. So would the glossy magazines and all those sad-rags you find in the dentists' waiting rooms. Then there's telly. They're bound to want you on *This Morning*. It's a shame Jeremy Kyle's no longer on.'

'Robyn, will you stop. I have no intention of selling my story, and I've absolutely no desire to go on TV. This is my life, and it's private.'

'You're missing out on some serious cash, babe.'

'I don't care. You'd better not tell anyone either. I mean it, Robyn. This is personal.'

Robyn's face softened. 'You're right. I'm sorry. I was getting ahead of myself. You must be going through hell right now.'

I pulled into the space and turned the engine off. 'To be honest, I don't know how I'm feeling. I was shocked, obviously, but... well, Dominic has always denied killing Stephanie. He's spent twenty years in prison. Without this Fenadine business, he'd only have another five years left, then he'd be out on licence anyway. He's served the majority of his sentence, so why not just admit killing her if he did it?' I frowned.

'Do you think he's innocent?' Robyn asked.

It was a while before I replied. 'I have no idea.'

'You must think he is, or you wouldn't be going to all this trouble. If there was a hint of doubt in your mind, you wouldn't be pursuing it like this.'

'Do you think?'

'Definitely. You're not the type of person to risk everything, knowing there's no chance of winning.'

I looked out of the windscreen at the concrete car park. It was overcast, and there was a stiff, cold wind blowing – I could feel it through the gaps in the car where the sealing had perished. Robyn was right. I did believe my father could be innocent.

Chapter Twenty

We walked to the coffee shop in comparative silence. I was about to meet with the woman whose daughter my father was accused of murdering. Although Barbara had been understanding and kind to me when we met before, she had spent the past twenty years despising the man who killed her only child, and I seemed to be hell bent on having his name cleared. I suddenly felt very ashamed of myself.

'You're very quiet all of a sudden,' Robyn said.

'I don't think I should meet her.' I stopped in my tracks.

'What? This was your idea.'

'I know it was. It's just… What if Dominic is innocent? I know it's a long shot, but what if he is? Barbara is going to be back to square one. In fact, it'll be worse, as she'll have spent twenty years in limbo without knowing it. She may never know who killed her daughter. I'm raking all of this up, and I don't—'

'Dawn.' Robyn stepped forward and put a comforting hand on my arm. 'You can't think like that. For a start, you don't know if Dominic is innocent. You're one of nature's fence-sitters, you always have been. Look, no offence or anything, but maybe you only think it because you want him to be, so you don't have to tell people your father is a killer. Until you have all the facts, you can't make a firm decision.'

I took a deep breath. 'You're right. I know you're right. I'm being hysterical, aren't I?'

'Just a tad, but it's fair enough, given the situation.' She smiled. 'Keep an open mind. Don't believe everything you hear. You're in the legal profession. You should know the majority of people are liars.'

'Not everything is black and white, is it?'

'No. There's at least fifty shades of grey that we know of.' She laughed.

That made me smile.

'Come on. We're going to be late.' Robyn linked arms with me, and we headed for the coffee shop.

We were five minutes late.

Barbara was already sat at a table with a small Americano in front of her. She smiled when she saw me, but for the brief second before she noticed us, I saw the look of utter sadness on her face. I apologised for being late and blamed it on not being able to find a parking space.

'I never drive into town,' Barbara said. 'I've never been a confident driver, and I panic in heavy traffic. Besides, I get extra reading time on the bus. It's my book club tomorrow evening, and I'm not finished with *Jude the Obscure* yet.'

'I haven't read that one,' I said.

She lowered her voice. 'I'm not really enjoying it. You're not missing out on much.'

I smiled. 'Mrs White—'

'I wish you'd call me Barbara. We're not in school anymore.'

'Sorry. It feels wrong calling you by your first name, but I will try. Barbara, I'd like you to meet a friend of mine. This is Robyn. Robyn, this is Barbara White, Stephanie's mother.'

They shook hands and exchanged the usual pleasantries. I went to the counter to buy the drinks. Barbara said she was fine with what she had, while Robyn asked for a large mocha and a chocolate twist. I decided not to make a pig of myself, electing for a medium black Americano.

We were sat uncomfortably in an oddly shaped triangle around a circular table. None of us wanted to be the first to get the serious conversation going. We all exchanged awkward smiles as we sipped our drinks.

'Another cold day,' Barbara said, looking out of the window.

'Yes,' I agreed. 'Lovely and warm in here though.'

'It was a cold night, too. It went down to minus four according to the weather this morning.'

Robyn joined in. 'It's been a long winter.'

'Long time until spring,' Barbara said.

We fell silent again.

'Barbara, have you ever heard of Robyn Shelley before?' I asked.

'No. Should I have?' she said, before smiling at Robyn.

'She gave a statement at the time Stephanie went missing. The next day at school, in fact. She gave a very good description of a man she saw speaking to Stephanie at the back of the shops in Winlaton, but the statement wasn't used in court, and Robyn was never asked to be a witness at the trial.'

'I don't understand why she wouldn't have been.' Barbara frowned. She was nervously playing with her fingers. 'No other witnesses ever came forward. If Robyn gave a statement, then it was the only one, and would definitely have been used. I'm sure of it.'

'I did give a statement,' Robyn said firmly.

'The thing is,' I said, not making eye contact with Barbara, 'something happened that we think may have been the reason why her statement was removed from the files.'

Barbara swallowed hard, preparing herself. 'Go on.'

Robyn took a deep breath and told Barbara all about the man she knew to be Stephanie's father coming to the house, demanding to know who she had seen with his daughter. She said how upset she and her mother had been, how he'd punched her father, and how the detective who had come to the school had been called and marched Harry White out of the house.

Barbara placed a hand over her mouth. Tears filled her eyes. She shook her head. It was a long time before she spoke.

'I am so sorry,' she said softly.

'You've nothing to apologise for.' I leaned forward and placed a hand over hers.

'The man you described definitely sounds like Harry, and the detective is Ian Braithwaite. They were partners. Ian was the Senior Investigating Officer looking for Stephanie. He must have removed your statement from the file to stop Harry getting into trouble. They always were close. They still are.' She closed her eyes and shook her head as if trying to make sense of it all. 'The man you saw with Stephanie,' she began, looking directly at Robyn, 'was it Dominic Griffiths?'

'I honestly don't know. In my head, when I think back to that day, I see someone I think could possibly be Dominic, but that may only be because I've been led to believe Dominic was the killer for all these years.'

'Can you remember any of what you said twenty years ago?' Barbara asked. There was desperation in her voice.

Robyn shook her head. 'I wish I could. I was twelve years old. Twenty years is a long time.' She crossed her legs and tucked her hair behind her ears.

'But if you concentrate,' Barbara pleaded.

'I've tried. All I see is Dominic. I'm not sure if that's the truth or what my mind is telling me to see.'

'I suppose that's understandable,' Barbara said, looking crestfallen.

I glanced from my neighbour to my former teacher. 'Barbara, are you going to mention this to Harry?'

'I think I have to. Will you excuse me a moment?' She stood up and headed for the toilets.

'Poor woman,' Robyn said, draining what was left of her mocha. 'She hasn't really been living for the past twenty years, has she?'

'Not really. I suppose Dominic pleading his innocence all this time is bound to have some kind of effect. It'll have planted the seed of doubt in her mind, and now we've come forward with a positive sighting of a man, she'll be even more full of doubt. Listen, Robyn, do you mind making your own way back? I was thinking of offering Barbara a lift home. I'd like to speak to her alone.'

'That's fine. I need to pop into the market for more material anyway.'

'Thanks.'

Barbara came back to the table. Her eyes were red.

'I hope you two don't mind, but I think I'll head back home. I've got a lot to think about.'

'Would you like me to give you a lift?'

She smiled. 'There's no need. The bus isn't far.' She put on her coat and began buttoning it up.

'I really don't mind. I was going to visit my mum at the florist anyway. It's not far from you.'

We walked to Eldon Square car park in silence. We were surrounded by the noise of shoppers and vehicles, but the silence between us was palpable. It wasn't until we were in the car and I had put the key in the ignition that I finally said something.

'I'd just like to apologise in advance if we break down and the AA end up taking you home. I'm afraid this car is on its way out.'

'It does look like it's seen better days,' she said, glancing around the car with a worried expression.

'It's perfectly safe. There's nothing to worry about. It's just a tad temperamental.'

The engine started on the fifth attempt, and I reversed out of the space and headed for Winlaton.

'Do you think I should say anything to Harry?' Barbara asked, once we were on the dual carriageway.

'I'm afraid I can't answer that, Mrs— Barbara. It all depends on whether you think you can forget about it. Should I not have told you about Robyn seeing Stephanie? Would you have rather not known?'

'No. I needed to know. I just wish it had been Harry or Ian who'd told me.'

'Can't you speak to Ian now?'

'Ian's stroke was very severe. The doctors said he was lucky to survive. Sometimes, I think it might have been better all-round if he hadn't. There are times he doesn't even recognise his own son.'

'I'm so sorry.'

'You're too young to remember, but this case hurt a lot of people. We had the world's press descend on our doorstep. They wouldn't leave us alone for months. The aftermath was felt for years. I'm still feeling it now. Dominic didn't just kill my daughter, he killed my sister and my mother. He destroyed Ian, and he ended my life as I knew it.' She spoke with sadness, as she sat back in the seat and looked out of the window, watching the cold, dreary Newcastle landscape pass by.

When we pulled up outside Barbara's house, she invited me in. She asked if I'd like to see Stephanie's room. I wasn't sure if I did or not, but I hesitantly agreed.

The house was neat and tidy. There was a hint of furniture polish and the scent of flowers in the air. Barbara went into the kitchen and flicked the kettle on. She instructed me to follow her upstairs. She opened the bedroom door and stepped back to allow me to go in first.

'She certainly liked Newcastle United,' I said, with a laugh in my voice.

'You could say that. Football mad. It's strange, you're only the third person to come in here in twenty years.'

'Really?'

'Yes. Harry rarely comes in. It's usually just me. From time to time, I get a bit maudlin, and I like to sit on the bed, look around and remember Stephanie how she was.'

'She was very pretty.' I picked up a framed picture on the desk.

'She really was. Lovely big eyes.' She sat down on the bed and picked up the pillow, squeezing it to her chest.

'Why did you want me to see the room?'

'I don't know. But I feel I can understand what you're doing. You've just found out who your father is, what he's done, and you're trying to make sense of it. What he did was pure evil, and I don't mind saying that I wish we still had the death penalty. Sorry if that's hard for you to hear, but he ripped apart my life. You being here, though, is a comfort to me in a strange way. I understand that you're just trying to work everything out and none of the blame lies at your feet. We're both victims in a way; I feel for you, love. There's a lot about the case online, I've often looked myself, but only a few people know the real Stephanie. I think it's important for you to know more about her than her just being a murder victim.'

'Do you mind if I sit down?'

'No, of course not.'

I sat next to her on the bed. 'It's a sad fact that the victims are often forgotten. We all remember the names of killers like Jack the Ripper, Myra Hindley, Fred West and Peter Sutcliffe, but it's the victims who should be remembered. The killers, the evil murderers, should be left to rot.'

I looked around the room and tried to picture Stephanie in here, listening to music, reading a football programme. I couldn't feel any presence, but just imagining what she would have been doing in here made me smile.

'Tell me about Stephanie.'

Barbara's face lit up. It was obvious she'd been waiting for me to ask her.

'She was a wonderful child,' she said softly. Her eyes glistened with tears. 'She never gave us an ounce of bother. She was bright, always smiling. She played in goal for the school football team, the first female ever.' Barbara beamed with pride, then she chuckled.

'What is it?' I found myself smiling.

'I remember going to see her in a game once. It was absolutely bloody freezing. Me and Harry stood on the sidelines. I don't think either of us saw the game – we were just watching Stephanie in goal. It was hardly a World Cup match, but she took it incredibly seriously. I kept telling her it was all in fun, but she and Harry didn't agree. Every game was do or die. Anyway, something happened, I don't know what, as I'm not up on the rules, and the other team was awarded a free kick. Stephanie, at the top of her voice, shouted, "There's no way that's a free kick, you wanker." I was mortified. All the other parents turned to stare at me. I'm sure I went bright red. Harry couldn't hold his laughter for long, and soon, all the parents were laughing. Well, the men were. I certainly had a few words with her that night,' Barbara said. Despite her daughter swearing at the referee in front of her parents, there was a hint of a smile on Barbara's face. The memory it brought back was of a passionate girl, full of life, enjoying herself.

'Barbara, in the car on the way over, you said that Dominic hadn't only killed Stephanie, but your mum and sister, too. What did you mean?'

Barbara sniffed and wiped away her tears. 'As I'm sure you can imagine, Stephanie going missing and then being found dead consumed us all. Everything else went out of the window.' She took a deep breath. 'My sister, Angela, she was younger than me. She couldn't have children, and she doted on Stephanie. When she was killed, Angela went to pieces. Well, we all did. But it hit Angela hard. By the time she noticed a lump on her breast, it was too late to do anything about it. The cancer quickly spread, and she was dead by the end of the summer.'

'I'm so sorry,' I said to fill the heavy silence.

'My dad died when I was young, so my mother brought me and Angela up on her own. Losing her granddaughter and her daughter in such a short space of time destroyed my mum. Less than a month after Angela's funeral, my mum went to bed and didn't wake up again the next morning. A severe heart attack, the coroner said, but we all knew she died of a broken heart.'

'Oh my God,' I said, deflated, my head bowed. 'That must have been…' I had no words.

'I lost my daughter, my sister and my mum within the space of a few months. It was the hardest time of my life.'

I shook my head.

We sat in silence for a long time. I looked around the room at pictures of Stephanie in her school football kit, in action, posing for a team photograph, at the soft toys and posters of Alan Shearer on the wall.

'Barbara, I'm so sorry. And to think my father was responsible for it all. I just want everything to be better, but I have so much I need to work out and understand. I have a dilemma,' I began. 'I'm sure you've heard about this Fenadine drug that Dominic was taking at the time he killed Stephanie. His solicitor is using its side effects as a defence…'

'I heard. It makes me sick,' she said, with venom.

'The thing is, say the evidence is there that Dominic did kill

Stephanie, even though he perhaps wasn't in control of his own mind. How can I accept him as my father, knowing that he actually did commit murder?'

Barbara let out a heavy sigh. 'That is not an easy question to answer. However, you're in a better position to answer it objectively now than if you'd known your father before he went to prison. At this stage, you've never met him. You don't have any feelings towards him because you don't know him as a person. Yes, he's your father, but you can still walk away and not be hurt any more than you already are.'

'But he'd always be in here.' I tapped the side of my head.

'Stephanie is always in here,' Barbara said, tapping her own head in the same place. 'And they always will be. The thing to do is keep busy. Eventually, the memory will fade. You'll meet someone, get married, have children, and when you think of him, you'll be surprised that ten years have gone by.'

'I'm not sure if I can believe that right now.'

'Maybe not right now, but you will. I know it.' She smiled. 'Looking back, sometimes it seems incredible that twenty years have passed. Other times, it seems like only last week. When I think of the days following Stephanie's body being found, I wonder how I ever managed to get through it. How did I attend the funeral of my own teenage daughter without collapsing? But I did. I made it out the other side. I survived. It's what we do.'

Downstairs, the front door opened. We both listened. We could hear voices as the door was closed.

'Barbara, are you in?' Harry called out. 'I've got Terry with me.'

'Oh God,' Barbara said.

'Everything all right?'

'Yes. Fine.'

'I should probably go,' I said, after seeing the look of worry on Barbara's face.

'I'll show you out.'

We went downstairs, Barbara leading the way. In the living room, Harry was taking off his coat and gloves. Next to him was the man I presumed was Terry. He was tall and very slim with a mound of tangled brown hair. He wore black trousers, scuffed shoes and a white shirt that had been washed so many times it was almost grey.

The smile on Harry's face dropped when he saw me.

'Harry, Dawn just popped round again to say hello.'

'Did she? What were you doing upstairs?'

'I was showing her Stephanie's room.'

'Why?'

'I asked if she wanted to see it. She was interested.'

'I bet she was. Sorry, Terry, you won't have met Dawn, will you?' he said, with resounding sarcasm. 'Dawn, believe it or not, is Dominic Griffiths' daughter.'

Terry's eyes widened in surprise. 'Oh.'

'Yes, we said something similar when she just turned up on our doorstep last week.'

'I should probably be going,' I said, edging out of the living room.

'Harry, there's no need to be rude.' Barbara gave her husband a sharp look. 'Dawn, there's really no need to leave. Terry is an old friend of the family, Ian Braithwaite's son, in fact. He's a policeman now too, aren't you, Terry?'

Both men stood looking at me without saying a word.

'Nice to meet you, Terry. But honestly, Barbara, I really must be off. It was nice to see you again. And you, er, Mr White. Goodbye.'

I was at the front door and pulling it open before Barbara could get there.

'I'm so sorry about Harry. He's really struggling—'

'Don't be,' I interrupted. 'There really is no need.'

Out on the empty driveway, I noticed there were no new cars

in the cul-de-sac. That must mean Terry had come on foot. I got in the car, drove to the end of the road, turned left, pulled over and waited.

It was an hour later, and I was hunkered down in my seat. I was freezing cold, as the icy northerly wind was blowing in through the gaps in the car. It was starting to get dark already as a deep grey sky descended. A few flakes of snow began to fall.

Out of the corner of my eye, I saw Terry come down the driveway, hands plunged firmly in his pockets, collar of his jacket up around his ears and his head down, as he took large strides, heading, I assumed, for home.

I opened the car door, just after he passed by.

'Terry,' I called, but there was no reaction. He either hadn't heard me, or he was purposely ignoring me. 'Terry!' I shouted louder.

He stopped and looked back over his left shoulder. 'I had a feeling you'd wait for me.'

'I wasn't aware I was so predictable,' I said, with a nervous smile.

'You know, you've really upset Harry and Barbara. They're like a second family to me.'

'I'm sorry. It was never my intention to upset them.'

'Then what was your intention?'

'I... To be honest, I don't know. Barbara taught me at school when I was doing my GCSEs. She was my favourite teacher. I really admired her. When I found out who my father was, what he'd done, I felt... I don't know. I felt like maybe she should know.'

'And what's all this about a girl seeing Stephanie on the day she disappeared?'

'Ah. She told you?'

'Yes. Are you making this up?'

'What?' I asked, astonished.

'Is this some cruel trick you're playing to get your father pardoned?'

'No, it isn't. Look, I haven't even met my dad yet, and I don't know if I'm going to. I'm trying to decide if I want him in my life or not. He's always denied killing Stephanie. He was taking a drug that shouldn't have even been on the market. He didn't know his own mind.' I wondered why I was defending him all of a sudden, but Terry's face kept getting darker the more I did.

'Look.' Terry grabbed me by the elbow and pulled me to the edge of the road. We stood toe to toe, and he lowered his voice as he leaned down. 'Harry and Barbara have been through a great deal over the years. The last thing they need is some amateur Jane Tennison thinking she can uncover a miscarriage of justice. Dominic Griffiths killed their daughter. Your father is a murderer, and the sooner you accept that the better. Now, if I find out you've been here hassling them again, I will have an injunction slapped on you so fast you won't see it coming. Do you understand?'

I winced under the pain of Terry's grip.

'I said, do you understand?' he repeated through gritted teeth, gripping my arm firmer.

'Perfectly,' I said quietly.

'Good. Now, piss off home and get on with the rest of your life, and stay away from here.'

He let go, pushing me backwards, before turning on his heels and striding away.

I rubbed my arm, shocked and trying to catch my breath. I watched him retreat into the distance before turning back to my car. I could understand him being protective of Harry and Barbara, but there was no need for him to be so aggressive.

Chapter Twenty-One

It was another cold night. I sent a fourth email to my landlord about my heating not working, but I wasn't hoping for a reply. He never replied. One day, in the height of summer, I was sure an engineer would turn up to mess around with the boiler, hit it with a spanner and say it was working fine. Then, come winter, I'd turn it on, and nothing.

I steamed a chicken breast and had it with a few vegetables. It was time I ate more healthily and made a real effort to lose some weight. I wouldn't mind getting down to a size fourteen by the summer, maybe twelve by Christmas. It was an achievable goal and one that would require minimal change to my day-to-day life. I was up for the challenge.

By eight o'clock, I was hungry. I had a box of Maltesers in the freezer. It would be a shame to leave them until they were past their best and had to be thrown out. I'd properly start my diet once all the chocolates and biscuits had gone, and I wouldn't replace them.

Sitting up in bed with the box of Maltesers open next to me, I pulled the duvet up around me to keep warm and continued to make my way through my grandmother's diaries.

I picked up where I'd left off and read about another miscarriage. It was sad reading of her desperation to get pregnant. All she wanted was to be a wife and a mother. She had no intention of being a career-driven woman. She didn't want to run marathons or climb mountains. Her only aim in life had been to get married, live in a nice house and fill it with kids. Unfortunately, the kids bit hadn't happened.

Then, in 1981, Dominic came along. The first few entries after his arrival were about how blissfully happy she was being a mother, and how it wasn't too late for her to have more. The journals were filled with photos of a smiling happy baby and beaming parents. It seemed that Dominic was the perfect baby. He ate well and slept through the night. Motherhood was a breeze. His formative years went without a hitch. There was no mention of the stories Clare Delaney had told me about when he'd slapped a girl so hard she'd lost the hearing in one ear, or about the boy he blinded. Once he became a teenager, that's when the trouble set in, and Carole's entries grew darker.

Wednesday, 2 February 1994

I had a knock on the door around seven o'clock. I don't usually answer the door after dark, but there was something urgent about the knock. At first, I thought it was the police, that something might have happened to Anthony. When I opened it, I saw Mr and Mrs Clarke from number 178 on the doorstep. Their faces were like thunder. I didn't get a chance to say hello or welcome them in as Mr Clarke just exploded into a tirade of vitriol, calling Dominic evil and a devil-child.

Apparently, he's been touching their Sophie – putting his hand up her skirt and getting her to put her hand down his trousers. He's been explaining to her in detail what men and women do together in bed.

Sophie has been in tears for weeks and finally, tonight, she told them what had been happening.

I managed to assuage Mr and Mrs Clarke by telling them Anthony will be home at the weekend, and he'll sort it out. They've told me Dominic isn't allowed contact with Sophie again, and I agreed with them.

When Anthony called just before I went to bed, I told him what had happened. He didn't seem shocked or upset but said he would have a word on Saturday, and I wasn't to worry about anything.

I always feel better after talking to Anthony. He has a way of calming me down. I sometimes feel guilty about having to make these stories up, but it's the only way I can get Anthony to notice me, to be the man and tell me what I should do. On the bright side, when Anthony does come home at the weekend, he'll spend some time with his son, chatting, maybe go for a kick-about in the park. It could help them bond. It's a win–win situation.

'Bloody hell.' I looked up from the diary. Carole had made up a story about her son sexually interfering with a young girl, just so Anthony would spend some time with him. She'd started the entry as if it had really happened, like she was practising convincing herself it was true. I frowned as I shovelled another handful of Maltesers into my mouth and turned the page.

Monday, 21 February 1994

I've been given tablets to help me sleep. I told the doctor I spend all night alone, while Anthony's at work, sitting up in bed, fearing to fall asleep because I'm scared of Dominic. It's not natural, is it, to be scared of your own child? I can hear him in his room now, just pacing up and down.

Anthony left this morning. He's driving to Wales then on to Plymouth. He won't be home until the weekend. I've got a whole week on my own with that devil-child.

What's wrong with him? I've been the best mother I know how to be.

I've given him everything he's wished for and never shouted at him or chastised him, yet he repays my kindness with his acts of evil.

I flicked back through the entries to see if I'd missed any examples of Dominic's so-called bad behaviour, but Carole hadn't given any. She spoke about not sleeping, hardly eating, wishing Anthony was home and struggling to cope on her own, but she didn't back up her woes with any evidence. Was she lying? There was nobody for me to ask who could give me an honest answer. Anthony hadn't been there often so wouldn't have seen what was going on, and if I asked Dominic about his childhood, could his replies be trusted? Their former neighbour, Sylvia, talked about his unruly behaviour, but tipping over dustbins was hardly the work of the devil.

Monday, 11 April 1994

There's a new doctor at the surgery. He wouldn't give me a repeat prescription as I've been taking the anti-depressants too long, and he said he was more interested in tackling the cause rather than dulling the pain with pills. He wants to see Dominic.

Thursday, 14 April 1994

We went to the doctor today. I had to sit in the waiting room while Dominic went into the consulting room to speak to Dr Glebe on his own. One of the receptionists went in to act as an appropriate adult. They were chatting for over twenty minutes. All sorts were going through my mind while he was in there. Eventually, the receptionist brought him out, and I went in. According to Dr Glebe, Dominic told him about feeling isolated and lonely. Children won't go near him at school because they've heard about his mood swings and are worried he'll attack them. He has to sit on his own in classes, and he feels tired and drained when he gets home so goes straight to his room. He feels sad all the time as he doesn't have any friends. My stories seem to have worked.

Dr Glebe said there is a new drug on the market called Fenadine that will help to stabilise Dominic's moods and, hopefully, improve his behaviour so he is more acceptable and approachable among his peers. I'm to be slowly weaned off my medication while Dominic will begin his on a small dose of only 10mg per day.

I've always known my son was ill with psychological problems. I've been telling people for years his behaviour is dark and frightening. Now I'm finally being believed. It's a huge relief.

I had to stop reading as I couldn't see the words anymore. Tears were blurring my vision. Carole had lied to anyone who would listen, saying that Dominic was disturbed, and people had accepted what she said as the truth. She'd lied to her husband, to doctors, and it had led to Dominic being given a drug that changed his mood and led him to murder Stephanie Griffiths. And the reason Carole had killed herself must have been because she knew her lies had led to the poor girl's murder, and she was unable to live with herself.

Tuesday, 3 May 1994

I don't think Dominic's tablets are working. There's no improvement. I'm going to make an appointment with Dr Glebe tomorrow to see if he can increase the dosage.

I flicked through the pages and landed on one at random.

Wednesday, 18 September 1996

I mentioned to Dominic about leaving his dirty trainers lying around the house, how he should put them in the cupboard under the stairs instead of on the carpet in the hallway. I've told him time and time again. He looked at me with that cold death stare of his, and he struck me. He swiped me so hard across the face I almost fell over. I'm so scared. I wish Anthony was here.

Tuesday, 24 November 1998

The moment Dominic left the house, I secured the chain on the door, so he wouldn't be able to sneak back in, and I went upstairs to look around his room. He's put a padlock on the door, but we have a similar one on the shed and the same key fitted, which was a surprise. I can't remember the last time I was in Dominic's room, well over a year, and I was shocked by how much it had changed. The walls were still covered in Newcastle United posters, but it was a complete mess. His desk and bookshelves were full of comics and magazines and junk. Every surface was covered in something. There was dust in the air, and it stuck to the back of my throat. I looked in all his drawers; I wanted to find out as much as I could about what he's getting up to. He seems to have thrown nothing away for years – empty chocolate wrappers, full packets of crisps, old socks, outdated football programmes, boxes and boxes of tablets, a shoe box with the pair of trainers I bought him for Christmas last year that still had their tags on. I hate to say this about my own flesh and blood, but Dominic is seriously abnormal. I'm not sure if I should tell Anthony tonight when he phones. That's if he does phone. He didn't ring at all last night.

There were three polaroid photos that accompanied this entry, all depicting Dominic's mess of a bedroom. I leaned in close to get a good look at the images. All I could see was what appeared to be the bedroom of a normal teenage boy.

'Dominic, you poor, poor man,' I said, as I wiped away the tears.

It really was Carole who should have been on medication. She had been forcing an illness onto her son. What was it called… Munchausen by Proxy?

I closed the diary and tossed it onto the floor. I couldn't read any more. I was so angry. Carole had been mentally ill and nobody could see that. Her actions had led her son to be so heavily medicated that it messed with his brain patterns and led to the attempted rape of Joby Turnbull and the murder of Stephanie White.

I snuggled down under the duvet and wrapped it around myself to form a protective cocoon. I couldn't help but feel sorry for my father. My father the killer; my father the victim.

Chapter Twenty-Two

I was behind the wheel of my car impatiently trying to get it to start. Fourth attempt, fifth attempt, sixth – there was no life in the engine at all.

'Fucking car,' I screamed. I hit the steering wheel hard, breaking a nail in the process.

'I heard that.'

I jumped, turned, and saw my mum standing on the pavement beside me.

'Jesus! Sorry, I didn't see you there.' I opened the door and climbed out.

'Car trouble?'

'You could say that. I think it's finally died.'

'Well, it has been through two world wars.' She smiled.

'And one of them was the Crimean.' I chuckled. I looked ahead and saw the florist van Mum had come over in. 'Listen, you couldn't give me a lift somewhere, could you?'

'Sure. You're early going to work, aren't you?' Mum asked, looking at her watch.

'Ah. I'm not actually in work this week. I've taken some time off.'

'What for?'

'It's a long story.' I opened the back door of the Golf and took out the shoe box containing the diaries and my handbag. 'Mum, don't roll your eyes or have a go at me or anything, but I need you to drive me to Langdale Crescent. I wouldn't ask, but it's really important.'

'Who do you know at Langdale Crescent?'

'Anthony Griffiths.'

'Oh, Dawn, no, please don't tell me you're getting mixed up in all of this?' she said, a look of genuine concern on her face. 'You're going to end up ruining your career at this rate.'

'I'm not. I've been given compassionate leave. Will you give me a lift, or am I going to have to get myself further into debt by getting an Uber?'

'You know, blackmail is a serious crime, Dawn Shepherd,' she chastised.

I gave her a wide smile, hoping it would win her over.

'Go on then. I've got a delivery in Winlaton anyway. What's in the box?' she asked as we set off towards the van.

'Gwyneth Paltrow's head.'

We pulled up outside Anthony's home. I took off my seatbelt, but Mum remained still with the engine ticking over.

'Are you coming in?'

She thought for a moment. 'No.'

'Why not?'

'It's you who wants to see him, not me.'

'He's my grandfather. Don't you want to say hello, see how he is?'

She looked down. 'Dawn, if you want to build some kind of a relationship with him then that's fine – I've no issue with that. But please don't get me involved. Between Dominic and his mother, I've had enough of the Griffiths family to last me a lifetime.'

'He's an old man. He's on his own. He's lonely. Jesus, no wonder the elderly feel unappreciated in this country. The British are great at holding grudges. It's a shame it isn't an Olympic sport.'

'All right,' she said, holding a hand up to silence me. 'I'll come in. But don't expect some kind of big family reunion with lots of tears and hugging.'

I smiled. I felt warm inside, despite being frozen on the outside.

I rang the bell and stepped back. I turned to Mum and grinned. She rolled her eyes.

Anthony opened the door.

'Dawn, I didn't expect to see you again so soon.'

'No. I've a few things I want to discuss with you. Anthony, this is my mum. Mum, this is Anthony. My grandfather.'

I watched as they looked at each other, and neither of them said anything for what seemed like hours but was probably a few seconds.

'It's lovely to meet you,' Anthony said. There was genuine warmth in his voice and a twinkle in his eye. He held out his hand for Mum to shake.

'And you,' she replied, accepting his hand.

'Would you both like to come in? The kettle's not long since boiled.'

'I can't stay long,' Mum said quickly.

'Long enough for a cup of tea, though,' I added just as quickly.

We followed him into the dimly lit hallway. I closed the front door behind us and showed Mum into the living room while Anthony went into the kitchen.

Mum stood in the doorway, looking around the room. Her eyes fell on the photo frames on the cabinet.

'That's his wife,' I said, following my mother's gaze.

'I'm aware of who she is, Dawn,' she said, an edge to her voice.

'She was very pretty in her younger days, wasn't she?'

'I suppose. Difficult to tell how pretty someone is when they're screaming at you and calling you every name under the sun.'

'I was very ashamed about that,' Anthony said.

We both turned quickly, not realising he'd come into the room. He was holding a fully laden tray in his hands that looked too heavy for him. I went over and took it from him, placing it carefully on the coffee table.

'I had no idea she'd been round to see you until much later,' Anthony continued. 'I came round to apologise.'

'Did you?' Mum asked.

'Yes. It took me a while to work up the courage. You weren't there, but I spoke to your parents. They were a lovely couple.'

'Yes,' she smiled.

'They really wanted to protect you. I told them all about Carole and Dominic, and we decided it was probably best if he wasn't involved in Dawn's upbringing.'

'That wasn't really your decision to make, was it? It was my baby. It was up to me who should have an input in her life.'

Anthony smiled. 'Your mum said exactly that. However, it wasn't long before… well, what happened, happened.'

'Shall we sit down?' I asked.

Anthony took his usual place in his armchair, while Mum and I made ourselves comfortable on the matching sofa. I took it upon myself to pour the tea. I felt comfortable here.

'You've raised a wonderful daughter, Mrs Shepherd.'

'Thank you.' She smiled. 'And it's Rita, please. She has her moments, but I'm very proud of her.'

'You've read the diaries?' Anthony asked, clocking the shoe box.

'I'm working my way through them. Have you?' I asked.

'Not for a very long time.'

'But you know what's in them?'

'I do.'

'Is that why you wanted me to read them?'

'What you have to remember about Carole is that she wanted to be a mother so badly, and it just wasn't happening for her. We assumed that we couldn't have children, and it devastated her. By the time she found out she was pregnant with Dominic, she'd given up hope. She'd resigned herself to never becoming a mum.'

'But surely, news of a miracle baby should have made her happy.'

'It did. For a little while. But… I knew Carole had been ill for a long time. Depression set in long before Dominic was born. I thought a baby would have been the cure, but it wasn't. It made everything worse, and I didn't help by not being at home very much.'

'You were a lorry driver, weren't you?' Mum asked.

'Yes. Long-distance. Money was tight, and I was getting well paid. I thought I could make up for my absence by providing my family with material things, so I started accepting more hours. Longer hauls for more money, so I could buy nice things for them both.'

I removed the lid of the shoe box and picked up one of the hardback diaries. 'The behaviour Carole talks about – Dominic being disruptive, touching girls, hitting boys, terrorising the neighbourhood – it wasn't true, was it?'

Grandad seemed to deflate in his chair. It was a while before he answered. 'No.'

'But when I was looking for you and spoke to your ex-neighbour, she said Dominic was a problem child.'

'If you're told something often enough you start to believe it. It wasn't long before visitors stopped coming to the house, people stopped chatting to us in the street. Carole isolated herself even more through her lies.'

'And children stopped wanting to play with Dominic,' I added.

'That's right.'

'Which is why he withdrew and became sad and lonely. He thought there was something wrong with him, because that's what he had been led to believe.'

'Yes.'

'So, when the doctor offered medication to improve his low mood, he took it.'

'Yes,' he said, not making eye contact.

'And that medication – Fenadine – caused him to lash out at Joby Turnbull and kill Stephanie White.'

'Who's Joby Turnbull?' Mum asked.

'I'll tell you later.'

'Yes, it did. And that's why Carole killed herself,' he said, turning towards his wedding photo on the table by his chair.

'When did you find out it was all a lie?' I asked.

'After Carole died, and I read those diaries.'

'She never told you?'

'No. It must have been eating away at her, what she'd done. She couldn't live with the guilt, I suppose,' he said, looking at his wife's photograph again. Despite what she'd done, I could tell he still loved her.

'It was Carole who needed help? Not Dominic?' Mum asked. I nodded. 'So, when she came to my house ranting and raving, it wasn't because she wanted me to stay away from her son—'

'I suppose she was worried the attention would be taken off her with a grandchild in the picture,' I interrupted.

'So, where does all this leave Dominic?' Mum asked.

'Languishing in prison for committing a crime he was manufactured to commit,' I said.

Mum took a deep breath. 'So, at the trial, if everything had been taken into consideration, he would have been found not guilty of murder but guilty of manslaughter?'

'Involuntary manslaughter,' I said.

'And that wouldn't carry a twenty-five-year prison sentence?'

'Probably not.'

I looked at the expressions on the faces of my mum and grandad. Judging by their blank stares, neither of them relished the prospect of Dominic being released back into the big, wide world.

Chapter Twenty-Three

The majority of my spare time was spent reading Carole's diaries. I tried to put myself in her shoes.

She was missing Anthony immensely as he worked away during the week and spent most of the weekend resting and preparing for the working week ahead. He phoned her most nights from wherever he was in the country, but it appeared Carole spent most of the conversations lying to him about the evil acts Dominic had supposedly been committing. Was she saying these things for sympathy, or was she hoping Anthony would race home and promise to look for a job locally? From Anthony's point of view, it was understandable why he continued to work away so much.

In the middle of all this was poor Dominic. His mother's lies isolated him. He was ostracised and prescribed a drug that altered his state of mind. If Carole's illness had been detected, maybe Stephanie White would still be alive today.

It upset me to think of the twenty-year anguish Barbara and Harry had been forced to endure. They were victims of Carole's behaviour, just like Dominic was. As much as it would upset the Whites, Dominic deserved to be released.

I couldn't put it off any longer. The visiting order Dominic had sent me was still on the coffee table. I kept looking at it, my mind constantly changing between using it and tearing it up. In the end, I decided to use it. Clare Delaney had emailed me several times, asking if I was visiting and if I wanted her to give me a lift to the prison. I knew it was all for show. She didn't care about bringing a father and his long-lost daughter together; she was just thinking of how it would look in the papers and how much weight it would give to her case against Maxton-Schwarz. However, I no longer had transport, I couldn't ask my mum to drive me, and Cruella de Vil had that gorgeous car... Why not use her like she was using me?

Friday soon came around, and the drive to the prison took less than an hour. I was loving the smooth ride and soon relaxed in the huge Range Rover. It smelled of newness, and I was very impressed by the touch screen controls, the heated leather seats and the purr of the engine. I wondered how much a car like this would cost – probably more than my flat.

'Are you nervous?' Clare asked, once we'd left Gateshead and were on the A1.

'I am. I'm not sure what to expect. The only photos I've seen of him were taken twenty years ago.'

'He's certainly changed since then. Prison does that to a person.'

'Is he looking forward to being released?'

Clare thought for a moment. 'He's apprehensive. Twenty years is a long time to be locked up. The world has changed. It'll take some getting used to. He's looking forward to reconnecting with his family,' she said, with a smile.

'There's only me. I don't think his father is too keen on having him back in his life.'

'He's absolutely thrilled about meeting you.'

'Really?' I could feel a smile spread across my face.

'You've given him hope, Dawn.'

I took a deep breath. Despite the confident air I tried to project, walking with my head held high, rocking my own sense of style, I was finding the weight of being a stranger's only hope for twenty years a lot to carry. Dominic might not adjust to freedom after two decades. There was evidence that long-term prisoners preferred life locked up, as that was all they knew, and would reoffend just so they could get back inside where it was safe and familiar. What if Dominic did that? What if Dominic killed someone just to get back to his version of normal? I didn't think I would be able to handle that guilt.

I pulled the visor down and examined my appearance. Once again, I had decided against wearing all black. I didn't want to frighten my father by sitting opposite him looking like the offspring of Frankenstein's monster. I was contemplating dyeing my hair a lighter colour, maybe a chocolate brown. The panda eyes I normally spent ages perfecting in front of the mirror were gone, and my lashes were no longer severe. I wore a knee-length black skirt, black tights, and cream shirt. Adding colour to my style was still something I struggled with. When I had stood in front of the full-length mirror that morning, I had thought I looked like a fat pint of Guinness.

'We're here,' Clare said, pulling into the car park.

I looked out of the window at the imposing building. Behind those walls were men who had committed unlawful acts. They were locked away because they were deemed a menace to society.

Dominic Griffiths had been at HMP Holme House for six

months and was gradually being prepared for life in the outside world. He was undergoing counselling and psychological treatment. He was allowed supervised days out to get used to what 2019 was like beyond prison walls. He was being informed of what was expected of him, what his rights were and what benefits he would be entitled to. His release date was looming, and soon, he would be on his own. As I waited outside the visiting room, I wondered how he would be feeling when the day came to take his first steps as a free man.

We were taken into a large room that had tables and chairs uniformly placed. The visitors went in first and sat down. There was a quiet hush while we waited for who we'd come to see. Once everyone was seated, the prisoners were allowed in. It suddenly dawned on me. I was meeting my dad. The day I had longed for my entire life was finally here. I was meeting my father for the very first time. Oh my God! My heart was hammering, my palms were sweating and I had to remind myself to keep breathing.

I watched as the door opened, and men of every age and race entered. Their expressions were downcast and hardened until they saw a friendly face, then they smiled and hurried to greet a family member. I smiled as I watched men wrap their arms around their wives, mothers, fathers, children. It was heartwarming.

'Here he is,' Clare said, standing up.

I looked up but couldn't see anyone who resembled an older version of the twenty-year-old man I'd seen pictures of. As a man approached, I took in his shorn dark brown hair, his sad brown eyes with the dark circles beneath them. His skin was dull and lifeless. His shoulders were hunched, and his strolling gait was that of a man resigned to a life behind bars. He wore faded blue jeans and a blue sweater that had been through the washing machine far too many times.

Our eyes locked. He looked nervous. I guessed I did too.

'Dominic, it's lovely to see you again,' Clare said, holding out a hand for him to shake.

I watched. His grip looked light, almost limp. He smiled at his solicitor.

'Dominic, I'd like you to meet Dawn Shepherd, your daughter. Dawn, this is your father.' The excitement in Clare's voice was palpable. I would have bet everything in my savings account she wished she could have had a film crew present.

Dominic held his hand out towards me. 'It's lovely to meet you at last,' he said. He spoke in a soft Newcastle accent. He smiled, which softened his features slightly.

Hesitantly, I held out my hand. I was terrified. I took my father's clammy hand in my own and shook it lightly. I had no idea what to say, so I just smiled.

'Shall we sit down?' Clare said.

We all sat. Dominic was unable to take his eyes from me while I looked over his shoulder at the rest of the room.

'Clare has told me a great deal about you,' Dominic said.

'I didn't know Clare knew a great deal about me.' If in doubt, be light-hearted.

'I've been telling him about your efforts – how you're helping to strengthen his case that he wasn't culpable for the murder, and how you want to be supportive in his life once he is released.'

I had never agreed to help his case for compensation. Nor had I said I would be there for his rehabilitation. I had a life of my own, a career of my own, to concentrate on.

'Do you think we could chat alone?' I asked, turning to Clare.

'Oh. Of course. I'll be in the waiting area. I'll be in touch soon, Dominic.' She stood up and took her time walking away from the table.

'She's quite a forceful woman, isn't she?' Dominic said, once she'd left.

'That's one word for her.'

'I really am pleased you've come to see me,' he said, with a smile. 'I've thought about you often over the years.'

'I've thought a great deal about who my father could be over the years too.'

'I'm guessing I've come as a bit of a disappointment.'

'Well, there were times I wondered if my dad was a famous actor, a member of the royal family or possibly a secret agent, but not once did I imagine he was a murderer.' I was aiming for levity, but it fell flat.

Dominic looked crestfallen and bowed his head.

'There isn't a day goes by that I don't regret what happened. I should have called the police as soon as I found the body in the shed. I just… I panicked. I didn't know what to do. I thought, if I hid the body and waited until Dad came home, he'd know what to do.'

'Are you saying, hand on heart, that you didn't murder Stephanie?'

He placed his hand on his heart and looked deep into my eyes. 'I didn't do it.'

I inhaled deeply. I chewed the inside of my mouth. 'You weren't at the shops in Winlaton on that day?'

'I don't know where I was. I'd lose hours sometimes and not know what I'd been up to. Those tablets I was taking really spaced me out. I know I shouldn't have been driving, but Mum wasn't an easy person to live with. I'd go out for a drive to escape her constant nagging. When I got back home, I couldn't say where I'd been or if I'd seen anyone. How I didn't cause a pile-up, I've no idea.'

'Do you think it's possible that you did see Stephanie that day, that you did kill her, and you just can't recall it?'

'Over the years, I've seen many different counsellors and therapists, and I've asked them that exact question. They've said it is highly unlikely I could have kidnapped someone off the streets, driven her to the allotment and killed her without any memory of it. Dawn, I know you don't know anything about me, and you've no reason to believe anything I say, but I have no knowledge of seeing Stephanie on that day. I'm not a killer. I didn't murder her.'

I didn't say anything.

'I'm getting released from here in a few weeks. Clare's probably told you the date. I'd really like to get to know you. I know I don't have any rights to be a father to you, but I'd love to be a part of your life, no matter how small.' Hesitantly, he reached forwards and placed his hands on top of mine. It felt strange, cold. 'You're my daughter.' He beamed. 'I'm your dad.'

I smiled. I couldn't help it. His smile was infectious. Gone were the boyish good looks of twenty years ago, the dark floppy hair and the sparkling eyes, but when he smiled, there was a hint of the man he used to be shining through. The twinkle, although dulled, was still there.

'I would like to get to know you too,' I said. I could feel I was smiling, but inside, I was shaking like a leaf in a force nine gale.

The relief on his face was evident. 'That's... that's the best news I've ever had.' He squeezed my hands and tears pricked his eyes. 'I can't make up for twenty years of absence, but I can be there for you as a friend, or whatever, as and when you want me.'

'Thank you,' I said, with a catch in my voice. 'Do you know what you're going to do when you're released?' I asked, withdrawing my hands from his and sitting back.

He mirrored my movements. 'I don't. I'll be in a halfway house for a while, until I find my feet. The first thing will be to get a job. I've not been idle in here. I've taken courses and got qualifications. I've got a degree in English Literature,' he said, with pride.

'Really? That's good. I studied English Literature and Law at university.'

'We have something in common,' he said, looking even more proud. 'I love reading Chaucer, and I'm a big Shakespeare fan.'

'I like my classics. I could read Brontë and Austen on a loop. I'm re-reading *The Tenant at Wildfell Hall* at the moment.'

'I've not read that one.'

'You should give it a try. It was Mrs White who…' I tailed off, suddenly remembering who Mrs White was and where she fitted into our story.

'Mrs White?'

I took a deep shaking breath. 'Barbara White – Stephanie's mother – was my English teacher at school.'

'Oh. Small world.'

'Incredibly small.'

He looked away and sighed. 'It's always going to be there, isn't it? It doesn't matter that I say I'm innocent, people aren't going to believe it. They're going to see me as a cold-blooded killer. We can't even have a simple chat about books without something ruining it.'

'It will get easier. It will just take time.'

A bell rang. Visiting was over.

'Time for me to go,' I said, standing up.

'Well, I am very grateful to you for coming to see me,' he said.

He stood up and held out a hand for me to shake. I did, but then I leaned in and kissed him on the cheek.

'It was lovely to finally meet you… Dad.'

His eyes lit up, and his bottom lip began to wobble. 'And you.'

Chapter Twenty-Four

It was a cruel twist of fate that Dominic was to be released on the day before the twentieth anniversary of Stephanie White's murder. Had the Prison Service realised this, would they have delayed it by a couple of weeks? Although I doubted Clare Delaney would have been happy about that. I had decided to be there when Dominic came out of prison. I didn't know what the future would hold for us, but for now, it felt like the right thing to do.

On the drive over to the prison in temperatures below freezing, Clare filled me in on the progress of the case against Maxton-Schwarz. Now that Dominic was released from prison, they could push ahead for a court date, so she could state categorically that the British government had accepted that Dominic Griffiths was not responsible for committing the heinous crime he had been imprisoned for and that one of their drugs had been the driving force behind him committing such a despicable act. Dominic should be compensated for losing twenty years of freedom. She was almost ecstatic at the prospect. I sat in the plush car, listening impassively.

It was eight o'clock in the morning, and the sun was beginning to appear on the horizon. The clouds were thick and heavy with snow. Winter was still maintaining its stranglehold. We stood outside the prison in the stiff breeze and waited.

There was no press, but Clare had lined up several interviews for Dominic with the national media over the coming days and weeks. The more money she could squeeze out of this story, the better for all parties, apart from the poor Whites, whom I thought of often. I'd phoned Barbara and kept her abreast of everything that was happening. Despite our different positions in the situation, we had a strong bond, and she'd even invited me to join her book club.

I felt underdressed standing next to the resplendent solicitor, who stood tall in her expensive-looking boots and heavy winter coat. I wore low-heeled boots, black trousers and the second-hand coat I'd bought from the market. I was often proud of my bargains, but beside a woman decked out in brand-new designer labels, my shabby-chic style looked trashy.

The gates began to open. I could feel Clare staring hard at me as if committing my exact expression to memory for when she told the press all about the reunion between father and daughter.

Dominic walked out of the prison. He had a plastic carrier bag in one hand containing all his worldly goods. He shivered as the cold hit him. He looked nervous, petrified even. As soon as he saw two familiar faces, his eyes lit up, and a smile spread across his face.

I smiled and slowly approached him.

'I never thought this day would come,' Dominic said. 'I have no idea what words to use to thank you,' he said to Clare.

She smiled back.

'I've got you a gift,' I said. From my bag, I pulled out a Penguin Clothbound Classic edition of *The Tenant of Wildfell Hall*. I handed it to him. 'Look inside.'

He opened the cover and read the inscription. 'Thirteenth of February 2019. To Dad, something for us to talk about over coffee. Love Dawn.'

He looked up. There were tears in his eyes. 'This is the best present I've ever received. Thank you so much.'

He pulled me into a tight embrace, and I hugged him back.

Clare took her expensive iPhone out of her pocket and took a couple of photos of father hugging daughter. I wouldn't have been surprised if she already had a tabloid newspaper lined up to buy them off her for a few hundred pounds each.

'Well, Mr Griffiths, your car awaits,' Clare said.

'I really can't believe all of this is happening. I'm just so overwhelmed.'

'It's a lot to take in, Dad, I know, but you'll get through it,' I said.

'Absolutely. You're a free man now, Dominic. This is your time.'

Clare got behind the wheel, while I got into the back with Dominic. We had a lot to talk about, a lot to plan for, and there was no time like the present to begin.

Part II

ONE YEAR LATER

Chapter Twenty-Five

Thursday, 2 January 2020

Dawn Shepherd really wasn't in the mood for being out of the house today. She'd had far too much to drink on New Year's Eve with Robyn and her boyfriend, Chris, who, on the stroke of midnight, had got down on one knee and proposed. Robyn had said yes, of course, and the rest of the night had been a blur of bottles of champagne and dancing. Dawn had no idea how she'd made her way from Robyn's flat to her own bed, but needless to say, New Year's Day had been a write-off, and she hadn't spent much time anywhere else but under her duvet.

The next morning, she had showered, put on a touch of make-up and styled her dark brown hair – having swapped the severe black beehive for a stylish bob – and left the flat, wrapping her long coat around her.

There had been a heavy frost the previous night, and it took a while for her to scrape it off the windscreen of the second-hand Peugeot she'd bought last summer. She missed her Golf but felt much more confident behind the wheel of something made this century.

With Dusty Springfield playing on the stereo, she drove along the streets of Newcastle to Atlantic Road, where her father lived alone in a two-bedroom semi-detached house.

The second of January usually marked the day most people returned to work after the Christmas and New Year break, but Dawn had learned from previous years' experience and had booked a couple of extra days off work to allow time to get over the hangover.

She pulled up outside her father's house. The curtains were still closed in the living room, but then, it was a dull start to the day. She climbed out of the car and made her way up the front path. She rang the doorbell and stepped back.

The door of the house two doors along opened, and a woman came out. She was wearing a dressing gown and slippers. She lifted the lid of her dustbin and dropped a heavy black sack into it. Dawn looked towards her. She was going to say good morning, wish her a happy New Year, but the woman looked daggers at her. They all knew who lived in this house, and they would have no doubt Dawn must be of the criminal class, by association. Dawn shook her head; the narrow-mindedness of some people never failed to shock her.

She rang the bell again.

There was no reply and no sound of movement from inside. She dug around in her handbag for the spare key Dominic had given her for emergencies. This wasn't technically an emergency, but it was freezing cold, and she was in urgent need of a pee.

'Dad, it's me. Are you decent?' she called out, as she stepped inside. It was as cold indoors as it was outside. She knew her dad struggled with things like paying bills and getting the heating to work after being in prison for twenty years. He couldn't get used to having to do everything himself, but she had helped as much as she could. She thought she'd explained his heating system enough for him to be warm and comfortable in his own home by now.

The small hallway led to a living room. She pushed open the door and stopped dead in the doorway. The room was a mess. The widescreen TV had been pulled off the wall. The sofa had been overturned and the coffee table smashed.

'Oh my God,' Dawn said to herself. 'Dad!' she called out.

She went all the way into the room and surveyed the damage. There wasn't a single item of furniture that wasn't broken or damaged in some way. She rummaged around in her pocket and pulled out her phone. With shaking hands, she dialled her mother, who answered on the second ring.

'Mum, it's me. I'm at Dad's. I think there's been a break-in.'

'What? Are you sure?'

'Yes. I'm in the living room. It's a mess, Mum. It's been completely destroyed.'

'Oh my God, that's awful. Where's your dad?'

'I don't know. He's not here,' she said, as she walked through the living room to the kitchen. The back door leading to the garden was wide open. She looked out but didn't see anything. 'What shall I do, Mum? Should I call the police?'

'Have you tried calling your dad?'

Dawn went back into the living room and stopped. Straight ahead, behind the table, on the floor, she found her father. He was lying in the corner, slumped against the wall. His face was a patchwork of cuts and bruises, and a large carving knife was sticking out of his chest.

'Dawn? Are you there? Dawn?'

Dawn stood frozen, staring at the father she had known for less than a year. There was nothing she could say.

Chapter Twenty-Six

Barbara White looked around the living room. It seemed bigger now the Christmas decorations had been taken down. She was relieved the festivities were over with for another year. Christmas was always a difficult time for her, even after all these years. She went into the kitchen and looked out of the window at the bleak landscape. The lawn was white with a layer of frost, the trees were bare, the thick gnarly branches reaching up into the sky, like cold, naked arms. On the ground, pathetic twigs stuck out of the soil. It was hard to believe, a few months ago, they were resplendent rosebushes, standing proud, their sweet-smelling scent floating on the warm summer breeze. Now, the ravages of winter had decimated the garden she loved. It would be ages before she'd be able to get out there and bring it back to life. The winter was dragging on, and there was no end in sight.

She released a heavy sigh. Turning her back on the window, she flicked the kettle on, looked at the kitchen and wondered when was the last time it had been decorated. It had to be nearly ten years ago. Maybe she should take advantage of being kept indoors on these cold January days and give the house a makeover.

The front door opened and slammed closed.

'Barbara, are you in?' Harry called from the hallway.

'Of course I'm in. I'm always in,' she replied. There was a hint of sadness in her voice.

Harry and Barbara would be celebrating their thirty-fifth wedding anniversary in August. As much as Barbara wanted to look forward to a lavish celebration, she couldn't help remembering those who should be part of it and wouldn't be. She couldn't have expected her mother to still be alive, but her sister should be, and her daughter *definitely* should be.

At six foot one, Harry stood a good eight inches taller than Barbara. He was wrapped up against the elements in a long beige overcoat, thick grey trousers and grey walking shoes. His woollen gloves, scarf and matching hat were all in the same tired-looking dull grey. He looked like he'd stepped out of a Seventies Littlewoods catalogue.

'It's parky out there,' he said, slamming the two heavy carrier bags on the table.

Barbara went over to unpack them.

'What have I told you about buying Christmas food?' she admonished, pulling out a Christmas pudding.

'It was on offer. Only a pound.'

'Don't you think we've eaten enough of this stuff already?' She pulled out three boxes of mince pies and a Christmas cake.

'They'll keep.'

'The shops love people like you. It's their own fault they have to reduce these things. If the prices weren't so high in the first place, they wouldn't have so many left over.'

'They're bargains.'

'We don't even like Christmas cake. It's not a bargain if it's just going to take up space in the cupboard gathering dust.' She began putting the useless shopping away, slamming doors and drawers closed.

'I bought this for you, too,' he said with a grin, pulling out a dark Chocolate Orange. 'Only one pound fifty.'

'They're only a pound in Morrisons.'

'Are they?' His smiled dropped. 'The robbing buggers.'

The kettle boiled, and Barbara went to fill the teapot. 'Harry, I've been thinking. Why don't we redecorate?'

'Redecorate?' he asked, as if he'd never heard the word before.

'Yes. We could strip the wallpaper in the living room, repaint the kitchen, and I'd love to get rid of that carpet on the stairs.'

'What's brought this on?'

'Nothing. I just thought it would be nice to have a change.'

'I don't know, Barbara, not with my back.'

'I'm not asking you to lay the carpet, just help me choose one. I'll help out. I like stripping wallpaper. It's therapeutic.'

'I'm not sure.' He pulled a face. 'All that mess and upheaval. Do we really need that at our time of life?'

'You're sixty-five, Harry, not eighty-five.'

'It just seems like too big a project.'

'Fine. Forget it.' She turned her back on her husband and poured hot water into the teapot.

'Is everything all right?' he asked, after he watched her throw the spoon into the sink and slam the teapot down on the table.

'Everything is absolutely fine,' she replied unconvincingly. She stood back and folded her arms tightly across her chest.

'Barbara, sit down,' he said, pulling out a chair at the breakfast table.

'I don't want to sit down, Harry. I want to pop down to B&Q and pick up some paint samples.'

'Sit down,' he said, raising his voice.

Reluctantly, she sat.

He sat opposite her, took her hands in his and squeezed them gently.

Barbara looked down at their joined hands. She saw liver spots, gnarled fingers, cavernous wrinkles and dulled skin. Getting old was cruel.

'Tell me what's going on.'

'Nothing's going on.'

'You've been in a mood for weeks now. Is it that seasonal affective disorder thing?'

'Oh for God's sake, Harry,' she said, snatching her hands back. 'No, it is not.'

'Then tell me. Come on. If you can't talk to me, who can you talk to?'

Barbara looked up at her husband. She stared into his eyes. 'You're right. Who else can I talk to? There isn't anyone left, is there? It's just you and me,' she said, barely above a whisper.

'Barbara, what's wrong?' Harry asked, tilting his head to one side like a dog hoping for a treat. 'You've been distant for a while now. I thought you'd have bucked up over Christmas but…' He trailed off.

Barbara reached forward and held her husband's hands. 'Harry, why don't we go away?' she asked, an expectant smile on her face.

'Away?'

'Yes. You know, a holiday.'

'We are going. Cornwall in June, like always.'

She resisted the strong urge to roll her eyes. 'I don't mean in the summer, I mean now.'

'Now?'

'Yes.'

'But it's January. Nothing'll be open.'

'I'm not talking about bloody Cornwall, Harry. I'm thinking about going for some winter sun. Imagine it, Harry – sat by a pool with a cloudless blue sky above us, sun beating down, a glass of cold beer in one hand and a good thriller in the other. Meals on the terrace of some Jamaican hotel overlooking the sea, watching the sun go down on the horizon.'

'Jamaica?' He wrinkled his nose.

'It doesn't have to be Jamaica. Spain. Greece. Turkey. Florida. Anywhere the sun is shining at this time of year.'

'I don't think so, Barb. You know I don't like flying.'

'Well, forget America then. We could have a driving holiday. Go through the Tunnel then down to southern Spain for a week or so and drive back. We could stop off at a few hotels on the journey for a few nights. A real road trip.' She gripped his hands harder and looked at him with a smile on her face, her twinkling eyes wide open.

'A driving holiday? All that time in the car? I'd seize up, Barbara. You know I'm not good on long journeys.'

She released his hands and closed her eyes tight in exasperation. She bit her bottom lip hard, to stop her from saying what she was thinking.

'Fine,' she said calmly, even though she was seething beneath the surface. 'Fine. We'll just stay here, shall we? Winter in Newcastle. Cold nights. Cold days. Frost. Ice. Snow. Wind. Rain. Bliss. I think I'll mix myself an Ovaltine cocktail and sit outside with a good book wearing five layers of woollen clothing.' She jumped up from the table and stormed out of the kitchen.

'Barbara, what the devil's got into you lately?' he asked, going after her.

At the bottom of the stairs, Barbara paused, her hand on the banister. She took a deep breath. 'You don't get it, do you, Harry?'

'Get what?'

She bit her tongue. 'It doesn't matter,' she said, a heavy sadness to her voice. She made her way slowly up the stairs.

'Is this about Dominic Griffiths?' Harry asked, from the bottom of the stairs.

She stopped, halfway up, and lowered her head.

'Barbara, we've been over this so many times.' He tried to placate her with a soothing tone.

She turned to face her husband. 'You can justify that man being released from prison as much as you want. I'm aware what the law says. He was sentenced by a jury of his peers. He served his time and is now free to go about his life—'

'He's not free,' he interrupted. 'He's out on licence. He has to…' He sighed. 'I'm not getting into this with you again. He's paid his debt to society, and that's that.' He headed back to the living room.

'For fuck's sake, Harry,' Barbara screamed, running back downstairs. She rarely swore. She hated swearing, but sometimes the situation called for it. 'Stop talking like a detective. You haven't been one for years. Talk like a father for once.'

'I haven't been one of those for years either.'

Barbara recoiled. 'You bastard,' she said. 'Stephanie may be dead now, but she was alive for thirteen years. We had her for thirteen years, and she will always be in here.' She tapped her head. 'And in here.' She tapped her heart. 'She is still our daughter. I am still her mother. And you are still her father. I can't even look at you right now.'

She went back up the stairs slowly. She felt sick and numb. Her legs were heavy, and a tension headache had taken hold of her brain, squeezing it hard like it was in a vice.

At the top of the stairs, she looked at the door next to her bedroom. Stephanie's room. She had last gone in there on Christmas morning to wish her a Happy Christmas. She wanted to go in there now, pull back the Newcastle United duvet, dive underneath, pull it over her head, go to sleep and never wake up again. She had nothing to live for anymore.

Chapter Twenty-Seven

Dawn was in the back of a police car, sitting next to a female uniformed officer who had sprayed far too much fragrance on that morning. It was an assault on the senses.

Dawn couldn't take her eyes off the house her father had lived in. White-suited forensic officers had arrived not long after the first attending officer on the scene. She had watched them suit up from the back of the car.

The police officer next to her spoke in faux soothing tones. 'I'm so sorry for your loss. Were you close? Try not to think of how you saw him just now; remember the good times.'

Dawn tuned her out. She wished she'd just shut up and leave her with her thoughts.

A car pulled up, and a man stepped out whom she vaguely recognised. She watched as he took a coat from the back seat and put it on. It looked too big for him, hanging from his shoulders as if from a coat hanger in a wardrobe. He looked up at the house. Dawn followed his gaze but had no idea what he was looking at. He shivered as a gust of cold wind seemed to chill him. He pulled the coat tightly around him and headed for the front door. He flashed his ID to a uniformed officer freezing to death on the doorstep before signing something and stepping inside.

Terry Braithwaite. Dawn remembered him from when she'd visited Stephanie's parents' house. He'd warned her to stay away from them. It was obvious he had hated her father and didn't agree with him being released. Surely he wasn't going to be involved in the investigation of his murder?

A white van turned the corner too quickly and screeched to a halt to avoid crashing into a forensics van. Dawn looked up and saw her mother had arrived.

'That's my mum. Can you let me out, please?' Dawn asked the officer.

Dawn rapped on the window to get her mother's attention. Rita saw her and ran over to the car, pulling open the door.

'Oh, Mum,' was all Dawn could say, before the tears started to fall again.

Rita lifted her daughter out of the car and pulled her into a tight embrace.

'Oh, sweetheart, I'm so sorry. What happened?' she asked the police officer.

'We don't know yet. It's possible he disturbed a burglar.'

'Mum, you should have seen him,' Dawn said, pulling herself out of her mother's embrace. She wiped her eyes. 'He'd been beaten. He looked a mess. And there was a knife…' she said, before the rest of her words were lost to tears.

'Can I take her home?'

'I think DI Braithwaite will want to have a word with her first. He'll be leading the investigation. She'll need to give a statement.'

'Will you stay with me, Mum?'

'Of course I will.' Rita held her daughter once more and looked back at the house.

It was an alien sight for Rita. She had only ever seen a crime scene on television dramas and had often wondered what they were really like. Seeing white-suited people milling in and out, she realised how spot-on the dramas were. She held her daughter tighter and closed her eyes. She had known something like this was going to happen. She had known Dawn meeting her father was going to end in tears, and she'd be left to pick up the pieces.

Bloody Dominic, she thought. *Why couldn't he have simply died in prison and saved us all this heartache?*

Chapter Twenty-Eight

Anthony Griffiths wrapped himself up against the cold. He was wearing a thick sweater, a heavy coat and his usual matching hat, scarf and gloves set he'd had for years. His socks were thick, and his walking boots were heavy. He locked the front door of his bungalow behind him, checking it was secure several times, before he tentatively made his way along the uneven pavement of Langdale Crescent, treading carefully to avoid patches of frost and ice.

He made his way slowly. His breathing was laboured as the cold breeze cut into his exposed face. His cheeks were red, his bulbous nose shining. He dragged his feet over the cracked concrete, his eyes firmly fixed straight ahead. He knew his destination.

Anthony hated cemeteries. He hated to see the fallen gravestones, whether it was at the hands of youths who thought destroying a person's final resting place was a good source of entertainment, or just destruction caused by the harshness of the North-East weather.

As he passed them, he couldn't help but steal a glance. Some were beautiful – black granite with gold lettering, ornate stonework, some even had pictures of the deceased. He offered a sympathetic smile when he read the dates of birth and death. It brought a lump to his throat when he saw graves for people younger than he was now.

He arrived at Carole's grave and slowly cracked his back as he bent down to replace the wilted flowers with a fresh bunch. He licked the corner of a tissue from his pocket and wiped away the bird shit on top of the marble.

'Happy birthday, love,' he said to his wife. 'I won't say your age out loud. I know how sensitive you always were about that. I've decided to bake you a cake this year. I don't have your flair, but I'm going to try and knock up a Victoria sponge. I've got a Mary Berry recipe.'

Anthony always felt self-conscious talking to his dead wife, as if someone might be listening and sniggering at him for talking to a slab of marble. He looked to his left. Further along the row, a young woman tidied up a grave, talking to whoever lay there. He couldn't hear what she said, just the mumbled utterances caught on the breeze.

'Dawn said she'll pop over later, and we'll have a bit of a tea. She often asks about you, what you were like and if you'd get on. I think you would have done. She's a bonny lass, Carole. I often think what would have happened if you'd… well, if we'd have let Rita be a part of our lives, and we'd known Dawn from the beginning. You'd still be here now, I think.'

He looked back at his wife's grave through blurred eyes as his tears began to fall. 'I…' He couldn't say what he wanted to say. The words stuck in his throat. He stayed silent, staring at the gravestone, his eyes watering as the cold stung them.

Anthony always struggled for things to say when he visited his wife. Alone at home, he'd look at her photograph on the mantel, and he'd not be able to shut up as he reminisced about the good times, the old days, how much he missed her, how much he still loved her. But actually coming to see her here at Blaydon Cemetery, his mind went blank.

'I'm going to get off now. I'm cold. Your fault for having a birthday in January. If you'd been a July baby like me, I could stay with you all day. I'd have brought some sandwiches, and we could have had a proper chinwag.' He half-smiled. He remained crouched in silence for as long as he could manage it before his legs began to stiffen. 'Sleep well, sweetheart.' He struggled to stand up, using the gravestone as leverage.

Anthony turned and walked away, wiping his tears as he left. She would have been seventy years old today. Fifty-one was no age to die. He kept looking back over his shoulder, until he could no longer see her grave, then he headed for home. A quick stop off at the Co-op, then back to his bungalow. He had a cake to make.

Chapter Twenty-Nine

Dawn felt like a criminal. She was sat in the back of the police car being driven through the streets of Newcastle to the station on Forth Banks. As she looked out of the window at the people heading for the shops or to work, wrapped up against the elements, she couldn't help thinking they were all looking up at the sight of a brightly coloured police car, glimpsing the person in the back and thinking she was guilty of something. She suddenly felt incredibly nervous.

Once in the station, she was taken straight into an interview room. She'd asked if her mother could sit in with her but that wasn't allowed, apparently. She felt like she should have known that, working in the legal profession. Being denied access to her own mum made Dawn feel even more like she'd done something wrong.

Twenty minutes later, the door opened, and DI Terry Braithwaite entered with a female colleague. He looked even thinner than when Dawn first saw him last year, older, too. His hair was flecked with more grey, and he had two-day stubble, which, Dawn admitted, looked sexy on him. His face looked lived in, but there was no getting away from those ice-blue eyes. Piercing. Electric. Hypnotic.

He introduced himself, then his partner as DS Kyra Willis. She was at least a decade younger than him, a good few inches shorter, but not much thinner, despite her being slight. Her shiny brown hair was pulled back in a tight ponytail that looked almost painful. Her face wasn't creased or lined. There were no marks, blemishes or scars. It was a perfectly smooth caramel colour. Dawn hated her on sight. At only twenty-two, she was already using anti-wrinkle cream and a serum to help fade the dark circles beneath her eyes.

'Ms Shepherd,' Terry began. 'You're not under arrest. You're free to go at any time. However, this interview will be recorded for investigative purposes. Do you understand?'

'Yes,' she said, her voice quivering slightly.

'First of all, I'd like to say I'm truly sorry about your father's death,' he said earnestly. 'We will do everything in our power to make sure whoever did this is caught.'

Dawn gave a weak smile.

'Now, when was the last time you saw your father?'

'New Year's Eve,' she said, without having to think. 'I went over there at lunchtime to have a coffee and a chat.'

'Did he have any plans for New Year?' Kyra said. Her accent wasn't local, and Dawn couldn't place it.

'No. He was staying in.'

'Was that unusual?' Kyra asked, making a note in her pad.

'Well, seeing as I'd only known him for about ten months, and he'd been in prison for twenty years before that, I doubt he *usually* did very much on New Year's Eve,' Dawn replied, an edge to her voice.

'Sorry,' Kyra said quietly.

'How did he seem on New Year's Eve?' Terry asked.

'Same as always. Relaxed.'

'There was nothing worrying him?'

'No.'

'No money or health problems?'

'Not that I'm aware of.'

'Had he received any animosity from his neighbours?'

'Well, they didn't know who he was when he first moved in, so he'd receive smiles and the odd hello then. But it wasn't long before the rumours started. When news got out, the smiles stopped, and people kept a wide berth. Some even crossed the road when they saw him.'

'How did that make him feel?' Kyra asked.

'Like a leper. He'd expected it, though. He tried to make out it didn't bother him, but I could see it did,' Dawn said, playing with her fingers.

'Was he considering moving out of Newcastle?' Terry asked.

Dawn looked up. She could see in his eyes he wasn't asking this question as a detective, but as someone close to Stephanie White and her family.

'Why should he? He was born and raised here. His father's here. I'm here,' she said, with defiance.

'When you first found out who your father was, how did it make you feel?' Kyra asked.

'Is that relevant to how he died?'

'I'm just trying to understand your relationship with him.'

'We had a good relationship. It wasn't easy discovering the father I didn't know I had was a convicted murderer, but the more I looked into it, the more I researched, the more I understood that he did not mean to kill Stephanie White,' she said, looking at Terry for his reaction when she mentioned Stephanie's name.

'Do you honestly believe that?' Terry asked.

'Yes. I do. Because it's the truth. Look, why are you questioning me like this? You should be out there trying to find out who killed him. Or don't you give a toss because he's a murderer who killed the daughter of one of your own?'

'We take every single case incredibly seriously, Ms Shepherd,' Terry said, a heaviness to his tone. 'I don't care what your father did in the past, but I will find out who killed him and make sure they answer for their crime to the full extent of the law.'

'But you do care. I can see it in your eyes,' Dawn said. 'When I mentioned Stephanie just now, you flinched. It was only slightly, but I still saw it. Are you really the right person to be leading this investigation?' she asked, leaning forward on the stained and scratched table.

'Ms Shepherd, I am a professional. I've been a police officer since I was twenty years old. I am more than capable of leaving my emotions at the door and doing the job to the best of my ability.' His fists were clenched, there was a vein throbbing in his neck and his leg was jiggling involuntarily under the table.

Dawn maintained eye contact. She allowed the silence to envelop them both. Kyra Willis might as well not have been in the room.

'So, what if the killer turns out to be Stephanie's father, former Detective Inspector Harry White? What if he went around to Dominic's house and killed him for what he'd done to Stephanie all those years ago? Would you arrest him?'

Terry swallowed hard. 'Yes. I would.' His reply lacked conviction.

'Really? The man is your father's best friend. He's a career template for you. You'd handcuff him, lead him to the car with everyone watching, caution him, interview him, inform the CPS to prosecute, and watch while he was handed a life sentence, a sentence which he wouldn't serve because, at his age, he'd most likely die in prison.'

Dawn could see Terry's nostrils flaring as he breathed deeply in and out. His lips were pursed, his blinking had increased. In the silence of the room, she thought she could even hear his heart pounding in his chest.

'Ms Shepherd, I understand you're upset, but we're deviating from our line of questioning,' Kyra said, clearing her throat. 'Could you tell us where you were from yesterday evening onwards?'

Dawn still kept her eyes locked on Terry. It was a while before she turned away. 'Yes. I was in bed for most of the day. I'm afraid I celebrated a little too hard on New Year's Eve. A good friend of mine had got engaged just after midnight.'

'Where was this celebration?'

'In their flat. We live in the same building.'

'What time did you get back home?'

'It was very early in the morning. Maybe three, four o'clock?'

'Did you go home with anyone?'

'No.'

'So, from four o'clock on the morning of the first of January until later that day, nobody can corroborate your story.'

'Actually, from four o'clock in the morning until early this morning, nobody can corroborate my story. I didn't see anyone. I spoke to my mum on the phone in the evening, but I was on my own until I left the flat this morning.'

'So, you have no alibi for the time of your father's death?'

'It would appear not.'

Dawn was told she could leave. There was no reason for her to stay, but they'd be in touch if they had more questions, Kyra told her, as she was led out of the police station with her mother in tow.

Terry watched from the door of the interview room. He waited until she was out of sight before he stormed off and took the stairs two at a time.

He was seething as he strode down the corridor. He entered the open-plan CID office, barging his way through the maze of desks, before throwing open his office door and chucking his notebook across the room.

He looked to see if Kyra was behind him. She was, but she'd had to run to keep up with him.

'What was that all about? Asking if I'd let the killer go if it turned out to be DI White who killed him?'

'She's upset. Her father has just been murdered, and she knows your history with the case,' Kyra said, moving a pile of paperwork from a chair and sitting down. 'Everybody in this station knows about Harry White and what he went through. Even I do, and I wasn't even living in Newcastle when his daughter was killed. It's as much a part of this city's history as coal mining. When I got my posting here, Stephanie White was the first name that came to mind. It's understandable that Dawn Shepherd is questioning how the investigation into Stephanie's killer, her father, is going to be run.'

Terry was by the window, looking out over the bright, but freezing cold, morning. His breathing had slowed. He was beginning to calm down.

'Maybe I'm not the right man for this case,' he said, not turning back. 'I think about Stephanie a lot, more so this past year. We were best mates. Her parents are like a second family to me. I don't think I can be objective in this.'

Kyra shrugged. 'Then go and see the Super and ask to be reassigned.'

'There's nobody else. DI Hillary is doing that undercover drugs case. DCI Markham has got cases coming out of his ears, and DI Sheffield is still on long-term sick leave.'

'Okay. Then here's what you do,' she said, a forcefulness to her voice. 'You strike while the iron's hot. The interview with Dawn this morning was a train wreck, but what you need to do – what *we* need to do – is show them how professional we are. Interview everyone with a possible motive. Wait for forensic results and see where we are. If we identify a suspect, whoever it is, we arrest them. Look, I'm not as close to this as you are, I'll arrest whoever it is, if it comes to it. I've no qualms about that.'

Terry turned from the window for the first time and looked at his DS.

'You'll need balls of steel for this case.'

'Not being equipped with actual balls, I ordered mine from Amazon, and I ensured they were made of the strongest stuff available,' she said, with a smile.

A hint of a smile spread across Terry's face. His cold eyes began to sparkle.

'I've got a dark feeling about this case. I feel like we're going to unearth something that should be left buried.'

'Maybe. But I'm prepared to do the digging, if it gets us to the truth. Are you?'

He took a deep breath. 'Yes,' he said, without conviction.

'Good. Then let's get started. Who are we going after next?'

He thought momentarily. 'Dominic's father.'

Chapter Thirty

Rita Shepherd drove Dawn back to her shop in Blaydon. She unlocked the door and shivered as she stepped inside. It was as cold in as it was out. The scent of flowers made Dawn sneeze. Rita turned on the lights, went into the back room and flicked on the kettle.

'Come and sit down,' Rita instructed her daughter. 'How are you feeling?'

Dawn sat, her coat hugged tightly around her. 'I don't know. All I know is the police aren't going to investigate this properly.'

'Yes, they will, Dawn. Their jobs will be on the line if they don't. They'll treat this like any other murder case.'

'That's rubbish, Mum, and you know it. If they don't find a suspect, they'll shelve it. I can see it happening. They won't find Dominic's killer, and they won't care.'

Rita set about making the tea. She took a pint of milk from the fridge, gave it a quick sniff to make sure it was still okay and poured it into two mugs. She glanced back at her daughter. 'Why don't you have a word with someone from work? They're bound to know people in the police.'

'They probably do, but something like this, well, the police all band together, don't they?'

'What about Dominic's solicitor? What was she called? That Delaney woman.'

'Clare Delaney.'

'That's her.'

'She won't care anymore. She got Dominic his big settlement fee, took her cut, and now she's on to the next case. I bet if I did go to see her, she'd start the clock and charge me a hefty amount for a five-minute consult.'

'You're calling him Dominic again,' Rita said, as she handed Dawn a mug.

'Sorry, what?'

'Since he was released from prison last spring, you've been calling him Dad. Now it's Dominic again. What's changed?'

Dawn held the hot mug in both hands. She was freezing, and it was slowly warming her up, fingers first, then hands and arms, as the warm blood started to flow through her veins. 'I don't know,' she said. Her bottom lip began to wobble. 'I suppose, if I call him by his name, then it gives me a bit of distance.' A tear fell from her left eye. 'It's a lot to deal with.'

Rita put down her mug and went over to her daughter. She wrapped her arm around her shoulders and pulled her close to her chest. 'Life is incredibly cruel at times, Dawn. We have to be on our guard, because if we take our eye off the ball for even a minute, something will come along to ruin everything.'

Dawn wiped her eyes with her coat sleeves. 'You said something like this would happen, didn't you? That it would all end in tears.'

'I did.' Rita nodded. 'But I had no idea it would end in someone being murdered.'

Anthony Griffiths was sifting self-raising flour into a mixing bowl. He was wearing an old apron of his wife's he hadn't realised he'd saved. As he began to mix the ingredients, the doorbell rang.

'Typical,' he said to himself. He wiped his floured hands on his apron and limped to the door. His left leg had seized up slightly – the effects of the cold weather, he guessed.

'Mr Griffiths?'

'Yes.'

'I'm DI Braithwaite. This is DS Willis. We're from Northumbria Police. Could we have a word?' Terry asked.

Anthony looked at each of them in turn. They were dressed smartly in black trousers and similar overcoats. They shivered on the doorstep.

'Oh. Yes. Of course. Come on in,' he waffled, stepping back and letting them enter the warmth of the house. 'Go on through to the living room, I shan't be a moment,' he said, as he began to untie the apron.

He went into the kitchen and turned off the oven that was preheating. He washed his hands and ran his bony fingers through his thinning hair before joining the police in the living room where he found them standing in the middle of the room like spare parts at a wedding reception.

'Sit down. Please. I'm sorry, I forgot to ask if you'd like a tea or coffee or something.'

'We're fine, thank you,' Terry answered for them both.

'Are you sure? It's very cold out.'

'Honestly, we're fine.' Kyra smiled.

They both sat, and Anthony took his usual place on the armchair. 'Sorry, I'm in a bit of a state,' he said. 'It would have been my wife's birthday today. I'm making a cake. We're having a bit of a tea later.'

'We?'

'Me and my granddaughter,' he said, with a smile.

'Mr Griffiths, I'm afraid we have some bad news,' Kyra began.

'Oh?'

'Your son, Dominic, was found dead in his house this morning.'

Anthony's mouth fell open. 'Dead? Good grief. What happened?'

'We think he might have disturbed a burglar,' Kyra continued.

'What does that mean? Did he have a heart attack or something?'

'He was murdered, Mr Griffiths,' Terry said. 'He was found stabbed.'

'Oh, good Lord,' Anthony said, closing his eyes and sinking into his chair. Something suddenly came to him as he sat bolt upright. 'Does Dawn know? His daughter.'

'Ms Shepherd found him this morning,' Kyra said.

'Oh, the poor girl,' he said, slapping a hand to his chest. 'She must be devastated. Where is she now?'

'I don't know. She gave a statement earlier. Her mother took her home, I presume.'

'I should go and visit.' He stood up.

'Mr Griffiths, we have some questions we'd like you to answer before you do that,' Terry said.

'Oh. Of course, yes. Sorry.' Anthony sat back down. 'Fire away.'

'Mr Griffiths, do you know anyone who would want to kill your son?'

'I don't understand. I thought you said he surprised a burglar?'

'That's one theory we're pursuing. However, it could just as easily have been someone who broke in with the prime intention of killing your son,' Terry stated firmly.

'I see.' Anthony frowned. 'Well, no, I don't. I mean, I'm sure you know about his past. He's not exactly popular, and I suppose there could be some people out there who were against him being released. Getting all that compensation probably didn't win him any friends either.'

'What compensation?' Kyra asked.

'I'm sure you know.'

'We do,' Terry said, nodding to Kyra. 'The amount was never released though.'

'No. It was all done out of court. His solicitor is a very cunning woman. She knew exactly the right things to say and do to make sure everything was done in private.'

'But him winning the compensation was made public, just not the amount?' Kyra asked.

'Yes. It made all the papers. I didn't agree with it myself. He was released from prison. He should have been content with that.'

'Do you know if your son received any threats?' Terry asked.

'You'd have to ask Dawn about that.'

'Surely he would have told you over a daughter he barely knew.'

Anthony adjusted himself in his seat. He looked in pain. 'I didn't see Dominic,' he said slowly.

'What do you mean?'

'The last time I saw Dominic was in September 1999 when he was sentenced to life in prison. I didn't visit him. I wanted nothing more to do with him.'

'But he was released almost a year ago,' Terry said. 'He was living less than a twenty-minute drive away.'

'I know. He wanted us to meet, but I didn't want to. I couldn't forgive him for what he'd done. It wasn't just Stephanie he killed. I blame him for his mother's death, too.'

'I have to ask this,' Kyra began. 'Where were you last night?'

Anthony gave a chuckle. 'You think I could have killed him? I have to have a sit down and catch my breath just getting dressed in the morning. But to answer your question, I was here all day. I watched a DVD until about ten o'clock, then went to bed.'

'Can anyone confirm that?'

'No, my dear, they can't. However, you're more than welcome to call my consultant up at the hospital and ask if a man riddled with bone cancer is physically capable of stabbing someone to death.'

'Oh.' Kyra physically paled. 'I'm sorry.'

'There's no need to apologise. You weren't to know. Are there any other questions you'd like to ask?'

Kyra looked to Terry who shook his head.

'No. I think we have everything, thank you.'

They both stood up. Anthony followed.

'We may need to talk to you again.'

'I'll be here,' he said, with a smile.

Anthony stood and watched as the detectives made their way to the front door.

'DI Braithwaite,' he called out.

Terry stopped and turned back.

'Are you a relation of—?'

'Yes,' Terry interrupted. 'I'm his son.'

'This must be extremely difficult for you.'

'All in a day's work,' he said, with a faint smile.

'It's not, though, is it? I really am incredibly sorry for what your father went through.'

'Thank you.'

'Is he still—?'

'Alive? Yes. Retired now, obviously. Goodbye for now, sir.'

Anthony watched them leave and the door close behind them. He went back over to his armchair and slumped into it. He was no longer in the mood to bake a cake.

Chapter Thirty-One

Terry's personal interest in the Dominic Griffiths case was playing on his mind. He hoped more than anything his godfather, Harry White, hadn't decided to take the law into his own hands. One way to find out was to ask him, but he needed to do that on his own. He told Kyra to make her own way back to the station and take a team out to the crime scene to do house-to-house enquiries – talk to Dominic's neighbours, find out what they had heard and seen the previous night.

He drove away from Langdale Crescent at speed, oblivious to Kyra standing on the pavement wondering how the hell she was going to get back to the city centre.

Terry's mother, Helen, had died from breast cancer when he was four years old. Despite knowing what she looked like thanks to the many photographs his father had taken of their life together, he couldn't conjure up a single memory of his mum, as hard as he tried.

His dad fell apart following the death of Terry's mum. He avoided being at home, where her memory lingered in every room. He threw himself into his work and allowed cases to consume him. He'd fall asleep in his office from exhaustion and run home whenever he had a quiet five minutes to shower and change his clothes. He neglected Terry. That's when Barbara had stepped in.

Barbara and Harry White were Terry's godparents, but they had become so much more, like his substitute parents really. Barbara had picked him up from school and taken him home. Sometimes, there would be a note scrawled on the back of a receipt or bill from Ian saying he might not be home that night, and Barbara would take charge. She'd tell Terry to grab a few clothes for tomorrow and his pyjamas, and he'd go home with her and Stephanie. If he was honest with himself, Terry had preferred being at the Whites' house. He knew he'd get a hot meal, his clothes washed and ironed, a comfortable bed in a warm room. He was loved there. Stephanie was his best friend and was like a sister to him. Then she went missing.

Terry pulled up in the Astra at the bottom of Harry and Barbara's driveway. Harry's Peugeot was parked outside, and there was a light on in the living room. He had no idea how they would take the news of Dominic's death. Harry and Barbara had been living with the aftermath of their only child's murder for twenty years. They had tried to move on and live comparatively normal lives, but whenever something happened to Dominic in prison, it made the newspapers. Whenever a child went missing, Stephanie was mentioned. Dominic's release and his compensation payout from Maxton-Schwarz had made headlines around the world, and once again, it had brought back the torment Stephanie had suffered at his hands. They never seemed to be free from the pain of their daughter being murdered. They would never forget her, but they were never given the chance to move on. Now, with Dominic's murder, Stephanie would be splashed all over the papers once more, and the nightmare would continue.

He knocked on the door and stepped back. He looked up at the house that had been his second home for most of his childhood. He had good memories here. He also had disturbing dreams that were set here. Watching Barbara and Harry fall to pieces after Stephanie was found, gathering in the living room for the wake after the funeral and listening to his father apologising over and over again for failing to find their daughter alive. This was a house of grief and sadness. It leached from the walls. Even birthday and Christmas celebrations couldn't be relaxing and happy. There was always a hint of melancholy in the air.

Barbara's face lit up when she opened the door and saw a familiar face. He was welcomed in with open arms, shown into the living room and told to sit down.

'You've lost weight,' she said. 'You're not looking after yourself, are you? When was the last time you had a cooked meal? That shirt could do with a good iron, and the hem is coming down on those trousers. You can come over here any time you want for something to eat. This is your house as much as is it ours. Tell him, Harry.'

'I don't need to. You've told him for me,' Harry said, with a smile and a roll of the eyes as Barbara headed into the kitchen. 'Barbara's right though, you don't need to wait for an invitation to come round.'

'Thanks, Harry,' Terry said. He proffered a smile, but it didn't reach his eyes. He felt uncomfortable here today. He sat on the edge of the armchair, taut like a coiled spring. He had no idea how he was going to bring Dominic Griffiths back into their lives without having to watch them falling apart all over again.

Barbara came in with a tray. She always was a good host. Terry turned down the offer of a sandwich, or a bacon butty, or scrambled egg on toast. A cup of tea was enough.

'So, how are things at Northumbria Police?' Harry asked.

'Oh, you know, the usual. Overworked, understaffed.'

'Nothing changes.'

Terry took a sip of his tea. He knew he was stalling.

'I need to tell you both something,' he said, not making eye contact. 'There's been a murder that I'd rather you heard about from me than the news outlets.' He swallowed hard. 'There's no easy way to say it, so I'm just going to come straight out with it.' He took a deep breath, still unable to look at them. 'Dominic Griffiths has been killed.'

He was still looking down into his teacup. When neither of them spoke, he looked up at two blank faces staring at him.

'How?' Harry asked quietly.

'I'm waiting to hear back from forensics, and the PM hasn't been done yet, but we think he may have interrupted a burglary. He was stabbed.'

'Oh' was all Harry could say.

'Barbara?' Terry prompted.

Her face was impassive. 'I don't know how to react. I feel like I should be pleased.'

'Barbara!' Harry chastised.

'Well, what am I supposed to say? I can hardly feel sorry for the man, can I? Anyway, I said I *feel* like I should be pleased. I didn't say I was pleased. I'm… I don't know how I feel, to be honest.'

'Have you identified a suspect yet?' Harry asked.

'No. I've got a team interviewing his neighbours.'

'Who found him?'

'His daughter.'

'Dawn?' Barbara asked. 'Oh, that poor girl. She must be in pieces.'

'Is she a suspect?' Harry asked, knowing the person who found the body was often the most likely perpetrator.

'Harry! Of course she isn't,' Barbara said.

'She doesn't have an alibi, but I don't think so,' Terry said.

'Well, it's karma, isn't it?' Barbara placed her cup on the tray and stood up. 'An eye for an eye and all that. He got what was coming to him.' She folded her arms across her chest and went over to the mantelpiece, picking up a photograph of Stephanie.

'It's not right, though,' Harry said. 'Nobody has the right to take the law into their own hands. Justice always prevails. I've said that all my life.'

'Well, it didn't in this case, did it?' Barbara said, almost shouting. 'Where was the justice for us, for Stephanie? He got life in prison, then he was let out twenty years later and given a million pounds to live comfortably for the rest of his life. That's not justice. That's sticking two fingers up at the law. That's rewarding someone for taking a life.'

'Barbara, not again. Not now,' Harry said, his face wrinkling at the notion of having to repeat the same argument. 'He wasn't just released. He wasn't a free man.'

'He should have been locked away without the possibility of parole. He cut my daughter into fifteen pieces. I don't care what kind of medication he was taking; he knew exactly what he was doing when he stuffed her into those bin bags.' She looked at Terry with tear-filled eyes. 'I'm not sorry he's dead. I'm glad. I'm thrilled that someone decided to stand up and take the law into their own hands. When you find out who did it, I know he'll have to go to prison for what he did, but I'll go see him, and I'll shake his hand and thank him for what he did.'

'Barbara!' Harry barked.

She replaced the photo of Stephanie on the mantel and slowly left the room and headed upstairs.

Harry and Terry fell silent while they listened to Barbara's footsteps. They heard a door open then slam shut.

'She's gone into Stephanie's room,' Harry said. 'She always goes in there when she needs to have a good cry.'

'I had to come and tell you, Harry.'

'Of course you did. Don't worry, she'll be fine.'

Terry cleared his throat. 'Harry… I have to ask…'

'You want to know where we were at the time of his death.'

'I'm afraid so.'

'When was he killed?'

'Some time last night.'

'Well, I was with your dad until gone eleven. I drove straight home and was back about half-past. There was very little traffic on the roads.'

'And Barbara?'

'She was at home all night. She doesn't go out on her own after dark. She was in bed by the time I got back.'

'Why didn't she go with you to see my dad?'

'Because I took my Clint Eastwood box set with me.' He smiled. 'She's never been a big fan of westerns.'

'Understandable.'

'Are you thinking this was some kind of vigilante delivering justice for him being released early?'

'I have to consider that possibility. A quick recce of the house showed there wasn't anything missing. He had a decent-sized TV, but it was smashed up rather than stolen.'

'You're going to hit a wall of silence – you know that, don't you?'

'This is not going to be an easy case to solve.'

'I wish you all the luck in the world, Terry.'

'I'm going to need it.'

Chapter Thirty-Two

A dejected Terry Braithwaite walked into the open-plan CID office. He was dragging his feet, and he had the hang-dog expression of a Basset Hound. While everyone sympathised with Harry and Barbara White for having lost their daughter in such a cruel and tragic way, and people had rallied around his father when he had found the body, and for his subsequent breakdown and, more recently, his stroke, nobody had ever asked Terry how *he* was coping. In the past twenty years, not one person had asked how the murder of his best friend at the age of thirteen had affected him.

After the murder, he had adopted the same strategies his father had used. He bottled up his emotions. He kept quiet and retreated into the background. Upon his return to school after the funeral, he had been subjected to lingering glances from fellow pupils. It was obvious they wanted to ask the gory details, but they were too afraid to. Teachers treated him like he was made of glass, and his friends distanced themselves from the new quieter, unsmiling, timid Terry Braithwaite.

And that's how he'd been ever since. College, university, police training. He'd kept his head down. He didn't make waves, he didn't stand out and he performed his duties to the best of his ability. He got results, but he didn't get the recognition and the glory, because he didn't want them.

Terry leaned over Kyra's shoulder and asked her to pop into his office.

'The Super was looking for you,' she said, as she closed the door and sat down. 'I told him you were informing the Whites of the murder before it leaked out to the press.' Terry looked at her with wide-eyed surprise. 'I'm psychic.' She smiled.

'You wish.'

'I do actually. I'd love to know what you're thinking right now,' she said, crossing her legs and staring at him.

'You really don't,' he scoffed.

'How did they take it?'

'The Whites? As you'd expect. They won't be shedding any tears.'

'Understandable. Neither will his neighbours.'

'You've spoken to them all?' He pulled out his chair and sat down.

'It didn't take long. Talk about trying to get blood out of a stone. Not one of them heard or saw anything.'

'Really?'

'Considering the violence of the attack and the level of destruction in the living room, it would be unlikely nobody heard any signs of a disturbance – furniture breaking, cries of pain, et cetera – but they all claim to have had the TV turned up loud or been asleep.'

'That's bollocks.'

'That's exactly what I said. Well, I didn't, but you know what I mean.'

Terry released a heavy sigh. He chewed on his bottom lip, his sign that he was deep in thought. 'Have forensics finished?'

'Yes. There are several different sets of fingerprints. Obviously Dominic's, and we're guessing his daughter's, but there are others. Let's hope they're on our system and there's a match.'

'We could do with another chat with the daughter. She'll have known him better than anyone. She'll know who his friends were, if he had any. Also, try and get hold of Dominic's solicitor; find out how much his compensation was and when he received it. I remember reading about it in the papers last year. There was talk of a seven-figure sum, but he was living in a semi in a crappy area. What happened to the money?'

'Will do,' she said, making a note. 'Before I forget, a jacket was found in the house that doesn't belong to Dominic.'

'How do you know?'

'It's a size small, and Dominic would have been a large, judging by his build.'

'Could it belong to his daughter?'

'There's no way she's a small. Besides, it's a man's jacket.'

'A friend could have left it.'

'Could have.'

'You don't think so?'

'It's the middle of winter. It's bloody freezing. Would you go round to a friend's house and go home without your coat on?'

'True. Okay, get it off to forensics, see if they can find a hair on it or something.'

'Speaking of hairs, they also found a single, long, black hair on the floor by Dominic's body.'

'And Dawn has brown hair.'

'Exactly.'

'Okay. Well, at least we've got something to go on.'

'We've had the press on the phone.'

'I'm shocked.' He grinned.

'What do you want me to say?'

'Nothing. We'll issue a press release later today, just giving the basic facts. Apart from that, we say nothing.'

'This is going to be a big deal.'

'I'm aware,' he said, running his fingers through his hair. 'But I don't want this turning into a circus. I don't want the press raking everything up from twenty years ago again.'

'You know they're going to,' Kyra said, trying to sound sympathetic.

'I know. It's what they're good at. I just don't want them upsetting Harry and Barbara.'

Kyra studied her boss for a while. 'You're very fond of them, aren't you?'

'They were like parents to me when I was growing up. They still are in a way.'

Terry had a wistful look in his eye, and his mind seemed to drift as he stared into space.

'Right then,' Kyra said, standing up. 'I'll go and find this solicitor.'

She stood in the doorway and turned back to look at the sad expression painted on her boss's face. She couldn't help but feel this case was going to have an adverse effect on him. The Superintendent should never have laid it on his shoulders. He wasn't strong enough.

Chapter Thirty-Three

There was still one person Terry hadn't told about Dominic Griffiths' death – his father, DI Ian Braithwaite. Terry visited him often in the residential home he was now living in, but it was a fifty-fifty gamble whether Ian would be lucid or not. There were times he didn't even recognise Terry. That was heartbreaking. Despite Harry and Barbara being excellent substitute parents, there was nothing like the real thing, and Ian was the only true family member Terry had left. He decided he'd pay him a visit that night after work, and if his dad was of sound enough mind to hear the news, Terry hoped he'd take it in a similar way to the Whites and not descend into a deep depression.

From the police station, Terry drove to Dawn's flat in Ryton. For the purpose of the investigation, he needed to know what Dominic had been up to in the year since his release from prison.

He pressed the intercom and stood back, looking up at the grey building. He wondered if he should sell his dad's house and go for something cheaper and smaller. He didn't need to be living in a four-bedroom house. He never understood why his father had bought it in the first place. The residential home wasn't cheap, so Terry could certainly do with the funds.

'I wondered when you'd come calling. Push the door.'

Terry raised his eyebrows at Dawn Shepherd's stern tone. He pushed open the heavy security door and made his way to the top floor. By the time he reached it, she was already standing in the open doorway.

'Ms Shepherd. I'm not sure if you remember me—'

'From this morning? Of course I do.'

'I meant from… Well, it was about—'

'Last year, you mean? When you threatened me? Yes, I remember.' She turned and went back into the flat. He followed, closing the door behind him.

'I did not threaten you, Ms Shepherd.'

'You stated, very clearly, that I was to keep away from Barbara White and her husband. Your tone was threatening. You actually frightened me.'

Dawn was stood by the kitchen units. She had her arms tightly folded across her chest. She was wearing black tracksuit bottoms and a dusky pink top. Her dyed brown hair was resting on her shoulders. It was damp, and her face was red from the heat of a recent shower. There was a scent of fragranced shampoo in the air.

'I'm sorry,' he said, looking down at his feet. 'That was never my intention. Harry and Barbara have been through a great deal over the years. I feel very protective towards them.'

Dawn's face softened. 'I can understand that. Shall we put it behind us and move on?'

'I'd like that,' he said, an awkward smile on his face.

'Would you like a cup of tea or something?'

'I'd love a coffee. It's cold out there.'

'I'm afraid it's not much warmer in here,' she said, as she set about making them both a drink. 'I've finally got my landlord to repair my boiler, but if I try and get the thermostat any warmer than fifteen degrees, the boiler can't cope, and it dies on me. Thank goodness for woolly jumpers.' She looked over her shoulder and smiled at him. 'No need to stand on ceremony. Take a seat.'

'Thank you.'

He sat on the sofa and looked around the flat. It was basic and compact, but it had everything Dawn would have needed. There was a small table and chairs in front of the window, which she obviously used more for work than eating, judging by the open laptop and files next to it. A large-screen TV dominated the feature wall, and a table was placed beneath it. There was one door leading off, which Terry guessed led to the bedroom and bathroom.

'Milk and sugar?'

'No milk. One sugar, thanks.'

She brought the drinks over and placed them on the heavily stained coffee table. She went back to the kitchen area, picked up a plastic tub and plonked it next to the mug. She removed the lid, and Terry saw it was full of chocolate bars. She told him to help himself after she extracted a Mars and a Twix.

'I shouldn't really. I've been on a big diet for months, but I eat when I'm nervous. Actually, I eat when I'm excited, scared, sad and angry. Food is my comfort blanket.'

'Do you need a comfort blanket?' he asked, while rifling through the tub.

'My father has just been murdered, of course I do.'

'Sorry. That was insensitive of me.' He opted for a Crunchie. He unwrapped it, picked up his coffee and sat back, crossing his legs at the knee. 'What can you tell me about your father?'

'What do you want to know that you don't already?'

'What has he been doing with his life since he was released last year?'

'Adapting,' she said, dunking the Mars into her coffee and

swirling it around. 'Well, trying to adapt. It's not easy getting used to life on the outside when you've been locked away for twenty years. It took him a while to get used to the changes. I didn't realise how difficult it would be for him.'

'How do you mean?'

'Well, he did a few courses while in prison on computers, so he was able to use them, understand the basics, but things like social media, iPhones, flat-screen TVs, self-service tills in supermarkets – that was all another world to him. I had to show him how to do everything, and he hated not being fully independent. He had to keep reminding himself that he was still only forty-one, because he felt like an old man with dementia at times.'

Terry looked away. That's what it was like dealing with his father.

'But he managed to adapt?'

'Oh yes. He had a job.'

'Where?'

'The supermarket in Blaydon shopping centre. I used to go to school with a girl who works there. I asked her if she could have a word with the manager, and he got him a job in the warehouse and stacking shelves after the store closed. It wasn't what my dad wanted to do, but we were treating it like a confidence booster, a stepping stone to something better. It gave him a wage, independence and the chance to meet new people.'

'Did it work?'

'He'd only been there for four months.'

'Plenty of time to make friends.'

'I'm not sure he did make friends. He never talked about anyone.'

'What did they think of him working there, given his past?'

Dawn adjusted her position on the pine dining chair at the table. Her eyes danced around the room.

'What are you not telling me?' Terry asked.

'We thought it would be best if people didn't know who Dominic was.'

'We?'

'Me and Dominic.'

'His name was splashed all over the papers in the run-up to him being released.'

'Yes, but there was no new photograph of him – just the ones of him taken twenty years ago. Prison is hardly a health centre. He'd aged a great deal in those two decades locked away. He was unrecognisable.'

'What are you saying?'

'Well, we just got him the job using his middle name rather than his first name.'

'What was his middle name?'

'Rupert. After his grandfather.'

'So, everyone at work knew him as Rupert Griffiths, not Dominic?'

'Yes. It's not a crime, is it?'

'No. No, it's not. And nobody at work twigged his real identity?'

'If they did, he didn't tell me about it.'

'Were there any incidents at work, anything that you can think of which might have led to someone wanting to kill him?'

'I thought you said it was a burglary gone wrong?' Dawn said, as she opened the Twix.

'That's one theory. Obviously, given Dominic's past, we can't rule out the possibility of a vigilante.'

Dawn closed her eyes and shook her head. When she opened them, a tear rolled down her cheek.

'At the back of my mind, I always feared something like this would happen.' Her voice was softer. 'Whenever we went out anywhere together, I'd constantly be on my guard, looking around for people who might recognise him. I got a bit paranoid about it at times. I wanted him to live a normal, happy life. I didn't want anyone ruining it for him.'

'And did they?'

'No. It didn't stop me worrying though.'

'How did he manage to get the house on Atlantic Road?'

'His dad found it for him.'

'His dad?' Terry looked confused. 'I was led to believe Anthony Griffiths didn't want anything to do with his son.'

'He didn't, but that halfway house Dominic was staying at wasn't ideal. Also, a few of the people there took against him, who he was, despite them being murderers themselves. A couple of them attacked him. Anthony saw the house was for rent and told me about it. I set the wheels in motion.'

'It's nice to know he had people around who were there for him,' Terry said, though it stuck in his throat to have any sympathy for someone who had murdered and cut up his best friend.

'I was disgusted at first, when I discovered my dad was a killer, but I could see he was sorry for what he'd done. He genuinely wanted to repent. I think he did.'

'Despite always maintaining his innocence?'

'Despite being unable to remember the truth,' Dawn corrected him.

'The compensation claim,' Terry said. 'The amount was never disclosed in the press.'

'No. We all discussed it and thought it was best to keep as much of it private as possible. We didn't want Harry and Barbara getting more upset.'

'How much was it?'

Dawn paused. 'It was a million pounds. Obviously, Dominic didn't get that amount. His solicitor took a cut and there were fees to pay.'

'Huh. But he must have received a substantial amount.'

'He did,' she said, her face impassive.

'Yet he was still living in a rented semi on Atlantic Road.'

'Yes. He liked it there.'

'Forgive me, but I've been in Dominic's house. Apart from the big TV, there's nothing there that screams luxury.'

Dawn sighed. 'When you've been in prison for twenty years, simply having a door on the toilet is classed as a luxury. There was nothing Dominic wanted beyond a decent-sized TV and a few books.'

'What was he planning to do with the compensation payout?'

'I believe that is none of your business,' she said, a stern expression appearing on her face. 'Now, if you wouldn't mind, I'd like to spend some time on my own. I saw my father with a knife sticking out of his chest a few hours ago, and I'm struggling to keep hold of my sanity, and my emotions.'

'Of course,' Terry said. He drained what was left of his coffee before standing up. 'Thank you for your time. And the coffee.'

'You're welcome.'

Dawn remained on the pine chair. She didn't move and didn't watch Terry as he went over to the front door and let himself out.

She stared at the wall, shrouded in silence. DI Braithwaite seemed like a competent detective, but it was obvious he was a man haunted by his past, a past that was connected to Dominic Griffiths. Despite it being proven that Dominic had not been in control of his own mind when he killed Stephanie, the fact still remained that he had killed her. How deep would Terry dig to find the murderer of the man who had caused so much upset in his life? Would he care all that much if Dominic's killer was allowed to remain free?

Dawn leaned forwards in her seat and rummaged around in her snack tub. She smiled when she found a packet of Maltesers. They were her favourite.

Chapter Thirty-Four

'Kyra, have you been to see the solicitor yet?' Terry asked, standing outside Dawn's block of flats with his phone to his ear. A strong gust of wind made him shiver. He seemed to be feeling the cold more lately. He was going to have to change his lifestyle. There were days when he'd hardly eat, surviving only on coffee and whatever was in the vending machine at the station.

'No. I've got an appointment at three o'clock.'

He looked at his scratched watch. He'd make it into town in plenty of time. 'Text me the address of her office, and I'll come with you.'

'Something up?'

'Possibly. Before we meet, could you do me a favour and try and get hold of Dominic's bank statements?'

Kyra had been vague about the details when arranging the meeting with Clare Delaney. She had told her it was related to one of her clients but didn't say which one. Before they entered the building of Ripley, Blumenthal and Partners, Terry checked with the station, and online, that the story of Dominic's murder hadn't been released. He didn't want Clare being forewarned. He knew how sneaky solicitors could be. Fortunately, the press was still clueless.

'How much do you reckon they charge for the hour?' Kyra asked in a low whisper.

They were sat on Chesterfield sofas in the expensively decorated waiting room.

'I shudder to think,' Terry replied, not bothering to whisper. 'Don't be intimidated though. I bet, behind the scenes, the rooms the public don't see are a complete shithole.'

'Do you think?'

'Of course. Look at that chandelier – it's caked in cobwebs. But how many people look up? The law business is shallow. It's all about impressions. Nothing else. Don't be fooled if she starts talking about the importance of justice. That goes out of the window the moment you get your name engraved on a brass plaque.'

'Your cynicism is incredibly sad at times,' Kyra said.

'On this occasion, it's spot-on.'

The door opened, and Angelina led them towards Clare's office. The receptionist didn't smile once.

Clare stood up from behind her unnecessarily large desk when the detectives entered the room. She was wearing a pin-striped suit, white shirt and dark grey tie. Her dark red hair rested on her shoulders. It was huge, like a mane.

'Clare Delaney. Lovely to meet you,' she said in a strong, deep voice that screamed insincerity.

'Detective Inspector Terry Braithwaite. This is Detective Sergeant Kyra Willis,' Terry said, emphasising his Geordie accent.

They all shook hands, and Clare told them both to take a seat. She waited until they were seated before she did the same. She seemed to know all the rules in the book about how to give the impression she was powerful and in charge.

'So, you want to talk about one of my clients. Before you do, I must remind you of the laws relating to client confidentiality.'

Terry was itching to make a sarcastic comment but decided against it, for now. 'We are aware of the law, Ms Delaney. First of all, just to confirm, you were the solicitor who represented Dominic Griffiths in his early release from prison and his subsequent compensation claim against Maxton-Schwarz?'

'I was,' she said, with a proud grin.

'When was the last time you saw Dominic?'

She seemed taken aback by the question. 'It would have been the day we settled the claim. We were prepared to take the case to court. That was my intention. However, at the eleventh hour, Maxton-Schwarz made a generous offer that Dominic chose to accept. I arranged the paperwork, he signed, we shook hands and that was that.'

'On to the next claimant?' Terry couldn't hide the derision in his voice.

'You make is sound so cold, Detective. I'm sure you're exactly the same. You arrest someone then move on to the next case. You don't go and visit the murderer in prison to see how they're coping, do you?'

He couldn't help but smile. 'I suppose not.'

'What's this all about?'

Terry looked at Kyra and gave her the nod.

She cleared her throat. 'I'm afraid to say that Dominic was found dead at his house earlier this morning.'

'Good grief,' Clare said, slapping a hand to her chest. She looked genuinely shocked by the news. 'How did he die?'

'He was murdered,' Terry said, almost matter-of-fact.

'Murdered? That's deplorable.'

'Indeed. Obviously, given Dominic's history, we need to explore who might have wanted to kill him. Is there anything you can tell us about him that may help in our investigation?'

She thought for a moment. 'I'm not sure. I don't think so. I try not to get involved in my clients' personal lives. I've made that mistake in the past. Some start to believe you're their friend and latch onto you. When you move on to the next case, they can take offence. It can get quite ugly.'

'So you wouldn't know where Dominic was living or working?' Kyra asked.

'Well, we have his address on file, I'm sure. I wasn't aware he was working, no.'

'Purely for elimination purposes, could you tell us where you were last night?' Terry asked, with a smile.

She returned the smile. 'Of course. I finished here around six, went home and had dinner with my husband. We went to bed around eleven, and I slept until the alarm went off at seven o'clock this morning.'

'You worked on New Year's Day?'

'Only for a few hours in the afternoon. I have a case in court on the fourth.'

'I hope you don't mind me asking, but was Dominic's compensation claim on a no-win, no-fee basis?'

'Yes, it was,' she answered clearly.

'So, when a settlement was reached, he received one hundred per cent of the claim, and your costs were paid by Maxton-Schwarz?'

'That's correct,' she said, the smile disappearing.

'I only ask because Dominic's daughter, Dawn Shepherd, told us his compensation was for one million pounds. Yet' – Terry made a play of reaching inside his coat pocket for the bank statement Kyra had given him outside – 'his bank statement clearly shows a payment of only eight hundred thousand pounds going into his account.'

Clare's eyes darted around the room, while she searched for something to say. She blinked rapidly and swallowed hard.

'That's correct,' she said eventually. 'It was a gift.'

'A gift?'

'Yes. Dominic wanted to give me a gift for all my help. I told him it wasn't necessary, but he insisted.'

'Isn't that against the rules?' Kyra asked.

'Not at all. Providing the gift is declared, it's fine.'

'Did you declare it?' Terry asked.

'Yes, I did,' she replied, looking away.

'Really? Tell me, Ms Delaney, do all of the claimants you deal with *offer* you a gift? Or do they not even realise they're giving you one?'

'I'm sorry?' Her eyebrows shot up.

'If Dominic was the one giving you a gift, then the whole one million pounds would have gone into his account, then two hundred thousand pounds would have been transferred to you. His statement clearly shows just eight hundred thousand pounds went into his account from the company account of Ripley, Blumenthal and Partners. There was no gift, was there? You told Dominic Griffiths that your cut of the claim was twenty per cent, and he accepted it.'

'You're wrong,' she said, fingering her collar.

'I don't think I am.' He stood up, and Kyra followed. 'I think we're done here, Ms Delaney. I'm working on a murder investigation, and I don't consider you to be a suspect so there's no reason for us to talk again. However, you will be hearing from someone in the fraud squad, and I'm guessing the lovely people at Her Majesty's Revenue and Customs will be in touch. Have a good day.'

'You enjoyed that, didn't you?' Kyra said, when they left the building and stepped into the cold afternoon air.

'Call me a flawed human being if you like,' he said, with a grin. 'I don't get much to smile about in this job, but occasionally the right situation presents itself.'

'I wonder how much she's been creaming off her clients over the years?'

'I wouldn't be surprised if it runs into millions.'

'She'll go down for it, won't she?'

'If she's been keeping the money for herself then Ripley and Blumenthal will throw her to the lions, and she'll get a very long time inside. If they're in on it too and taking their own share, it'll be so deeply hidden that they'll lie and cheat their way out of the worst of it and probably just get a hefty tax bill.'

'I'll keep my fingers crossed the lions will have something to snack on soon,' Kyra said, with a grin.

'Ooh, if I didn't know you better, Kyra, I'd say you were being bitchy.'

She looked at him over the roof of the car. 'I *was* being bitchy. Sometimes it's necessary. Where to now?'

He looked at his watch. 'Do you mind if I drop you off at the station? Check up on forensics then take an early night. We'll need to be bright and early for the post mortem in the morning, and I doubt we'll be able to hold the press off much longer. Tomorrow is going to be a long day.'

Her face lit up at the mention of an early finish. 'Would you like to come round to mine for your tea? It's Matthew's turn to cook, and he's doing chicken cacciatore. It's delicious.'

'Thanks for the offer, but there's somewhere else I need to be. Some other time?'

'Sure.'

By the time Terry dropped Kyra off at the station, the day was starting to fade into night and the streetlights were coming on. The suggestion of a home-cooked meal had sounded wonderful. He couldn't remember the last time he sat down to a proper meal and enjoyed it. Unless he had a takeaway, his culinary skills only went so far as piercing a film lid and throwing the container in the microwave for three minutes. If Kyra had lived alone, he would have accepted her offer. A bite to eat with a colleague was manageable. But the prospect of making small talk with Kyra's husband filled him with dread. He didn't do light-hearted conversation. He was much more comfortable chatting over a post-mortem report or gruesome crime scene photos. No wonder he had very few friends.

From Forth Banks, Terry drove through the busy city centre streets, until he hit open country. He turned up the volume on his playlist and slammed his foot down on the accelerator. It was a long drive to his father's nursing home, and he enjoyed breaking the law to get there.

Chapter Thirty-Five

Lavender House Nursing Home was on the outskirts of a village called Edmundbyers in County Durham. It was twenty-five miles away. There were many homes closer to the city that could cater for Ian's needs, but this was the only one Terry could afford without having to sell his father's house. That was something Ian would not allow to happen.

After Ian had suffered the stroke two years before, it was decided that he could no longer live on his own. Terry had sold the flat he hated and moved in with his father, but his demanding job wasn't compatible with his being a sole carer. Harry and Barbara helped as much as they could, but Ian needed specialised care from qualified nurses. Reluctantly, Terry had admitted defeat and began looking for nursing homes that could accommodate his father.

Lavender House was a privately run home. It catered for residents who had suffered massive strokes or were in the final stages of dementia. Despite the newness of the building, the soft lighting, the plush furnishings and the smiling staff in their pastel-coloured uniforms, the atmosphere was heavy and depressing.

Even to a visitor just sitting in the car in the car park and looking up at the bright place with its well-manicured lawns, neatly trimmed hedges and rooms with balconies, the place gave off an atmosphere of false hope and abandonment.

The staff knew Terry by name and greeted him like a friend. He didn't need to explain who he was visiting or be shown where to go. He just signed in, exchanged a few meaningless pleasantries with the receptionist, then headed for the stairs to the third floor.

Terry tried to remain positive when visiting his father, but the more visits he made, the more he was there to witness his dad's slow decline, the more painful they became. He could feel his hope ebbing away with every step along the overheated pastel corridor.

He pushed open the door to his father's room and entered. When he'd first started visiting, the intense heat used to stifle him. It was energy-sapping, and he often felt himself nodding off in the easy chair. Now, he was used to it and sat by his father in exhausted comfort. He could already feel his shirt sticking to his back.

Ian was sat up in bed. He looked a decade older than his sixty-two years. His eyes were wide and devoid of their old sparkle, and they were blank as he stared at the far wall. He was unable to feed himself, dress himself or even bathe himself, and his memory was patchy.

He recognised his son, and Harry and Barbara, when they visited. However, once they were gone and staff asked if he'd enjoyed their visit, he wouldn't recall that anyone had been to see him.

'Hello, Dad,' Terry said, taking his father's hand and shaking it.

'Who is it?'

'It's me. Terry. Your son. You feeling all right?'

'I'm tired.'

'Aren't you sleeping well?'

'Not that kind of tired.'

Terry bit his bottom lip and dropped his gaze. He quickly changed the subject. Living in denial of the inevitable wasn't easy but ignorance really was bliss at times. 'Dad, do you remember me telling you about Dominic Griffiths being released last year?'

'Bastard,' he spat.

'Dad, he's dead. Someone killed him.'

Ian turned to look at his son. The sparkle in his eyes was back. 'Dead? Someone murdered him?' Terry nodded. Ian clapped his hands together and let out a hearty laugh. 'Excellent. That's wonderful news.'

'Dad!' Terry admonished.

'Oh, come on, Terry, the man was a killer. There are very few people who witnessed first-hand what he actually did. I was one of them. I had to pick Stephanie's body parts out of bin bags. Do you really expect me to mourn that evil bastard?'

'No. No, I don't,' Terry said, taking his father's hand.

'Who did it?'

'I don't know.'

'Are you investigating?'

'I am.'

'Don't bother.'

'What?'

'Leave it. His killer doesn't need putting away; he deserves an OBE. Tell your boss you've hit a dead end. He won't even care.'

'Dad, I can't do that.' Terry was shocked. He was surprised his father was even suggesting it.

'Of course you can. He deserved everything he got. I hope he rots in hell. Have you told Harry and…?' He struggled to find Barbara's name in his memory. Terry didn't help him. His dad liked to remember himself rather than be reminded. 'Barbara. Barbara. Have you told them?'

'I have.'

'I bet they were elated, weren't they?' he asked, with a grin.

'No, Dad, they weren't.'

Ian looked at his son suspiciously. 'Hmm. I bet when you left, they were dancing around the living room. Oh, Terry, that's the best news I've heard in a long time. Stephanie can finally rest in peace now that fucker's dead and gone.'

'There are people mourning him. He's got a daughter. I told you, remember?'

'Harry has a daughter?'

When Ian became confused, his eyes changed. It was as if a fog had descended. He was looking at Terry, but he wasn't seeing him. Terry knew not to push the conversation. If Ian couldn't remember, it would only make him more agitated. Terry stood up.

'Where are you going?' Ian asked.

'I'm going to check your bathroom, see what you need.'

Ian's room was designed to be a small flat. There was an en-suite bathroom and an off-shot kitchen. A table for two beneath a window. It was warm and cosy, but he wasn't at home, and that's what Ian wanted more than anything else.

Terry came out of the bathroom, making a note in his mobile of the things his father needed.

'Can you put a few more books on here for me?' Ian asked, holding out his tablet.

'More books? You read those quickly.'

'What else have I got to do all day? I can't even go out into the gardens because it's too bloody cold.'

'Has Harry been to see you?'

'Has he fuck,' he said, tutting and rolling his eyes.

Terry knew he'd forgotten. Harry had been there just yesterday. And Barbara was always popping over with something she'd baked for him.

'You've read all the Lee Child novels. Shall I choose a new author for you?' Terry asked, scrolling through his tablet.

Ian crawled off the bed and went over to the window. He looked out at the barren winter landscape.

'Dominic had a daughter,' he said.

Terry looked up. 'I know, Dad. I told you.'

'She'll know who killed him.'

'Why will she know, Dad?'

Ian turned back from the window. 'Because she knew him. She'll have spent the most time with him over the last year.'

'I've spoken to her twice, Dad – she doesn't know.'

'Do you believe her?'

'I've no reason not to.'

He sat back on the bed and picked up the tablet. 'You've every reason not to. *The Firm*. Wasn't that a film?'

'Yes, it was,' Terry said, a frown on his face.

Terry stayed with his father for another hour. He always felt a lump in his throat when he was leaving, just in case it would turn out to be the last time he saw his dad. He could have another stroke that could kill him. He could become confused and fall, crack his head open on the toilet or something. Ian was the last blood relative Terry had. He wasn't ready to say goodbye to him yet.

On his way out, Terry wanted to ask the receptionist to check the visitor book and see if Harry's alibi stood for the night of the murder, but nobody was behind the desk. He made a mental note to follow it up another time and made his way outside. He felt uneasy. It was more than just a niggle in his brain. What Ian had said about Dawn was right. He didn't know much about her at all, and now her father was dead, she would inherit his compensation claim. Money was the biggest motive for committing murder, and who needed money more than a trainee paralegal with a massive university debt hanging over them?

Chapter Thirty-Six

Terry lived only a five-minute walk from Harry and Barbara. On his way home from seeing his father, he decided to turn off and pop in for a visit. It was pitch-dark outside, yet not quite ten o'clock. He guessed they would both still be up.

Harry was dressed in comfortable trousers, a cardigan and slippers, while Barbara looked more relaxed in pyjamas and a dressing gown.

'Harry, telly off, Terry's here,' she said, as she led Terry into the room.

'Don't turn it off on my account. I just stopped in on my way home.'

'Been to see your father?' Harry asked.

'Yes.'

Harry and Barbara exchanged glances. They noticed the sad look on Terry's face, the way he said 'yes' with a heavy sigh, and the way he dropped into the armchair.

'Can I get you anything, Terry?' Barbara asked.

'I'm fine, thanks.'

'Something to eat? There's some shepherd's pie left.'

'No. Honestly, I'm fine. Thank you.'

'How is your dad?' Barbara sat down and placed her hands in her lap.

'The usual.'

'Did you tell him about Dominic?' Harry asked.

'Yes. He practically danced around the room.'

'Well, I can understand that,' Barbara said.

Harry looked over at his wife and gave her a blank stare. Terry could see what he was thinking. He couldn't get her to see how Dominic's murder was not the solution to the problem. They wouldn't suddenly get their daughter back. Their grief wouldn't be lifted. Nothing would change for them.

'How's the investigation going?' Harry asked.

'Who cares,' Barbara muttered under her breath.

'I care,' Harry almost shouted. 'I'm interested. A man has been murdered. It's important his killer is caught and faces justice.'

'We're waiting for forensics to come back on a few items found at his house, but we've hit a brick wall when it comes to witnesses,' Terry said. 'The neighbours all claim to have heard nothing, but if you'd seen the state of the house, someone must have heard something.'

'They're not talking because they don't want to get involved,' Harry said.

'No. They're not talking because they don't care. It's good riddance to bad rubbish,' Barbara injected.

Harry visibly baulked. He jumped up. 'I'm not going through this with you again.'

'We'll be having this conversation time and time again, until you admit that man got his just deserts,' she called after him, as he went into the kitchen. She turned back to Terry who looked uncomfortable in the armchair. 'Sorry about that.'

'It's okay. I understand. It must be difficult for you both.'

'It's always difficult for us. It's got worse since Dominic was released.'

'Is there anything I can do?'

Barbara looked over her shoulder to see if Harry was coming back into the living room. He wasn't.

'Don't find his killer,' she said, her voice hardly a whisper. 'I'll want to recommend him for a knighthood while Harry will say prison. It'll drive an even bigger wedge between us. I don't want to end my life hating the man I'm married to.'

Terry looked at her with wide-eyed fear on his face. He had always been under the illusion Harry and Barbara had grown closer following Stephanie's death, that their grief had bonded them and made them stronger. He had had no idea how fragile their relationship really was.

Chapter Thirty-Seven

STEPHANIE WHITE'S KILLER MURDERED

Dominic Griffiths, the killer of thirteen-year-old Stephanie White, has been found stabbed to death at his home in Winlaton.

Griffiths, 41, was released from prison last year following the introduction of new evidence that he was taking a now banned prescription drug at the time of the killing which had altered his mental state. He went on to receive an undisclosed compensation payout from the makers of the drug.

Northumbria Police were at the rented semi-detached house in Atlantic Road all day yesterday, and a post mortem is due to be carried out today. Leading the investigation is DI Terry Braithwaite, son of DI Ian Braithwaite, the detective in charge of the case which secured Griffiths' conviction for the murder of the tragic teen. The junior DI Braithwaite was unavailable for comment last night.

Police sources have told the *Chronicle* that neighbours have put up a wall of silence and are claiming to have heard and seen nothing at the time of the murder. One neighbour, who doesn't want to be named, told us: 'It's understandable nobody is saying anything. That man was pure evil. The Bible says an eye for an eye, and he certainly got what was coming to him.'

DS Kyra Willis turned into Atlantic Road and pulled up outside Dominic Griffiths' house. Now the story of his murder was in the public domain, there was more pressure on the police to find the killer, and quickly. This was a huge story, and the media would be feeding on it for a long time to come. A child-killer, one of the most hated men in the country, had been murdered. The tabloids would be stoking the flames, and if the killer wasn't swiftly caught, it could lead to copycat crimes and other vigilantes taking the law into their own hands.

Kyra stood on the pavement and looked around her as she buttoned up her coat. The road was silent. Kids were still on holiday, but nobody was playing outside. Yes, it was too cold to be sitting in the front garden, but they'd have received bikes and skateboards for Christmas. They should be out on them before the novelty wore off. She thought she saw a few curtains twitching and could feel the eyes of every resident burning into her.

There were five pairs of semi-detached houses and one detached on Atlantic Road. Cars lined both sides and some residents had turned their gardens into driveways. Built in the Fifties, the houses were spacious, and they all had chimneys, something lacking from modern-day new-builds. They also had character. Each one would tell a fascinating story about the families who had lived in them over the past seventy years.

Kyra headed up the path of the house next door to Dominic. If anyone had heard anything on the night he died, it would be the people who lived directly next door. She could hear her footsteps resounding around the eerily silent street. She shivered and not from the cold. She knew she wasn't welcome here, and it was simply because she was investigating a crime nobody wanted solved.

She rang the doorbell and stood back. She'd left her notes at the station and couldn't remember who lived here, but she would need to come across as friendly and approachable if she was going to have any chance of them opening up to her. She tried to soften her face from the frown she was wearing and blew out a breath she hadn't realised she was holding.

The door was opened by an elderly woman in her early eighties. She was bathed in a warm glow from behind, and Kyra could feel the heat from the central heating reaching out to her, almost pulling her in.

'Good morning, I'm DS Willis from Northumbria Police,' Kyra said, showing her ID. 'I'd like to have a word with you about your neighbour, Dominic Griffiths.' She smiled her warmest smile and hoped it didn't look too creepy.

'Oh.' The elderly woman's face dropped. She looked over Kyra's shoulder at the rest of the street, her eyes darting left and right. 'I didn't know him,' she answered quickly. 'I don't think I said more than a dozen words to him in all the time he was living here.'

'I can understand that, but I need to know if you saw or heard anything on the night of his death. There are several lines of investigation we're following, and one of them is that he was killed when he interrupted a burglar. Obviously, one less burglar on the street will make us all sleep easier in our beds at night.' Kyra's smile was starting to make her face ache, but if she could just get inside and chat to the woman, she might be able to get her to open up.

'Oh. I didn't realise. I suppose you'd better come in.' The old woman stepped to one side and allowed Kyra to enter.

While showing Kyra into the living room, Milly Preston told her a potted history of how she had ended up living on Atlantic

Road. She'd moved there twenty years ago, after she divorced her husband when she was sixty-three. They'd been married for thirty years, and she'd woken one morning, realising he bored the living daylights out of her and she'd go mad if she had to spend the rest of her life with him. For her, life had begun at sixty-three, and she was loving it.

Milly's home was modern and stylishly decorated. Framed photographs adorned every surface, showing Milly and various other people grinning at the camera against backgrounds of famous landmarks around the world. Kyra couldn't help but smile.

'So, you think it was a burglary gone wrong then?' Milly asked. 'I do have a pretty good security system, but technology advances so quickly these days, doesn't it? Do you think I should upgrade?'

Kyra felt bad about frightening her. 'Not necessarily. Though it wouldn't hurt to have a review, I suppose.'

'I'll give them a call. Ask them to send someone round,' she said, the worry leaving her face.

'Mrs Preston—' Kyra began.

'Milly, please.'

'Milly. We believe Dominic was killed at some time in the night on New Year's Day. We've been round to every house in the street, and nobody seems to have heard anything. I can understand people's reluctance to get involved, but it really is important we find out what happened to him. He has a daughter. She's only in her early twenties, and despite what he did, he is her father.'

Milly nodded. 'I can understand that.'

'I don't suppose you saw or heard anything on the night he was killed, or you've seen anything suspicious lately?'

Milly leaned back in her comfortable armchair. 'I remember the Stephanie White case. Well, who doesn't? It was one of those cases that had the whole country hooked. She was a pretty little girl.

Mind you, he was a handsome lad, if memory serves me correctly. Although he looked completely different when he moved in here. You wouldn't have thought it was the same person. Prison does that to you, I suppose. He was a good neighbour though. Never any trouble. He took a few parcels in for me. I'm always ordering from eBay, and then I forget I've ordered and bugger off out.' She laughed. 'I chatted to him a couple of times.'

'What about?' Kyra asked.

'Just general chit-chat really. I asked if he was settling in, and he said he was. He was busy decorating when he wasn't working. He said he wanted the place all done up in time for Christmas. To tell you the truth, I'm a bit of a nosy sod,' she said, with a devilish grin. 'I asked if he was married, any kids, you know, like you do when you want the gossip.'

'What did he say?'

'He said he wasn't married, but he had a grown-up daughter.'

'Did he have any other visitors that you noticed?'

'No. I never saw… No, I tell a lie, I did see one woman come to visit him. She came twice. Well, I didn't see her the second time, but I saw her car parked outside. A great big brand-new Range Rover it was. Personalised number-plate.'

Kyra knew who that was straightaway. Clare Delaney.

'I don't know who she was, but I didn't like her on sight. She looked up and down this street like she had a bad smell under her nose. Stuck-up mare.'

Yes, that was definitely Clare Delaney.

'Anyone else?'

'No, love. Like I said, he kept himself to himself. He went to work; he came home. That was it. He put his bins out when he should, and he didn't leave them at the edge of the road like some people around here.'

'What about the night he was killed? The neighbours who did talk to us said they didn't hear anything.'

'They would do. Him that lives next door, Ray Fisher, now he might not have heard anything. He's out almost every night and often comes back with a different woman. Dirty bugger. Her at number nine, she's got three small kids by three different fathers. They're only young, so they would have been in bed at the time he was killed. She must have heard something, and if she said she didn't, she's lying.'

'Thank you,' Kyra said, making a note in her pad.

'Now, what was I doing on New Year's Day?' Milly smiled to herself. 'Same thing as I do every night – sitting and watching TV. All I heard was the cars.'

'Cars?'

'Yes. Slamming doors. I was down here, watching *Pride and Prejudice*. You'll be too young to remember Colin Firth as Mr Darcy, won't you?' Kyra shrugged. 'Do yourself a favour and watch it. Best version I've ever seen. I like to watch it every now and then. It makes me smile. Anyway, I was watching that when I heard bam, bam, bam. Three car doors slamming shut. Then I heard tyres squealing. I got up and had a look through the crack in the curtains, just as a Peugeot 206 was turning left at the bottom of the road.'

'You're sure about the type of car?'

'Definitely. I had one myself for years, until some bastard nicked it from the car park in the Metro Centre.'

'You didn't get the number-plate by any chance?'

'No, love. It was dark, and I only saw it for a few seconds.'

'Is there anything else you can remember? Anything leading up to him being killed?'

Milly thought for a moment. 'Now you come to mention it, yes, there is. That car. The 206. It wasn't the first time I'd seen it. It had driven up and down here a few times. I saw it just before New Year. It drove down here, slowly, and then turned left at the bottom.'

'Do you know what day that was?'

'No. I was… actually, I'm lying again. Hang on.' Milly went over to the solid oak sideboard. She opened a drawer, took out a slimline Betty Boop diary and brought it back to the sofa. She licked her finger and flicked through the pages. 'Here we are: Monday, the thirtieth of December, Christmas tea at Alice's. A week late because she was in hospital from the fifteenth. She slipped on ice and bruised her coccyx.'

'That was two nights before Mr Griffiths was killed. He was murdered on the night of the first.'

'So he was.'

'So the car was driving up and down on the night of the thirtieth, obviously checking to see if the coast was clear.'

'Do you think so?'

'Where were you when you saw it?'

'I was getting out of a taxi.'

'Did the driver of the Peugeot see you?'

'He must have done because the taxi was blocking the road.'

'Did you see the driver?' Kyra asked, almost daring to get excited.

'No. It was dark. I was cold and just wanted to get in. Here, do you think they were going to kill him that night but saw me and decided not to?'

'I'm not sure. It's possible, I suppose.'

'Oh, I don't like that.' She shivered.

'No. Me neither,' Kyra mused. 'Thank you so much for agreeing to talk to me. You've been a big help.' She stood up.

'Have I? I haven't told you anything though.'

'You've given us a lead to follow. That's something. I might need to call on you again, is that all right?'

'That's fine, dear, any time. Although I'm going to Cancun at the end of the month. That's still all right, isn't it?'

Kyra smiled. 'Only if you take me with you.'

Milly laughed. 'There's six of us going and not one of us is under eighty. You'd be bored silly.'

On the doorstep, Kyra stopped and turned back. 'Sorry, I have to ask – why Cancun?'

'Why not?' Milly shrugged.

Chapter Thirty-Eight

Terry had been due to attend the post mortem of Dominic Griffiths first thing, but by the time he got off the phone to the Press Office trying to find out how the hell the story had been leaked to the media, he was too late. He was pleased. Attending a post mortem was never the highlight of the day, and when the person was the man you despised more than anyone else, it was difficult to find any compassion for how he had died.

Terry sat in his office with the door closed. He knew he was the wrong man to lead this investigation, but there was nobody else. In every murder investigation he'd ever conducted, he'd sympathised with the victim and their family and wanted justice to be served. This time, it wasn't so clear-cut.

He put his head down on his desk and closed his eyes. He had some serious soul-searching to do. He couldn't go to the Super and ask to be reassigned, because he didn't want to risk coming across as weak or unprofessional. He was a good detective, and he didn't want anything to interfere with his professional reputation. He loved the job. He needed it. It was all he had.

That left only one thing he could do, and that was to try and put his personal feelings aside and solve this case as quickly as possible.

'I've been looking all over for you.' Kyra Willis approached Terry, who was sat at a table in the canteen. She pulled out a chair and sat down, unable to take her eyes from his scrambled egg on toast. 'You don't look like you're enjoying that.'

'I'm not.'

'Eggs made last week again?' she asked, with a smirk.

'No. I'm only eating it because I felt a bit faint. I'm not enjoying it.'

'You're far too thin, Terry. It's not healthy.'

'I just don't seem to have much of an appetite lately,' he said, pushing it away only half-eaten.

'Aren't you finishing that?'

'No.' He looked at her, as she licked her lips. 'You can if you like.'

'Thanks,' she said, pulling the plate towards her. 'There wasn't enough milk for cereal this morning, so I only had a crumpet.' She cut off a few large chunks of toast and chewed.

'How did it go on Atlantic Road?' Terry asked. 'Did you have to threaten any of the neighbours with a taser to get them to talk to you?'

Kyra quickly chewed and swallowed. 'No. I put on my little-girl-lost look, and a sweet old dear told me all about a Peugeot 206 seen cruising the area over the past couple of nights.'

'Why didn't she tell us yesterday when uniform knocked on her door?'

Kyra shrugged. 'She didn't want to get involved.'

'So, why get involved now?'

'Because uniform don't have my expertise when it comes to chatting to elderly ladies.' She grinned.

Terry wasn't listening. 'What car does Dawn drive?'

'What?' Kyra was taken aback by the sudden change of direction. 'A Peugeot.'

'Colour?'

'Black. It's not a 206, though.'

'You don't happen to know the reg plate, do you?'

'No. It's not brand-new though.'

'Last year, she was driving a shitty Golf that didn't look like it could get out of second gear without bursting into flames.'

'How do you know?'

'I... just know,' he said. 'What I'm saying is, how can she afford a newish car, when she's on a trainee paralegal's salary, lives on her own and has several thousand pounds' worth of university debt hanging over her?'

Kyra thought for a moment. 'Maybe her mother helped her out.'

'Her mother runs a florist's. She's hardly Alan Sugar.'

'Maybe her dad bought it for her out of his compensation claim.'

'Along with the large TV in her flat.'

'There's nothing wrong with a father buying his daughter gifts. My dad bought me a slow cooker for Christmas.'

'What if he didn't buy them for her? What if she asked for them? What if she laid on the guilt trip, saying he owed her after not being in her life from day one? What if she asked for more, and he said no?'

'You don't think Dawn killed her own father, do you?'

'She doesn't have an alibi. She got home in the small hours on the first and spent most of the day in bed, recovering.'

'As did a large majority of the country.'

'But we only have her word for it. Look, go and see her, find out exactly who she was with on New Year's Eve and see if their stories match.'

'Really?' Kyra asked, with a screwed-up face. 'You're really considering her as a suspect?'

'Dominic Griffiths isn't your normal victim. I don't believe this was a burglary gone wrong. I believe someone wanted him dead for what he did twenty years ago, and they succeeded. That could be anyone: his neighbours who took against him living on their road, his colleagues, his own daughter, her mother, even his own father.'

'And what about the Whites?'

'Sorry?'

'Harry and Barbara. If we're talking motive, they have the best one of the lot. Are they suspects too?'

It was a while before Terry replied. 'Yes,' he said, matter-of-factly. 'Although I have spoken to them, and they have an alibi for the night of the first.'

'Really?'

'Yes. They were home together,' he lied. But it reminded him he needed to check up on whether Harry was at Lavender House like he claimed.

'Not much of an alibi, is it? Each other.'

'Come on, Kyra, they're in their sixties, for crying out loud.'

'So? Sixty isn't old. Matthew's dad's in his late sixties, and he still runs marathons. Milly Preston is in her eighties, and she's off to Cancun at the end of the month with her friends.'

'Harry and Barbara aren't the running type. They're not the jet-setting type, and they're certainly not the killing type either,' he said harshly.

'I'm sorry, sir, but they're exactly the type. He murdered their daughter, cut her up, and he was rewarded with a million pounds. Putting myself in their position, I'd want Dominic dead.'

They sat in silence, both of them contemplating the implications.

Terry had known Harry and Barbara his whole life. Surely he would be able to detect a change in their behaviour that would reveal they'd just killed a man. But Harry was a detective, too. He'd know what Terry would be looking for and would know how to hide it.

'Jesus,' he said, his head falling to his chest.

Kyra reached across and placed her hand on his. 'I'm sorry, sir. I didn't mean to upset you. I know how close you are to them.'

'I'm too close to this.' He looked up. There were tears in his eyes. 'If Harry and Barbara…' He couldn't finish his sentence.

'I'm sure it's not them,' Kyra said quickly. 'I was just playing devil's avocado.' She winked. 'Look, I'll go back to Dawn and check on her alibi. We need to solve this as quickly as possible, before it eats away at you. And, no offence, you can't afford to lose any more weight.'

He smiled and remained seated as Kyra walked out of the canteen. He looked around him. Others were giving him sidelong glances. They'd all read the papers. They all knew what case he was working on. He couldn't stand the sympathetic looks. He needed to get out of the station.

Chapter Thirty-Nine

Dr Jamie Glendenning was in his office eating his long-delayed lunch of an egg mayo sandwich and a packet of ready salted crisps. He looked up when he heard a tap on his door.

'Detective Inspector Braithwaite, I expected you here at nine o'clock.'

'Yes. Sorry. I—'

'You ask me to make Dominic Griffiths a priority, put him to the head of the very long queue, and then don't bother to turn up? You certainly know how to make a man feel worthless.'

'I gave you an expensive bottle of whisky at Christmas.'

'Which my wife thoroughly enjoyed,' he said, looking at Terry over the top of his glasses. 'Anyway, I'm not one to hold grudges. Pull up a chair, and I'll give you all the gory details you missed out on.'

'The highlights will do.'

'Look at the name on the door. Does it say Gary Lineker? I do not give highlights, Detective Inspector.'

'You really hate your routine messed around with, don't you?'

'I do. Especially when today was supposed to be my day off. I was called out on Christmas Day to a suspicious death in Cramlington and on Boxing Day to Ogle. I've had exactly six hours with my family this festive season.'

'Ah.'

'Indeed. Now, your chap Dominic Griffiths,' he began, selecting the file on his laptop and opening it. 'He certainly made my start to the year an interesting one. Every single one of his ribs was broken.'

'You're joking?'

'I'm aware of the police's penchant for gallows humour at a crime scene, but it does not enter my autopsy suite. I never joke,' he said flatly, his face emotionless.

'Sorry. Go on.'

'His nose was broken, as were several of his teeth, a number of which we found in his stomach. His last meal, by the way, was a chip sandwich. His body was covered in contusions, abrasions, and he was hit around the trunk of his body with something long, narrow and cylindrical.'

'Like a pipe?'

'More like a baseball bat, I'd say. His liver, by the way, was a couple of punches short of exploding. It was almost treble the size it should have been. He also suffered a fractured skull and a subdural haematoma. To you that's—'

'Bleeding on the brain,' Terry interrupted.

'You're learning! Well done.'

'So, what actually killed him?

'Unsurprisingly, it was one of the stab wounds. He was stabbed four times in the chest. A direct hit to the heart. It wouldn't have taken long for him to die. He was already badly beaten by then. I would've thought it was a blessing for his body.'

'If he hadn't been stabbed, would he have survived?'

'Highly unlikely.'

'Then why stab him after beating him to a pulp?'

'Fortunately, that's a question I don't have to answer.'

'Could a woman have done this?'

'Of course she could have. A few whacks with a baseball bat to incapacitate him, then she could have her fun. So to speak. Why, do you have a suspect in mind?'

'I'm afraid to say I do.'

'Isn't that usually a cause for celebration, rather than disappointment?'

'Usually. However, I get the feeling the person who has done this is incredibly clever and will have covered every single one of her tracks.'

'Then I wish you the best of British luck, inspector.'

Anthony Griffiths opened the door to find Rita and Dawn on his doorstep. Rita was holding a bunch of flowers, and both women had grim expressions on their faces.

'I'm sorry I didn't come around yesterday, Anthony. I know you wanted to celebrate Carole's birthday, but after—'

'You don't have to apologise. I understand. Come on in.' He held the door open wider for them to enter, and closed it firmly behind them. He shivered from the cold.

'I brought you some flowers from the shop.' Rita handed him the bunch. 'I was going to bring them yesterday for the birthday, but, well…' She faltered.

'They're lovely. Thank you. Would you both like a drink?'

'Shall I make it?' Dawn asked.

'If you would. You know where everything is.'

Dawn took the flowers from him and went into the kitchen. Anthony returned to his usual armchair, though it seemed to cause him pain to sit. Rita perched precariously on the edge of the sofa.

'Are you all right?' she asked. He looked at her. 'Sorry, silly question. Have you taken your medication today?'

He nodded. 'It doesn't seem to be working anymore. I've been on to the doctor, and he's increased the dose. Hopefully, it'll kick in soon. So then, what about this business with Dominic?' he asked, changing the subject.

'Yes. I'm very sorry about it,' Rita said. She leaned forward and placed her hand on top of his. 'It's just so horrible.' Her voice was full of emotion, but there were no tears in her eyes.

'Thank you, Rita. But I suppose he got what was coming to him. There was a lot of ill feeling about him being released from prison.'

'I know, but for someone to have killed him. Well, it's disgusting. I mean, what kind of a country are we living in where people think they can take the law into their own hands?'

Anthony winced in pain and looked down. He played with his fingers but didn't say anything.

'Have the police been in touch? Do they know who's done it yet?' Rita asked.

'They came by yesterday. I don't think they have any idea who's responsible, though.'

'Listen, Anthony, if you need anything, you only have to ask,' she said, with a smile.

'Thank you, Rita. That's very kind of you.'

The phone started to ring, but Anthony didn't move.

'Would you like me to get it for you?'

'No. It'll be someone from the papers. They've been ringing all day. I should unplug it really.'

Rita took a deep breath. 'Anthony, would you like to come and stay at mine for a few days? There's plenty of room.'

'No. I couldn't impose like that. I just want to be on my own.'

Dawn came into the room carrying a tray with three mugs on it and a large Victoria sponge cake in the middle. Despite Anthony not being in the mood to make the cake after the police had left, that morning he'd thought it would be a good activity to take his mind off things. After all, he'd bought the ingredients and hated things going to waste.

'I thought we'd cut into this. It looks lovely, doesn't it, Mum?'

'It looks better than any I could make. Dawn, tell him about the cake I made for your sixteenth.'

'Oh my God. She made this cake that was supposed to be three layers, but she used the wrong flour. She didn't notice and still iced it. It looked like a big biscuit rather than a cake.'

Anthony gave a weak smile.

'You still ate it, though,' Rita said.

'I never say no to cake.'

Dawn cut into the cake Anthony had made and handed out three slices. Hers was the smallest. Her new diet allowed her the odd treat, but she didn't want the taste of those delicious calories to undo all the work she'd done in the past six months to remove the weight. The phone started to ring again, and they all ignored it.

Anthony waited until the ringing stopped before he spoke. 'How are you doing, Dawn?'

'I'm okay. I don't know… I can't seem to settle.'

'You're in shock,' Rita said, munching on the cake.

'I think we all are,' Anthony said. He was using his fork to turn his slice of cake into crumbs. He hadn't eaten any. 'To be perfectly honest, I wanted him to die in prison. I always imagined getting a phone call or a letter from someone telling me he'd been beaten up or he'd committed suicide. I didn't want him being released and returning to Newcastle. I knew something like this would happen.'

'You couldn't have known, Anthony,' Rita said.

'He was my son,' he said, with a broken voice. His eyes filled with tears. 'He was my…' He couldn't finish. His words were lost to his emotion.

Dawn, the nearest, stood up and perched on the edge of the armchair. She placed an arm around his shoulders and held him to her.

'It's all right, Grandad. It's all right to be upset.'

She looked at her mother, who was looking down at her cake, her bottom lip wobbling slightly as she struggled to contain her tears. Dawn knew her mother. She was a very emotional person and always cried when she saw other people crying. She cried whenever anyone died in a TV soap or a child hugged his grandfather in an advert for life insurance.

'I just…' Anthony tried again but still couldn't speak. He waited a moment then wiped his eyes on his sleeves. 'I just keep thinking about Carole. If someone had done this twenty years ago, she might still be alive now. That's why I'm upset. I miss her so much.' He fell into Dawn's arms again, and she held him tighter.

Anthony was crying for his dead wife. Rita was crying just because Anthony was crying. Dawn's eyes were dry. Dominic had been dead for little more than twenty-four hours, and nobody was crying for him.

Chapter Forty

Terry drove to Lavender House. He wanted to talk to his father. He had no idea what about, but he couldn't help wondering if Harry and Barbara might, in some way, be capable of murdering Dominic Griffiths. It was a ridiculous notion. The level of violence inflicted upon him had been savage. Yes, they hated him, but could they murder him with such intensity? It was time to find out if he needed to consider them suspects.

He parked, got out of the car and made his way to the reception desk. He asked the smiling receptionist if he could check the visitors' book, and there, on 1 January at 7.30 p.m., was Harry's signature. Terry let out an audible sigh of relief. Harry was in the clear, and there was no way Barbara could have attacked and killed Dominic on her own. He felt like the weight of the world had been lifted from his shoulders.

Terry thanked the receptionist and walked down the corridor, entering his father's room with a couple of carrier bags. One contained fresh toiletry supplies for the bathroom, the other had a sandwich for each of them along with some fruit, chocolate bars and a couple of paperback novels.

'Terry, I didn't expect to see you today.'

Ian was sitting by the window, looking out over the back gardens. They were usually landscaped and vibrant, but at this time of year they had an unkempt, abandoned look about them. He was reading his tablet and had a cup of tea on the table in front of him. It would be easy to look at him and think he was simply having a lazy afternoon reading a book and enjoying his retirement. Sadly, the truth was very different.

'I thought I'd pop over with some things.' Terry raised the bags. 'I've brought you a sandwich from that shop in town you used to like, with the crusty rolls.' He took out a paper bag and placed it on the table. 'Hot roasted pork with apple sauce and stuffing.'

Ian's eyes lit up. 'Delicious.' He tore open the paper bag, took the huge sandwich in both hands and held it up. He inhaled the aroma and closed his eyes. 'It's been years since I've had one of these.'

It was a couple of months ago, actually, but Terry didn't say anything.

Ian took a bite and chewed slowly, savouring every morsel.

Terry sat opposite his father at the table and tucked into his own sandwich. He hadn't realised how hungry he was.

'How's the book?' Terry asked, to break the silence.

'I'm enjoying it. This John Grisham bloke used to be a lawyer himself.'

'Did he?' Terry asked, though he already knew.

'Yes. It was a film. I looked it up on that website you told me about. Tom Cruise and… can't remember his name.'

'I'll get the DVD for you if you like.'

'I'd like that. We could have a film night.'

'Sounds good,' Terry said, with a smile. 'Listen, Dad, can I ask you something about Harry and Barbara?'

'Of course you can,' he said, taking another bite of his sandwich.

'I know Barbara's always wanted Dominic to rot in prison, but what were Harry's feelings towards him?'

It was a while before Ian replied. He chewed slowly, swallowed, licked his lips and frowned as if in deep thought.

'Harry was a born detective,' he eventually said. 'Always on the side of law and order. If anything happened, he said the law would sort it out. It didn't matter what case we were on – murder, rape, kidnapping, drugs, domestic abuse, riots – Harry trusted the law would see the perpetrators caught and sentenced accordingly.'

'But what about when the law didn't work? What about when some smart-arse lawyer got a killer off on a technicality? How would Harry react then?'

'He'd blame himself.'

'How?'

'He'd say he hadn't worked hard enough to secure the conviction.'

'Sometimes, things are beyond our control,' Terry said, placing his sandwich down on the paper bag they were both using as a plate.

'I agree. Criminals don't want to get caught. And they'll do everything they can to get away with their crimes. They'll lie, cheat, deceive, blame others, even kill, to save their own skin.'

Terry couldn't help but feel a warm glow inside. His father was lucid today. He knew who he was; he knew his own life, career and background, and they were having a regular father and son conversation. He'd missed this.

'That's happened to me a few times,' Terry said. 'I've arrested the right bloke. I know I have. Yet he's managed to worm his way free because someone has lied for him or it's his word against someone else's.'

'Maddening, isn't it?' Ian asked.

'Painfully so.'

'You just have to take it on the chin. Chalk it down to experience and move on.'

'Is that what you did?'

'Yes. You have to, or it'll drive you insane. What could you have done differently? What could you have done better?'

'Was Harry able to chalk things down to experience and move on?'

'No. He was one of the few who allowed things to eat him up.'

'That's not healthy.'

'No, it isn't. That's why he exploded the way he did after Stephanie went missing, when he went round to that witness's house. He was a man possessed. I couldn't pull him off the poor girl's father.'

'It was a horrible time,' Terry said, looking down.

'It was. It changed Harry into someone I didn't recognise. That time he came to the station and saw—' He stopped in his tracks.

'What?' Terry asked, looking up into his father's eyes.

'What?' Ian replied innocently.

'You were going to say about the time he came into the station and saw someone. Saw who?'

'I don't know.'

'You do, Dad.' Terry edged closer. 'Who did he see? What happened?'

'I can't… remember. It's fuzzy.'

'No, it isn't. Your memory is good today. Who did Harry see when he came into the station? Was it Dominic? Did he see him there after you'd arrested him?'

'It was a very dark time for us all,' Ian said quietly. He placed what remained of his sandwich down on the paper bag and pushed it away. 'It was twenty years ago. It was a different world back then.'

'What happened?'

It was a while before he spoke. 'We couldn't get Dominic to talk. We didn't know he was taking that drug he was on. If we had, it might have given us an insight into his behaviour. He kept saying he couldn't remember. He didn't know Stephanie. He'd never met her. He didn't know how she came to be on his allotment. We questioned him for hours and hours, going over the same thing, and he wasn't budging.'

'Surely Harry wasn't questioning him?'

'No. I didn't even know he was in the station. I was in that interview room for hours. Someone…'

'Go on,' Terry prompted, when his dad fell silent.

Ian turned to looked out of the window. He couldn't look at his son. 'Harry had come to the station. He was always turning up, even though he was on compassionate leave, asking how we were getting on, if we'd arrested anyone yet. Someone let him into the observation room without telling me. He watched the entire interview with Dominic.'

'Oh my God.'

'We were charging him for hiding the body, but we couldn't do him for the murder. Not then anyway. We put him in the cells and let him stew for a while. We all needed a break. You know what it's like when you're trying to break a suspect. I needed some air. I smoked back then, as you know. I was in the car park. It was bloody freezing, but I needed some nicotine inside me. I'm standing there smoking. I turn around and I see DS bloody Jason Carr going into the cell block with Harry. I couldn't get in there fast enough.'

'Do I dare ask what happened?'

'When I got there, Jason was nowhere to be seen. He'd unlocked Dominic's cell door and left Harry to it.'

'What was he doing?'

'He had him by the scruff of his neck, pinned against the wall.

He literally had him off the ground. He was right in his face, telling him to confess. He said he knew he'd killed Stephanie, and he needed to hear him say it.'

'What did you do?'

'I grabbed Harry and eventually managed to pull him off him. Dominic dropped to the floor, then... Harry kicked him.' Ian looked down, ashamed.

'What?' Terry was almost out of his seat. The shock went through him like a charge of electricity. He had never known Harry to be violent. 'Where did he kick him?'

'The stomach. He only did it the once. I managed to stop him. I pushed him out of the cell and closed the door.'

'Bloody hell, Dad. Did Dominic confess?'

'Yes. Soon afterwards. Then his parents got him a solicitor, and it all came out about him being a bit depressed and moody, and he retracted his confession and stuck with the story that he didn't know what he was doing at the time Stephanie was killed, and then said he had no memory of confessing. By then I wanted to kick him myself. It was all a big mess.'

Terry remained quiet and watched his father pick up the remainder of his sandwich and return to looking out of the window. He finished it in three bites, chewing slowly before swallowing.

'Would you like me to make you a drink? I've brought biscuits.'

'Thank you.'

Terry smiled and rose from the chair. He went over to the off-shot kitchen and filled the kettle. When he turned around, he jumped. He hadn't heard his father come up behind him.

'You won't say anything to Barbara, will you?' Ian asked. He looked worried.

'No. Of course I won't.'

'Or Terry.'

'Sorry?' Terry frowned.

'I don't want Terry to find out. He used us as a career template. He looks up to us, Harry. It'll break his heart if he knows what happened.'

Terry wanted to cry. There was an earnest look on his father's face. He genuinely thought he was talking to Harry. This confusion and the memory blackouts couldn't just be a result of the stroke, surely. Maybe he should have a word with the matron and have his dad tested for dementia. He hated seeing his father like this. The body and the mind were so incredibly fragile, and it was fucking cruel to see them crumble.

'Your secret's safe with me… Ian,' Terry said, with a lump in his throat.

Chapter Forty-One

Anthony made himself beans on toast for tea. He wasn't hungry, but he had to eat in order to take his pills. He turned off the television. He couldn't stand early evening programmes. It was all quizzes and soaps.

He shuffled into the kitchen, turned on the light and pulled two slices of white bread out of the bread bin before slipping them into the toaster. He turned to the cupboard behind him for a small tin of baked beans, and something outside the window caught his eye. He stopped and looked out into the blackness. He couldn't see anything. There were no cars on the road and no people around, yet he was sure he'd seen something.

Putting it down to a trick of the light, he returned to making his tea. He opened the can of beans and tipped them into a bowl. He put it in the microwave and timed it for two minutes.

While waiting for them to heat up, he put a plate and cutlery on a tray to take into the living room. He rarely sat at the dining table to eat. He didn't see the point when it was just him to cater for. He had thought of getting rid of it, donate it to charity or something, but that would leave a huge gap on the far side of the room. It would make him feel even more lonely than he already did.

Something caught his eye again. He quickly turned to look. There was someone outside – he was sure of it. The doorbell rang.

Anthony hardly ever received visitors. Only Dawn and Rita, and they called first, so he knew to expect them. He tried to look out of the kitchen window without getting too close, so whoever was outside wouldn't know he was in, but all he saw was his own reflection looking back at him.

The doorbell rang again.

He jumped. The toast popped up. He jumped again. The microwave beeped. His tea was ready, but he didn't want to move.

Another knock on the door.

'Shit,' he said, under his breath.

He had to answer it. Whoever was out there knew he was inside. He should have had a security chain fitted, but he'd never felt vulnerable in his own home before… Not until now.

The doorbell rang again.

'Shit,' he said again. Tears were forming in his eyes.

Anthony dug in his cardigan pocket for the house keys. They jangled as he approached the door. He hadn't realised how much he was shaking.

He swallowed hard and took a deep breath as he turned the key and pulled open the door.

There wasn't just one person standing on the doorstep but a whole group of people. Something flashed and blinded him. He closed his eyes, but all he could see was brilliant white light. He opened them and more flashing caused him to stagger back in confusion.

'Mr Griffiths, what can you tell us about the murder of your son?'

'Who would want him dead?'

'Is it true you haven't visited him since his release from prison, even though he only lived twenty minutes from here?'

'Do you have anything to say to the parents of Stephanie White?'

The questions from the sea of journalists came in quick succession. They all held out mobile phones and recording devices to catch anything he said. More photographs were taken, momentarily lighting everything up in a brilliant, blinding white.

Anthony stepped back and slammed the door. He was visibly shaking as he turned the key in the lock and bolted the door at the top and bottom. The doorbell started to ring again, and someone knocked on the door.

The letterbox was lifted. 'Mr Griffiths, if you'd just answer a few questions, we'll leave you in peace.'

He didn't believe a word they said.

'Go away!' he shouted. He didn't recognise his own voice. It sounded nervous, frightened, petrified. He was in fear in his own home.

He staggered to his bedroom, holding onto the walls for stability. He slammed the door closed and went over to the window which looked out onto the back garden. He pulled the curtains shut, plunging the room into darkness. He fell onto the bed face-down and cried into the pillow.

When Anthony woke up, he was surrounded by silence. A ticking clock in the distance, probably the small carriage clock on the mantel in the living room, and the hum from the fridge were all he could hear. He hoped the journalists had gone, and he'd be left in peace.

He must have fallen asleep within minutes of throwing himself down on the bed. He sat up, wiped his eyes and turned on the bedside lamp. Next to it was a framed photograph of his wife. It had been taken on the day they'd moved into their first home just after they married. She was standing on the doorstep, the front door wide open behind her. The sun was shining on her, and she smiled to the camera. She was proud, pleased, happy to be living in her own home with the man she loved. It was the beginning of their journey together. They were both full of hope and optimism, but that had died so quickly.

He picked up the frame and held it close. He looked deep into his wife's beautiful eyes. She really was beautiful. Smooth skin, full lips, shiny hair, gorgeous figure, tiny ears, button nose. He loved every inch of her.

Anthony hugged the frame, holding it tight to his chest. Tears rolled down his cheeks.

'I miss you so much, Carole,' he choked. 'It's a physical pain being apart from you. Every day is torture. I just want us to be together. I want to hold you. I want to kiss you. I want to smell your hair. I'm sorry I didn't appreciate you as much while you were still alive. I hate myself for not realising you needed help. It was all such a tragedy, all such a big mistake – every bit of it.'

He looked back down at the photograph. He smiled through the tears.

'I'm so, so sorry, Carole. I love you.'

He put the photo, face-down, on the bed next to him. He swung his legs off the bed. He was weak from crying, from lack of food, from exhaustion.

Anthony took several deep breaths and managed to grab a hold of his emotions. He braced himself by placing a hand on the bed either side of him. The tears stopped flowing, and his mind began to clear. He knew what he had to do.

He looked at the calendar box of tablets on his bedside table. He hadn't taken any today, and he should have had three at breakfast time, two at lunch and two this evening. He had missed a full day's dose. No wonder he was feeling so ill. He took a pad of paper and a pen out of his bedside drawer and started writing. He took his time, choosing his words carefully, and when he had finished, he felt a sense of peace he hadn't felt for years. He sealed two letters in two envelopes and left them on the bedside table, before taking the photo of his wife in his hands and kissing it one last time.

'I hope you're waiting for me, Carole.'

Chapter Forty-Two

DI Terry Braithwaite was at his desk, leaning back in his chair, head slumped down on his chest, snoring gently.

The door opened and DS Kyra Willis entered. She coughed but that didn't wake her boss. She coughed louder, and he jolted up with a start.

'Sorry,' he said, wiping the drool off his lips with the back of his hand. 'I sat back to have a think and must have nodded off for five minutes.'

'Is everything all right?' she asked, with a frown.

'Fine. Why?'

'You look… rough,' she said, unable to think of a better word.

'Thank you, DS Willis. You didn't pass that charm school course, did you?'

'Sorry, it's just… when did you last have a full night's sleep?' She pulled out a chair and sat down, crossing her legs.

'Last night, actually,' he said, not looking her in the eye.

'Really? What time did you get in this morning?'

'I haven't been here long. About half an hour maybe.'

'I parked next to your car in the car park. The bonnet was cold. I checked.'

'Of course it was, it's cold. It's below freezing out there.'

'It's one degree. There is also a layer of frost on your car. You've been here longer than half an hour.'

'So, do I call you DS Holmes now, or DS Marple?' he said, with a smirk.

'I'm not getting at you – I'm worried. In the past year, the weight has dropped off you. You hardly eat. You rarely sleep, and you're in this station day and night. It's not good for you.'

'We have a lot on at the moment,' he said, acknowledging his heaving in-tray.

'You're not a one-man police force.'

'Did you come in here for a reason, Sherlock, or just to see how far you could push me before you ended up assigned to marshalling the next Magpies home match?'

'Sorry,' she said, genuinely meaning it. 'The forensics results are back from the long black hair found at Dominic Griffiths' house.'

'That didn't take long. We usually have to wait ages.'

'Since the story hit the press, orders have come from on high to get this solved as quickly as possible.'

Terry gave a wry smile. 'It wouldn't look good for the Super to have a vigilante killer roaming the streets. What have we got then?'

She opened her notebook. 'The black hair was twelve inches in length, and it was synthetic.'

'You mean it wasn't real hair?'

'That's right.'

'So, a wig or hair extensions, then?'

'It looks like it.'

'And I'm guessing no wig was found in the house?'

'No.'

'Huh,' Terry said, sitting back in his chair, a pensive expression on his face.

'What are you thinking?'

'Dawn Shepherd had black hair last year.'

'That would have been dyed, though, wouldn't it?' Kyra said. 'Forensics will have been able to tell the difference between a dyed hair and a plastic one.'

'What I'm getting at is, she changes her appearance. She had it whipped up into a kind of beehive. Also, she wore a lot more make-up than she does now. She was almost goth-like this time last year.'

'And in the space of a year, she's gone from that to shoulder-length dark hair, understated make-up and, well, a conservative dress style.'

'Exactly. It's a big change.'

'So, you think she disguised herself, put on a wig, then went around to her dad's house and beat him to a pulp before stabbing him?'

Terry thought for a very brief moment. 'No. I don't know. It's possible,' he waffled.

'But why wear a disguise? Surely, she would have wanted to gain entry to the house as easily as possible, and with Dominic knowing her, he would have just let her in. There's no reason for her to change her appearance. Also, she had a key. She had let herself in when she found the body.'

'Unless she didn't want anyone else in the street to recognise her. She's been visiting him on an almost daily basis for the best part of a year. The neighbours will have seen her come and go.'

'So, you think she deliberately softened her image over the last year and then disguised herself to confuse the neighbours?'

'It's a possibility,' he said, wondering whether it really was.

'And what's her motive?'

'Money. There's eight hundred thousand pounds sitting in his bank account. In the last year, she's changed her car, and there's a massive TV on her wall I'd love to have in my living room. She has a motive and no alibi. That reminds me, did you speak to the friend she went out with on New Year's Eve?'

'I did. She confirmed what Dawn said. There were three of them in this Robyn's flat. They were having a few quiet drinks, until Robyn's boyfriend, Chris, got down on one knee and proposed. The drink started flowing a bit more after that. None of them left the building at all. Although Robyn and Chris have no memory of Dawn leaving. They woke up the next morning in painful positions on the sofa. She didn't see Dawn again, until after Dawn had found her father dead.'

'So that means Dawn's name is definitely on our suspect list.'

'I wasn't aware we had a list.' Kyra smiled.

'It's a very short list.'

'I'll jot it down on a Post-it.'

'What about the hairs on the jacket?'

'They should be able to extract DNA, but these things don't happen overnight. They'll let us know.'

'So much for a rush job. Did we get a match on the fingerprints found at the scene?'

'No. There was a very good set lifted from the back of a dining chair that's not on the system and doesn't belong to Dominic or Dawn. We just need to get a suspect to match them to.'

'You make it sound so simple,' Terry said, flippantly.

'Where do we go from here?'

'I want to chat to the staff at the supermarket where Dominic worked. He was working there under his grandfather's name so as to avoid revealing his real identity. If anyone had found out who he really was, they could well challenge Dawn for the top spot on our most wanted list.'

'Should we bring Dawn in for more questioning?'

'Not yet,' Terry said, standing up and grabbing his jacket from the back of the chair. 'If she is the killer, she will have gone to great lengths to cover her tracks. We need firm evidence to present her with.'

'How are we going to get that?'

'We'll consider that once we've explored all other avenues, which begins with chatting to Dominic's colleagues. Come on, Sherlock, you can tell me what they each had for breakfast by looking at stains on their shirt cuffs.'

Chapter Forty-Three

'Do you think it'll snow?' Kyra said, climbing out of the car and buttoning her duffel coat.

Terry looked up at the greying sky. He thought for a moment and inhaled deeply. 'I'm not sure. The wind is coming from a north-north-easterly direction at a speed of twenty-seven miles per hour. I believe the jet stream is to the south of us—'

'You're not going to drop this Sherlock shit, are you?'

'I've got to get my kicks from somewhere.' He smiled, zipping his jacket up and heading for the supermarket.

Terry introduced them both to the first member of staff they saw and asked to speak to the manager. She limped over to the customer service kiosk and asked an elderly woman to radio for him and say there were two police officers to see him.

'I don't suppose you'll let me do a bit of shopping while we're here,' Kyra said, as they waited.

'No,' he replied flatly.

'It would save me battling rush-hour traffic this evening if I could pick up a few mushrooms, onions and pasta, seeing as we're standing in a supermarket.'

Terry snorted a laugh.

'What?' Kyra asked.

'I find it funny you think you'll be finishing in time for rush hour this evening.' He turned to her and proffered a broad grin.

The manager was a Mr Roberts, according to a name badge on his shiny black jacket, yet he asked Terry and Kyra to call him Bob. As they made their way to his office, Terry couldn't help but wonder why someone would name their child Robert Roberts. Surely that bordered on child cruelty.

On the way to the office, Kyra stopped and nudged Terry.

'What is it?'

'Over there.' She nodded.

Terry looked to where she was staring. By the entrance to the café, a member of staff in the store's garish green uniform was chatting to Dawn Shepherd.

'What's she doing here?' Kyra asked.

'Well, she doesn't live far, and her mother's shop is just across the parade.'

'Do you stand and chat to the staff in your local supermarket?'

'This is my local supermarket, and no, I don't.'

'Everywhere we go she seems to be there,' Kyra pointed out.

Terry couldn't take his eyes from Dawn. She seemed to be having a very familiar chat with the staff member.

Bob's office was smaller than Terry's. There were several boxes around the room and an underlying smell of rotting vegetables coming from somewhere. Bob sat at his desk. He was the older side of fifty, the larger side of fifteen stone and the shorter side of five foot seven inches. His teeth were crooked, and the broken capillaries on his bulbous nose told Terry he took advantage of his staff discount in the alcohol section.

'We'd like to talk to you about one of your employees, Dominic Griffiths. I believe you knew him as Rupert Griffiths.'

'Ah,' he said. 'An error of judgement on our part, I'm afraid. I hold my hands up and claim all responsibility.' He literally held his hands up. 'In my defence, we were very short-staffed last summer. Our hiring policy may have gone out of the window a bit.'

'Are you saying you wouldn't have hired him knowing he was an ex-con?' Terry asked.

'I'm not saying that at all. We're an equal opportunities employer, and we take all staff on their merits and ability to do the job. Age, ethnicity and sexual orientation play no part in how we pick out—'

'Calm down, Bob,' Terry interrupted. 'You're not giving a statement to the press.'

'Sorry.' Bob pulled a tissue from the box on his untidy desk and began dabbing at his forehead. 'You have to be so careful these days when employing people. It's more of a box-ticking exercise than whether they have the right qualifications. There are more questions you can't ask than what you can. What I meant was: Rupert – Dominic – came to us recommended.'

'By who?'

'An already established member of staff.'

'Which one?'

'Selina Baxter.'

Terry looked up, as he thought. 'Dyed blonde hair, slim, about five foot five, bright red lipstick.'

'You know her?' Bob asked.

'Do you think we could have a word with her?'

'Of course. I'll go and fetch her.'

Bob stood up and left the office.

'Who's Selina Baxter?' Kyra asked.

'She must be the friend Dawn Shepherd asked to recommend her dad for the job, and I'm guessing she's the woman Dawn was talking to as we came in.'

'She's just coming,' Bob said, as he re-entered the office.

'How was Dominic's work?' Terry asked.

'We had no complaints. He worked in the warehouse mostly, helping with unloading deliveries, and when the store was closed, he stacked shelves. He was only with us for about four or five months, but he was a good worker, reliable.'

'Did he get on with other staff members?'

'I believe so. I'm afraid I rarely get time to leave the office, so you'd need to ask the other staff.'

'Would we be able to chat to them?'

'Of course. I'd prefer if you did it in the staffroom though, rather than on the shop floor.'

'No problem.' Terry smiled. 'I'm guessing the news of Dominic Griffiths' release from prison was quite a talking point last year. How did people feel about it?'

Bob looked slightly uncomfortable. 'I'm not sure.'

'How did *you* feel about it?'

'Me?' he asked, his eyes darting between Terry and Kyra.

'Yes.'

'I… I didn't have any feelings really.'

'I find that hard to believe. You have a thick Newcastle accent, so you're obviously from around here. I'm guessing you were here when Stephanie was killed twenty years ago. Surely you remember it.'

'Yes. I remember it.'

'And were horrified by it.'

'Well, yes, I suppose I was.'

'And therefore, have an opinion about Dominic being released early.'

'Well, I-I-I didn't think… I mean…'

The door opened, and Selina Baxter breezed into the office, bringing with her a fragrance of whatever perfume she was wearing mixed with chips.

'You wanted to see me, Mr Roberts?'

Bob couldn't jump out of his chair fast enough. 'Selina, yes, come on in. These are police officers. They'd like to ask you a few questions about Rupert… Dominic. Dominic Griffiths.' He grabbed her by the shoulders and steered her towards his seat. 'Well, it's getting a bit cramped in here, isn't it? I'll leave you all to it.' He rushed out of the office, closing the door firmly behind him.

'Is he all right?' Terry asked Selina.

'I'm not sure.' She frowned.

'He seemed to get disturbed when we brought up how he felt about Dominic Griffiths being released from prison.'

'Ah. He would. Something happened to his sister years ago. Nobody knows what, but she died, and whoever did it was never caught. I'm afraid he was very vocal when the news broke about Dominic Griffiths being released.'

'Understandable,' Kyra said, making a note in her pad.

'How did you know Dominic?' Terry asked.

'I didn't. I went to school with his daughter. Dawn. Dawn Shepherd. I ran into her last year, here in the store. It was a surprise seeing her again after all this time. She's certainly changed. We met up for a drink and a catch-up. She told me all about Dominic being her real father. She never knew who her dad was, you see. It was a story and a half, like something out of *EastEnders*.' She laughed nervously. 'Anyway, she asked if there was any chance I could put a word in for him here, if a job came up. We were taking on extra staff at the time. I just thought I was helping.'

'Whose idea was it for Dominic to use a false name?' Kyra asked, without looking up from her pad.

'Dawn's, I think. I remember her saying that it would be for the best if people didn't find out who he really was.'

'Did anyone find out?' Terry asked.

'Not that I know of.'

'What was Dominic like to work with?'

'I didn't work with him much. I'm on the tills mostly. Sometimes I supervise the self-service, but I hate doing that.'

'You said Dawn had changed since you last saw her at school. In what way?' Terry asked.

'Well, she's bigger for a start. She was never slim, but she's piled on the weight. And last year she had jet-black hair. At school, she was mousey, more like she is now. I hardly recognised her at first.'

'Selina, did you tell anyone who Dominic really was?'

'No,' she answered, too quickly. She suddenly had a shifty look about her, as her eyes darted around the room.

'You did, didn't you?'

Her eyes filled with tears. She nodded. 'I told my mum. I tell her everything. And I told Scott, my boyfriend. He wanted me to pack in working here.'

'Because of Dominic?'

'Yes. He said, if a man has killed once then he could kill again, and it would be easier the second time around. He also said, if you looked at a photo of Stephanie White and then at me, you'd think I was a grown-up version of her, and I might be his next victim.' She burst into tears.

Kyra leaned forward, snatched a few tissues out of the box and handed them to the crying girl. Selina squeaked a thank you and blew her nose.

'I think your boyfriend may have been watching too many detective programmes, Selina,' Kyra said.

Selina laughed. 'That's exactly what I told him.'

'Selina,' Terry began, 'is there anyone among the staff who took against Dominic being released when it was announced?'

'We all had something to say on that subject.'

'But was there anyone who you thought might take matters into their own hands if the opportunity arose?'

She looked confused. 'I don't know what you mean.' She gave a weak smile.

'Would anyone here have attacked Dominic, if they'd learned his true identity?'

She thought for a moment. More tears pricked her eyes. She nodded.

'Who?'

'Do I have to say?'

'It would help.'

Selina led Terry and Kyra to the staffroom along the corridor from Bob's office. Bob was in there with a few of the workers, all dressed in identical green uniforms. They were sitting on mismatched chairs, chatting among themselves with a mug of tea or coffee in their hands. Nobody offered the detectives anything to drink.

'I liked Dominic. He was lovely,' a woman in her mid-fifties called Margaret said. She had a thick local accent and a deep voice, evidence of a lifetime smoker. 'Obviously we didn't know him as Dominic, but he was a nice bloke, hard worker, not like some,' she said, glancing over at a fat man asleep on a battered sofa. 'Intelligent too, well read. I like that in a man.'

'Margaret fancied him,' a young woman said.

'Piss off, Linda, I didn't. I just liked him. He was different.'

'In what way different?' Terry asked.

'He wasn't your typical mouthy, leering sleaze you sometimes get working in warehouses, and trust me, I've worked in enough warehouses to tell you plenty of stories. He got on with his work and said hello.'

'We know why he was quiet now, though, don't we?' Linda said. She was a mousey woman in her late twenties, stick-thin, with bad teeth and greasy hair. 'He was hiding his past. My mum said, you always have to watch the quiet ones.'

'No. He was quiet because he wanted to get on with his life. He was trying to put his past behind him. He'd served his time. You can't blame him for that,' Margaret said. 'Can you imagine what it would have been like here if we'd known his real name? His life wouldn't have been worth living, bless him.'

'Especially with Andrew and his lot.'

'Who's Andrew?' Kyra asked.

Selina shrank in her chair. She'd already mentioned Andrew to Terry and Kyra in the manager's office. She gave a very brief description of his character, saying she wasn't qualified to make a judgement about him. Terry could see she was scared of sticking her head above the parapet so decided to let her off.

'Andrew works in the warehouse,' Bob said.

'He thinks he's a supervisor, but he's not,' Margaret muttered. 'When it was in the papers last year about Dominic being released, he really kicked off.'

'Did he?'

'Oh God, yes, it was embarrassing,' Margaret said. 'Going on about bringing back hanging and having him castrated. I told him, this is the twenty-first century, Andrew, we don't go around publicly flogging people anymore.'

'Is Andrew here?'

'No. He's off sick.' A man standing at the back of the room who had been observing the whole conversation butted in. He was tall with a heavy brow and a brooding scowl. He wore a navy beanie hat and had dark stubble around his strong jawline.

'What's wrong with him?'

He shrugged. 'Dunno. Look, don't go singling him out as some kind of dinosaur. He's not the only person who thinks the death penalty should be brought back for some crimes. I remember the Stephanie White case. What that Dominic did to her was fucking disgusting. He shouldn't have been allowed to move back around here.'

'He was Newcastle born and bred,' Margaret said.

'Do any of you know of anyone who would want to have harmed Dominic?' Kyra asked.

'Stick a pin in the phonebook, love,' the man said. He crushed his plastic cup, threw it in the bin and stormed out of the room.

'Ignore him. He likes you to think he's hard, but he's all talk. It's that Andrew you want to watch. I've seen him when he's had a few drinks. A proper Jekyll and Hyde.'

'Where will we find Andrew?'

'I can give you his home address,' Bob said.

The atmosphere in the small room had darkened. Terry thanked them for their time and told them they'd all been very helpful.

Terry and Kyra walked back to the car in silence. Both looked thoughtful.

'So, what did you deduce from that? Any thoughts?' Terry asked.

'Well, the main thing I'm thinking is why anyone would call their son Bob when his surname was Roberts. It's like me having a son and calling him William.'

Terry laughed. 'Yes, I thought the same. William Willis. He certainly wouldn't thank you for that.'

Kyra unlocked the car, and they both climbed in.

Terry looked at his watch. 'If you're quick, you can go and buy your mushrooms.'

'Really?'

'I'll not say it again.'

'You're an angel. Do you want anything?' she asked, a huge smile on her face.

'You can buy me a Mars and a bottle of water.'

She jumped out of the car and ran back to the store before Terry had a chance to change his mind and call her back.

Terry pulled out his mobile and opened the notes app. He'd already written Dawn's name down, but now he added Andrew Dickens and the manager Bob Roberts as possible suspects. The list was growing, but he didn't feel any closer to solving this case.

Chapter Forty-Four

Dawn had asked for compassionate leave from Schofield and Embleton. In the past year, she had impressed them with her skills and had established herself as an invaluable member of the team. She had soon advanced from a glorified office junior to helping out with cases as a proper paralegal. She conducted research and often accompanied solicitors in court. She was loving her work, and it pained her to have to take time off, but following the death of her father, the murder of the father she had known for less than a year, it was understandable.

She woke up and for the briefest of moments, everything was right with the world. Then reality dawned. She threw back the duvet and almost fell out of bed. The energy seemed to have been drained out of her. She was cold. Bloody heating. She wrapped her dressing gown around her and went over to the window. Pulling open the curtains, she looked out at the dark, grey, uninspiring view. Another freezing cold day.

Dawn sat back down on the bed and looked at her reflection in the mirror above her dressing table. She looked old, somehow, dark lines beneath her eyes, downturned mouth and a sallow complexion. She shivered, padded into the bathroom and turned the shower on to as hot as she could stand it.

Sitting in front of the mirror again, her hair washed and tied back in a neat ponytail, she applied a little make-up. Her appearance was important to her, and she wanted people to see her as a happy, positive person. She had trained herself to walk down the street with her head high and shoulders back, to ooze a confidence she didn't necessarily feel. However, it was imperative, in her line of work, to project an image people could admire, respect and trust. This morning, she felt more of a fraud than ever.

She ignored breakfast. Usually, as per the new diet, it was a strong black coffee, a slice of granary toast and whatever was overflowing from the fruit bowl. This morning, she couldn't face anything. She put on her coat, snatched up her bag and car keys and left the flat.

'Dawn, are you all right?' Robyn was coming out of her flat next door as Dawn was leaving. 'I've been texting you, and you haven't replied. I knocked on your door for ages last night, and you didn't answer.'

'I'm so sorry, Rob, I've not felt up to talking. I actually fell asleep early last night. I was just so drained.'

'Understandable. Do you want to come in for a chat?'

'No thanks. I'm going over to see my grandfather.'

'How's he taking it?'

'I'm not sure, to be honest.'

'Listen,' she said, stepping closer and lowering her voice despite there being nobody else in the foyer with them. 'I had the police round yesterday asking if I could confirm what times we were together on New Year's Eve. They really went into detail. I felt like I was being interrogated. They don't suspect you of having anything to do with your dad's death, do they?'

Dawn gave a weak smile. 'No. It's just that I found the body, and the police are incredibly suspicious of whoever finds the victim. They're just double-checking everything. You know what us solicitors are like when we get a detective on the witness stand – we do everything we can to pull them apart.' She grinned.

'So you're not a suspect?'

'No.'

'Oh good,' she said, hand firmly on her chest. 'I was beginning to think I was going to have to look for a new chief bridesmaid.' She laughed nervously. 'Are you eating?'

'Yes, I am.'

'Good. I know you're on a healthy-eating kick at the moment but try not to lose too much weight before my wedding. I don't want you looking sexier than me.' She grinned. 'Listen, do you fancy coming around tonight for a few drinks?'

'I'm still not over the last drinking session,' Dawn said.

'I know. We went a bit mad, didn't we?'

'A bit? How's Chris? Isn't he usually a bit of a lightweight?'

'He's a big drama queen. He's finally come round to accepting he's just had a massive hangover and not alcohol poisoning. I think I might have "in sickness and in health" taken out of the vows, if he's going to be this much of a hypochondriac.' A car beeped from outside. 'That's my Uber. I'd better go. I've got twin girls to measure up for christening gowns in half an hour. Look after yourself. Text me any time.' Robyn kissed Dawn on the cheek and ran out of the building, leaving her behind in the foyer.

Dawn waited until Robyn was in the Uber and it had pulled away from the kerb and driven out of sight before she left the building. It was strange how much things had changed in the last few days. Robyn was engaged and beaming with happiness at the thought of settling down, while Dawn's father had been murdered and a heavy cloud was hanging over her.

Dawn parked outside Anthony's bungalow on Langdale Close. She needed to pull herself together for him. He wasn't well, and she worried about him. The last few days had been a rollercoaster for both of them, and she would need to keep a close eye on him, at least until after the funeral.

She knocked on the door and stepped back. The kitchen curtains were drawn, but she thought nothing of it. Looking up at the grey sky, she wondered if it was ever going to brighten up today.

'Dawn.' She turned at the sound of her name being called.

The woman next door, whose name Dawn could never remember, stood on her doorstep in sensible clothing and pink carpet slippers. She had recently celebrated her eightieth birthday – Dawn remembered seeing banners up on her front door, thanks to the efforts of the woman's grandchildren.

'Good morning,' Dawn replied.

'Is your grandfather all right?' she asked in a soft voice.

'Yes. Why?' Dawn replied, concerned.

'The press were hounding him last night. They were outside here for ages. Knocking on the door and ringing the bell. I phoned him and asked if he wanted me to call the police, but he said he was ignoring them.'

'Oh. He didn't call me or anything.'

'He probably went to bed early or something. I'd have been scared witless if it had been my door they were knocking on.'

Dawn was rummaging around in her bag for the key she had for emergencies. 'I'm sure he's fine.'

'Tell him I was asking after him.'

Dawn nodded. She unlocked the door, stepped in and closed it behind her.

'Grandad, are you up?'

The house was in darkness. It was colder than her flat. She needlessly pressed her hand against the radiator in the hallway. The heating was off. She went into the living room and turned on the light. The curtains were drawn and the room empty.

'Grandad? Is everything all right?'

Back in the corridor, she turned to his bedroom. The door was closed. She hoped he'd put in a pair of earplugs, gone to bed early and was having a lie-in. She placed a hand on the cold handle and leaned in to check for any noise coming from behind the door. All she heard was her own heartbeat thumping loudly.

She knocked lightly. 'Grandad. Are you in there?'

She waited. There was no movement.

She took a deep breath and pushed open the door.

The bedroom was in full darkness thanks to the blackout curtains. She couldn't see her hand in front of her face. She fumbled on the wall for the light switch, and the room was suddenly lit up in a brilliant glow.

On the bed lay Anthony Griffiths. He was wearing the suit Dawn recognised from his wedding photograph in the living room. Next to him was Carole's wedding dress. They were lying side by side, and the cuff of the wedding dress sleeve was in Anthony's hand, as if they were holding hands.

Dawn leaned back against the wall. A tear rolled down her cheek. Her grandfather's face looked peaceful, content, and there was a slight smile on his lips. She had never seen him look so happy before.

Chapter Forty-Five

Dawn was sat on an uncomfortable sofa in the police station at Forth Banks. Her mother was beside her. Dawn hadn't stopped crying since she had called the police from Langdale Close and told them about her grandfather. She hadn't wanted him to be alone, so when DI Terry Braithwaite arrived at the bungalow, he had found Dawn sitting by the bed next to her grandfather, holding his hand.

Terry had been surprisingly sympathetic. He hadn't rushed her as he gently eased her up and walked her slowly to a waiting car where he told a PC to take her to the station, sit her in the family room and call her mother.

An hour had passed, and Dawn hadn't said anything to her mum. Rita had made the right placatory noises and hugged her daughter, but Dawn seemed to be in a state of shock.

The door opened, and Terry breezed in with Kyra Willis behind him. They closed the door and sat on a matching sofa opposite.

'Dawn, how are you?' Terry asked in a quiet, soothing tone. 'Are you up for answering a few questions?'

She gave a brief nod in reply.

'When was the last time you saw your grandfather?'

Dawn's face was blank. She looked to her mother.

'It was the third of January,' Rita said. 'We were due to go around on the second as that was Carole – his wife's – birthday, but, well, with everything that had happened, neither of us felt like it. We went the following day.'

'How did he seem?' Terry asked Dawn.

'He was sad. Reflective,' Rita said. 'He missed his wife terribly.'

'Did he mention his son at all?'

'Yes.' Rita continued speaking for Dawn. 'He said…' She trailed off.

'Go on,' Terry prompted.

'Well, the thing is, his wife killed herself because of what Dominic had done. I think Anthony thought that if someone had killed Dominic in prison all those years ago, or he'd killed himself when he first went to prison, then Carole would still be alive, and they'd be happy.'

'He blamed his son for his wife's death?'

'Yes.'

Terry and DS Kyra Willis exchanged glances.

'What's going on? Why the look?' Rita asked.

'In Anthony's bedroom, we found an envelope addressed to me,' Terry said.

From a folder, Terry took out a white envelope and placed it on the coffee table between them.

'In it,' Terry continued, 'Anthony states that he killed Dominic.'

'What?' Dawn exclaimed. 'No. That's not possible.'

Terry took a single sheet of paper out of the folder and opened it. 'He says that he didn't believe he had long left to live, and he felt justice needed to be served. So he killed him, and then himself.' Terry left the revelation hanging in the air before continuing. 'He had told us he was ill, but why did Anthony believe he didn't have long left to live?'

'He has bone cancer. Had bone cancer,' Rita explained. 'He was diagnosed around September last year. It was spreading quickly. There was nothing the doctors could do other than try to ease the pain. He was taking medication, but I don't think it was working. There were days when he looked in agony. He never complained though.'

'The thing is, we don't think Anthony murdered his son. The level of violence inflicted upon Dominic is not something a man in his physical condition could have managed. Why would he admit to a crime it's so obvious he didn't commit?'

'I don't know.' Rita shrugged.

'Dawn?' Terry asked.

She didn't say anything.

'My years of experience tell me he's confessed to cover up the identity of the real killer.'

'Why would he do that?' Rita asked.

'Because he wants to protect them.'

'But...' Rita started to speak then trailed off. 'You think... You think he confessed to protect Dawn? That he thought Dawn killed her own father? Why would he think that?'

'Why would I want to kill my dad? I'd only just met him. I was getting to know him. I helped him find that house. I got him a job. I had no reason to kill him,' Dawn said, her words tripping over each other as she finally started to speak.

'How are your finances?'

'What?'

'You live on your own. You run a car. You've not long left university. You can't be earning much as a junior paralegal. Your father had been awarded a million pounds in compensation. I'd say that was motive enough for killing him.'

'What? No,' Rita exclaimed. 'She wouldn't. I can't believe you're even suggesting this. I've brought Dawn up on my own. I've taught her that if she wants anything in this life, she has to earn it herself. She had two jobs while at university. She saved and saved for everything she needed. I wanted to buy her a car, but she wouldn't let me. She bought that old Golf for a few hundred pounds.'

'And how much did the Peugeot cost?'

'That is none of your business,' Rita said.

'It is my business. I'm investigating a murder.'

'My daughter is innocent.'

'Then she won't mind answering a few questions about her finances.'

'She bought the car on finance,' Rita said.

Terry turned to Dawn. 'Did you?'

It was a while before Dawn answered. 'My dad bought it for me.'

'What? You told me it was financed,' Rita said. She removed her hand from Dawn's.

'He offered.'

'So you lied to me?'

'I didn't think you'd understand.'

'What's there to understand? It's nothing to do with me if he wants to buy you a car. Why lie, Dawn?'

'I'm sorry,' she said, tears rolling down her face.

'And the large-screen TV in your flat?' Terry asked. 'Did Dominic buy that for you too?'

'Yes,' she replied, her voice barely audible.

'Did he buy you anything else? Diamonds? A Caribbean cruise? First class tickets to New York?'

'Don't be flippant,' Rita said. 'He was her father. He hadn't been in her life for twenty years, and he suddenly came into money. He had every right to buy her things.'

'He didn't buy me anything else,' Dawn said. 'I didn't want anything else.'

'As his next of kin, you will inherit what is left of his compensation claim. You have no alibi for the time of his death. Your grandfather confessed, it seems, to cover up for someone. That someone, I can only assume, is you.'

'He was my dad,' Dawn cried.

'He was a child murderer. It's not going to look good for a paralegal to have a convicted murderer for a father, especially one who was able to cheat the system and get one million pounds in compensation. It would make for a very nice nest egg if your career takes a nosedive when clients find out your true parentage.'

'Is she under arrest?' Rita asked.

'No.'

'Then we're leaving.' She stood up and practically dragged Dawn off the sofa. 'If you want to ask her any more questions, you can do it in the presence of a solicitor.'

Rita wrapped her arm around Dawn, pulled open the door and pushed her through. The door slammed closed behind them.

'Do you think Dawn's the killer?' Kyra asked.

Terry inhaled deeply and let the breath out slowly. 'I think she might be, but if she is, she's playing a very good game.'

'How do we catch her?'

'By playing a better one.'

Chapter Forty-Six

Anthony's funeral was a week later, on 11 January. There was a very small crowd in attendance. Dawn and Rita and a few of Anthony's neighbours. Five people standing around the open grave in Blaydon Cemetery as he was lowered into the ground to join his wife. Dawn had cried throughout the service and as she followed the coffin on its journey to the grave.

It was a cold morning. The sky was dull, and there was a stiff breeze blowing. When prompted, Dawn stepped forwards, picked up a handful of earth and threw it onto the coffin. Her mother did the same.

'It was a beautiful service,' the woman who lived next door to Anthony said, as she approached Dawn and shook her hand.

'Not many came.'

'No. But it's not the number of people that matters – it's what those few meant to him. He spoke of you often. He was incredibly proud of you.'

'Thank you.' Dawn smiled through the tears. 'It was lovely of you to come.'

'It was my pleasure. You take care now,' she said, patting

Dawn's hand. 'You know where I am if you want to call in for a chat.'

Dawn smiled, said goodbye and linked arms with her mum. As they headed down the incline, Dawn stopped in her tracks when she saw a woman in black approaching her.

'I didn't want to come to the church. I wasn't sure if I'd be welcome,' the woman said. 'How are you?'

'I'm getting there,' Dawn replied. 'Mum, this is Mrs White. Barbara. Stephanie's mum.'

'Oh,' was all Rita could say. 'Nice to meet you.'

'Likewise.'

'I read about Anthony dying in the local paper last week. It must have been a blow to you, only just getting to know him after all this time.'

'He'd been ill for some time. It was his way of taking back what little control he had.'

'It takes a brave man to do that,' Barbara said. She shivered as a cold wind buffeted them.

The three women remained silent. Dawn and Barbara didn't break eye contact.

'If you ever want to talk, you know where I am,' Barbara said.

'Thank you. How are things with you and Mr… Harry?'

'We're fine. Plodding along as usual. One day at a time.' Her smile looked painful. 'Well, I'll not intrude. You're a strong woman, Dawn.'

'I don't feel like I am at the moment,' Dawn said, with a hint of a chuckle.

'No. These things take time. But you are. You've been through the mill this last year, but things'll calm down now. I'm sure of it.'

'I hope so.'

Barbara stepped forwards. She tentatively held out a hand for Dawn to shake. It was an awkward gesture. Their handshake was stilted, but the smiles were warm and genuine.

'Put the past behind you, Dawn. You're only young. You've got your whole life ahead of you. Grab it by the horns and be the best person you can be.' A tear rolled down her cheek, and she didn't wipe it away.

Before Dawn could say anything, Barbara turned on her heel and headed down the path towards the gates.

'So that was Stephanie's mum,' Rita said, as they watched her walk away.

'Yes.'

'I remember her from when you were at school. She was your favourite teacher.'

'She still is.' Dawn smiled.

'What was all that about? Be the best you can be?'

'I don't know. She probably wants me to do all the things her daughter was unable to do, all the things *she's* been unable to do. She's been living in the past for twenty years. Just like Grandad was. It's not healthy.'

'No,' Rita said, turning towards the exit. 'Come on, let's go. I'm perished.'

Parked a few metres away from the gates of Blaydon Cemetery, Terry hunkered down behind the wheel of his Astra when he saw Barbara White enter. She was dressed in funereal black and had a sombre look on her face. There was only one place she could have been going dressed like that, and that was Anthony's funeral. But why? It wasn't long before she came back out. She passed his car and wiped away a tear. She hadn't been there long enough to watch the burial service. At first, he wondered if she hadn't realised it was Anthony's funeral today – maybe she had been intending to visit Stephanie's grave, saw the service and decided to leave. But she wouldn't wear all black clothing to visit

Stephanie, she never did. Why would she want to witness the funeral of the father of the man who murdered her daughter?

A few minutes later, Dawn and Rita left the cemetery. They wore grim expressions as they headed for Dawn's car.

Anthony's will hadn't been read yet, but Terry knew the solicitor and had asked for a sneak preview. Dated six months ago, Anthony had left everything to Dawn. His house and its contents, his shares in various companies and money from several savings accounts totalling more than fifty thousand pounds had all been bequeathed to the granddaughter he had known for less than a year. The granddaughter who had conveniently discovered his body a few days after finding the body of her murdered father. Add on the money she would inherit from her father, and Dawn was going to be a very rich twenty-two-year-old.

Terry watched them drive away. They headed in the direction of Ryton, where Rita lived. He couldn't help but think he was watching a murderer drive away. If only he had the evidence to prove it.

Chapter Forty-Seven

There was a knock on Terry's door. He looked up from the latest overtime report he was struggling to write and saw a smiling Kyra Willis on the other side of the glass. He signalled for her to come in.

'Hello, stranger,' he said. Since Anthony Griffiths' death, the investigation into who had killed Dominic had stalled. The forensics hadn't turned up anything useful, they had no leads on the origin of the synthetic hair and their follow-up interviews with Dominic's co-workers hadn't led anywhere. Kyra had been reassigned, and Terry had been told not to spend all his time on it. Another week or so, and the case would be shelved. It would then be down to the cold case squad to review it every eighteen months or so.

'Why is it every time I see you, you look paler and thinner?' Kyra said as she came into the small office and sat down.

'Did you want something?' Terry was well aware of his weight loss, as he'd had to bore another hole in his belt. Some cases made a home for themselves in his mind and wouldn't leave until they were solved. Dominic Griffiths' murder was such a case. It was a constant headache that neither paracetamol nor alcohol would evict. He spent his free time either with his father or sitting in his dark living room, mind whirling over how clever Dawn Shepherd had been at covering her tracks. That's if she was the murderer. Maybe he was too close to this case to accept that Harry and Barbara White were the culprits. It caused Terry sleepless nights, loss of appetite and a yearning to get in his car and drive to a new life. If only he could leave his head behind.

'First of all, I'd like you to sign my holiday form,' Kyra said, placing it on his keyboard in front of him.

'Going anywhere nice?' he asked. He signed without even reading it.

'Matthew's taking me to Niagara Falls in July. I've always wanted to go.'

He looked up and saw she had a beaming smile on her face. He wondered if he'd ever been that happy. Probably not. He'd never had a relationship that lasted longer than a month. He'd never been on a romantic holiday with a girlfriend. In fact, he'd never been on a holiday. What was the point if he didn't have anyone to go with?

'I'm sure you'll have a lovely time,' he said, as he handed back the form.

'Also, I've had a call from forensics. They've finally got the DNA back on those hairs from the jacket found in Dominic Griffiths' living room.'

'It took them long enough.'

'They have a backlog. This was labelled as priority. We could have put a rush on it, but we'd get charged extra for that.'

'I'm aware of costings, Kyra, thank you,' he said, as he glanced at the next report he was having to write, justifying the budget for his department. It wasn't even his department. DI Sheffield should have been writing the report, but he was on long-term sick leave due to burn-out.

'Anyway, they've managed to extract DNA from the hairs, but whoever they're from is not on the database.'

'How did I know you were going to say that? Anything else?'

'No. That's about it.' She stood to leave. She reached the door then stopped. 'Erm, there *is* something, but it's not work-related. It's personal.'

Terry sat up and folded his arms. 'Are you wanting to report someone?'

She smiled. 'No. It's nothing like that.' She retook her seat. 'Look, speaking as a friend, you let cases get to you, and you shouldn't. I know this isn't a regular job that you can switch off from at the end of the day, but you don't just take the work everywhere you go, you absorb it. It's obvious you're not looking after yourself.'

Terry could feel a wave of emotion burn inside him. He knew Kyra was right but hearing it out loud was upsetting. He couldn't tell her to leave, because he couldn't be sure what would come out of his mouth if he opened it.

'Now, do you know Sergeant Morton in uniform?'

He shook his head.

'Yes, you do. About my height, dark red hair, slim, Yorkshire accent. You wrote that character report for her when she thumped that rapist last year.'

He nodded and smiled. 'I remember her, yes.'

'Well, she's always had a bit of a soft spot for you. And I thought, before you lose so much weight you disappear completely, you might like to take her out for a meal.'

'Did you?'

'Yes.' She grinned. 'I could always be in the local this evening with her for a drink, you pop by, and then I get a strange phone call from Matthew telling me I'm urgently needed at home and leave you both to it.'

Terry couldn't hide his smile. 'Thank you, Kyra. I know you're trying to help, but—'

'No,' she interrupted. 'No buts. Terry, I'm being serious now. There is more to life than the job. Please don't turn into a cliché detective.'

'Let me think about it. Ask me again on Monday.'

She jumped up from her seat, excited. 'You do realise I won't be taking no for an answer on Monday.'

'I do.'

'Excellent. See you later.'

Terry watched her leave then turned back to his report. His heart sank. She was right. The job was consuming him. He did need to let things go. Unfortunately, it was easier said than done.

When Ian Braithwaite had bought his four-bedroom townhouse in Greystones Mews, he had done so with one thought in mind: he'd be able to hand it down to Terry and his wife and kids to live in. That didn't look like it was going to be happening any time soon. If ever. Terry was rattling around in a house with three floors, like a ghost. The only positive Terry could find to living there was it was within a five-minute walk of four decent pubs and two dives, two Indian takeaways, a Chinese and three pizza places. He could have a different meal each night. Tonight, he fancied pizza and texted his order when he was a ten-minute drive away. It was ready as he pulled up outside. He wasn't sure if the bloke behind the counter knowing his name was a good thing or a sign he should learn how to cook.

He parked in his designated space and climbed out – pizza box in one hand, pack of four cans of lager in the other.

He kicked the front door shut behind him, turned on the light with his elbow and went into the kitchen, slapping the pizza box down on the counter. From his back pocket, he took out his mobile and fired off a quick text to Kyra: *You win. Arrange the phoney meet with Sergeant Morton for some time next week.*

The truth was, he didn't want to be alone. He had a big house, and he needed someone to share it with.

Later, Terry woke from a doze on the sofa. He was in that state where he knew the television was on – he could hear the sound – but he couldn't process it. For some reason, he was fighting sleep. The pizza box, with only three slices eaten, lay open on the coffee table in front of him, and he'd only drunk one can of lager before his eyelids had grown heavy and sleep tried to claim him.

His mobile burst into life. His eyes shot open, and he sat up. He scrambled for the remote and turned off the television. He must have been asleep. There was no way he would have consciously been watching a cookery programme.

Terry's iPhone was dancing around the coffee table. He picked it up and blinked a few times for the screen to come into focus. Kyra was calling. He swiped to answer.

'Kyra. What time is it?'

'It's half-past nine.'

'Is it?' He looked at the clock on the wall. He'd only been dozing for a few minutes. It felt much later.

'Oh. What's up?'

'We've got him,' she said, the excitement evident in her voice.

'Got him? Got who?'

'Dominic Griffiths' killer. Uniform arrested him an hour ago.'

'Him?'

Terry squeezed his eyes tightly shut. The news had come out of the blue, but it was a huge relief, and he could feel his entire body starting to relax already. He thought of Harry and Barbara and his father, of everything they'd been through over the past twenty years, and it still wasn't over with. Maybe now it finally would be. Maybe now they could all finally move on.

Chapter Forty-Eight

'You're going to have to do something about your appearance if you want to have any chance with Bella,' Kyra said upon seeing Terry enter the police station in a stained and creased shirt with his jacket half hanging off his shoulders.

'Who the hell's Bella?'

'Sergeant Morton.'

'I didn't know she was called Bella. I may have to reconsider. Tell me what you've got,' he said, as he headed down the corridor to his office.

'Andrew Dickens, thirty-nine years old, lives in Prudhoe. He was arrested for—'

Terry interrupted. 'Andrew Dickens. Why do I know that name?'

'He works at the same supermarket Dominic Griffiths worked at. His name came up when we chatted to some of his colleagues.'

He nodded. 'I remember now. He had some very draconian views on prison sentences. So, why's he been arrested?'

'He was arrested for driving without due care and attention, endangering lives, criminal damage—'

'Bloody hell, what did he do?'

'Drove into a bus shelter.'

'Is that all?'

'There were three people in it at the time. They had to jump out of the way.'

'Okay. So how do we get from that to murdering Dominic Griffiths?'

'His fingerprints are a match for the set lifted from the chair in Dominic's house. We've also taken a DNA sample to see if it's a match for the hairs on the jacket, but it'll be a few days before we get the results.'

'So, his fingerprints are found in Dominic's house, big deal. They worked together. Maybe he went over for a Christmas drink or something.'

'Ever since he was arrested, uniform have said he's just been apologising over and over again saying he didn't mean for it to go so far.'

'Maybe he's talking about crashing into the bus stop.'

'You really are a glass-half-empty person, aren't you? The jacket found in Dominic's house is also Andrew's size.'

'Am I allowed to be sarcastic about that one, too?'

'No. You're not. I'm missing date night for this. This is a huge leap for us. You should be bouncing off the walls.'

He turned to look at Kyra. She had a smile on her face.

'Hmm,' Terry mused. He entered his office, turned on the light and slumped down into his chair. He looked at the black mirror of his computer screen, saw his hair sticking up in all directions and tried to flatten it.

'You don't look happy,' Kyra said.

'It's not what I was expecting.'

'You wanted it to be Dawn Shepherd, didn't you?'

'I didn't want it to be, but that's where everything was pointing.'

'Surely you should be happy that it's not. A young woman, career just getting off the ground… She's not gone and ruined her life.'

'No.'

'You still don't look happy.'

'I never look happy, Kyra. You should see photos of me as a child. I was born a miserable bastard.'

'I can believe that. Do you want to interview Andrew now or wait until morning?'

'Was he drunk?'

'No. Breathalyser came back negative. The on-call doctor has cleared him to be interviewed.'

Andrew Dickens looked like an extra from *The Walking Dead*. He was slumped at the table in the interview room, head in his arms. He looked up when he heard the door open. His dark, receding hair was all over the place. He had a sheen of sweat on his red face and a couple of days' worth of salt-and-pepper stubble. He had an athletic frame, and from the veins protruding on his muscular arms he was no stranger to the gym.

The room stank of desperation and sweat, and it wasn't only coming from Andrew. It leached out of the walls – a legacy of the number of nervous interviews that had taken place in the room over the years.

Andrew had a large plaster stuck at an angle on his forehead, and judging by the mark on the bridge of his nose he was going to have two black eyes in the morning.

Terry pulled out a chair and sat down. Kyra sat next to him.

'How are you feeling?' Terry asked.

'Like I've just spent a night sleeping in a cement mixer,' Andrew replied in a gravelly voice.

Terry gave the nod to Kyra. She started the recording equipment and stated the people present.

'Mr Dickens. I'm going to ignore the reason you were arrested earlier, as I want to talk to you on a different matter. Do you know a man by the name of Dominic Griffiths?'

The spine seemed to have been yanked out of Andrew's back. He slumped to the table once again. His head was in his arms which muffled his sobbing.

'Mr Dickens,' Terry prompted.

Andrew looked up and wiped his nose with the bottom of his polo shirt. 'Yes. I know him. We worked together.'

'Did you know him well?'

'No.'

'Did you socialise with him?'

'No.'

'Did you ever see him out of work?'

'No.'

Terry and Kyra exchanged a glance. Kyra struggled to stop from grinning.

'You know what happened to him on New Year's Day?' Terry asked.

He nodded. A tear rolled down his cheek. He didn't wipe it away.

'Is there something you want to tell me about Dominic's death?'

He shook his head. His face was screwed up with complex emotions. His bottom lip was wobbling uncontrollably, and more tears began to fall.

'For the benefit of the recording, I'm showing Mr Dickens a photograph of a jacket found in Mr Griffiths' living room.' Terry pulled a photo out of the cardboard folder in front of him and placed it slowly in front of Andrew. 'Mr Dickens, do you recognise this jacket?'

He nodded.

'For the benefit of the recording, Mr Dickens nodded his head. Does this jacket belong to you?'

He nodded again and Terry confirmed this for the recording.

'On the collar of this jacket were several hairs which we had analysed. We were able to get a DNA profile from them. Unfortunately, that person wasn't on our DNA database, but we've taken a DNA sample from you so I'm guessing they'll match. We also found a set of fingerprints in Dominic's house on one of his dining chairs, which are a match for your prints. As you say you never met Dominic Griffiths outside work, can you explain how your jacket came to be left in Dominic's living room?'

It was a while before Andrew replied. Judging by the plethora of emotions that swept across his face, he was struggling to decide what to say.

'I… I liked him,' he said quietly.

'You liked Dominic Griffiths?' Terry asked.

'He wasn't known as Dominic Griffiths when he started work. He was calling himself Rupert. He was quiet. Shy. But he was a hard worker, and he knew a lot about football. I liked him.'

'Then you found out who he really was.'

He nodded. 'I've got kids of my own. Three girls. The oldest is the same age as Stephanie was when she was killed. I was born in Winlaton. I know all about what happened to her. It shaped my childhood. He should never have been released from prison. And he was compensated for it, too. He was given taxpayers' money, for fuck's sake,' he spat. 'He killed and cut up a thirteen-year-old girl, and he was being rewarded for it. I'm doing shitty shift work in a supermarket. My wife lost her job. We're having to use fucking foodbanks. And Dominic Griffiths is given a million pounds.'

'It made you angry,' Kyra said.

'Of course it made me fucking angry. Wouldn't you be?' His hands were clenched so tight, his knuckles were white.

'What did you do?' Terry asked.

'We went round. Had a word with him.'

'We?'

'Me and two mates.'

'Their names?' Kyra asked, pen poised.

'I'm not a grass. We just wanted to have a word with him. We wanted him to know we knew who he was and that he wasn't welcome around here.'

'So, what happened?'

He took a deep breath. 'I think, if it hadn't been for the compensation, I'd have been able to get over it. I walked into that house, and I saw a real Christmas tree and a big fuck-off television on the wall and a leather sofa. We couldn't even have a real tree this year. I couldn't afford one. My mum gave us her old plastic one. From that point, I wasn't interested in talking. I saw red.'

'You hit him?' Terry asked.

'I've never hit anyone before in my life. Ask my wife. I'm not violent. I don't even like violent films. I just—'

'You saw red,' Kyra answered for him, repeating his earlier remark.

'I did. I punched him. Hard. In the face. He fell back and landed on the floor. My mate, he laughed. That egged me on, I think. I took my jacket off. I rolled up my sleeves, and I went at him again. I couldn't stop.'

'What were your mates doing while you were beating seven shades of shit out of a defenceless man?' Kyra asked.

He thought before answering. Clearly not wanting to mention the names of his friends. 'One of my mates pulled the telly off the wall. My other mate started kicking him.'

'So, you're punching him, your mate is kicking him... who stabbed him?'

'None of us.' He looked up with wide eyes.

'Bullshit,' Terry said. 'We've placed you at the scene, Andrew. Which one of you stabbed him four times?'

'None of us. I swear.'

'According to the post-mortem report, Dominic would have probably died from his injuries, whether he'd been stabbed or not. Every single one of his ribs was broken. His liver was two kicks away from exploding. He had bleeding on the brain, a ruptured spleen and a punctured lung. He was a dead man before the first knife was plunged into him. You'll be getting charged with murder, regardless,' Terry stated.

'No. No. We didn't stab him. We didn't murder him.'

'Then who did?' Terry shouted.

'I don't know. But it wasn't us. We were interrupted. We did a runner. That's why I left my jacket behind.'

'Who interrupted you?'

'His parents.'

'What?' Terry frowned.

'J… One of my mates, he looked up and looked out of the window, and he saw someone coming up the path in the back garden. He said something like "Fucking hell, it's his parents," so we did a runner.'

Terry and Kyra exchanged glances.

'His parents? He definitely saw two people?' Terry asked.

'Yes.'

'Andrew, Dominic's mother died in 2001. His father had bone cancer. He wasn't well enough to kill his son.'

'Well, I don't know for sure who they were – they might not have been his parents. But my mate definitely said his parents were there, and we all panicked and ran off. I swear, hand on heart, on the lives of my three daughters, none of us stabbed him.'

'What do you think?' Kyra asked.

She and Terry were back in his office with a mug of coffee each. It was pitch-dark outside, and the room was lit up by the unhealthy yellow glow of the strip-lighting above.

'Why lie about not stabbing him?' Terry asked. 'I've basically told him Dominic would have died anyway without the stab wounds, yet he still swears he didn't stab him. Why?'

'Because stabbing would mean a murder charge, or manslaughter, at least. If he stands by his claim of just wanting to give him a bit of a slap, but it got out of hand, it'll carry a lighter sentence.'

'It'll still be manslaughter. With or without being stabbed, Dominic would have died. It's as simple as that.'

'Then Andrew has no incentive to lie.'

'What? So you think that Dominic Griffiths' mother came back from the dead after nineteen years, and she and his father decided to pay him a night-time visit?'

'His mate only assumed it was Dominic's parents. It obviously wasn't. Don't forget, that hair found at the scene was synthetic. Whoever came to the house could have been wearing a wig. Maybe *they* stabbed him.'

'Two separate parties came on the same night to kill him? It's a bit of a stretch of the imagination, isn't it?'

'I suppose. What do you want to do?'

'Charge him with what he was arrested for tonight and with the murder of Dominic Griffiths. That'll buy us more time to question him. We need him to give us the names of his mates. I want to know exactly what his mate saw through the window.'

Kyra stood up and made to leave the office. Terry called her back.

'Kyra, get me a photograph of Dominic's parents.'

'Will do. We're close, aren't we?'

'Very close,' he said, with a whisper of a smile on his lips.

Kyra left the office and closed the door behind her.

'Too close,' Terry said out loud.

Chapter Forty-Nine

Terry didn't bother returning home to Greystones Mews. It wasn't his home, and he didn't feel comfortable there without his dad. He might as well be uncomfortable in his office; he'd probably get the same amount of disturbed sleep slumped over his desk as he would get in his bed.

He pulled the blinds closed, turned the radiator up a notch and slumped in his chair. It wasn't long before his eyelids grew heavy, and sleep claimed him.

Unfortunately, it didn't claim him for long. Every time he woke, he looked at the time on his phone. He saw every hour of the remaining night: 12:07, 01:14, 01:52, 02:44, 03:31, 04:19.

There was a knock on the glass door. He jumped up from his slumber. He looked at his phone: 05:54.

'Yes,' he called out, in a hoarse voice.

The door opened, and the custody sergeant popped his head through the gap.

'Have you spent the night here?'

'Do I really need to answer that?' Terry asked, yawning, stretching, running his fingers through his knotted hair.

'I suppose not. Have you considered having your post redirected?'

'You're a funny man, Adam. What can I do for you?'

'The bloke who was brought in last night for driving into that bus stop, Andrew Dickens. He's been ranting and raving since gone three. He says he wants to talk to you. Normally, I'd wait until regular hours but as you're not normal—'

'Thanks.'

'—I thought I'd give you a nudge and see if you wanted to speak to the gobshite now, before I have to charge myself with GBH.'

'Put him in an interview room. Give me five minutes to have a coffee and a wash, and I'll come down.'

'Five minutes? That's optimistic, isn't it?' He left before Terry could say anything.

'Interview with Andrew Dickens at seventeen minutes past six on Thursday, the sixteenth of January 2020. Those present are myself, that's Detective Inspector Terry Braithwaite…' Terry turned to the PC by the door.

'PC Ben Kent.'

'And…'

Terry indicated towards Andrew.

'Andrew Dickens,' said Andrew.

'Mr Dickens, for the benefit of the recording, I'd like you to state that you've requested this interview at this time and have not been pressured into it.'

Andrew cleared his throat. 'No. No pressure. I wanted this interview.'

'Once more for the benefit of the tape, do you wish to have a solicitor present?'

'No. Let's just get on with it.'

'Right, let's begin.'

'I know I said I wouldn't grass on my mates, but there's no way I'm going to be sent down for something I didn't do. I didn't see Dominic's parents coming up the path, and if you say his mother's dead, then it obviously wasn't her. My mate would be able to give you a better description.'

'Okay. Who are your mates?'

He took a deep breath, clearly still unsure if he was doing the right thing. 'Paul Cummings and John Wheatley.'

'Do they work with you at the supermarket?'

'Yes.'

'Whose idea was it to go round and give Dominic a hiding?'

He looked down. There was obvious regret for his actions.

'It was a joint thing.'

'About what happened last night. Why did you crash into that bus shelter?'

Andrew shook his head. 'I wasn't thinking straight. I haven't been thinking straight since we… since New Year's Day. I must have lost concentration or something. I don't know. I…. I can't believe… I can't believe I had it in me to…'

'Kill a man?' Terry suggested.

'I didn't kill him,' he said.

'He died following your attack on him.'

'Look, talk to John. Ask him to tell you who he saw coming up the path. We didn't stab him. *They* obviously did. They're the ones who killed him.'

There was nothing more Terry could do. Once daylight broke, or what passed for daylight in January in the north of England, two teams were sent to the homes of John Wheatley and Paul Cummings to arrest them for the murder of Dominic Griffiths. Wheatley resisted and had to be restrained, cuffed and practically dragged to the police car by three uniformed officers. Cummings accepted his fate and headed for the waiting car with his head down.

By the time they were ready to be interviewed, DS Kyra Willis had arrived, freshly showered, with clean clothes and minty breath and looking bright and sharp, ready to face the day. She spent the first twenty minutes chastising Terry for his appearance before revelling in how fast the case seemed to be moving.

First up to be interviewed was John Wheatley.

John had a face riddled with pockmarks. His blond hair was a buzz cut, and his blue eyes were dull. He had an indecipherable tattoo on his neck and wore a blue hooded sweater that had been through the wash too many times. His expression was stern. He resented being arrested. There was a deep-seated hatred for the police there, and the look he gave Terry and Kyra as they entered the room should have struck them down dead.

Kyra started the recording. Terry filled John in on the overnight developments of Andrew Dickens confessing to the beating of Dominic Griffiths. Now, it was John's turn to speak.

'The bloke was a nonce. He had it coming to him,' John said, in a thick Geordie accent.

'Stephanie White was not sexually interfered with. Dominic Griffiths was not a paedophile,' Terry stated.

'He killed a child. He deserved a beating.'

'Did he deserve murdering?'

'We didn't kill him,' he said, pointing a grubby finger at Terry. 'I'll hold my hand up to giving him a slap, but we didn't stab him.'

'Who did?'

'You're the filth. You tell me.'

'Andrew Dickens said you called out that Mr Griffiths' parents were coming up the back garden path, which is why you all ran.'

'That's right.'

'How did you know they were his parents?'

'Because they looked like his parents.'

'How do you know what his parents look like?'

'There was a photo of them on the fireplace. I was looking around the room at his stuff while Andrew and Paul were giving him a kicking.'

Terry frowned. 'Can you describe the people you saw coming up the path?'

John let out a heavy sigh. 'I only saw them briefly through the net curtains. The bloke had a hat on, like a beany hat. The woman had dark hair down to her shoulders. She was wearing a long, grey coat. She was a few inches shorter than him. They were exactly like they were in the photograph.'

From the folder in front of him, Terry took out a black and white photograph Kyra had found in Dominic's house. It showed Anthony and Carole Griffiths in the back garden of their home in 1977.

'Is this the couple you saw coming up the path?'

'Yes. Definitely. I'd stake my life on it.'

'Carole Griffiths –' Terry pointed at the photograph '– died in 2001. Anthony Griffiths died last week. At the time his son was killed, he was living with bone cancer. He was in a great deal of pain and wouldn't have been able to kill his son by stabbing him four times in the chest, especially considering one stab went through his ribcage and pierced his heart. Do you see why I'm having trouble believing you?'

John sat back. His eyes widened. There was fear on his face. 'We didn't kill him,' he said, his voice no longer harsh and threatening.

'You have a history of violence, don't you, John?'

He closed his eyes and shook his head. 'It was a long time ago.'

Terry opened the folder. 'The fourteenth of February 2015, you were arrested for threatening your wife with a knife.'

'It was a misunderstanding.'

'The twelfth of March 2014, you were arrested for assaulting Jamie Pratt.'

'He threatened my sister.'

'The second of November 2012, you were charged, along with your brother, with beating up two Liverpool football supporters.'

'Things got out of control. They were taking the piss because they beat Newcastle. We'd had a few drinks.'

'And then there's this one: the tenth of August 2010. Perverting the course of justice. Lying under oath.'

'My sister already had points on her licence. She'd have lost her job if she couldn't drive.'

'Lying under oath,' Terry repeated. 'Why should I believe you when you say a ghost and a terminally ill man killed Dominic Griffiths, when you freely admit to being in the house and taking part in his assault?'

'Because it's true.'

Terry looked at his watch. 'Interview terminated at 09:37.'

The interview with Paul Cummings was even shorter. He hadn't seen anyone coming up the garden path. He echoed Andrew's words, more or less verbatim, when quoting John as shouting, 'Shit, his parents are here', before all three of them ran out of the front door. He admitted kicking Dominic a few times in the trunk of his body, but claimed Andrew performed most of the assault.

He was full of remorse and spent most of the interview wiping away tears with the sleeve of his sweater. He stated that he would never have gone to Dominic's house if it hadn't been for Andrew and John egging him on, telling him that Dominic should be taught a lesson.

'Paul, do you drive a car?' Terry asked.

'Yes.'

'What make?'

'A Peugeot.'

'Colour?'

'Black.'

'Did you use your car to travel to Dominic's house on the night of the first of January?'

He nodded. 'Andrew hasn't got a car, and John's only got a van. Andrew said the van would stand out a mile.'

'How long were you planning this assault?'

'We didn't plan on assaulting him, just scaring him,' he said, with frustration.

'How long?'

'I don't know. A few weeks maybe.'

'From the beginning of December then?'

'Maybe. I don't know how it started. Andrew said that some girl at work had told him who Dominic really was. We all knew him as Rupert.'

'Who was the girl at work who told Andrew?'

'I don't know. Everyone gossips in that place.'

'So, you planned to scare him. You chose which night to do it, and you had your car to get to and from Dominic's house.'

'Yes.'

'Which makes this premeditated. Paul Cummings, I'm charging you with the murder of Dominic Griffiths. You do not have to say anything, but it may harm your defence if you do not mention, when questioned, something you later rely on in court. Anything you do say may be given in evidence. Do you understand?'

'We didn't kill him,' he pleaded.

'Don't worry. You won't be on your own. I'll be charging your two accomplices, too.'

It was almost lunchtime by the time Terry arrived back at Forth Banks. He'd showered, changed, had a quick bowl of cereal and a strong coffee. Now, in his office, he was eating an egg salad sandwich he had picked up in the canteen and was washing it down with his umpteenth coffee of the day.

Kyra entered without knocking. She pulled a face when she smelled the sandwich. 'I don't know how anyone can eat eggs like that. The smell alone turns my stomach.'

'Did you want something?'

She looked down at her pad. 'Andrew Dickens said the woman who told him Dominic's real identity was Selina Baxter. Apparently, she's well known for being a bit of a gossip.'

'So much for Selina only telling her mum and her boyfriend.'

'Exactly. And I've run Paul Cummings' registration number through ANPR, and it was picked up on Scotswood Road just after eleven o'clock on the night of the first. Scotswood Road isn't far from Atlantic Road.'

'A couple of minutes, if that.'

'Case closed?'

'It would seem so,' he said, glaring into space.

'You don't sound convinced.'

'That synthetic hair keeps popping back into my mind. Andrew, Paul and John weren't wearing a disguise. They just knocked on the door and walked in. So, who went to the house wearing a wig, and who were the couple walking up the garden path?'

Kyra pulled out a chair and sat down. 'Are we sure that couple even exists? Only John claims to have seen them, very briefly, and after looking at a photo on the mantelpiece. Is it possible it could have been a trick of his imagination? Andrew said they'd had a few drinks in the pub before they went round to Dominic's house.'

Terry thought for a while. 'Okay, I can probably accept he was half-pissed and thought he saw something he didn't, but that doesn't explain the hair.'

'It might have been there for days.'

'Even if it was, it still means that someone visited Dominic wearing a disguise. Why?'

Kyra chewed her bottom lip. There was a pensive look on her face. 'I really don't know. I'm sorry. I suppose it's going to be one of those unanswered questions.'

'I don't like those.'

'No. But the tourist industry at Loch Ness has managed to turn them into a boon,' she said, with a smile.

Chapter Fifty

Dawn opened her front door to find DI Terry Braithwaite standing on the doorstep with a bottle of wine in his hand.

'The woman downstairs let me in. I've brought you this.' He held out the bottle.

'Is this so you can get my fingerprints to set me up for something?'

'Why do people have such a negative impression of the police?'

'I'm not sure.' Her tone was laced with sarcasm. 'Maybe it has something to do with you accusing them of murder while they're grieving for their father and grandfather.'

Terry sighed. 'That's why I'm here. I'm sorry. Please. It's a peace offering.'

She stood back to let him in. She took the wine and looked at the label. 'Very nice. Not cheap. You really must be sorry.'

'Mind if I sit down?'

'Go ahead.'

He sat on the sofa, looking at the large TV on the wall as he did so.

'We've arrested someone for your father's murder.'

'You have? Oh, that's wonderful,' she said, hands going to her chest. A satisfied smile appeared on her lips. She sat down at the table. 'Who?'

'Three men who worked at the supermarket with him.'

'Three? Oh my God. He must have been so scared. How did they even... No.' She stopped herself. 'I don't want to know. You've caught them. That's the main thing. Have they admitted it?'

'They're admitting to beating him, but they claim they're not responsible for the fatal stab wounds. Forensic evidence and the autopsy results should work in our favour. I just wanted to come over and apologise for my behaviour towards you.'

'You thought I'd killed my father, didn't you?'

It was a while before he answered. 'I'm afraid I did, yes.'

'You're lucky I don't hold grudges. This can't have been an easy case for you. It must have brought back some very unpleasant memories.'

'It did. Still, whoever said life was easy obviously didn't work in the police service.' He gave a weak smile. 'How are you doing after everything that's happened?'

She took a deep breath. 'I'm not sure. I'm glad I got to know who my father was for myself. And it was lovely spending time with my grandfather.' She smiled. 'But I don't feel like I've missed out on anything growing up. My mum was both parents to me.'

'How is the relationship between you and your mum?'

'It got a bit damaged when I said I wanted to get to know Dominic, but we repaired those bridges.'

'That's good. I'm glad. Well, I'll not take up any more of your time,' he said, standing up. 'I just wanted to let you know the latest developments.'

'Thank you. I appreciate that.'

'Erm, I know this is going to sound strange, but did Dominic do anything for Halloween last year?'

Dawn was taken aback by the random question. 'Halloween? No. I don't think he did. Are you asking if he went out trick-or-treating?'

Terry smiled. 'No, nothing like that. Did he attend a party, get dressed up at all?'

'No. He didn't,' she said firmly. 'Why?'

'Just curious.'

When Terry told Harry and Barbara White about the arrest of three men for Dominic's murder, their relief was evident. Now they could start to put it behind them. Harry stood up and shook Terry's hand.

'Well done, son,' Harry said. 'I'm pleased for you. You've done a grand job.'

'It's not been an easy case.'

'What will happen to them?' Barbara asked. She was sitting in her usual armchair, a newspaper folded on her lap.

'We've charged them with murder. Life in prison. Minimum term.'

She looked down, almost crestfallen.

'Barbara, they're killers,' Harry said. 'It doesn't matter who the victim is – they committed a crime, and they need to pay for it.'

'Excuse me.'

Barbara stood up, left the room and walked quickly upstairs.

'Is she all right?' Terry asked.

'No. She's not. She's been a changed woman ever since Dominic came out of prison. Her head's all over the place.'

'She's a smart, intelligent, law-abiding woman,' Terry said. 'Suddenly, she finds herself wishing a man dead and hoping his killers get away with it. She's got hugely conflicting messages running around her mind. It can't be easy for her.'

'No. I suppose not,' Harry agreed. 'We've had a few rows.'

'Well, hopefully things will calm down a bit now.'

'I hope so. Are you going to visit your dad?'

'Yes. I'll pop round this evening and tell him.'

'I really am proud of you, Terry,' Harry said, looking at his godson with a beaming smile. 'Your dad is as well. I know his mind isn't what it was, but I know for a fact he's proud of how you've turned out.'

'Thank you. That means a lot.'

'Now, you need to concentrate on yourself, Terry. Find yourself a good woman and think about settling down.'

'I've got a date arranged for next week, actually,' Terry said, blushing slightly.

'Good. And remember, until you find yourself a good woman, there's no harm in going out with a few bad women.' Harry winked.

It started raining when Terry left the Whites' house. By the time he arrived at Lavender House Nursing Home, it was pouring down. He ran from the car park into the building where he signed in, had a chat with the receptionist, then made his way to his father's room.

'I love the rain,' Ian said. He was by the window when Terry entered. 'I could stand here and watch it for hours.'

'Remember when I was a child, and I used to stand and watch thunderstorms?'

Ian turned to his son, a huge smile on his face. 'I do. I do remember that. You always wanted to go outside in the back garden.'

'Mum was terrified I'd get struck by lightning.'

Ian returned to looking out of the window. 'We don't get good storms anymore, do we?'

'No.'

'Just a lot of rain.'

'Are you all right, Dad? You look a bit down.'

'I'm worried.'

'What about?'

'Barbara and Harry.'

'They're all right. I've been to see them this afternoon.'

'Terry, you'll go easy on them, won't you?' Ian asked, a desperate look on his face.

'Dad, I don't know what you're talking about.'

'Harry and Barbara. Stephanie's parents.'

'I know who they are, Dad. Look, come and sit down. Talk to me.'

Ian went over to the bed and sat down on the edge. 'Terry, I know you're a detective, and you have to arrest people when they've done wrong, but Harry and Barbara are my friends. They'd been abandoned by a greedy society. They saw no alternative.'

'Dad? What are you trying to tell me?'

'Harry and Barbara killed the bastard. They killed Dominic Griffiths.'

The visit to see his father didn't last much longer after that revelation. It didn't seem to matter what Terry said to Ian, the old man wouldn't calm down. When he started crying, Terry called for one of the nurses. She took him in hand, offered to make him a cup of tea and watch television with him for a while. Terry sank into the background. It distressed him to see his father in this state. Nobody knew what was going on in his mind, and he was unable to express himself competently. Could what he said be trusted? Dominic's killers had been arrested; the case was closed. Harry and Barbara couldn't possibly have done it, could they? He felt sick. After Ian had settled and was in the capable hands of the nurse, Terry left. He needed to get to the bottom of this, once and for all.

Terry sat in the car and listened to the sound of the rain lashing down on the roof. He didn't turn on the engine and didn't bother with the windscreen wipers. He wanted a few minutes alone with his thoughts.

Ian seemed adamant that Harry and Barbara had killed Dominic Griffiths. They both visited Ian often, sometimes together, sometimes alone. He guessed Barbara would be more outspoken when she visited alone, saying how she hated Dominic for being released and how much she wanted him dead. Had these conversations become convoluted in his mind, and he'd formed the conclusion that his best friends had indeed committed murder? Or was he telling the truth? Had they confessed to Ian that they had murdered Dominic to get it off their conscience, knowing, and hoping, he would forget as soon as they'd spoken the damning words?

The image of the couple walking down the garden path came to Terry's mind. Maybe John Wheatley had genuinely seen someone approaching the house. But he had said they were of a similar height, give or take. Harry was just over six foot, and Barbara wasn't much taller than five foot. It didn't make sense.

There were three men in custody, charged with Dominic's murder. Terry had never been one hundred per cent satisfied they were guilty, but the facts were there, and they had admitted to the beating. Was it possible someone had been waiting in the shadows to strike the final blow?

Chapter Fifty-One

Harry and Barbara were sat opposite each other at the dinner table. She'd made a shepherd's pie and loaded their plates with fresh vegetables. It was Harry's favourite meal, and his eyes lit up when she placed it in front of him. He tucked in straightaway, shovelling in huge forkfuls while Barbara merely picked at hers.

'They've forecast snow for the weekend,' Barbara said, breaking the silence.

'Really? I'll pop to Morrisons tomorrow, buy a few bits, just in case it comes down heavy.'

She smiled. 'You always prepare for an avalanche. I doubt it'll be even ankle deep.'

'You never know. How are we doing for candles?'

'We have more than enough,' she said, a stern edge to her voice.

'I'll get some batteries for the torches.'

'Maybe a few distress flares, too,' she said, with a twinkle in her eye. Then, after a few mouthfuls, she said, 'Harry, I've been thinking. We've never really moved on, have we?'

'From what?'

'From Stephanie dying. We've sort of been living in a limbo state for twenty years.'

'I did mention moving years ago, but you wouldn't have it.'

'No. I know. I don't want to move. I like our house. But, well, maybe we could have a clear-out.'

'A clear-out?' he asked, wiping his mouth with his napkin.

'Yes. Starting with Stephanie's room.'

Harry's mouth fell open. 'Really? What's brought this on?'

'We've lived in the past for too long. As much as I like to think I feel Stephanie's presence every time I go into her bedroom, I know I don't. She left a long time ago. We need to move on. I need to move on. And I can't while I'm still clinging to what might have been.'

Harry reached across the table and took hold of his wife's hand. 'We will do whatever you want to do.'

'There are a few things I want to keep, obviously, but there's plenty that can go to the charity shop or the skip.'

'I'd better add black bags to my list tomorrow.'

'I'm doing the right thing, aren't I, Harry?'

'If you think it will help, then yes, you are.'

'We could clear out the attic, too. There must be all kinds of junk up there. And the shed.'

'New year, new start.' He smiled.

'You've got football programmes going back to the Eighties you never look at.'

'Steady on, Barbara,' he said, with a horrified look on his face.

Barbara let out a genuine throaty laugh – her first in a very long time.

Chapter Fifty-Two

It took Barbara and Harry two days and a gallon of tears to decide which of Stephanie's belongings they wanted to keep and which to get rid of. The photographs, the drawings, the teddy bears, Barbara wanted. They were personal items which were special to Stephanie and would always remain special. The duvet covers, the curtains, the carpet, the clothes, the posters were all expendable.

'Shall I take these curtains to the charity shop?' Barbara asked. 'There's nothing wrong with them, though I might have to give them a quick wash,' she said, smelling them.

'You can't give those to charity.'

'Why not?'

'Look at the bottoms – the moths have been at them.'

Barbara looked down and saw tiny holes along the seam. 'Oh my God, I didn't notice. I don't want people thinking we're mucky.' She sighed and looked around the rapidly emptying room. 'Do you think we should just have a bonfire and throw the lot on?'

'Good idea. Let's wait until dark, though.'

'Why?'

'Her next door has just hung out a load of washing.'

'Fair enough. Right, we need two piles: one for what we're going to keep and one for the bonfire.'

'I'll get a couple of those plastic crates from the garage – we can put what we're keeping in there,' Harry said.

'Good thinking. Oh, is there anything else we want to get rid of, while we're in a burning mood?'

'I don't think so. What were you thinking of?'

'Your football programmes?'

'Barbara, they'll be worth something one of these days. I'm not getting rid of them.'

Barbara rolled her eyes. 'What about those Christmas sweaters?' she called out to him as he went downstairs.

'Why is it all my things you want to get rid of?'

Barbara smiled and left the question unanswered. She turned back to look at the room she had spent twenty years wallowing in. It hadn't taken long to turn it from a shrine into a simple spare bedroom. The thought suddenly struck her: what would they do with it once it was empty?

By eight o'clock, everything for burning was stacked up in a pile in the back garden. Harry was getting a bonfire lit in the centre of the lawn, using old pieces of wood from the garage. While he was battling with the elements to get it lit, Barbara ran upstairs for one final box.

'What do you think?' Harry asked, standing back and marvelling at the flames.

'I feel like I should be holding a sparkler and making baked potatoes,' she said, smiling.

'Ooh, I could just eat a jacket spud, with baked beans and melted cheese on top.'

'Shall I pop a couple in the oven? They'll be ready by the time we've burned this lot.'

'Go on then.'

Harry was wrapped up in a thick winter coat with gloves and a bobble hat. Despite the heat of the roaring bonfire, he was cold. Barbara came out to join him. She stood well back while Harry added items to the flames. Dressed in layers like Harry to stave off the cold, she fought back the tears, watching the last remnants of her daughter's life going up in flames. It was too late to change her mind now.

She looked down at the pile still to be burned. The last box she had added was still there.

'You're not wanting to burn these, surely,' Harry said, rummaging through a box.

'What?'

'These old annuals.'

'Harry, we've been through all this. We'll be here until midnight if you start going through them again. Just lob them on the fire. Here, give them to me.'

Barbara took the handful of books from her husband, walked over to the bonfire and threw them into the centre of the roaring mound. She turned around and slapped her hands together. 'See, that's how you do it. Your lips are turning blue. Would you like me to make you a mug of hot chocolate?'

'I'd love that, thank you,' he replied.

Barbara went into the cold house and set about making them both a hot drink. She looked in the fridge to see if there were any KitKats left to keep them going until the potatoes were baked. She turned around to find Harry standing in the doorway.

'Oh, bloody hell, Harry,' she said, a hand slapped to her chest. 'You scared the life out of me. Shouldn't you be out there, keeping an eye on the fire? We don't want it getting out of control. If her-next-door's fence goes up, there'll be hell to pay.'

'I found this in one of the boxes,' Harry said, taking a long grey coat from behind his back and holding it out to her.

'So?'

'So, it isn't Stephanie's.'

'No. Well, like I said, while we're burning things, we may as well see if there's anything else we want to get rid of.'

'It's not yours either.'

'I know it's not. It belonged to Angela,' she said, referring to her sister. 'Remember, when she died, I cleared out her house. I kept a load of her clothes and just stuck them up in the attic. They've been there fifteen years or so. May as well get rid of them now.'

'And what about this?' Also from behind his back, Harry produced a black shoulder-length wig.

'It's what she wore when she had cancer, Harry. Don't wave it around like that, just throw it on the fire.'

Harry didn't say anything. He stood there with a stony expression, glaring at his wife.

'Harry, what's wrong?'

'A long synthetic black hair was found in Dominic Griffiths' house the day after he was killed.'

'What?' Barbara asked, steadying herself against the worktop.

'Those men who beat Dominic half to death said they were interrupted by a couple coming up the path. The woman was wearing a long grey coat and she had dark shoulder-length hair.'

'Oh, come on, Harry, you don't seriously think it was me, do you? How long have you known me?'

'I know you've wanted Dominic dead ever since he was released. I know you've been trying to convince me from day one that he should have paid with his life.'

'Well, he should have.' She tried to laugh off his ridiculous notion. 'Harry, wanting a person to spend their life in prison, or wishing them dead, is one thing. It doesn't mean to say I'm going to go out there and actually do it.' The kettle boiled, and she turned to finish making the hot chocolate.

'I need to call Terry.' Harry turned away and went into the living room.

She slammed the kettle down on the worktop. 'What? Why?' she asked, running after him.

'They can do tests. See if that synthetic hair matches this wig.'

'Harry, don't be ridiculous. All synthetic hairs are the same. It will probably match with a thousand different wigs. Harry, please,' she said, pulling on his arm.

Harry stopped as he reached the telephone on the coffee table. He turned to look at his wife. 'Barbara, look me in the eye and tell me you didn't kill Dominic Griffiths.'

'Why are you even asking me that? You should know I couldn't do something like that.'

'Then say it.'

'This is ludicrous.' She half-laughed.

'You're not denying it, though, are you?'

'Okay. I didn't do it.'

'Look me in the eye and say it.'

'Harry,' Barbara pleaded, on the brink of tears.

'Oh my God.' He sank into the sofa. 'You did, didn't you? You killed him. What did you do? Did you put those three men up to beating him up, too?'

'No, of course I didn't,' she said, lowering herself to his level.

'I can't believe this. I was a detective inspector. I worked for the police for almost thirty years. How did I not see this?'

'Harry.' She sat on the armchair. She allowed a silence to develop for a few seconds, though it felt like hours. She softened her voice. 'I didn't do it for you. I didn't do it for me. I did it for Stephanie,' she said, tears rolling down her face.

'Stephanie's dead!' he screamed.

'I know she is. And her killer should be too. That's the way it should be. A life for a life, Harry.'

'Not in the eyes of the law.'

'The law isn't working. How many times do I have to tell you? For people like us, the law is not working. We're left to suffer and grieve and be in pain for the rest of our lives, while people like Dominic Griffiths are allowed to carry on as if nothing's happened. The law isn't on our side. It looks after the criminals but not the victims and not the families of victims. God forbid you put a murderer in solitary confinement – it's against his human rights. What about *my* human rights?' she screamed, slapping herself on the chest. 'What about *Stephanie's* human rights?' She pointed at the photograph on the wall.

'Nobody has the right to take the law into their own hands,' Harry said, slowly losing the will to continue the argument.

'When the law allows killers and rapists to go free, we have to act to show we're not going to give in to them. The liberal do-gooders in their ivory towers make the law, but they're never on the receiving end of the consequences. How many politicians in the cabinet do you think live within a five-minute walk of a paedophile, or a rapist, or an arsonist, or a killer? None. And why? Because they don't give a toss about the regular people. All they think about is what's in it for them. They give themselves pay rises above the rate of inflation, they line their own pockets, and fuck the regular hard-working members of society like me and you, Harry. So, yes, from time to time, we have to take the law into our own hands, because we cannot trust the lawmakers to do it for us.'

'I'm phoning Terry,' Harry said eventually, turning to pick up the phone.

'No, Harry, please,' Barbara begged. 'Please don't. I'll be arrested. I'll be sent to prison.'

'I'm a detective, Barbara. I can't sit back and watch a crime go unreported.'

'You're not a detective anymore. You're retired. You're just a member of the public, like me. Dominic killed our daughter,

Harry. In cold blood. He kidnapped her, and he killed her.' She ran over to the picture on the wall and snatched it down, holding it up to show Harry. 'Look at her. Look at our daughter. She was thirteen years old, and Dominic stole her from us. He killed her and cut her up. He deserved to die.'

Harry, with the phone receiver in his hand, stopped and turned to his wife.

'I don't know you at all. I'm calling Terry.'

'No!' She snatched the phone out of his hand, gripping it firmly in both hands, holding it tight against her chest.

'Barbara, give me the phone,' he said, holding out his hand.

'I'm sorry, Harry, but no. I won't let you do this.'

They were at an impasse. Neither of them moved. Their eyes were locked on each other.

The doorbell rang. Barbara's eyes widened. Still, neither of them moved. The doorbell rang again.

Slowly, Harry headed for the door.

Barbara went over to the sofa and slumped down onto it. She placed the phone on the cushion next to her and picked up the framed photograph of Stephanie. She looked down at the smiling face with tear-filled eyes. She was suddenly aware of Terry's voice in the hallway. Why had he come here? What did he want? Barbara jumped up from the sofa and ran into the kitchen. Her mobile was on the windowsill next to the back door. She grabbed it, scrolled through the contacts and made a call. She impatiently chewed her bottom lip while waiting for it to be answered.

'It's me. Harry's found out,' she said quietly. 'I need you to come round. Bring everything with you.' She hung up.

'Barbara, Terry's here,' Harry called out.

She replaced the mobile on the windowsill and walked slowly back into the living room. She didn't want to look at Terry, her godson. She knew she would see disappointment all over his face. When she finally looked up, the tears came.

'Barbara, it's not true. Surely?' Terry said.

'I'm so sorry,' she said, barely above a whisper.

Terry went over to her, put his arms around her shoulders and guided her to the armchair. He sat her down. 'Barbara, tell me everything that's happened.'

'I don't want to hear this,' Harry said, making to leave the room.

'Harry, sit down,' Terry instructed.

'No. I refuse to listen. She knows the law. She knows how I feel about vigilantes. There's no excuse for what she's done.'

'And there's no excuse for going into a prison cell and beating up a young man because he won't confess,' Terry said, looking at Harry over his shoulder.

'What?' Harry asked.

'Is this true?' Barbara looked up at her husband.

Harry took a deep breath. He walked over to the sofa and sat down. He closed his eyes and composed himself, releasing the breath he had been holding.

'When Dominic was arrested all those years ago, he wouldn't talk at first,' Harry said, his voice shaking with emotion. 'He refused to admit what he'd done. Ian was doing everything he could to get him to talk, but… Anyway, I went into the cell, and I… I hit him.' He looked down at the floor in shame.

'You hit him?'

'I know. I know it was wrong. As soon as Ian dragged me off him, I felt guilty. I regretted it. If Dominic had told anyone, I could have jeopardised the whole case.'

Barbara stood up and walked slowly over to her husband. She sat on the sofa next to him and took his gloved hand in hers. 'Why didn't you tell me?'

'I didn't want you to think any less of me.' He looked up at her. There were tears in his eyes.

'I would never have done that,' she said. She reached out to touch his face, but he recoiled.

'The thing is, Barbara, I felt guilty straightaway, and there hasn't been a day that's gone by when I haven't thought about how low I sank. If you tell me that you regret what you've done, I'll find it in my heart to forgive you.'

Barbara took a deep breath and looked into her husband's eyes. 'If I feel regret, it will mean that I'm sorry for what I did, and I'm not. He stole my daughter away from me.' Tears began to fall. 'He snatched an innocent thirteen-year-old girl from the streets for his own sick pleasure. He cut her up into fifteen pieces and hid her in his attic. Imagine the pain and fear she must have gone through in her final moments. My only regret is that I didn't get my hands on him twenty years ago.' She spoke slowly and calmly, but anger flashed behind her words.

It was a while before Harry spoke. 'I don't know who you are anymore.'

Chapter Fifty-Three

Wednesday, 1 January 2020

Barbara was late arriving at the gates to Blaydon Cemetery, where they'd arranged to meet. She opened the back door to the Peugeot, climbed in and slammed the door behind her.

'I'm so sorry. Harry wouldn't go.'

Dawn was in the driver's seat, with Anthony next to her. All three were disguised. Dawn wore a navy trench coat and had a hat pulled down over her hair. She'd bought a pair of reading glasses from the local chemist too and put those on, amazed by how different a cheap pair of glasses made her look. Anthony wore a black beanie hat and a black coat he hadn't worn in years that he had found in the back of his wardrobe. He purposely hadn't shaved for three days to allow stubble to grow in. In the back, Barbara scratched at her head. The wig she'd found in the attic had belonged to her sister, and it was making her scalp itch. They were all wearing gloves, so they'd leave no trace of what they were about to do.

'Will you be back before he gets home, do you think?' Anthony asked. He didn't turn around in his seat, his gaze remaining fixed straight ahead. His voice was shaking slightly from nerves.

'I managed to persuade him to take his Clint Eastwood box set with him. They love westerns, and they can never watch just one.'

Silence filled the car. Their nerves were palpable. 'Are we ready?' Dawn asked.

The others nodded. She turned the key in the ignition and pulled away from the cemetery.

It was New Year's Day. Most people had been celebrating the night before and would have spent the day recovering. Traffic was light, and Dawn stuck to the speed limit. The last thing she needed was to be pulled over.

She found a space in a poorly lit street which was a good ten-minute walk from Atlantic Road where Dominic lived. She knew all about ANPR cameras and the risk of her registration number being picked up during the subsequent investigation, if she drove too close.

It was a freezing cold night, and as they made their way on foot to Dominic's house, their shallow, quick breaths formed puffs of smoke in the frigid air. It was a while before any of them spoke. They were all nervous, reflective.

'Are you sure they're there?' Barbara asked Dawn.

She nodded. 'I've been following Andrew for weeks, ever since Selina told him Dominic's true identity. They were going to go the other night but got spooked by a woman getting out of a taxi. I was within seconds of ringing you both when they shot off. Fortunately, Andrew seems to be one of those people who, when he gets an idea into his head, sticks to it.'

They approached Dominic's house from the back way, having to walk through overgrown scrubland to do so. When they reached the garden gate, Dawn stopped.

'I'll go up first, make sure they're there, then you come up, okay?' she whispered.

Barbara and Anthony nodded. They both looked nervous, but behind the wide-eyed stares was a sense of determination to see justice finally done.

Dawn slowly pushed open the gate. She looked up at the house. There was a light on in the living room. Through the thick net curtains, she could see shadows of people moving around. She took a deep breath and walked quickly, but quietly, up the pathway, until she was at the back door. She placed her ear against it, listening intently. There was nothing but silence. Had they left already? She hoped not. Suddenly, a loud crash made her jump, and she slapped a gloved hand over her mouth to stop herself crying out. She heard muffled cries from within. She looked back towards the garden gate where Barbara and Anthony were watching and gave them the nod.

Slowly, linking arms, Anthony and Barbara came up the garden path. Dawn risked moving towards the living-room window. She gave the glass a knock with the back of her hand, hoping someone inside would look up and see a couple resembling Dominic's parents coming up the path.

It wasn't long before she heard scrambling from inside, and someone shouted to 'get the fuck out'. Then there was the sound of the front door slamming shut. They'd gone. From the inside pocket of her coat, Dawn pulled out a bunch of keys, inserted one into the lock and opened the back door.

The kitchen was in darkness, but the door to the living room was ajar, and the light from in there gave just enough brightness for Dawn to see where she was going and not bump into anything. Barbara and Anthony followed closely behind her.

As Dawn headed for the living room, she passed the countertop and stopped. She carefully lifted a carving knife out of the wooden block and wrapped her gloved right hand firmly around it. She turned back to Barbara and her grandfather.

'Ready?' she mouthed.

They both looked at each other before turning to Dawn. They nodded.

Very slowly, Dawn pushed open the door to the living room. It was a mess. Andrew and his mates had caused some serious damage, and Dawn hadn't been prepared for what she saw. She'd been in this room so many times over the past ten months, playing the dutiful daughter, but now she didn't recognise it.

She heard a muffled noise ahead and looked up. In the corner of the room, by the four-seat dining table, Dominic was slumped on the floor. His face was a mess of blue and purple bruises. One eye was swollen shut, his lip was split, blood was pouring from his nose. He seemed to be having difficulty breathing, as if every intake of breath caused him pain. Again, this was not what Dawn had been expecting. She almost felt sorry for him. Then she remembered the evidence.

She stood perfectly still, her eyes fixed on her father. He looked towards her, and his eyes filled with relief. She fully entered the room and stood to one side, allowing Barbara and Anthony to witness the carnage.

Anthony closed his eyes and briefly looked down at the floor. He breathed deeply a few times, finding the confidence and energy from somewhere deep within to look back at the son he hadn't seen for twenty years. Barbara clamped a hand to her mouth. Whether it was the state Dominic was in or coming face-to-face with her daughter's murderer, she hadn't properly prepared herself for this. Neither of them had.

Dawn walked over to her father, careful not to disturb the detritus, and squatted down on her haunches. She studied him closely and listened to his laboured breathing.

'Can you hear me?' she asked, her voice barely louder than a whisper.

He nodded.

'I've brought some people to see you. Do you recognise your father?'

It was a while before he reacted, but eventually, he nodded his head.

'The woman with him is Barbara White. The name will sound familiar to you. She's the mother of Stephanie White, the girl you murdered in 1999.'

Dominic whimpered, and a tear fell from his sealed eye.

From her inside coat pocket, Dawn took out a photograph. 'When your mum and dad first married, your mum kept a journal of married life. Her intention was to pass it down to her children and grandchildren, a sort of historical document. She included photographs as well. This one here is of your bedroom.' She showed it to him. 'I looked at this picture a few times, and I didn't spot it at first, but then it just seemed to jump out at me. Do you know what I'm referring to?'

Dominic looked at the photo then back to his daughter. He didn't try to say anything.

Dawn took out another photo. It was a blown-up version, concentrating on a specific part of the room.

'Have a look now.' She held it close to his eyes. 'Under your bed were several boxes of Fenadine. They've never been opened. You were prescribed them, but you didn't take them, did you? You never took one single tablet of that drug in your whole life, did you?'

Dominic breathed in and out, but it was causing him serious pain. He was uncomfortable and every movement hurt.

He shook his head.

'I need you to say it,' Dawn said. 'I need you to look Barbara and your father in the eye and tell them you never took a single tablet of Fenadine.'

Dominic looked at his dad. His gaze moved to Barbara, then back again.

'No,' he said, barely audible. 'I never… took Fenadine.'

Barbara turned away and wiped her eyes.

'You lied. For twenty years, you lied and said you were innocent, hoping someone would listen and try to get you released. You must have thought it was Christmas when Clare Delaney contacted you. Not only could she get you out, but she could get you compensation too. You'd be set for life. You managed to fool everyone. But you're not a victim, are you? You're a cold-blooded psychopath. You attacked kids at school, you attempted to rape Joby Turnbull, but worst of all, you saw a happy, smiling thirteen-year-old girl, and you kidnapped her. You strangled her. You cut her body into fifteen pieces, and you hid her in your attic. You did all of that, and you knew exactly what you were doing. Didn't you?'

'Yes,' he spat, blood dripping down his chin.

Dawn turned away. There were tears in her eyes. Her father, the man who gave half his DNA to make her, was pure evil, and he'd finally admitted it. She felt angry, betrayed, deceived, sick. With one swift movement, she picked up the knife she'd placed on the carpet beside her and plunged it deep into his chest.

'That's for Joby Turnbull.'

She pulled out the knife and held it out for Anthony to take.

He stepped forwards. He held the handle firmly in his shaking right hand and walked slowly up to his son. He leaned down. He didn't have much strength for the thrust into his chest, but it was enough to break the skin and cause his son to wince in pain.

'That's for your mother,' he said, his voice full of emotion. He pulled out the knife with both hands and handed it back to Barbara.

She took it from him. Despite wanting this man to pay for what he'd done to her daughter, she couldn't look him in the eye. She stepped forwards and plunged the knife firmly into his chest.

'That's for Stephanie.' She let go and stepped back, turned on her heel and headed for the kitchen.

Dawn reached for the knife handle. She pulled the knife out of her father's chest and slammed it into him once more.

'And that's for your dad.'

She looked up at Anthony and smiled.

Chapter Fifty-Four

'I can't believe any of this,' Terry said, after Barbara had told him everything.

On the coffee table in front of them lay the long grey coat and black wig. Terry looked up at Harry's pale and stony face. Barbara's eyes were full of tears. She was anxious and frightened. Terry was numb, disappointed and shocked.

'My dad…' Terry began. His voice croaked. He cleared his throat and started again. 'My dad said something about not blaming you both for what you've done. Did he know?'

'I haven't done anything,' Harry said.

All eyes turned to Barbara.

'He may have become confused,' she said quietly. 'I needed to unburden myself. I needed to tell someone I could trust with what I'd done.'

'He's not well, Barbara,' Terry chastised.

'I didn't… I just wanted someone to understand.'

'And did he?'

'Yes. He did. He hated Dominic just as much as I did—'

'He wouldn't have wanted you to murder him,' Harry interrupted.

'That's where you're wrong. I told him everything, and he hugged me. He said he wished he had had the strength to do it himself.'

'He didn't know what he was saying,' Harry shouted.

'He knew exactly what *I* was saying. For crying out loud, Ian spent hours in that attic with the pathologist while they opened those bin bags and took out Stephanie in fifteen pieces. He was her godfather, for Christ's sake. What do you think that did to him?' She wiped her tears away. 'He was never the same after that. He bottled everything up. He stored it all, up here.' She tapped her head hard. 'And it caused him to have a stroke that almost killed him. Dominic did all of that.'

'You had no right—' Harry was interrupted by the doorbell. 'Who's that?'

Barbara didn't reply. She stood up and went to the door.

Terry and Harry looked at each other with confused expressions. They listened intently, trying to hear who was at the door, but they couldn't. Outside, the crackling fire was slowly dying as Stephanie's belongings were finally consumed and the wood burned out.

Barbara walked back into the living room. Dawn Shepherd followed her, carrying a shoe box. Both had blank expressions.

'What's going on?' Harry asked.

'Harry, I need you to be calm and listen carefully to what Dawn has to say.'

'She knew?' He pointed. 'But she's his daughter.'

'Can someone please tell me what's going on here?' Terry said.

The atmosphere was tense. They all sat down. The only place for Dawn was on the sofa next to Harry. He scooted over to the far end. He didn't want to be anywhere near her.

'I think you'd better start from the beginning, Dawn,' Barbara said.

'When I found out who my dad was, when I found out what he'd done, I felt sick to my stomach,' Dawn began. She didn't look at anyone. Her voice was low, and her head was bowed.

'I was filled with all these conflicting emotions. I wanted to get to know him because he was my dad, but at the same time I didn't want anything to do with him because he was a murderer. But I wasn't sure if he was guilty. The more I looked into what happened, the more it became clear that he had murdered Stephanie – all the evidence pointed that way. But I also discovered that maybe he wasn't completely responsible for what he'd done. I heard about that drug he was taking, Fenadine, what it had done to other people who'd taken it. It was a lifeline. It gave me hope that maybe Dominic wasn't the cold-blooded killer the press made him out to be. Maybe my dad really was a mixed-up, confused young man.

'I met his father, my grandad.' She smiled. 'He was a sweet man. He loved his wife, that much was evident from the minute I met him. He wanted to protect her memory. At the same time, he could see I was eager to know everything I could about Dominic and what he was like. He gave me his wife's journals.' She removed the lid of the box but didn't take out any of the hardback notebooks. 'He knew exactly what she'd written. He'd read them all many times since her death. He knew what I'd find out when I read them, but he never mentioned it. He let me discover the truth for myself.'

'What truth?' Terry asked.

'Carole Griffiths started writing these journals just after she was married. After several miscarriages, she resigned herself to the fact that children just weren't on the cards for her and Anthony, but then she became pregnant. The problem was, she'd become severely depressed as a result of facing the prospect of not being able to have children, and Dominic's birth didn't lift her out of it, like you'd expect it to. She couldn't bond with him. Anthony worked away a lot, so she was left to bring him up on her own, and she just physically and mentally couldn't do it. Dominic began acting out, like a child who isn't taught right from wrong would, but Carole exaggerated it.

'Carole began taking medication for depression, but one particular doctor realised it was probably Dominic who needed the medication, not her. Again, she lied to the doctor. I suppose, nowadays, she'd have been diagnosed with Munchausen by Proxy or something, but at the time, nothing was picked up. There's one entry in here where she categorically states that Dominic is ill. She believed it herself. In fact, there was nothing wrong with him that a bit of guidance wouldn't have sorted out. He didn't get that, and he went off the rails.'

'Tell them about Joby Turnbull,' Barbara said.

Dawn took a breath. 'When Dominic was seventeen years old, he had a friend, Joby Turnbull. Joby was struggling with his sexuality. He turned to Dominic to confide in and told him he was gay. That night, Dominic attempted to rape Joby.'

'What?' Terry exclaimed.

'We didn't know anything about that,' Harry said.

'It was never reported. There was no physical evidence as Joby managed to fight him off. However, it was believed that Dominic was taking Fenadine at the time of the assault. He wasn't. He was prescribed it, but he never took a single tablet. The attempted rape was all down to Dominic.'

'I don't understand,' Harry said, squeezing the bridge of his nose.

'All of Dominic's bad behaviour was put down to him taking this drug,' Barbara said. 'But he lied about taking it.'

'But he was taking it when he killed our Stephanie.'

Dawn rummaged around in the shoe box and brought out a

dark red book. A page had been marked with a Post-it note. She opened it.

'Carole was very thorough in her journals. Sometimes, it's difficult to work out what is the truth and what's made up, but photographs don't lie.' From her handbag, Dawn took out a magnifying glass. She handed the journal and the spyglass to Terry and pointed out a photograph for him to study.

They all sat in silence as Terry leaned over the notebook and cast his eye over the picture. Dawn turned to Barbara and gave her a weak smile. They had both known this day would come, and they'd arranged what they were going to say.

'His bedroom's a mess. There's crap everywhere. It's like *Where's Wally?* What am I supposed to be looking for?' said Terry.

'The drawer under the single bed is open. Look inside it.'

Terry leaned further forwards and squinted. 'Boxes of something. Is that… Fexa…?'

'Fenadine. They're his tablets.'

'So, he was a hoarder. I've got empty boxes piled high in the garage,' Harry said.

'Those boxes aren't empty. There's a protective tab on each one, and they're still sealed. They were never even opened. Dominic was prescribed Fenadine, but he never took a single dose.'

'What?' Terry asked, his mouth agape.

Dawn took a photograph out of her pocket and handed it to Terry. It was the blown-up shot, clearly showing the sealed tablet boxes.

'When Anthony and Carole were moving out of their house, not long after Dominic was sent to prison, Carole couldn't bring herself to go through her son's things, so Anthony did it. He confirmed that every single box of tablets Dominic had been prescribed was untouched beneath his bed. He threw them out and never told his wife. We confronted Dominic with the evidence, and he admitted he'd never taken Fenadine.'

'So, his defence, based on the effects of the medication, was a lie?' Harry asked.

'Yes,' Barbara confirmed clearly.

'Dominic Griffiths knew exactly what he was doing when he tried to rape Joby Turnbull, and he knew exactly what he was doing when he kidnapped your daughter and killed her,' Dawn said. 'He saw this whole Fenadine business as a way to get out of jail early. He lied. I went to visit him in prison before he was released and asked him if he killed Stephanie. He said he couldn't remember a single moment of it. He lied to my face. I hate to say this about my biological father, but Dominic Griffiths was evil and rotten to the core.'

Dawn fell silent and allowed her revelation to sink in for Terry and Harry.

'Not only was he a murderer, but he conned the judicial system, and a pharmaceutical company awarded him one million pounds for what he'd done,' Barbara said. 'He was laughing at us, Harry. He was rubbing our noses in it. Yes, he served twenty years for killing Stephanie, but he hadn't learned anything at all. He hadn't atoned. He wasn't remorseful, and he didn't feel any regret. He'd lost twenty years of his life. He was forty and had a million pounds in his pocket. We had to do something.'

'We?' Terry asked.

Barbara and Dawn exchanged glances. Barbara nodded.

'It was all my idea,' Dawn said. 'Barbara didn't want anything to do with it at first. I had to convince her that it was for the good of everyone involved.'

'And you inherit his compensation and live happily on blood money for the rest of your life,' Harry said, with bitterness in his voice.

'No. I don't want a single penny of it. Me and Barbara have

made a list of charities that support people who have lost someone to murder. The money will go to them.'

'You have it all worked out, don't you? Like father, like daughter,' Harry said, standing up and moving to the other side of the room.

'Harry!' Barbara said.

'It's all right,' Dawn said.

'No, it isn't.' Barbara followed her husband, who was stood by the patio doors, watching the fire die. 'You talk about justice, Harry. You talk about leaving everything to the legal system. Well, this is what your legal system has done. Yes, he was found guilty of murder, but he was a manipulating, evil, cold-blooded bastard. He saw a loophole, and he jumped right through it. If he was released after twenty-five years, full of remorse and sorry for what he'd done, I *might* have been able to accept that and move on, but he didn't. There was no reaction to medication, because he never took it. He saw our Stephanie on the street, and he kidnapped her. He lured her to his shed. He murdered her. He cut her body up into fifteen pieces. He knew exactly what he was doing, and he didn't care.'

Barbara didn't take her eyes off Harry. She watched as the reflection of the flames danced on his face. His eyes were full of tears.

'I can't condone what you did,' he said quietly.

'I'm not asking you to. But you need to understand why I did it. Why we did it.'

'Why did Anthony confess to the murder in his suicide note?' Terry asked from the other side of the living room.

'Anthony was dying,' Dawn said. 'Around autumn last year, he was told the cancer had spread, and there was nothing the doctors could do apart from manage his pain. He told me that when the pain became too much, he'd take his own life. He didn't want to die in a hospice hooked up to a load of machines. When I discovered the truth about Dominic, I talked about it with Anthony, and the conversation moved on to us enacting our own justice for Stephanie. And for Carole.'

'Enacting your own justice?' Harry spat with venom. He turned from the patio doors and faced Dawn. 'You mean committing murder.'

Dawn stood up. 'Yes. All right. I'm not scared of saying it. We discussed murdering my own father. Anthony was all for it. He asked me to come up with a plan, so we couldn't get blamed, and he'd leave a suicide note for the police, confessing to the murder, when he took his own life. Everything would be wrapped up.'

'The perfect crime,' Harry said. His reply oozed with sarcasm. 'You're proud of what you did, aren't you?'

'No. I'm not, actually. The legal system you represented for almost thirty years failed you. There are people like Clare Delaney who are willing to exploit it. It's wrong. It's disgusting. Do you think I took any pleasure in killing my own dad? I didn't. But what I was doing was right, because the law, in this case, wasn't working.'

'Where do Andrew Dickens and his friends come into it?' Terry asked, scratching his frowning forehead.

Dawn sat back down. 'I knew I couldn't murder Dominic in cold blood. I'm not that kind of person. However, I knew from my friend Selina that there was a lot of bad blood towards Dominic in the supermarket. I'm not proud of this, but I used my friendship with her to get him a job there, so I could wait until he was settled, and the staff knew him, then make sure his identity was revealed.'

'How did you do that?'

'I know Selina. She's a massive gossip; it was only a matter of time before she'd let it slip who he really was.'

Harry scoffed. 'And you call Dominic a great manipulator. You're just as bad. A real chip off the old block.'

'I was doing what the police couldn't,' she said firmly.

'You set up three men to commit murder.'

'No. I set up Andrew to beat Dominic. My plan was for us to go in and finish it. I had no idea they'd go as far as they did. It wasn't easy, but I couldn't stand by and watch Dominic profit from killing an innocent thirteen-year-old girl. It was wrong and immoral, and he couldn't be allowed to get away with it.'

'You profited too,' Terry said. 'The new car and TV.'

'Look out of the window, and you'll see there's a for sale sign in the back window. I don't want it. He bought me that car when mine broke down. I didn't ask him for it. The TV is now listed on eBay. He bought it for me as a Christmas present. I don't want it. I want nothing belonging to him.'

'So, what are you expecting?' Harry asked. 'A round of applause, a recommendation for an OBE? If you're wanting forgiveness, you can forget it.'

'I don't need your forgiveness,' Dawn said.

Silence filled the room. Terry looked stunned, as if he couldn't believe everything he'd just heard. Barbara looked up at Harry. He looked down at her. Neither of them gave anything away in their facial expressions.

'Harry?' Barbara asked quietly.

Harry's bottom lip was shaking as he turned away and looked to Terry. 'You have to arrest them, don't you?'

Terry blinked hard, and a tear escaped his right eye. He quickly swiped it away.

'You have Anthony's suicide note,' Dawn said. 'Use it for what it was meant for.'

'The CPS will not believe a man with bone cancer could inflict so much violence on a healthy forty-year-old.'

'You've got Andrew and his mates for beating him.'

'You've got the wig and the coat, Terry,' Harry said. 'That's evidence.'

Dawn looked towards Harry. Was he really condemning his

own wife to spending the rest of her life in a prison cell? Behind him, she saw the fire in the back garden.

'There's a bonfire outside,' Dawn said to Terry. 'Throw them on it. Burn them. You suffered as much as Harry and Barbara did when Stephanie was killed. Look at what happened to your dad. You and Ian are as much victims of Dominic Griffiths as they are,' she said quickly, the words falling over each other.

'Terry is an upstanding detective. He will not compromise his professional integrity,' Harry said.

'Terry, this can all be over tonight,' Dawn pleaded. 'You've got Andrew and his friends for the assault. You've got Anthony's confession in his suicide note. Burn the coat and the wig, and we can all move on with the rest of our lives. None of us should allow Dominic to haunt us for ever. He was a cold, sick, violent, evil man. He would have killed again.'

'You don't know that,' Harry snapped.

'He tried to rape his so-called best friend. He murdered an innocent girl. These journals are full of examples of his violent behaviour.'

'You said yourself Carole made most of them up.'

'I've researched them, looked at school records and reports made at the time. I now know what's a lie and what's the truth. When he was five years old, he bit a girl on the leg and drew blood. When he was eight, he slapped a girl so hard on the side of her face she lost the hearing in her right ear. When he was ten, he stole and killed a neighbour's cat and left its body on the owner's doorstep. He was evil when he was born, and it would have continued. He needed destroying.'

'Terry?' Barbara asked, standing up. 'What are you going to do?'

Epilogue

Monday, 4 January 2021

One year ago today, Anthony Griffiths took his own life. The pain he was suffering from the bone cancer which had spread to his lungs and lymph nodes was insurmountable. His evil, murdering son was dead by his own hand, and he felt he could finally join his wife.

Dear Dawn,

Meeting you has been one of the greatest pleasures of my life. My only regret is that we didn't meet sooner. It would have been a joy to watch you grow from a beautiful baby into the strong, confident woman you are today. However, in the short time we have known each other, my life has felt richer than at any other time in the past twenty years.

You are a wonderful young woman, and a credit to your mother. I know for a fact Carole would have loved you, and I could not be prouder to call you my granddaughter.

As we've mentioned, I'm leaving now to join my wife, and although this is a sad occasion, I'm blessed that we will be reunited. I wasn't the best husband, but I did what I thought was right at the time.

I am leaving everything to you in my will. The house, the insurance policies, everything in the savings account, will all go to you. Do with it as you wish. I only have one stipulation; whatever you decide to do with your life, make sure you enjoy it. So many young people think they have all the time in the world, but before you know it, you'll turn around and you'll be fifty and realise you've done very little. So, waste it on fast cars and luxurious holidays, lose it in a casino, spend it on expensive jewellery and clothes, but enjoy every penny.

This last year has been very special. I will go to my grave with a smile on my face and you forever in my heart.

Love,

Grandad xxx

There had been two suicide notes in Anthony's bungalow when Dawn found him the morning after his death. As planned, Anthony had written one for the police, but she had seen the envelope meant for her eyes only and taken it with her. It was something she kept with her at all times.

It was a chilly morning. The sky was grey, and rain was forecast for later, but it was dry for now. There was a slight breeze, and Dawn was thankful for her heavy winter coat. She kneeled down by the grave and placed a bunch of deep red roses on it for her grandfather and the grandmother she never met.

'I can't believe it's been a year,' Dawn said, as she stood up.

'Time passes so quickly,' Rita said, standing behind her.

'I don't want a funeral.'

'Where did that come from?'

'Look around you, all these graves abandoned, lost to the past, and there's nobody to mourn them. Who will come here when I'm gone? I don't want a gravestone of mine being used by vandals for target practice.'

'You're very morbid this morning,' said Rita.

'Well, we are in a cemetery.'

Dawn smiled. She linked arms with her mother, and they headed down the incline to the gates.

They spotted Barbara coming towards them, a bunch of flowers in her hand. They all stopped, a distance away from each other.

The year 2020 had been one nobody would ever forget, thanks to a pandemic sweeping the planet. The whole of the country had been locked down, and shops, restaurants, libraries and coffee shops had been forced to close. Barbara and Dawn hadn't seen each other since the night in her living room almost one year ago. Barbara had aged terribly.

'I had a feeling I'd see you here this morning,' Barbara said. 'I hope you don't mind. I thought I'd lay some flowers of my own.'

'Of course not,' Dawn said. 'How are you?'

Barbara took a breath. 'I'm… fine,' she said, with a fake smile. 'It's certainly strange getting used to living on my own after all these years.'

'Mum, could you give us a few minutes?' Dawn asked Rita.

'Of course. I'll just… hover.' Rita smiled and left them alone.

Dawn waited until her mother was out of earshot. 'There's no chance of Harry coming back home?'

'No. I've given up trying. He's renting a flat close to town, and he seems comfortable enough, by all accounts.'

'Is he talking to Terry yet?'

'No. He said he'll never forgive him for throwing the coat and wig on the fire.'

'I honestly thought he was going to arrest us.'

'So did I. Did you know he's getting married?'

'Terry?'

'Yes. He got engaged on Christmas Eve to a colleague. Bella. She's a lovely woman.'

'Oh, that's good news. I'm pleased.'

Barbara linked arms with Dawn, and they walked slowly towards Rita.

'Does your mum still think Anthony killed his son?'

'Yes. Terry did well in keeping a lot of what happened out of the press. I hate that we've tainted my grandad's name by having him acting in cahoots with Andrew and his mates, but there was no way to hide what they did to Dominic. There was no chance anyone would believe Grandad could have beaten him with the severity they did.'

'Anthony didn't want anyone else to suffer. It was his decision to take the blame.'

'I know,' Dawn said, a catch in her throat.

'We know the truth. That's all that matters.'

'I'm sorry the way things have turned out for you and Harry,' Dawn said. 'I never expected him to leave you.'

'It's a small price to pay. We did the right thing. Nothing will ever change my mind on that.'

Barbara visibly brightened and changed the subject when they caught up with Rita. 'I was going to call you, actually, Dawn. The book group is starting up again next month. God willing. Will you be joining us?'

'Of course.'

'Excellent. I'll add your name to the email list. Mary's chosen the first book and has picked *Anna Karenina*. Do you know it?'

'I do, but I haven't read it.'

'I have, but it was many years ago. You're more than welcome to join us, too, Rita, if you wish. There's plenty of room.'

'I haven't read many classics,' Rita said, with an apologetic smile.

'Now's the perfect time to start.'

'Come on, Mum, it'll be fun.'

Rita thought for a moment. 'All right. I'll give it a go. There was one we read when I was at school I really enjoyed. What was it called? A Russian, I think. *Crime and Punishment.*'

Dawn and Barbara looked at each other, eyes wide. 'We've already done that one,' they said together.

Acknowledgments

This novel was originally written more than twenty years ago. The story of Harry and Barbara White losing their daughter Stephanie on her thirteenth birthday has been the main thread running through all the various drafts that were rejected. However, I couldn't let this story go and kept returning to it every couple of years, updating it, redrafting it, trying a new subplot. It's taken two decades to see it in print.

Many thanks to the following people for believing in this story:

Imogen Papworth and Josephine Lane at Audible and Jill Halfpenny and Mark Stobbart for bringing the characters to life in the original audio version.

My agent, Jamie Cowen, to whom this book is dedicated, is a fantastic supporter of my work and encourages me to keep writing even when I have the merest acorn of an idea. He's a wonderful confidence booster.

The brilliant people at HarperCollins and One More Chapter including Jennie Rothwell, Charlotte Ledger, Simon Fox, Arsalan Isa, Emma Petfield, Chloe Cummings and Lucy Bennett and so many others who helped to put this book together.

The technical people who help in my research: "Mr Tidd", Simon Browes, Andrew Barrett, and Philip Lumb.

The people who support me in everyday life: Mum, Chris, Kevin, Jonas, Chris. You all help keep me on the right side of sane. Just.

Finally, I'd like to thank the readers, the booksellers, the bloggers and the people who recommend my books through word of mouth to their friends, family and colleagues. *Vengeance is Mine* is my thirteenth published novel. Without you, I wouldn't have managed to write this many. Thank you all so very much.

DCI Matilda Darke will return in Autumn 2024...

Five perfect murders

When an anonymous email from a serial killer seeking notoriety finds its way into DCI Matilda Darke's inbox, it's a message she simply can't ignore.

Hidden in plain sight

Now Matilda is on the trail of a murderer who targets the most vulnerable people in society and, aside from the anonymous hand delivered '*With sympathy…*' cards addressed to the families of the victims, leaves no traces.

A killer's deadly game

As threats escalate and those closest to Matilda are targeted, she has no choice but to find and bring down her opponent before it's game over. After all, there can only be one winner in this game of cat-and-mouse and the clock is ticking…

Available for pre-order in paperback and eBook now!

The author and One More Chapter would like to thank everyone who contributed to the publication of this story...

Analytics
Abigail Fryer
Maria Osa

Audio
Fionnuala Barrett
Ciara Briggs

Contracts
Sasha Duszynska Lewis

Design
Lucy Bennett
Fiona Greenway
Liane Payne
Dean Russell

Digital Sales
Hannah Lismore
Emily Scorer

Editorial
Kate Elton
Simon Fox
Arsalan Isa
Charlotte Ledger
Bonnie Macleod
Jennie Rothwell
Tony Russell

Harper360
Emily Gerbner
Jean Marie Kelly
emma sullivan
Sophia Walker

International Sales
Bethan Moore

Marketing & Publicity
Chloe Cummings
Emma Petfield

Operations
Melissa Okusanya
Hannah Stamp

Production
Emily Chan
Denis Manson
Simon Moore
Francesca Tuzzeo

Rights
Rachel McCarron
Hany Sheikh
Mohamed
Zoe Shine

The HarperCollins Distribution Team

The HarperCollins Finance & Royalties Team

The HarperCollins Legal Team

The HarperCollins Technology Team

Trade Marketing
Ben Hurd

UK Sales
Laura Carpenter
Isabel Coburn
Jay Cochrane
Sabina Lewis
Holly Martin
Erin White
Harriet Williams
Leah Woods

And every other essential link in the chain from delivery drivers to booksellers to librarians and beyond!

A MISSING DETECTIVE

DCI Matilda Darke has been kidnapped and her nemesis, Steve Harrison appears to be behind it. He's currently residing in Wakefield Prison, so how could he possibly be responsible?

A SERIAL KILLER WITH A VENGEANCE

As Matilda's team race to find her, they're alerted to a body found in an abandoned car on the outskirts of Sheffield. With forensics scouring the woodland for clues, the last thing they expect is for the body count to rise.

A RACE AGAINST TIME

If Matilda's team don't find her soon, they might not find her at all…

Available in paperback, eBook and audio now.

On a cold February afternoon in 1990, seven-year-old Danny Redpath disappeared from his home. Four months later, his body was found in the nearby forest.

Apprehended while attempting to abduct another child, Jonathan Egan-Walsh was charged with the murders of more than a dozen boys. Convicted on all counts, he received life in prison, refusing to reveal the whereabouts of one of his victims, Zachery Marshall.

Twenty-five years later, Zachery's mother Diane is still searching for his body. When Jonathan dies in custody, she realises she will never know its location – until she receives a letter he left in his cell, in which he admits he was guilty of all the crimes of which he was accused, except the murder of her son…

Available in paperback and eBook now.

A CENSURED DETECTIVE WITH NO LEADS

DCI Matilda Darke and her team have been restricted under special measures after a series of calamitous scandals nearly brought down the South Yorkshire police force.

A BRUTAL ATTACK WITH NO WITNESSES

Now Matilda is on the trail of another murderer, an expert in avoiding detection with no obvious motive but one obvious method.

A DEPRAVED KILLER WHO LEAVES NO TRACES

When his latest victim survives the attack despite her vocal cords being severed, Matilda is more convinced than ever of the guilt of her key suspect. If only she had a way to prove it…

Available in paperback, eBook and audio now.

YOUR NUMBER ONE STOP
ONE MORE CHAPTER
FOR PAGETURNING BOOKS